THE GIRL UNDER THE FLOOR

An absolutely gripping crime thriller with a massive twist

CHARLIE GALLAGHER

Detective Maddie Ives Series Book 8

JOFFE BOOKS

Joffe Books, London
www.joffebooks.com

First published in Great Britain in 2023

Cover art by Nick Castle

ISBN: 978-1-80405-707-0

Coppers scare the best, because the ghost stories you hear, those myths and monsters that sound so ridiculous, we get to see that they're real.

PART ONE

CHAPTER 1

Lynn Hathaway knew fear. Even when it was just a breath pushed out hard enough to cause distortion down a phone-line. Real fear can freeze a hardened call-taker in their chair, it can stop the world for just a moment, sucking all the noise, movement and air out of a busy room of blinking call boards and banks of chatting emergency call-takers.

This was one of those calls.

999 police, what's your emergency?

A line Lynn had delivered a million times to a million responses. This time the reaction was another breath that tailed off into a whimper. It was enough. Lynn Hathaway knew voices too and this was young, a child for sure, the desperation thick enough to clot in her ear. Lynn ducked her head to focus, her right hand lifting to push the headset more firmly against her ear so she wouldn't miss a thing.

'Everything's OK, my name is Lynn and I'm here to help you.' She was off script now, there were other things she needed to be saying but fear needs one thing: reassurance. Lynn fixed on her two monitors, they were close enough for the green text standing out from the black background to hurt, she held her breath for the next words as if they were all she had been waiting for her whole life. There was just breathing at first, then a muted knocking sound: knuckles on wood perhaps, but distant. The bright green font glowed with a mobile phone number; it wasn't a number that had called before or her screen would be populated with linked information, something that might help.

'Can you tell me if you're OK?' Lynn's cursor flew across the screen, a trail left behind it where she had turned the function on in a moment of boredom. She was regretting it now. She clicked to send the phone number for fast-track subscriber checks. Someone in admin support would receive it as a request and start making enquiries with the phone company that had issued the phone. If it was on a contract, they would have the details in around twenty minutes or so, which, in the world of emergency assistance, was an eternity.

A muffled cry. This was distant too, then another knocking sound, finishing with a scuff and another cry that faded back to loud breathing.

'If you cannot speak to me and you require emergency assistance, press five-five on your keypad and we will respond.' Lynn was back on script, her words very deliberate, her eyes shut briefly, silently begging for those tones — anything. There were more gasping sounds, then scraping like the phone itself was being dragged against something.

Two tones.

The screen also confirmed the keys had been pressed. The BT Operator who had passed the call to the police had made the same request but not got a response. As per his own procedures, he had stayed connected and now recognised his cue to speak.

'Provider is Vodafone, Eastings are 603228, Northings 170385, confidence approximately 80 per cent, operator to clear the line.' The man's voice was nasal, he allowed a moment's delay for Lynn to come back in with any questions. There was nothing more to ask and a click confirmed he was gone. She typed in the coordinates given; they related to the nearest phone mast to the caller rather than the caller themselves and gave a rough area. It came up with the entire Isle of Sheppey.

Thirty-six square miles.

'This is being treated as an emergency assistance call. We have officers in your area, are you able to confirm your location?' The headset was pushed so tight against her ear it hurt.

'Mum!' The voice was still distant, the word rushed, spoken like the caller had turned back into a room, away from the phone. There was another thud, then the same voice but louder, another layer of fear. 'Mum, is that you?'

CHAPTER 2

Saturday

Four days later

Her husband had gone down hard. Their hallway flooring was wooden and the vibrations spread out enough even to shake the part of the floor beneath where she was on her hands and knees. It was a connection, a reminder that she wasn't just an observer to the horror, despite the separation provided by the slatted door of her hiding place. She was there, she was part of it.

She could hear him too. He was in pain, choking and sobbing into his gag while turned on his side towards her. As she watched, his foot lifted then fell back down for the heel to thump. She felt that too; she'd splayed her fingertips against the floor, seeking more of that connection, trying to make it last. She wanted to feel him, his movements at least, even if it was flailing in pain. She could almost convince herself that the connection was two-way, that she could send something back to remind him that he wasn't alone.

But she had to stay quiet and she had to stay hidden. Those were his hurried instructions, instructions that had started even before the knock on the door, and his intensity had been such that she had followed dumbly. *You have to stay quiet*! *You have to stay hidden*! *You have to stay safe*! he had begged her, his palms raised out towards her to exert an invisible force that pushed her to the back of this cupboard and halted her questions.

She'd never seen him like that before.

She'd never seen him like this before, either: injured and wailing, his wide eyes towards her, searching the slats of the understairs cupboard, unable to see in, though she could see out. She found herself edging forward, still fighting her instinct to kick out at the door and rush to his aid.

Her nose brushed the cupboard door.

The sensation caught her out in the darkness, making her jerk back, her left elbow catching the underside of the cupboard in a glancing blow that made a scuffing noise. It was as good as silent, but to her it sounded like the loudest noise she had ever heard.

She froze.

She could see the legs of the stranger who had entered their home and now stood over her husband. She could see white trousers tainted with vivid stripes of red where the weapon had been wiped — one side, then the other, in a rhythmic movement. The weapon was gripped in a bloodied blue glove, the blade twisted and stubby. The stranger was unmoving, their stillness contrasting with her squirming husband who writhed like a snapped slow-worm. The stranger only moved to lash out, then was instantly back to still, back to silent; no pacing, no gesticulating, no shouting threats or demands. Just still, silent and cold.

And now turned to face the cupboard.

She couldn't see the face, the angled slats blotted out the top half entirely. For all she knew the stranger was staring down at the same gaps in the cupboard door as her husband was, searching for the same eye contact. Her internal dialogue told her to stay calm, that there was no way she could be seen, no way anyone but her husband even knew she was home.

The cupboard was an odd shape, made bespoke to make the most of the space under the stairs in their hallway. It rose in a sharp angle upwards, left to right, to chase the incline. But the first third, where the stairs were at their lowest point, was a bench with a padded top. It was a place where she had sat a million times to kick off her boots after a walk on a carefree Sunday, the whole family returning to be swamped by smells of dinner in the oven. Never could she imagine she would be cowering under it, pushed into it as far as she could muster, head first, with coats pulled from the hangers above as a way of adding an extra layer of concealment.

Maybe she should have run out of the back. She could have run the mile or so it took to get phone reception and called for help. Then at least she would be doing *something*, then at least she wouldn't be lying a metre away watching another flash of violence and feeling her husband's reaction through her fingertips.

* * *

Police Constable Vince Arnold upped his pace as the old railway bridge came into sight. The target address was just a couple of hundred metres the other side and knowing that gave him a boost. His legs were burning, he was built for sprints more than distance, but he'd run some distance to get here.

His chest burned as he made the bridge, the sound of his footsteps bouncing back like someone was running across the arched roof above him, keeping perfect pace for them both to burst out of the other side at the same time. The road had a gentle curve left, which meant he couldn't yet see the address, or the front door, but he was close.

One final push.

* * *

You will answer my question. The truth. That is all you will say.

The stranger had a voice. It was strong, determined and unflinching. There was no feeling to it, no weakness either. No single word spoken in such a way as to give any hope.

Her husband rushed a nod. He was still side-on, still facing where she was pressed up against the slats, her knees aching, merged into the darkness. His hands were pulled tight behind his back, his legs still fidgeting to make patterns in his own blood on the floor. He was sweating from his pain, crying in panic, his eyes blotched red and sopping as they followed the twisted blade that now moved slowly across his view. It came to a rest between his cheek and the material tied tight against his face to make up the gag. Another violent jerk and the material was yanked down around his neck. Her husband was like a listing ship, he spat and coughed towards the floor. His face jerked back up as the stranger moved directly towards the cupboard that concealed her, momentarily blocking her view.

The seat creaked and flexed above her. Dust fell onto her cheek and into her eyes that were turned upwards to the noise. Two legs in white now parted to frame her view out, the material so close she could have touched it. Her husband stared over, her new front door was directly behind him, it had a frosted glass surround, the low sun giving it a halo effect that now encircled him. She remembered the pride she'd felt when they had fitted it as part of the renovations they had always wanted, but had taken fifteen years to start. The birth of their son that had prompted the move to a larger place had then removed the finances required to improve it. The door had been last, the finishing touch and she'd never been prouder of their home, of what they had achieved together. It was everything she'd ever wanted: a forever home for her family somewhere quiet, isolated and peaceful.

That same cold, determined voice came back to fill the hall. This time it was a question that finally revealed the entire reason for this invasion of her home. The words meant nothing to the hiding woman, they might as well have been in a foreign language, but her husband's reaction was despair scrunched tight enough that a tear had to struggle its way out. And, in that moment, she knew that he had been a fool, that her dream of the perfect home with a perfect family was gone.

* * *

The house was now visible to Vince. The car on the drive and the tall tree in the front garden acted as an effective landmark. It was quiet out here, isolated and peaceful. He had barely passed anyone since breaking into a run.

His chest was close to bursting. His thighs were tightening up and he could feel the acid building in his calves as he pushed himself forward. His footfalls were heavier, the soles of his shoes slapping harder as he was getting tired and his technique was falling away.

But he couldn't slow down, he couldn't let up. He could only pray that he wasn't out of time already.

There was a garden path just the other side of that tree that cut through the front lawn. It was made up of polished stones mixed up in concrete and it led to a solid door with a glass surround. His soles squeaked at the sudden change of direction, his footsteps still heavy.

He only needed a few more.

* * *

The silence hit her the hardest. Every strike or slash of the blade had been met with noise: cries of pain, begging, scuffs against the polished floor where her husband had recoiled, or the clamour of him going down to the ground in the first instance.

But not this time.

This time there was no further to fall, this time his ability to push out his heels and scrabble away from the blade was gone. This time his voice was silenced. His face changed, too. He had been panicked and terrified, his eyes shifting from tightly shut to open wide, unblinking and chasing around the room. Now they were still, one eyelid lower than the other like a half-pulled blind.

The fingertips that had been splayed out against the wooden floor were now pressed hard into her cheek to stop any sounds leaking out as she struggled to look away from her dead husband. She was back to holding her breath then letting it out in controlled bursts, her mouth as wide as it would go behind her hand so it wouldn't make any noise.

There was movement from the stranger, back towards her, then a spin and a sit. The wooden bench squeaked and flexed once more, more dust shaken free to be sucked in through her fingers as she struggled to control her panic. She gripped her nose where it tickled like she might sneeze.

The weapon hung down in front of the slats, now held lightly between finger and thumb, and she could imagine her husband's killer slouched forward, taking a rest perhaps, looking out over a job done. This time the twisted blade hadn't been wiped clean and clumps of black and red mixed with the sunlight still bundling through the frosted glass opposite to give off an unreal, orange glow. She dared moved forward. Slowly, gently, her neck aching as she arched her head up, desperate to see those legs move away and leave her house.

Her eye was drawn to movement. It was a shadow that flickered across the glass of the front door in a blink-and-you'll-miss-it moment. But she hadn't missed it and the light was still changing: *someone was coming to her front door*!

The stranger must have seen it too, there was sudden movement, more creaking as the weight was removed. But then something unexpected, the legs turned again, away from the door, away from the movement and the voice returned. Three words that sliced through the silence like a scalpel to make her jump, three words spoken slow and deliberate like there was a need to be clear:

'*Sandy. Louise. Blackman.*'

Just three words.

Her full name.

CHAPTER 3

Vince Arnold misjudged his momentum to thump into the door when he had meant to just glide over it with his fingertips. Tagging the door was his finish line and he lifted his watch in the same movement to jab at the screen.

'*Run paused*!' The patronising enthusiasm from the American Exercise Overlord stored in his smartwatch always made him want to smash it up. Just a little bit. He pressed a button again to finish the run, knowing that it would save to his phone and instantly produce reports seemingly designed to humiliate him and to illustrate how he was *trending slower*, when what it should say was *trending older*.

'Jesus, someone chasing you?' He had been using his front door to lean on and now it moved inwards to send him stumbling over the step. His girlfriend, Maddie Ives, must have seen his return through the glass. She looked him up and down, disapproval mixed with humour.

'Only my P.B.,' he said.

'Did it catch you?'

'I reckon it must have left five minutes before I did,' Vince said with a grimace. 'Seems you can't outrun getting older. I think I might start using a new fitness app, one that doesn't have data on me from when I was in my twenties.'

'A lot of things you can't outrun,' Maddie replied and, just like that, the tense atmosphere that had pushed him out for a run in the first place was back in spades.

'I'm sure you're right.' Vince avoided eye contact by bending to pull his running shoes off. 'I need a shower,' he said, starting for the stairs.

'We didn't finish,' Maddie replied, then she walked away too. She was heading to the kitchen and Vince knew he was supposed to follow. This was the issue with being in a relationship with *Detective Inspector Maddie Ives*; a police interview was effectively a controlled conversation and no one controlled a conversation like she did.

Vince's sigh was one of inevitability. He'd played the running away card too early, turning out to compete against records he'd set when he was more than ten years younger and suffering the inevitable defeat. He shuffled into the kitchen already resigned to the second in quick succession.

At least she had clicked the kettle on.

'I don't wanna argue, not with you, Mads. You know I'm not clever enough to argue with you!' He tried a grin. He had the sort of grin that got him into, and out of, all sorts of trouble. Maddie was already leaning on the counter with arms folded. There was only getting into trouble from here.

'Then don't. Agree to take Sammy to see his mother and this conversation is done and you can go take your shower. Lord knows you need one.' Maddie flickered a smile back, it was fleeting for a reason, a little sample where only agreement would bring the real thing back.

'I told you already, Becks doesn't know what she's doing, she's a bit all over the place right now ... she doesn't want him seeing her like she is, not until—'

'She'll only get worse from here!' And there it was, Maddie bundling her words and the delivery into a sucker punch. Rebecca Arnold — his big sister — was dying in a hospital bed. It was a fact Vince had tried burying deep, but Maddie was determined to not only dig it up, but to force him to face it head on. Every conversation with his sister since her diagnosis had been about *when she got better*. The plans for that outcome were too numerous to remember but the other outcome . . . he still couldn't consider. Maddie continued. 'Sammy's been asking, he doesn't ask you anymore because he thinks it makes you angry, so he asks me. I can't keep telling him *soon*, that he gets to see his own mother *soon*. He misses her and you said yourself that she misses him, so what are we doing here?'

'I'm trying to protect him.'

'From what?'

'From seeing . . . from that place, from . . . just all of it . . .' Vince's words and his energy ran out together.

'What do you think Sammy will think if he never gets to see his mum again, if she dies and he never got to say goodbye?'

'Jesus, Mads!' Vince coughed, winded by another blow. 'It's not as simple as that. Life isn't, is it?'

'I think it is,' Maddie said, then showed mercy with a change of direction. 'I know this is a tough time for you, a shit week, right?' She smiled again, this time it caught and she brought it closer, stepping into him, her hands wrapping round his back.

'Same shit as last week, Mads, nothing I can't handle.' Vince felt himself let go, Maddie lifting her hands to his chest, using it to push herself away enough to be able to look him deep in the eye, the way only she could, the way no one else had ever been able to.

'Are you sure? What happened would take its toll on anyone at any time, but when you have this with your sister, with her boy too, trying to take it all on at once. Maybe . . .'

'Maybe I'm just fine!' Vince chuckled, tapping Maddie lightly on her bottom. 'Did you ever think of that? I've still got you, how could I ever be sad with you around?'

Maddie was still fixed on him, it looked like she had more to say but she settled on just a nod. 'I suggest you take a shower, then; stupid, stubborn but stinky and you're on your own.' Maddie pushed him away more firmly, just as her phone started buzzing on the kitchen side. 'I'll bring the tea up,' she said, her eye on the phone.

'That your job phone?' Vince already knew the answer. 'Yeah, it's the boss.'

'Harry Blaker calling on a rest day?' Vince said, smiling through a sudden sense of disappointment. 'Just make sure you make my tea before you leave, yeah?' He got no answer, wasn't even sure if Maddie had heard him and stopped half-way up the stairs to listen. Maddie's tone was one of concern. He was too far away to make out exact words; the conversation was over before it had a chance to really begin and Maddie flashed across the bottom of the stairs.

'Everything OK?' he called after her.

Maddie reappeared, her phone still in one hand, the other lifted to run through her hair. 'I have to go. My love to your sister. Can you be here for when Sammy gets back from his sleepover?'

'It's a Saturday, Mads. We don't get many weekends off together and now I can't even get a cup of tea out of you. I thought maybe you could bring yours up too, maybe we could drink our tea in the shower, you know, do what normal couples do when they get some time off and when one half is as irresistible as I am.'

'Not sure any *normal* people think that drinking a cup of tea in the shower is a good idea ... On ice, Vince, which just means I now need to make it up to you.' She winked. Vince couldn't help smiling back and cursed himself for it. He wanted her to know he was pissed off. 'You're seeing your sister, that'll be a few hours anyway.' She continued out of sight, Vince heard the shoe cupboard open.

'And the boss called you in for something that's only gonna take a few hours, did he? What did he say? Something about this case?'

'He didn't say much. When does he ever?' Maddie called back.

'What does "not much" mean?' Vince was still talking to an empty hallway. Maddie reappeared, sighing. Stress showed as lines that crossed her brow.

'He just said *there's been another one.*'

14

PART TWO

CHAPTER 4

Just over an hour later, Maddie was on her third attempt at backing her Volvo into a tight space between two marked police cars. The sudden slope of a grassy bank was throwing her angles out. When she finally pushed her car door open, Detective Inspector Harry Blaker was grinning from his position perched on a wooden stile.

'There are some Advanced Driver courses coming up.' His usual growl was tinged with humour. 'I could put your name forward if you like.'

'Very funny.' She stepped out into the chilly air that was strongly scented by the surrounding countryside. 'I'm just happy to be parked. That is not a drive I want to do too often.' Harry's call had summoned her to the rural village of Lower Halston on the west side of Sittingbourne. It involved a long stint on the aging A2 that merged into the equally shambolic M2 motorway. The vibrations of every concrete joint and rumble strip still seemed to be a part of her and she stretched until her lower back cracked. It instantly felt better.

'Sorry to call you out on a weekend off. How is young Vince?'

'He'll tell you he's just fine.' She huffed.

'Struggling, then?'

'Anyone would, it's only been a few days since he stumbled into that house of horrors. His problem is he's got this big heart, he can't just deal with a job and walk away, he has to take a piece of it with him.'

'Better to be ice cold, like you?' Harry said.

'Exactly.'

'The girl?' Harry said, his words a grunt as he dropped off the stile and straightened his waxed jacket.

'None of us want to turn up to anything and see there are kids involved, but for Vince, the timing of it, there are some parallels. We're looking after Sammy, a similar age and we're a part of what he's going through with his mum.'

'His mum and Vince's sister,' Harry said, like he was reminding her. 'I get the impression they're very close.'

'Always have been, which means he's worried about her, about Sammy, about a little girl at a crime scene . . . and he always thinks it's down to him to fix it all.' She huffed. 'Maybe that's why I love him so much.'

'Love!?' They were walking now, and Maddie's vision had blurred a little, but her focus sharpened when she felt Harry shoulder her gently. He was grinning too.

'I guess so?' Maddie was a little stunned at herself. That was a big word; bigger still when used for the first time.

'Well, this is no place for words like that. We have a second house of horrors. Two people dead this time, tortured first.'

Harry's reality hit was enough to stop Maddie in her tracks. She took a moment to shake her personal life from the forefront of her mind and take in her location. She'd called the force control room on the way to get an overview but Harry's words cut straight through. On one side was a large field where the wild grass was being levelled by a flock of nervy sheep that had initially formed a curious and critical group close to the fence when she had been trying to park, dispersing quickly the moment she had popped her door. The *house of horrors* was on the opposite side of Breach Lane, Lower Halston, the tarmac narrow enough to limit the parking to a short burst where the bank was missing from the other side. The house was the only one she could see and her first impressions were of a solid, square outline with windows in each corner, a central front door and a tiled roof forming a triangle over the top of it all. The style looked as if a child had been asked to draw a house from memory.

The driveway was made up of stones and had been kept clear. All the police vehicles were parked out on the road, no doubt on the instruction of the occupant of the single "CSI"-marked van that was parked out front, the black spinny thing on its roof highly agitated by a cold wind that was rolling in unhindered across the flat plains, its direction suggesting its origins were out in the North Sea. Even Harry had the collar of his waxed jacket turned up and she was glad she had opted for the extra layer of fleece.

'What do we have?' she said. They were moving again, their pace quicker as they made for the house.

'Two bodies, one white adult male, fifty-four years old and a white adult female, his wife. She's forty-six. We've got names from paperwork found inside the house: Ron and Sandy Blackman. Both were left in the hallway; both look to have suffered fatal stab wounds. This is their home address.'

'*Left* in the hallway? So we're happy someone else left them here, we don't suspect a murder-suicide?'

'I don't. The husband's hands were tied, there's suggestion he was gagged for at least some of the time and . . .'

'And?' Maddie prompted.

'The wife . . . she's missing a couple of fingernails.' Harry creased his jaw.

'So that's what you meant by torture?' They had made the threshold of the cordon, close enough for the tape to flap against Maddie's middle as she stopped again, waiting for her answer.

'No. The fingernails *were* torn out, but they were found under deep marks in a cupboard under the stairs. Scratch marks.' Harry was matter-of-fact.

'She was dragged out,' Maddie said.

'Fighting all the way.' Harry turned his head to take in the house. 'There's something else as well.'

'Go on?'

'A ground-anchored safe has been compromised. It's coded but hangs open. The master bedroom's messed up too and it's the only one.'

'So a robbery then, with a torture element to gain access to the safe.' Maddie sighed. 'And I assume the torture element will be a familiar one?'

'Stabbings. Lots of them, something short, sharp and twisted. I got CSI to grudgingly agree that it could be a corkscrew . . .' Harry faded out, a haunted look to his eyes perhaps, certainly a deeper ridge to the wrinkles around them. 'So yes, familiar.'

Just like four days earlier, when Vince and his crewmate had been the first to respond to a 999 call from an eleven-year-old girl. They had found a mother stabbed to death, a corkscrew-type implement used, the fatal blow delivered to the neck but only after a long and painful ordeal.

'We need to put that out of our mind for now, process this one without any preconceived ideas,' Harry said, though even he must have known it was impossible.

'Before we do that, how far away are we from that very familiar-sounding crime scene of a few days ago?'

Harry shrugged out his answer. 'Twenty-minute drive, assuming the Sheppey bridge is playing ball.'

They were now front-on to the house and much closer, enough for the white-windowed box with a triangular hat on to reveal some homely touches. The front door looked solid — and brand new. It was navy blue, dark enough to have looked black from a distance and with an oversized brass knob in its middle. Either side of it were frosted panels of glass shaped to fit into the original arch above it. Each panel had a hanging basket accompaniment that swung in the cold wind, the colourful flowers inside bobbing their heads in unison.

The separate building to the left was the garage she had expected. The right side of it had an overhang, under which

19

a Volkswagen SUV was parked. The tall fence also looked new, running back from the garage until it butted up against the side of the house. A gate was cut out of it and hung open to offer a glimpse of a neat lawn, a glimpse that was quickly blocked by a white paper suit that flared in the low sun.

'Detective *Inspector* Ives!' The voice that came from it was cheery and muffled at the same time. 'Stay right where you are.' The blob of white turned a sharp right out of the gate and walked a curved route away, hugging the fence line then cutting across the front of the garage to loop back round towards them like it was avoiding an invisible force field, shedding bits of blue as it did. The first was the forensic mask, then the hood was pushed down and the gloves tugged, snapped and thrust into the clear bag that hung from the left hand.

'Charley, good to see you.' Charley Mace, senior CSI. Maddie hadn't seen her for a while — the fact she was the senior for the force meant that her allocation of jobs was the same as Major Crime, an area Maddie had only just come back to.

'Ma'am!' Charley grinned back. 'Congratulations on the promotion, very well deserved I would say.'

'Half promotion.' Maddie shrugged, then said, 'Temporary Inspector,' by way of explanation.

'Ah yes, I must say, the rank structure for you warranted officers makes no sense to me. What does that even mean?'

'I guess it means they don't know if they trust me yet. Hence the need to go down to the crypt and break out Mr Blaker here. I think of him as like an undead babysitter.' The women laughed together, but Harry didn't join in.

'Rather than talk about our job roles, how about we get on with them?' Harry said, his straight face threatening to set Maddie off all over again. Charley, however, was back to serious like a switch had been flicked.

'OK then. There are some suits in the van, I've just walked the Common Approach Path so now you know where to go. I'll wait.' The Common Approach Path, standard at scenes where a serious offence had occurred, was supposed to be set by the first wave of police attendees, but CSI were the best qualified. It was effectively the most unlikely route to the body or scene of the crime, the idea being that the numerous persons arriving as part of the investigation didn't trample or disturb the areas of ground most likely walked by the offender.

Maddie and Harry suited up, then followed the route with Maddie in the lead. Charley watched every step from back by the gate, her hands on her hips. The forensic suits were ill-suited to the chilly wind, which rushed Maddie via the gap in the neck, billowing her suit out with a layer of cold air, and she was glad to make it inside, through the back door.

The theme of the exterior was mirrored inside. The kitchen they entered into was modern, minimal and functional. The splash of colour that had been provided by flowers outside was present inside in the form of a bowl of fruit in the middle of the kitchen table. The only "mess" that stood out was on an American-style double fridge whose doors were spotted with a mishmash of pictures. The right sort of mess. There were family members making silly faces topped by silly hats in a strip of photo-booth images, a newspaper cut-out that had to be part of some in-joke, magnets mocking diet attempts and a *Save the Date* card for an upcoming wedding. It was a storyboard of the lives lived in here, a glimpse into the timeline of a happy family.

Charley interrupted Maddie's musing to prepare her for the knowledge that the end of this happy family had been an abrupt one.

'Before I take you through, usual rules apply. We have two bodies in the hallway, husband and wife. The son called it in remotely and wasn't involved.'

'Remotely?' Maddie said.

It was Harry who replied. 'He's in Cardiff at the moment; university. He got a call from his mother that worried him, like she was saying goodbye, saying how much she loved him and she seemed panicked. I've tasked the local force to get a full statement from him.'

'So, they were found by a local patrol?'

Harry continued with what he knew. 'The FCR put it out as a welfare check. The attending patrol could only see the female's head and the male's legs through one of the windows at the front. There was no movement when they knocked so they went in. The son gave up a hiding place for the front door key.'

'Let's go take a look then,' Maddie said.

Charley led the way over a strip of white plastic she had no doubt laid out herself. It led them out of the kitchen and into a central hall where their movements were governed by stepping plates leading them to a viewing position with their backs close to the front door. The ground floor was largely open-plan but Maddie could see the remnants of divisions where the house might have once had a more traditional lay-out of rooms. From the look of the place, the remodelling could have been recent.

The areas either side of them were furnished as a living room and a snug area respectively, while the stairs were straight ahead, running across the internal wall of the kitchen. The husband and wife lay between them and a cupboard painted white and built into the shape under the stairs. The first third of the cupboard on the left side doubled as a bench that would suit for a place to kick off shoes.

The left door of the cupboard hung open. The two victims were positioned top to tail and had the stillness and silence about them that only came with death. It was wooden flooring throughout and, in the hallway at least, that wood carried a thick layer of blood smeared in writhing patterns that offered a contrasting dynamic to *stillness* and *silence*. Maddie reckoned their final moments had been far from it.

'OK then,' she said. 'The wife left a fingernail or two inside the cupboard. That tells us a story, doesn't it?'

'She was fighting for her life. On three fingers the nails are snapped in half,' Charley said. 'Evidentially, I will be able to show that the wife was in the cupboard and that she was not restrained or locked in there, which would suggest someone hiding. The husband appears to be the main subject of the pain compliance. The killer took their time getting to the blow that ended his ordeal.'

'Let's just call it torture, shall we, so I know where I am?' Maddie said.

Charley shrugged. 'Call it what you like, his death was a long way from pleasant. He was stabbed fourteen times at different locations on his body. Mr Blaker has already tried to pin me down on my use of language here, so don't bother trying the same, but this could be described as similar to a previous crime scene.'

'Similar or the same?'

Maddie might have been a little too quick with her question. Charley bristled a little. 'The forensic pathologist will answer that beyond all doubt; I can't. We can all see what we have here and consider that we were all stood in a *similar* place looking at a *similar* crime scene a few short days ago. What you make of that is none of my business.'

'Other *similarities* include a suspected robbery motivation,' Maddie said as she paused to scan the interior again. There were no other signs of disturbance. 'Which would seem excessive.'

'Excessive?' Charley said.

Maddie gestured at the husband, Ron Blackman, who was wearing shirt and trousers, lying on his side with his back towards them. He was large, not obese, but not in shape either, even for his age. The trousers were torn and bloodied where he had been stabbed in both buttocks and further down in his hamstrings. Maddie had seen that the shirt was ripped open at the front, exposing injuries to his stomach and underarms where the blade had entered. All of his wounds were ragged, bright white twists of flesh with black middles — just like the week before. The weapon in mind for that was deemed likely to be a solid, one-piece corkscrew, the sort you might see in high-end restaurants as a straight handle with a twist of steel coming off and used to open your favourite red. It was over-engineered for the purpose, however, and would have no trouble at all piercing flesh to release another type of red altogether. In this case a fifty-four-year-old vintage.

'All that for a code to a safe?' Maddie said.

Harry's first word was coarse, like his throat had dried out. 'Maybe it wasn't about the code for a safe, maybe it was for the location of his wife.'

Charley continued. 'You can see the male was restrained, which isn't something we saw at that previous scene . . .'

Maddie focused on Ron Blackman's hands. They were tight against his back, palms forced towards her from being trussed together at the wrists. The restraints were tight enough for blood to linger as a purple line through the shocking white skin. 'PlastiCuffs,' Charley added.

Maddie knew PlastiCuffs well; they were issued to officers who policed public order situations, where a backup might be needed for the single pair of steel-framed cuffs that were issued. PlastiCuffs were crude, little more than a cable tie that ratcheted tight through a central piece of plastic, and the only way to remove them was by cutting them off. Crude but effective.

And less than a fiver on eBay.

'They do the job,' Maddie said.

'So it would seem,' Charley agreed. 'You can see numerous stab wounds, all to fleshy parts so we're talking thighs, calves, buttocks, sides of the torso and biceps, but cause of death for both victims will be determined as a single blow to the neck. We have bruising around the wounds consistent with a handled weapon with a short blade coming from its centre, the blows administered using a punching movement. The stab wounds themselves have visible tears of the subcutaneous consistent with a twisted blade—'

'So, a corkscrew then, identical to before,' Maddie tried again.

'Your friendly forensic pathologist will be able to give confirmation after their examination,' Charlie said, her irritation clear.

'Which will take place on the slab?' Maddie said, despite already knowing the answer. The job of the pathologist was to give an official cause of death. Television dramas often showed them attending scenes, bantering with the lead detective and throwing up key pieces of information that could be used to go on and "crack the case". Their information was key, no doubt about that, but they rarely attended a scene and there was little room for banter when the report was delivered remotely via an update to the case on a computer system.

'We're not expecting attendance,' Charley confirmed.

'Anything else we need to know here and now?' Maddie said.

Charley's hands found her hips. 'Well, on first inspection of the husband I can't see any signs of defensive wounds, which strikes me as unusual, especially if we think the wife started out as hidden.'

'Unusual, because you would expect him to put up a fight?'

'Exactly. If someone enters your home for possessions and your wife is hiding under the stairs, you put up a fight the moment they bring out the restraints, don't you?'

'Unless he was just playing ball, hoping they wouldn't look beyond him and go,' Maddie said, but if she was trying to convince herself, she was failing.

'Maybe. Fortunately for me . . .' Charley paused to show off a wide smile that had returned, 'I don't need to worry about any of that. You'll have my report with all the *facts* that are here. The rest you will need to figure out yourself.' She turned back to the blood-soaked scene, frozen in time in front of them. 'Good luck with that.'

CHAPTER 5

Hospitals are just like custody blocks, the similarities stark enough that even someone like Vince Arnold couldn't miss them as he walked the bland corridors of The Queen Elizabeth, Queen Mother Hospital — QEQM — in Margate, to be assaulted by strong and changeable smells. The patients, like prisoners, shuffled towards him in their standard-issue clothing, their heads hanging as if in shame, their arm held to lead them somewhere they would rather not go. But the most glaring similarity of all: everyone just wanted to go home.

Vince always sighed a little in relief when he left a custody block and he would do the same when the doors parted and the fresh air rolled over him on the way out of the hospital.

But that would come later.

His sister was first.

The Intensive Treatment Unit was just what it sounded like. Rebecca Arnold was surrounded by bleeping, hissing, moving machinery, their sole focus on keeping those on the ward alive. Rebecca was at least conscious. They had been told that she was beyond the point where medical assistance could improve her condition and anything attached to her was purely to manage her pain and to give her the best base possible. It was all down to her to recover now, to turn a corner and build her strength back to the point where treatment could start again.

'Sis!' Vince said immediately and Rebecca's grin was enough to fire up those eyes, the last part of her that looked familiar. Around them hung darkened skin, the bones of her face visible like shadows, her hair flaky and thinned enough to show a bruised scalp. She was wearing a white vest, the exposed skin on her arms and chest covered in a multi-coloured patchwork of bruises and sagging clumps where her strong physique had wasted away to nothing.

Rebecca was seven years older than Vince, the ideal amount to be the perfect older sister. When Vince started secondary school his sister was still talked about, her judo abilities still adorned the walls, a whole section dedicated to her competing for Great Britain helping to form a general consensus: you didn't fuck with Rebecca Arnold. Which meant you didn't fuck with her little brother either. In truth, Rebecca was no fighter, not outside of the dojo at least. She was built naturally strong and had then trained hard on it, fuelled by a competitive streak that bled over into everything she did. Vince could remember a game of chess that had nearly come to blows in a rain-covered caravan on some cursed holiday. They still laughed about that now — at least until one of them claimed to have been the victor.

Tough but fair. They bickered a lot less than when they were younger but it still happened occasionally and this was a phrase that had had them bickering the last time he had visited. Rebecca had said it, followed by *that's what I want you to say at my funeral.* She had been joking, purposefully winding up her brother just like she always had, but his sense of humour had evaporated in an instant. He wasn't coping well with her illness, Maddie had told him that, told him that he needed to prepare himself, but she hadn't spent her whole life watching Rebecca Arnold fight against the odds like he had. She might have made a career out of her judo, the Olympics was her dream for a while, it had looked realistic for a time, but the reason she'd missed out might just be what summed her up best. That competitive nature, strength and dedication to training took her close, but she lost out, her trainer forced to explain how she lacked the killer instinct to go that final step. Rebecca had been devastated but, tellingly, she quit rather than try to prove a point. The only time she had quit anything her whole life. Rebecca then, like Vince now, knew that her trainer had been right. The one missing ingredient was that nastiness needed to drive an opponent down to the canvas.

Vince was different.

He did have that instinct. His own mixed martial arts career — inspired by his older sister — failed for a different reason entirely: lack of discipline. Where Rebecca was all technique, concentration and respect, Vince was an uncontrollable ball of rage who took a painful hit personally and forgot everything he had been taught to start swinging. That same trainer who had dropped Rebecca pointed out that if he could merge the two Arnold siblings together as one fighter he would have a world champion on his hands — in any discipline. That was a sentiment that had stuck with Vince: together, the Arnolds could take on the world.

Vince couldn't contemplate them divided.

'How you doing, Becks?' Vince still hadn't worked out a better opener.

'You come back for that arm wrestle?' she replied and her grin was finally removed by a cough.

'Would it count? What with you being proper fucked an' all?'

'You still think you could beat me?' Rebecca goaded him.

'Nope, that's why I'm not going to do it. Can you imagine the shame at losing now?'

'You mean with me on my deathbed?' Rebecca said, and Vince flinched at the word. 'It's OK. I mean, as far as deathbeds go, this is pretty state of the art!'

'How's Mum?' Vince said, moving the conversation on and gesturing at the fresh flowers. Their mother, Kathleen (never Kath), was in the habit of bringing fresh flowers every day. It was ridiculous and just about every bed in there now had a smattering of pink carnation overflow where Rebecca might otherwise be swamped.

'You know how she is! You remember you promised you would look out for her, bruv, you remember you said that?' Rebecca's switch to serious was instant.

'Don't talk like that,' Vince said, like he always did.

'Like what?'

'Like you're giving up.'

'Getting affairs in order isn't giving up. They told me that in here. I just need to know that everyone's looked after if this turns to shit.'

It was the first thing that they had talked about, the next thing after Rebecca had broken the news of her illness. Rebecca had said that she was sick, she didn't give it a name then and she still wouldn't now, just that she was sick enough that she needed to be sure certain things would go on without her. Rebecca had chosen a pub called the White Horse to break the news, their local when they were younger. That conversation had been just a few months earlier, over a game of pool, coming at the end of a set of nights for Vince. Maybe his fatigue was the reason he hadn't considered the call for a drink in a pub they hadn't been in for years as a reason to be concerned. Vince had been worried about Maddie at the time, she'd just finished a case that had left its mark on her, would leave a mark on anyone to be honest and he didn't really know how to be around her. He talked it out with Becks, starting the moment he saw her and, of course, she had listened patiently. Then she had helped, given her big-sister advice and made Vince feel better. By the time he had finally got round to asking how she was doing they were on their third game.

I'm dying, Vince. And they don't know if they can stop it.

Just like that.

29

That game was still unfinished. They had tipped out into the pub garden so Vince could gulp down fresher air like it might help. It hadn't. It had been a beautiful day, part of a long, hot summer that would come to a spectacular and stormy end the night after. For Vince, his sister's downhill turn started there and then, out in that bright sunlight where, under closer scrutiny, he had seen an increased distance between the edge of Rebecca's sunglasses and her sunken cheeks. It was to get worse every time he saw her.

'And my big man,' Rebecca said, 'you'll look after him, make sure he grows up to be the best?'

Sammy. Nine years old was old enough to miss his mum horribly and wise enough to know he was being kept away for a reason — and not a good one. Vince was finding it tough to handle that. Both mother and son were burying their heads, talking every day on a video call about how they would get together in person just as soon as she was better, while the elephant in the room only grew, soon to start trumpeting for attention. Vince could understand it; as much physical and mental anguish as his sister and her son were suffering right now, there was a whole other well of pain that was ready and waiting the moment he walked in here. But Maddie had left a lasting impression, she had a way of saying something that left no room for any argument: *What do you think Sammy will think if he never gets to see his mum again, if she dies and he never got to say goodbye?*

'Don't you worry about him,' Vince's throat suddenly felt dry. 'If ever a lad had his whole life worked out!' He forced some sort of a chuckle.

'We all did though, didn't we, at nine I mean?' Rebecca said, those eyes starting to fire back up.

'I guess we did.'

'I'll need someone to be there if his life doesn't quite work out as planned. It didn't for us after all, I'm not an Olympic champion with a house in Vegas and you . . . what was your dream? That's right, you never did get to be the Milky Bar Kid, did you?'

30

'Very good!' Vince smirked.

'I still don't understand why, I mean, you've got the hair, you're weedy and you'd look great in a Stetson . . .'

'Once . . . just once I said it would be a great job,' Vince moaned, his throat loosening a little. 'I like Milky Bars and I would be on the tele, that was all I said and I was like, what, seven years old? You've never let me live that down!'

'Say it!' Rebecca teased him. 'I tell you what, I'll get some of the nurses over here and you can do a sort of audition, they're brutal round here with their honesty, they'll soon tell you if you're not up for it. Nanny! NANNY!' Rebecca was raising her voice, the strain hidden by the sudden glee on her face, her words directed towards a nurse standing over at his station.

'This had better be good, Arnold!' he bawled back, his face lit with humour, his bald head by the overhead lighting. He moved closer.

'Don't you think my bruvver here could be the Milky Bar Kid? You remember that, right?'

'I remember it was a *kid*, yeah.' With that he turned back to his station.

It was enough — Rebecca was suddenly laughing as hard as her condition would allow. 'Mugged off!' she managed. 'Seems he reckons you're weedy enough, it's just that you're past it!'

'Nanny?' Vince's reply was low enough not to be detected, his eyes flitting between his sister and the broad shoulders of the man she had just berated.

His sister shrugged. 'He nannies me, you know.'

'Sponge bath?' Vince said, lifting an eyebrow.

That twinkle in Rebecca's eye flashed its return for just a moment, 'Jesus, Vince, you know nothing about dying!'

Vince laughed too, but there was a silence that followed that turned awkward. Finally, he moved on to the reason for his visit.

'Your boy wants to see his mum,' he started, leaving a pause for a reaction. There was a question in there somewhere but he didn't want to ask it direct. 'Not on Facetime, not through some screen . . .' he said, instead.

'This again.' All trace of humour now lost among the shadows of her face.

'It's not going away, he's not going away. I can't be the one who stopped him coming, who stopped him saying . . .'

'Goodbye?' Rebecca finished it for him.

'He asks every day,' Vince continued. 'Not me, not you either when you talk on the iPad, he asks Mads and she don't know what to say.'

'That's not fair, not on her. I get that.'

'It's not fair on the boy either. Of course he wants to come see his mother.'

'You've changed your tune, bruv! Not so long ago I got the impression you were trying to keep him away.'

'I was being selfish, I guess I didn't want to deal with the fallout when we leave here and go home.'

'He's comfortable there, he likes it, I mean?' She changed direction, her look at him suddenly earnest.

'I think he does. It's a tough time, but we've made the place his as much as we can. He knows it always will be, too. If he needs it.'

'You don't mind? You and Mads . . . I know you've got it good but it's early days still and you haven't long bought that house together. I reckon you had plans for those spare rooms and it wasn't my kid—' She stopped at Vince's raised hand. This was a conversation that had played out any number of times. She must have recognised a man who wasn't about to do it again. 'I just want to be sure—'

'I know what you want, it's the same thing we all want. You don't have to worry about Sammy, not ever. But you do have to see him. Please, just think about it.'

'OK,' she said.

'OK, you'll think about it, or OK, OK?'

'Bring him in,' she said, her eyes suddenly moistening. 'It's hard . . .' she paused where her voice might break. Rebecca was just like their mother; he didn't reckon he had ever seen either of them cry, not since their father had died and even then he had been too young to really understand what was going on. Rebecca fought it off. 'I want him here, every minute of every day if I could, I just can't take seeing him upset, I can't take being the reason . . .'

'Maybe it will do you the world of good. He's a good kid, stronger than you think and he's no fool either, he knows what to expect when he comes here and it won't matter, I think he just wants to give his mum a big hug.'

'OK then,' she said again, her head a jerked nod, her hand lifting to run across her eyes. Still Vince didn't see any tears but he made a point of not looking too close and was delighted with an interruption. The nurse his sister had affectionately referred to as Nanny appeared to stand over him.

'You're not upsetting my favourite patient, are you?' he said, his voice carrying mock authority while he lightly touched Vince on the shoulder.

'Not on purpose,' Vince countered.

'My brother was actually asking about sponge baths earlier,' Rebecca said.

'A sponge bath?' The nurse raised his eyebrows. 'It's not a service we normally offer visitors but I can make an exception.' He was obvious in looking Vince up and down.

'I'll bear that in mind,' Vince said.

'Well, OK then. I didn't mean to interrupt but I thought I would get you a nice cup of tea. You know, seeing as we don't often get celebrity guests up here.' Nanny was deadpan and there was a moment of confusion before Rebecca erupted into laughter. She strained to lift her hand and high-five the nurse who set two cups down, then walked away humming *the milky bars are on me*.

'Good to see you've made an impression in here,' Vince said.

'What can I say, I got all the charisma, sorry about that.' Rebecca reached for the tea. Her cup was different, it had handles on each side and Rebecca used them both, the cup shaking a little as she brought it up to her mouth. Swallowing looked painful. Rebecca put the cup back down then sucked deeper breaths in through her nose, like the effort required more of the pure oxygen being pumped to just under her nostrils. 'How are you, anyway, after that horrible call?'

'I'm good, sis, people keep asking me that but you get jobs like that. Water off a duck's back by now!'

'Doesn't mean you don't take . . . a little bit away.' Her sentence was interrupted by a gulp for air. She was getting tired, looking it and sounding it now, Vince knew the signs, his time with her was coming to an end. He watched her struggle with lifting her tea the second time, biting his lip so he didn't ask to help.

'It's always tougher where there's a kid involved, a little girl, not much older than Sammy. You'd have to be made of stone for it not to drag you down a bit,' Vince said.

'Just as long as you can get back up again.'

'Of course. I'm here, aren't I? What else would I do? Go sit under a rock somewhere until the world's rid of all the shitty people?'

'You can't get them all, the shitty people I mean, that's not your job.'

'Isn't it?' Vince snapped, that anger that would have him swinging in a fight suddenly rearing its head.

'Sorry, bruv, I'm not so good at being clear these days. It's all the drugs.' She took another deep sniff of her air, and her eyes rolled a little, like she might be losing the battle with the pain medication and her exhaustion. 'I know Maddie worries.'

'She doesn't need to worry about me.'

'She adores you, Vince Arnold, and I ain't never seen you more in love with someone. It sickens me, to be honest! She's taken you on, she's taken my Sammy on and all without a word . . .' Another break, this time with a scowl like she was struggling to continue.

'It's OK, I know what you mean. Don't be worrying about us, your energy needs to be on yourself, on getting better.'

'This girl you found . . .' she said. 'This will sound harsh, but her mum and dad have the job of making it better for her. Your job is Maddie and Sammy.'

'She doesn't know her dad,' Vince said. 'And her mother's dead. She was stabbed fourteen times while this girl was an inch or two away. Someone came into her house and destroyed everything she had, took her future for good measure. That could have been my house, or yours. It could have been anyone's. It did have an impact and I'm not sure I want to get to the point where I'm not scared by that.'

His sister took another deep inhale of her oxygen, her watery eyes seemed to be searching Vince. 'I didn't think you coppers got scared!'

'Coppers scare the best, because the ghost stories you hear, those myths and monsters that sound so ridiculous, we get to see that they're real.'

'Jesus, bruv, and you . . . wonder . . . why . . . I worry!' Now it was individual words that were intersected by deep sucks on the air, the exertion clear.

'Crazy world, eh sis? Where everyone just sits around worrying about each other!' Vince slapped his thighs, a sign he was ready to leave, one his sister picked up on.

'You'd better get back out into it, then.' And she smiled, then took another couple of long sucks to reply. 'I'm out of small talk anyway, bruv, to be honest . . . and you're pretty depressing. Imagine that . . .' Rebecca faded out to combine sucking air in with laughter and coughing. 'The ward of death and you're the most depressing thing on it!'

Vince laughed a little with her. 'I can stay as long as you want.'

'I'm shattered, bruv. This is the longest I've been awake for a while and besides, you got me thinking about requesting a bed bath now!'

'I reckon I know what Nanny over there will say.'

'I reckon I . . . do . . . too . . .' Vince waited her out while she recovered. 'I reckon he'd be more up for giving you one.' Another deep suck of the fresh oxygen. 'When did you wanna bring my boy in to see me?'

'Tomorrow?' Vince said, watching closely for her reaction. 'He was at a sleepover last night, at Ryan's, I reckon he'll be there most of the day. But tomorrow . . .'

'Tomorrow!' Rebecca said, her eyes flitting from side to side like she might be considering it. 'Best I get my hair done then.'

'Best you do,' Vince said. 'I can't wait to tell him.'

'Tell you what, I'll tell him tonight. Get him to call normal time.'

Vince swallowed the last of a tea that had been served lukewarm. He stood up.

'You will tell him, bruv, won't you?'

'Tell him?'

'Sammy; about me. I don't want him coming in here without knowing that I look . . .' She faded out, her eyes shifting from side to side in hollow sockets while she searched for the right words.

'I'll tell him,' Vince said. Then he met his sister's outstretched hand to grip it tight round the thumb, an embrace that had taken the place of the hug that had become too painful. Vince lingered over her, waiting for that reassuring smile, the one his older sister had always had for him. It came, and he felt able to head for the fresh air of the exit.

CHAPTER 6

'What are we doing back here?' Maddie's agitation was clear, and she wasn't the sort to try and hide it. It was a Saturday afternoon, Harry himself had called her in to study a brand-new crime scene — and there was much to do on that — and yet he had now brought her back to the first murder scene, the one from four days earlier.

'I told you there was no need for you to come,' Harry growled.

'You also said this might be relevant.'

'It might.' Harry was infuriating and Maddie made sure her harumph was loud enough that her colleague couldn't miss it. At least the Sheppey Crossing had played ball that day. The island had a hard-earned reputation as a place you could not plan around. The whole of the UK could be wrapped in glorious sunshine, while the Sheppey Crossing presented as four lanes of sun-washed tarmac reaching out into a giant wall of fog, like the Rapture had arrived to consume all in its path, making a start on a small island just north of Sittingbourne.

Harry worked the key to gain access to a house that was no longer a police scene. CSI were last to leave and they had locked up on doing so, but the keys had remained in police possession since no one, it seemed, was in any rush to come forward and claim them on behalf of the family. The eleven-year-old girl — the only thing left alive when police forced entry — had at least been claimed, but this place, this venue that had played host to such evil, had been left sealed tight for the air to thicken, the only internal movement the slow dance of shadows.

Four days later and the air had stagnated to the point of being oppressive. The house was old, the original part at least. The kitchen at the back was a newer extension that broke the lines of the original build by pushing out to the side. It was the oldest part that met you head on, originally constructed in the seventeenth century with a front door positioned off-centre to give a lopsided impression. The ground floor was dotted with small windows, the first floor the same and their lead-lined tops brushed the start of the grey-slated roof. The house had a chimney on each end, one was part of a defunct inglenook fireplace with original bread oven, the other linked to an ultra-modern wood burner that worked well as a juxtapose. The kitchen was more retro-modern; a long, slim building set back and rendered in polished stones that caught the light at different angles like glitter. The main house was a bright white matching the gravel that marked out the footprint overall. It was bigger than the house they had been to that morning but the feeling was the same, the feeling of a family home with all of its colour, light and life sucked out at once.

Harry hesitated at the door. He had a tablet in his hand that he powered on.

'What's that?' Maddie said.

'Vince's body-worn footage.'

'We've seen that.' Maddie wasn't sure she wanted to see it again, either.

'I want to go through it again, here, I want to walk it through.'

'OK?' Maddie said, holding back a flurry of questions that she was pretty certain he wouldn't answer anyway.

She hoped, instead, that this would all start to make sense pretty soon. Response officers all have personal-issue cameras attached to their chest. The footage they record can often provide key evidence, but Vince's arrival here — and that of his colleague PC Siobhan Maddox — had been studied a good few times by numerous sets of different eyes and nothing had stood out. Maddie didn't know what might be different just because they were watching it where it had been filmed.

Harry pressed play, the tablet held so she could see it too. The footage started with a sway, the door they were standing in front of appeared in its digital version, blurring with the movement where Vince was running towards it. The footage had sound too, the crunch of gravel was quickly overrun by Vince barking at PC Maddox and then a solid beating on the door.

'*Can you see in?*' Vince was anxious, his voice fragile. The screen filled with a close-up of the door and PC Maddox's voice shrill with panic called back.

'*No.*'

'*I'm going to put it in. Brace it.*'

The viewpoint moved back and angled downwards at the gravel for a moment where a red-coloured steel enforcer was waiting. Vince grunted with the strain of picking it up. The enforcer is a handheld battering ram, it weighs about twenty kilos but in the right hands the force applied to the door is many times more. Vince was those right hands. His colleague sat down in front with her feet lifted to rest flat against the door, pushing out for all she was worth. He swung over her, the strike level with the handle, and the wooden door popped in one.

Police! PC Maddox scrambled to her feet to be first in but both stopped in the hallway, the camera swinging like Vince was unsure which way to go.

Harry paused the footage, leaving the two panicked officers frozen in time as he stepped into the house still suffering the same. The introduction of a breeze through the

39

door disturbed a piece of blue plastic that skittered away from them across the floorboards and Maddie recognised it as the backing tape from a police evidence bag. The shadows now slunk to the corners, pushed away by the burst of light, biding their time to take back over. The windows looked smaller still, from inside, small enough to focus the light into beams made of dust under a low ceiling that was visibly uneven.

Harry turned to the left to face the square reception room with the ancient fireplace, knowing that, four days earlier, those first officers had done the same. He restarted the footage and the tiny speakers were enough to fill the empty home with panic and anxiety all over again.

'*In here!*' The camera jerked left to the sound of PC Maddox's voice, then Vince piled through the door to where his colleague had stopped still, her back blocking the view. Maddie might have stopped it here. She had the last time, deciding she had seen this enough. But Harry still had the tablet angled for her to see and she felt like she had to. PC Maddox's right arm was out, bent at the elbow to form a triangle where she had stopped to cover her mouth, where shock had her frozen still. Vince didn't move either, struck the same, for a moment at least. PC Maddox then squatted out of the way to reveal the first glimpse of what was left of a fallen woman: Maria Mercer.

The blood stood out, even in the footage; Maria's blood. Harry paused it again to take a single step into the reception room. The blood on the floor was still there, but muted, subdued after four days of drying to look like a patch of autumn leaves swept into a pile and left to rot black. Four days earlier it had been viscid; a bright red, the shade entirely unique: *blood red*. Its appearance on the screen was stark, contrasting with the earthy colours of the décor and clumps of shadow to demand attention. Maria was among it in a dark top that had a wet look, catching the light as the camera moved forward.

'*Someone's under here!*' PC Maddox's shrill voice arced out like lightning. The camera moved to point down and the next part of the footage was what had remained with Maddie, replaying over in her mind every day since, leaving her wondering just what impact it would have had on Vince. At first there were just hints of something light-coloured moving under the floorboards, visible through a gap where the boards were not quite flush, then a flash where the sunlight caught the tops of the steel nails holding the wood down.

'*It's OK, we're going to get you out of there.*' Vince's anxiety now close to panic, the camera shaking as he clawed at the floorboards with little effect. His next words were shouted and indiscernible, coming as he stood back up, then stumbled to a sprint that took him — and his camera — out of the front door to their car where he pulled a claw hammer from the boot. He was clumsy, cussing almost the whole time — like he was whispering into the microphone — his voice a higher pitch than usual. The hooked end of the hammer was effective as a lever to ply up the boards, the sound of the splintering wood mingled with his whimpers of exertion and despair. His colleague could be seen in flashes, she stayed kneeling down, talking through the gaps, her right hand flat against the floor. PC Maddox would later write in her statement how she was desperately trying to make contact with fingertips pushed up from below. Her left hand was glued to the radio on her chest as she tried to hold it together to call for an ambulance, to call for backup, to tell the world that they had a woman dying, her blood oozing through the floorboards to where a child was trapped, also covered in blood.

It was chaos.

Chaos that Harry could press a screen to pause, to take a breath. Maddie was glad of it, she needed one too. She silently moved to the place where PC Maddox had been. The floorboards were still ripped up and scattered either side of an exposed void, the planks bearing the tool marks from the claw hammer like fresh scars. In the last few days, Maddie had learned how the house had a suspended timber floor, common in houses of this age as a combatant to damp, she had been told. The space this left under the floor was just enough to trap a person, a child for sure, and Maddie allowed her eyes to shut.

41

The terror of an eleven-year-old nailed into a tiny crawl-space in the floor still hung in the air like the disturbed dust. The location of the bruises on Jade Mercer's body told a story of how she was likely grabbed by the tops of her arms and held down by her chest while the boards were laid over her and hammered in. One of the nails had missed a joist to nick her right foot. Maddie wondered if she had even noticed while her senses were saturated with the sound of hammering on a board that was an inch from her face, while her throat and nose were layered with dust and dirt as she gulped panicked breaths and her mind whirling with the realisation of being sealed in, while her mother screamed and begged above her.

Nails in your own coffin.

Harry's attention was back on the tablet and this time, when it fired up, it was a sound file that played. Maddie recognised it straight away as the 999 call that had started it all. A male voice was the first to be heard, robotic almost — monotone, then the call was quickly handed over to the police call-taker: Lynn Hathaway. Lynn's reaction was different, more emotional as she reacted to the sound of a whimper, of panicked breathing, a noise of scraping against wood. Maddie had seen Lynn's statement too, where she explained an instant bad feeling, how she had somehow known from that first moment that she was talking to a child and how she had to focus on doing what she needed and not try to imagine what was going on. Peering down into the dusty void where that call had originated from, Maddie wondered if anyone could have imagined this. The sound file continued with Lynn asking for two buttons to be pressed if she could hear but couldn't speak. The tones followed soon after. Then came a voice, the first words from Jade Mercer; distant, faint, terrified: *Mum . . . is that you?*

Harry sighed, his head hung forward, his first sign of any emotion. 'She's a long way from the phone when she speaks,' he said, his voice broken.

'I agree,' Maddie said with a shrug. She had agreed the last time they had talked about it too.

'Which would make sense if she had the phone in her hand. She wouldn't have been able to bring it any closer to her mouth, she'd be pressed too tight against the wood.'

'We know all this, Harry.'

'We do,' Harry flared angrily, swallowing it before he continued. 'But maybe we missed something, maybe that's why it's happened again, because we missed something.'

'Is that why we're here? This wasn't your fault, this wasn't *our* fault.'

Harry ignored her to squat, his fingers running over the dried blood staining the sides of the exposed floorboards where it had run through. So much had dripped below that Vince and his colleague had been convinced — wrongly — that Jade had been stabbed too. Harry reverted back to the video footage. Again, pressing play brought immediate chaos with Vince wrenching up a board, exposing a little more of the girl underneath who reacted by reaching out with any part she could, desperate to be released. A hand appeared first, then a knee from under where another board was ripped up, then two arms and finally a head. Jade's mouth, when it could be seen, was wide in a scream that continued as she was wrenched to her feet and swept away. Then came another moment that had been constantly invading Maddie's thoughts in the days since she had seen it first. Jade turned back, but only one side of her face was visible where her hair was flattened over the other side in a sticky clump of blood that continued as a smear on her face. PC Maddox had her, Jade's arm wrapped tightly over the top of her back, but she stopped and then came a wail of anguish that seemed to start before her mouth was even open, piercing and guttural. Her lips did open but it still didn't seem like her mouth was the source; *she* was the source, like that sound was emanating from everywhere, from every pore and even from second-hand footage, Maddie knew it would have pierced Vince right through to his heart. Jade was led away; the wailing got quieter but lost none of its impact.

Harry paused it again.

'What are we doing, Harry?' Maddie tried again, her throat had dried up too.

'Testing our theory. We're saying a robbery. Two offenders at least, one to get control of the mother, one for the child—'

'We don't know it was two, we can't rule out a lone offender. Once Jade talks to us, maybe—'

Harry was shaking his head as he cut her off. 'She's not going to be able to help but think about it, if you were nailing my daughter under the floorboards you would have to kill me first.'

'They did.'

'But after. From the blood, we know Maria Mercer bled out after they were put back down. This was planned, if you're planning to get control of two people and you want to be sure, you don't do it on your own. At least two. That's before you start a search for whatever it is you're here to steal.'

'You're probably right, but we don't know until we know.' Maddie took no pleasure from offering Harry a quote right back at him. *You don't know until you know* was actually an old Major Crime adage, one that had stood the test of time for a reason.

'Putting the daughter under the boards can't be spontaneous, it was always part of the plan. Why?' Harry said, like he hadn't been listening.

'We talked this out too . . .' Maddie said, but Harry waved her away.

'That was before this morning. Let's talk about it again, there's something we're missing about what they did.'

'OK, so we said it would be effective if they were trying to get something from the mother, something like access to the safe or knowledge of where the expensive jewellery is.'

'It's overkill,' Harry said immediately. 'No way you would need to go to these lengths. Maria Mercer is a lone female at a remote location and let's assume she's facing multiple offenders for now. Maria also has a young child upstairs to protect; she couldn't be more vulnerable. There's no sign of any forced entry so we think she opened the door to be rushed. She's caught out and unprepared. From what we can see, we can assume extreme violence would have been used to get immediate control, or at the very least the threat of it.'

'So that's what happened. The daughter was part of that, part of convincing her to open the safe, to tell them where her good jewellery is. I'm confused as to why you can't see where that fits?'

Harry moved back out into the hallway. 'Because it was never necessary! If it were me . . .' He paused, his expression pained.

'Maybe you shouldn't . . .' Maddie stopped herself telling him not to think of what happened here using his own family. Of course he was going to compare it, his daughter had been the victim of a violent home invasion too; so violent, in fact, that she had never stood a chance. Maddie knew he had taken this one personally. There was always a little extra emphasis when there was a child victim, but for Harry, this was bigger still.

He ignored her again. 'We know they had a weapon; you would only need to mention my kids with something sharp in your hand and I would fold. That would be enough, take what you want. We found Jade's bed ruffled, her laptop on it and open in standby so she was probably sat on her bed when her mother opened the front door. They wouldn't even need to get her down here.'

'Maybe Maria refused. Maybe there was something in that safe that she couldn't give up easy. We know she brought her work home, her position at the local council meant she had access to some very sensitive information.'

Harry's headshake was more violent. 'It wouldn't matter, nothing would. Say she refused at the first ask, then you get Jade and take her to another room and describe what you are *going* to do. Any parent folds at that point.' Harry peered back into the void. 'You would never need to bury her under the floorboards in the same room.'

'It escalated.' Maddie shrugged and she could see her colleague was biting his tongue, maybe holding back the

45

retort he'd made when they had talked it out the first time: *You might understand if you were a parent.* He had retracted it, said it wasn't fair, but stopped short of apologising and she was in no doubt he'd meant it when he said it.

'You're saying the mother played hardball, refused to give them the answers, so the floorboards were a way of getting what they needed?'

'Maybe, or maybe she didn't refuse to answer at all, maybe she just didn't know whatever it was they wanted. What I'm saying is that we have a theory pieced together painstakingly over the last four days that fits.' Maddie couldn't help her frustration spilling out into her words. Harry started speaking again, but it was a mumble as he mimed through the series of events, starting at the front door.

'They knock,' he said. 'The mother is the adult so she answers. The offenders get control of her, make the threat to harm and at this point Jade is sitting on her bed.' Harry paced away from the front door, his eyes lifted up the stairs. Maddie had an image in her mind's eye of a woman with a hand grabbed over her mouth in the hall.

'They want something and they ask for it. Maria Mercer doesn't give it up straight away so Jade is brought down to add incentive. At this point they must have done something to prevent recognition — cover Jade's eyes or more likely they were wearing something to cover their own faces.'

'Because they're going to leave Jade alive,' Maddie said.

'Exactly. They might not have wanted to involve her at all, but it got to the point where they needed to show that they mean business, they need the daughter upset, terrified and appealing to her mother, but without harming her . . .' Harry stepped out into the hallway to take in the stairs, the route Jade would have walked — or been dragged down.

'Maria Mercer, at this point . . .' Harry started, turning back to face Maddie. 'At this point she tells them anything they want to know. So how does her daughter end up under those floorboards? That's the bit that doesn't make any sense.'

'Maybe they did it for fun, Harry, we talked about that. The things we've seen, the people we've met, that evil is out there and we know it. Is it such a leap to think that someone gets their kicks from burying kids under the floor while their mother bleeds out above them?'

'What did we see this morning?' Harry's words were blurted, giving a clue that he was about to come onto the real reason he had wanted to come back here.

'What do you mean?' Maddie said.

'This morning, two victims killed in the same way. The wife hiding in a cupboard.'

'But Charley seemed pretty happy that Sandy Blackman was forced *out*, not in.'

'Which doesn't fit. But the phone call might.'

'Phone call?'

'To the Blackmans' son. Think about it, that means we have the parents dead and the child involved; the same as what we have here!' Harry was talking more quickly, his words blending into a single, excited stream.

'How is a twenty-year-old son getting a phone call from his mother, and one that didn't even tell him what was going on, the same as an eleven-year-old girl being nailed under the floor and bled on? The son wasn't even in the same country.'

'It *is* the same.' Harry rounded on her. 'The *impact* is the same. The wife this morning calls her son hundreds of miles away to say goodbye. Can you imagine the internal battle for the mother not to cry for help? To tell him to send the police? Why do you think she didn't?'

'She was told not to? Someone was stood in front of her with a sharpened corkscrew, her husband already dead perhaps — injured at least, I bet — and she knew that saying something like that would mean it was all over?'

Harry shook his head again. 'Her son said she was calling to say *goodbye*, she already knew it was over for her. But the way she did it, from what the son said, it was goodbye without saying it specifically. He just thought she was acting

47

weird, telling him she loved him, to be happy no matter what, that sort of thing.'

'OK, I still don't see how it's the same?' Maddie said.

'Sandy Blackman was *protecting* her son, she didn't want to make him part of the trauma, part of what was happening to her, for his sake. Maria Mercer here, all she would have wanted to do was protect her daughter, to keep her out of it entirely . . . And then there was the phone . . .' Harry was pacing the hall, his excitement had him breathing deeper and he moved to the front door to take deep breaths where it was fresher. 'Jade called 999 from her mother's phone,' he said, 'that could only be unlocked by her mother's face or code.'

'And we know she couldn't see the screen from her position,' Maddie added.

'So, whoever killed the mother must have given Jade that phone, unlocking it first, maybe even dialling 999. We've listened back to the call so we know it was on speaker, that Jade was talking from some distance away.'

'Her mother could have given her that phone.' Maddie was playing devil's advocate — usually that was Harry's role.

'I don't see how. If you get control of someone by force you would take something like a phone off them. And how would she slip the phone to her daughter while the boards were being nailed over her?'

'So the offenders wanted her to be found,' Maddie said.

'And by the police,' Harry replied.

'Not necessarily. Maybe just by someone and 999's a pretty reliable way to guarantee it.'

Harry took a couple of paces back into the hall. 'This is where . . .' he mumbled, then dropped to his hands and knees to run his fingertips over wood worn smooth through decades of footsteps. 'There was some damp work done, some boards replaced, we found the paperwork as part of the search.' Harry was back to talking out loud rather than seeking confirmation.

'The hallway by the front door . . .' Maddie confirmed what she had read.

'They're newer, the screws,' Harry said, pointing downwards.

'Which matches with them being replaced. And we think they used nails rather than screws to secure Jade because it would have been quicker.'

Harry leaned closer to the floor. 'This one is scuffed,' he said. 'Like someone has tried to unscrew it with a thread too small, or one that hadn't gripped.' He shuffled backwards to the next, now on his knees. Maddie couldn't recall seeing him so animated. He was inspecting more screws, they were lined up two at a time at the end of each board and she squatted closer. 'Tool marks!' Harry announced, pointing at a slight scuff she could see in the wood. 'What did CSI do with the flooring in other parts of the house? Did they spend any time on it or did they just look in this room?'

Maddie didn't know. 'It's a murder scene, Harry, you know how they treat these things. You can ask them if they were thorough enough by all means, no way I'm doing that!'

'What I mean is I didn't direct them to look at the floor outside of the room where Maria was found. What if the offenders tried somewhere else first?'

'But the blood, the fact that the mother was laid on top of the daughter, we think that was part of it. Why would they look to lift the boards anywhere else?'

'We thought that before this morning happened. This morning when the son was called on the phone, the son who wasn't involved until that call connected. By that logic they didn't need Jade to be in the same room, just to be close enough. Having her out of sight might even be more effective. Maybe they couldn't get the boards up, they tried but the screws out here are newer from when they had the work done. The living room is full of rugs and furniture and probably too far away for the impact they needed so they settled on everything happening in the hallway.'

'Again, this doesn't get us anywhere, does it? Even if you're right?'

'But I think it does. It gives us a theory at least.'

'Am I missing it?' Maddie's annoyance would have been clearer than ever to Harry.

'These parents, threatened with harm against their children, would have done all that they could to prevent it — said anything, done anything. It escalated way beyond what should have been necessary.'

'I'm still waiting for a theory?' Maddie crossed her arms.

'What sort of a secret would you refuse to give up, even if your husband was killed for it? What sort of a secret would you refuse to give up until your daughter was nailed under the floorboards, terrified and, for all you knew, next? Because I can't think of a single thing.' Harry's attention lifted temporarily from the floor, then he moved, still on his hands and knees, to find more nails with scuffed threads. The wooden edge of the boards had marks too, in two places, marks that he pointed out could have been caused by a crude tool digging for a point of leverage. They did look recent. Harry stood back up, his focus seemingly back on the front door. 'We think Maria Mercer opened that door to the offenders, so maybe she let them in, maybe this wasn't her being overpowered straight away but it was more a conversation that changed in tone. Maybe they didn't make their demands straight away and then when they did . . .' Harry licked his lips for one final, maddening pause. 'Both sets of parents needed something extreme to convince them to talk and there's only one scenario I can think of where that would be necessary.'

'Out with it, Harry, so I can get back to work.' Maddie crossed her arms.

'These offenders, they weren't taken seriously at first, because the victims knew them as friends.'

CHAPTER 7

The suggestion that the Mercer family home had been invaded by someone who had been there before was not a new one to be discussed within the confines of Canterbury Police Station, it had actually been among the first. Eileen Holmans, their intelligence analyst, had taken it further, going hard on the theory that the house had been chosen purposefully based on prior knowledge, the contents of the safe included. It was something that had taken up a lot of her time in the last four days, which could explain why she sounded a little put out when Harry called her on the hands-free as they were coming away from the former crime scene to ask her to look at it again.

Which would suggest I didn't do it right the first time? had been the reply, leaving Maddie to step in and offer assurance that this was not the case. Maddie also took the opportunity to talk to her about searching for a link between the Mercers and the Blackman family, their victims from that morning. Again, the reaction was far from delight, more a *harumph* sound and then *of course this is a consideration*. Eileen's role as an intelligence analyst was a civilian one and, technically, it sat her on the bottom rung of the investigative team when it came to hierarchy, though, it seemed, no one had told her that.

She had made an unexpected appearance to assist with their previous case and had shown her worth. The analyst role is to interrogate police databases and compile stats, reports and intelligence products when instructed — and, when combined with Eileen's past as a secondary school teacher of thirty years, it seemed like a role that was tailor-made for her. Maddie got the feeling they had inherited her as someone no one else wanted, but that suited Maddie just fine. Maddie adored her, and she was pretty sure Harry had a soft spot for her too, not that he would ever say so.

After upsetting Eileen it was time for Harry to do the same dance with an equally ferocious force of nature: Charley Mace. As the senior CSI, she had managed the forensic work at the Mercer house and would be best placed to know if the floors outside of the kill room had been inspected in any detail. Maddie grimaced as her colleague asked the question, his words left to hang in the air, like Charley needed to gather herself for a moment or two before she could answer. Then Maddie got every word of the response, which was short, cold but suspiciously agreeable; like if a bear crossed his heart and agreed not to eat you the moment you turned away.

While licking his lips.

It appeared that Harry shared her thoughts. The silence when the call ended was heavy with the knowing and the unsaid.

'Are we heading back in?' Maddie said, eventually.

'No, actually.' Harry seemed to be making the decision on the spot. 'Seeing as we're on a roll here with upsetting people, let's go upset some more.'

* * *

Police officers very quickly get used to expressions moving from *annoyed* to *unimpressed* in the moments that follow a front door opening. Today it was two people Maddie could only remember as "Mac and Angie" that they were un-impressing. They were Jade Mercer's godparents and, in what had been a small mercy, they were also Emergency Foster Carers, active on a list held by the local authority. It had made Jade's move from her blood-soaked family home to a foster home seamless from a procedure point of view, though behind the bureaucracy there was still a child who had been wrenched away from all she knew to go and live with almost-strangers.

Maddie hadn't been expecting both to answer and Harry seemed caught out too. This meant that Mac and Angie's first action was to preside over an awkward silence that threatened to move to a full-on stand-off.

'Inspector.' Mac finally spoke, his tone flat, giving nothing away. He was in his early sixties, a professional who had held senior roles in local politics and still worked with the local council as an occasional consultant. He was a little dough-faced, the nose in the centre red and dry enough to flake, the colour standing out from the shocking white of his beard. The back of his hands were a chafed red, visible when he tucked both his thumbs behind braces that were tight against his belly, a habit of his. Maddie had liked him from the outset. Sure, there was a frontage of bluster and bullshit, but behind it all was a big heart and good intentions that he couldn't hide for long. In their first meeting, Mac had become angry the moment anything was said that might affect Jade's well-being and he saw the police as a very real threat. And he was right to. They still needed much more from Jade and Mac had positioned himself as a wall standing firm between an outside world clamouring to know what had happened in that house and an eleven-year-old girl who never wanted to think about it again.

'Good morning,' Harry said, then cleared his throat. 'I'm sorry to drop in unannounced, but I said I would keep you up to date. I just wondered if we could have a little chat?' Harry's tone was one he reserved for when he was try-ing to sound warm, his opening line suggesting all give and no take. Maddie was sure he would be fooling no one and half expected the door to slam in their face. Instead, Harry got a brief and suspicious scowl from Mac who then took a moment to lock eyes with his wife before they both stepped back into their home, leaving the door swinging for the over-sized brass knocker to catch in the sunlight.

Harry moved in before they changed their mind and Maddie followed. There had been a hint of something freshly baked as they stood on the doorstep, a few steps in and it was a flood of something sweet and bready that forced Maddie to hope that her rumbling stomach wasn't as loud as it felt. Mac stopped halfway down the hall and rounded on them to speak in hushed tones.

'I would ask that we wait until we're outside for any *chat*. Jade's in her room. I would rather she was not aware of police visitors.' Harry nodded and Maddie had a little smile to herself as his real message was clear: there was no way they would be getting to speak to Jade today. Through the kitchen, they passed a pile of freshly baked scones, the jam next to them in an unlabelled jar to suggest it was homemade too, and Maddie's stomach voiced another complaint.

'How can we help you?' Mac's question came when they were out on the balcony of their town house. The living room on the first floor was over an integrated garage, and the view was out over a golf course where a few hardy figures moved about its frosty greens. Mac was wearing a chunky knit beneath those braces and over jeans; he offered the two officers a seat with a gesture, then waved towards a basket of rolled-up blankets that both politely declined. Maddie was tempted to suggest that a jam scone would help her greatly at that moment thank you very much, opting instead for *nice view*.

'We think so.' Mac and Angie were a couple that rarely said — or did — anything without involving the other. Even on this point Mac looked to his wife, waiting for a nod back in agreement.

'DI Ives you know,' Harry rushed, like he had just remembered Maddie was with him.

'We met briefly, but it wasn't really the time to be get-ting to know police colleagues.' Mac's previous role with the local council had included him working closely with the police at times. He still had some involvement and liked to make it clear that they were *on the same team* as often as he could.

'Of course. DI Ives is working this investigation and will be a significant part of the team. Her previous role saw her working with a number of child protection elements, so we will be calling on her experience in working with Jade.'

'And what, in your experience, should the police be doing now for Jade?' All the focus was suddenly on Maddie, a test she needed to pass.

'The police have done quite enough for now, Mr McIlhenny, so we need to take a step back but keep up a dialogue with those closest to her, in case her needs change and we can help.'

McIlhenny — Nicholas McIlhenny, Maddie almost patted herself on the back as his name came back to her just at the key time. He had insisted on being called *Mac* from the first moment they had met but the more formal approach seemed effective in changing the dynamic of the conversation. Nicholas McIlhenny responded positively.

'Quite right. Well, at least we seem to have two sensible officers running this thing.'

'How has Jade settled in?' Maddie was keen to press home any advantage. Mac looked over at his wife again. He was freshly shaven, the rawness clear on both cheeks where he had shaped his beard and in a patch under his ear, visible now his head was turned.

'The night terrors are quite something. She's afraid to sleep to be honest. We're trying to get some routine to the evenings but that's a real struggle. We take turns sitting with her, we read the brightest, most colourful children's stories we can, but it doesn't seem to be helping. Her mind quickly darkens. We've even tried a few age groups below, simple child ditties, but still they come.' Mac's tone was now heavy with sorrow.

'Does she sleep at all?' Maddie continued.

'She snatches a few hours. The child psychologist has been helpful with suggestions and I think we are making progress. We have a smart speaker in her room that plays calming sounds or stories and that seems to have made some improvement. Her first few hours are restful but then, not so much. That makes sense, of course, we don't dream imme-diately. It takes her a little while to get to the point where she starts seeing what she sees . . . and I cannot imagine what that might be. She shouts and roars herself awake and seems compelled to get out of her bed. We often find her sat on her floor.'

'Shouts?' Harry's haste made his line of thought clear.

'Barely anything discernible, Inspector, certainly noth-ing of interest.' Mac gestured like he was waving him away.

'Sometimes we don't know what we can use until we hear it. Any words or phrases in there?' Maddie kept it up, her tone softer, her eyes moving from Mac to his wife who suddenly seemed like she wanted to speak.

Maddie was right. 'She was shouting about a drill last night,' Angie said. 'It was about the only word I could make out but then, when she wakes up, we don't ask for any expla-nation. It's all I can do to tell her it's going to be OK, over and over. That's what we've been told will help.' She had started loud only to get quieter, her eyes glazed like she was reliving the moment.

'A drill . . .' Maddie said, her mind filling with images of scuffed screws in hallway floorboards.

'What happened to her?' Mac said. 'We know her mother, dear Maria, was murdered, we know Jade was present in some capacity, that she was scared half to death and we know not to ask. But a *drill*, for goodness' sake! I like to know what I'm up against and just that word conjures all sorts of scenarios.'

'I'm sure it does. There's very little we know for sure right now, that's why Jade is so important to us. There is always a possibility in a case like this that the offender had been to the house before, maybe even as a friend of the fam-ily. Has she—'

'If I can stop you there.' Mac cut back in to stop Maddie in her tracks. 'I can see where this is going and the answer is no. Jade does not talk about what happened and she does not talk about *before* what happened. Not to us and she certainly won't be talking to the police at this time. I don't believe she will be of any use to you, I'm afraid. I'm not sure she remembers much at all. It's common in children suffering trauma, we are told; the mind blocks it, throws out the memory of what happened to try and limit the damage.'

'I understand that. I just thought—'

'No. And if she was to say something as significant as who murdered her mother — and our friend, don't forget — then you can be assured that we would make a phone call straight away.'

'I never doubted that.' Maddie suddenly felt a little foolish. She was supposed to, of course. 'I don't mean to be remiss; I know you and Maria were close.'

Mac sighed, the expulsion of air came with a movement, a gentle falling back like he had developed a slow puncture. 'We lost a very dear friend in very horrific circumstances. All we want to do now is what is right for the daughter she left behind, to protect her. And we will do so until our last breath.'

'I know you've already been asked this, but is there anything you can think of that might have made Maria a target?' Harry said.

Mac flashed a pained smile directed at his wife. 'That has indeed been asked of us and, of course, we have asked the very same thing to each other over and over. Maria and I worked very closely at one time, she was a regular here for dinner, or for a coffee and one of my wife's incredible scones.' The smile flashed again, brighter and warmer this time. 'Maria was very passionate about her work, about social care and protecting the vulnerable in our society, the abandoned kids especially . . .' Mac paused like he might be overcome, perhaps by the irony. 'When I left my role at the Council we lost touch for a while, we remained friends of course but I don't feel like we know her as well as we did. One thing I do know is that she was a wonderful woman, Inspector, a wonderful woman with morals above the likes of even the people in your organisation. This was an opportune evil, I am sure of it. She has a fine home, a fine frontage, one could easily assume she has items of value and if someone were that way inclined . . .' This time, when he faded out, it was clear he was not coming back.

'I understand,' Harry said. 'And regarding Jade, it doesn't have to be something she says, maybe something she does will give us an idea of what is going on in her mind. We're not expecting you to hit her with direct questions, that's why we haven't insisted on doing it ourselves, we just want to stay in touch.'

Angie cut in when her husband floundered. 'Normality, that's the best we can hope for right now. We need Jade to have something like it, something like what she had before, if that's at all possible. Seeing her friends, going out to the park . . .'

'Is she seeing friends?' Maddie asked.

'She hasn't yet. I know the police have told us to keep her in for now . . .' Angie added, a sudden panic on her face and Maddie smiled to let her know there was no need. 'She does have a close friend and her mother has already approached us for a play date when Jade's ready and we . . . I think it would be a good idea.' Maddie noted a quick exchange between husband and wife to suggest that they disagreed on this point. 'Not until she's ready, of course. I just wish I knew what was going on in her head. She's suffering, though, that's for sure. I think it's all a bit much, no child should be having such dark thoughts.'

'Dark thoughts?' Harry was again hasty.

Angie's expression was almost wistful, she took a moment then seemed to wave away her line of thought. 'It's nothing that's tangible. She draws, I think you know this already. She's been into her art for some time, before . . . before all this.'

'And she's still drawing,' Maddie said, aware of Mac's attempts to make eye contact with his wife.

'She still draws,' Angie continued, 'but there's a pattern forming.'

'A pattern?'

Mac finally caught her eye and she waited for his reaction; it was a nod. 'We already talked about her regressing a little . . .' Angie's attention was now beyond the two seated detectives and back into the kitchen. The door was pushed to, but she moved over to it to pull it until it clicked shut. She lowered her voice. 'During the day she'll draw childish-type stuff, stuff like my husband has already mentioned: Disney princesses or cutesy characters, or just blocks of colour and glitter. She has a talent with her art, a real attention to detail and these creations . . . they're beautiful. It's a little heart-breaking. Disney is all about happy ever after, isn't it? I think she's craving that innocence.'

'I'm sure there's something there, the child psychologist will be able to make more of that,' Maddie said.

'They will. They'll be able to make more of the *night drawings* too.' Angie was back to checking with her husband and got another nod. Maddie found herself sitting straighter for Angie's next words.

'Night drawings?'

'Hang on . . .' Angie stood back up, her walk back through the door she had just closed was on tiptoes. The wait was short, Angie came back with a piece of paper rolled up. She checked the kitchen area she had just left before unravelling it to face the two officers. Art was something that seemed to miss Maddie out, she'd never understood the reaction other people would claim it had on them. But Jade's drawing on that day broke her heart.

The bright colours were present, married with blocks of glitter, bits of which were falling away from the paper in the chilly breeze. But the colours were obstructed by thick, untidy strips of black paint smeared across the page with firm brushstrokes. The strokes were thicker on the left side, running to thinner, ragged edges. There were three wide strips, roughly drawn with gaps between and paint runs left to dry like black tears.

'Those dark strips you can see were added at night, the colour behind is what she drew during the day. It's like she can find the light and colour and cheer when the sun is up and we are around, but at night her mind goes to a darker place and with it, the urge to deface her own work . . . She'll shout out and we'll go in there and find the black paint still wet where she's crossed it all out.'

'Floorboards,' Maddie breathed, her mind throwing up a realisation that she couldn't hold in.

Angie seized on it. 'Floorboards? This means something to you?'

'It might.' Harry's growl was hurried. 'Would I be able to take this away with me?'

'I took it out of the recycling, Jade put it in there herself. I was keeping it to one side and I left a message with PC Arnold that it might be something he would be interested in. He told me the same as you did; anything, he said, anything that might help us find who did this.'

'Vince?' Maddie said, unable to hold it in, her voice leaking her surprise.

Angie's smile appeared to be as big as she could muster. 'He did tell me to call him Vince, but it didn't feel right then and doesn't now. A rare dot of sunshine on a very dark day. He has promised to call back in, I hope this means he still will, if you take that away, I mean.'

'I'll make sure he does,' Harry said.

Angie was still beaming. 'Jade adored him, PC Arnold, she asks about him a lot. When he came back the next day the atmosphere of the whole house lifted. You don't meet many people who can do that. I understand he's had a similar impact on you, Inspector Ives?' she said and winked.

'He . . . we're . . . close.' Maddie suddenly felt awkward, the teenager cornered by an aunt and questioned over her first boyfriend. To Maddie's surprise, Angie reached out to place her hand on top of Maddie's, her smile remaining though her free hand wiped a tear that sprinted down her cheek to settle on her lip. 'He brought Jade here, this big man all in black like he was made of shadow, a size to make Jade look smaller, more vulnerable. I was a little scared when I opened the door, but when I saw him with Jade . . .' She rolled the picture up, putting both hands back on top of Maddie's as part of handing it over, her smile surviving another tear. 'A big man with a bigger heart. How is he?'

'He's . . . he's been OK, he's fine. Vince is always fine!' Maddie chuckled the last few words, still a little caught out.

'He wasn't then, Inspector Ives, not really, you could see that, you could see a man smiling with a frown in his voice.' She paused to check with her husband, a smile had breached his lips too. 'He was doing that thing that police officers do, that we all do. You can't let yourself care too much or it can bring you down, right? We've been told the same as foster carers. We have all sorts coming through here, children abused in ways the rest of the world would barely imagine and I feel every one, I feel their pain and the loss of their right to be children and I don't put up barriers to that, I don't do anything to protect myself from their horror because I think I owe them that. That's how I understand them, that's how I look after them best. PC Arnold, I told him . . .' She took another pause. 'Don't ever lose that big heart.' Angie's tears were thicker, now streaming down her cheeks. The silence that descended was heavy to the point of oppressive. Even the shushing trees with their raucous lining of birds seemed muted.

Mac spoke first. 'I think we've done all we can for one day. I'm very aware that Jade will normally appear from her room at around this time.' He stood up, prompting Angie to take back her hands.

'Thank you for your time. This has been very useful. I'll call ahead in future but anything she says or does, things like this,' Harry gestured at the roll of paper, 'it just gives us a fuller picture, fills in some blanks too. Between us all we can work out what happened and then we'll know how best to help her.'

'Do you have *any* idea who did this?' Angie's voice seemed smaller, part shielded where she was wiping her face. 'You must have,' she pleaded. 'Is there anything you can tell us? It goes both ways after all and we're the ones looking after her, we're the ones keeping her safe. If I'm taking her to the park with her friend or to the supermarket, is there something or someone I need to be aware of, somewhere to keep her away from?'

Harry stayed away from the standard *we can't tell you anything* police line and Maddie was glad of it. Angie had a point and they deserved better. A risk assessment had concluded that Jade was not believed to be in any further danger and Harry explained the thinking.

'The offenders were in Jade's house for some time, with every opportunity to cause Jade harm and they didn't. Coming back to do it now makes no sense at all and we don't believe they will. But you need to be vigilant, of course, and you need to keep Jade's location to yourselves.'

'We've had that talk, Inspector, we know all this; I think what my wife is asking is where you are with finding the bastards that did this in the first place?' Mac blustered.

Harry took a moment. 'Aggravated burglaries like this, generally speaking, they're not carried out by first-timers. Our profiling suggests that this is a man, or a group of men who have committed theft-type offences before. Almost certainly thefts with violence attached and they have escalated in seriousness. They're aggressive, well organised and forensically aware so we're not looking for kids. Right now we don't have a named suspect but we are doing all we can. Jade could well be the key.'

'And you also think it could be someone known to the family?' Mac said.

'Someone Maria knew in some capacity perhaps, but it could be a tradesman she only met a few times; once, even. We just don't know, so anything Jade says . . .' Maddie said.

'We'll call, rest assured,' Angie breathed.

Maddie almost felt like she should tiptoe as they were shown back through the house with Mac following a little too close as a way of hurrying them. They had just about made it when a voice stopped them all dead.

'You're one of the police officers, I remember how you sound. Vince said you were big and important.' The voice was small in every way and Maddie turned to face it. Jade was sitting on the landing, her bare feet resting on the second step from the top. She wore leggings and a top with the sleeves pulled over her hands so just the ends of her slender fingers were visible. She was fixed on Harry Blaker.

'Hey Jade!' Harry's voice was different again, softer, warmer and full of surprise. 'I'm not important, not really, not as important as you are.'

'Is Vince here?' she said, her neck straining like she was trying to answer her own question.

'Not right now.'

'He said he would come back and see me.'

'And he will, Jade. We're letting you settle in here with Mac and Angie for a bit.'

Maddie hadn't yet been introduced to Jade, she hadn't been there for her conversation with Harry. It had been at the police station and it had been difficult. Jade couldn't talk about what had happened and Harry had made the right decision not to try and force her. As with any major job, the policing team had been pulled apart and all over the place. Vince had made himself available to drive Jade here when the placement was confirmed, and Harry had come along too, both wanting to play their part in making her safe, the slightest chink of light on a very dark day.

'I've still got Herb,' Jade said. The landing was a little darker than the rest of the house so, when she lifted a battered old cuddly tortoise up, it emerged from shadow. 'You will tell Vince, won't you? I'm looking after him so good.' Maddie took a moment to place it, the last time she had seen it, at least. It hadn't been long ago, prime position on Sammy's

63

bed, a gift from his mother that he would never admit he still took comfort from. Here it was, with Jade holding it up by its crinkled neck.

'I'll tell him! He'll be so glad he's being looked after,' Harry said, his voice suddenly made of glass.

'Did he say thank you to Sammy? That's right, isn't it? His son, he's nine.'

'I'm sure he did,' Harry said, while Maddie tried to catch his eye. The regression that Mac and Angie had talked about in Jade was clear. She seemed young for her age — younger even, than Sammy — striving for innocence, for a simpler time when you could believe that teddy bears were all you needed to keep safe. She had no choice now, she had to believe it, it was all she had left.

'We're sorry too, we didn't mean to disturb you,' Harry said.

'Did you come to talk about me?' Jade said.

'Only to check that you're doing OK, that you're comfortable here . . .' Harry left the sentence hanging like a question.

'I still don't remember. Not anything. You said that was OK, that it wouldn't matter. Vince said you would still find who did this anyway, he said you were the cleverest in the whole police. Did you find out yet? I just want to go home.' The little girl seemed to be getting smaller in front of them. She was hunched forward, her shoulders rolled in for her hands to meet in the middle of her lap to hold on to Herb. Her long, brown hair fell gently around her face. Maddie didn't know what there was to say to that and she recognised that Harry was floundering too. Jade didn't have a home, not anymore, and she might never find a place she could truly call that again. Emergency foster care — even with godparents — was often a torturous route to an unknown place.

'Not yet, Jade, but I'm going to come see you as soon as we've got it all worked out,' Harry said.

'Vince said he would too, he promised we would have ice cream, the biggest they do!' Her face lit up for just a moment, then flickered and died back to shadow.

'That sounds like a great idea.'

Jade didn't reply, it looked like she was done talking and Harry finally met Maddie's gaze, the sighs and shuffles now of a group of adults who knew the visit was done. But Jade wasn't quite done, one last question drifted down from the shadow.

'Will you lock them up, the bad people? Lock them up and throw away the key? That was what Vince said?'

People, not person. Maddie wanted to push her on that, ask what she meant: *Was it* people *that came to your house, Jade? How many people?* Harry might have been reading her thoughts, he turned to her for the first time in that hallway, his expression a clear message that this wasn't the time to push their luck. The relationship they had with Mac and Angie, that gave them access to Jade, was fragile and it was built on trust. They would need to make it stronger first.

'We are going to do everything we can and we're going to have that ice cream. This is your home for now and Mac and Angie care for you very much. If you need anything then these people will provide it for you, I know they will. And if you want to talk to us about anything at all . . .' Harry couldn't resist and, inevitably, Mac jumped in.

'Jade knows that, don't you my dear? Angie has been baking this morning and the police are just leaving so perhaps you want to come down and have a look at what there is?'

Mac reached out a hand for Maddie to shake, his grip like a vice. Harry was already on his way out.

It was time to go.

CHAPTER 8

Sunday

The Sunday roast was always one of those traditions that belonged to someone else, to *normal* families that Maddie had observed from a distance while she got on with her career. Now it was one of hers and, quite possibly, the one she liked the most. The weekends in general had developed into a pattern of a cooked breakfast on a Saturday morning to start the weekend off, then an activity on Sunday morning — swimming or a walk with Sammy — to ensure an appetite for the big dinner. The fact that it had been able to develop into a pattern, as Vince's shifts allowed, didn't mean Maddie was getting fed up of the repetition, quite the opposite.

The cooked breakfast on Saturday morning hadn't happened, but Maddie was determined that the Sunday tradition would remain and she was up early to peel the potatoes and prep a bird for the oven.

But today was already going to be different. Today they were taking Sammy to see his mother at the hospital.

Vince was up early too, perhaps motivated by the same determination to make the day as normal as possible. He appeared in tatty pyjama bottoms and equally tatty slippers, both of which he refused to dump on the grounds of comfort, and they talked about the timings of the day and when she should set the oven to start. Normal things, a normal conversation.

Only with three elephants silently skulking at the back of the room.

Rebecca was the obvious one and they danced around that, making plans to *travel* without mentioning where to. The next was what Maddie had learned yesterday, how Vince had felt compelled to promise Jade Mercer a result in this case, and the impact he had left on her, which was something that could wait until the right time. The final big-eared, big-trunked obstruction was the possibility that Maddie might, once again, need to abandon her weekend to go back into work — and this one couldn't wait. When Maddie cheerfully told Vince how she didn't need to go in that day, how the house-to-house-type enquiries were being covered by uniform colleagues and how Harry and Eileen were in the office to ensure the investigation had all the necessary momentum, the reaction from Vince was that of a man far from convinced.

'Harry doesn't need me, he's probably delighted to have a day when I'm not around!' Maddie insisted. 'And as for Eileen, she said she would only call if it was life or death!'

Life or death. Maddie's face instantly showed her realisation of what she'd said and Vince did that thing when someone pretends not to notice. Today was the day he was taking Sammy along to see that very fight — one his mother was currently losing.

The car journey was muted. Vince put Sammy's playlist on, the volume just loud enough to limit conversation.

'I can't wait to see Mum!' Sammy announced as they pulled through the barrier outside the QEQM Hospital. The car park was busy — it was always busy — despite the horrific hourly rate and it was two laps before they could find a space. Vince hesitated, staying put in his seat. Maddie did the same. Sammy fidgeted with his seatbelt in contrast, his movement only stopping when he realised he was the only one not sitting still. Vince turned to face him.

'She's sick, mate, our Becks.'

'I know that.' Sammy jutted his chin out in defiance.

'I know you know, I know you know everything, but . . . she's really sick, mate. I just don't want you to get upset, you know, it's not like seeing her on your screen. You might need to prepare yourself is all.'

Maddie watched as all the enthusiasm drained from Sammy in an instant. His wide eyes shuffled from his uncle to Maddie and back again. 'She's going to be OK though, in the end, I mean. You said, Uncle Vince, you said you wouldn't let anything happen to her!' His expression now one of confusion, doubting everything Vince had ever told him. Maddie remembered the conversation, it was early on, when Sammy was upset and Vince said the only thing he could.

'I can't fight this thing for her, trust me, mate, I would love to. She's fighting as hard as she can. Sometimes, though . . . there's nothing I can do, but you, Sammy, you have no idea how much it will help your mum to see you today. You have to be strong for her, you have to give her a big hug and tell her what you've been up to.'

'You're going to let her die!' Sammy exploded from nowhere. He pushed the door at the same time, stepping out into the sudden white noise of a busy car park. Vince was next out, Maddie slower to hang back as Vince set off after him.

Rebecca was worse than ever.

She was sitting up against a mound of pillows to push her forwards. The news of their visit had been shared with the nursing staff and a stack of gaming magazines perched precariously on one of the bedside chairs. Sammy saw them and ignored them to take in the form of his mother, having stopped out of her reach.

'My big man!' The smile that followed was laced with pain. Sammy was used to his mother sweeping him up in a strong embrace when she saw him, it hadn't been that long ago that she would swing him round in a sort of bear hug. He didn't answer. He looked for his uncle instead, his eyes full of questions he couldn't find words for. He looked as scared as Maddie had ever seen him.

'Can't they fix her?' Sammy locked on to Vince and wouldn't look away, like his mother wasn't even there.

'Becks is getting the best they've got, mate.'

'You said! You said you won't let anything happen to her!' Sammy sounded desperate now, like his mother was already dead in front of them, rather than sitting silently, one hand covering her mouth. His voice was broken, full of upset and desperation. Vince moved closer to him, placing his hands on the boy's bony shoulders, but Sammy slipped out and stepped back, stumbling as his eyes fell back on his mother. Then he turned, almost at a jog as he left the ward.

'Give him a minute,' Maddie said, stepping across to where Vince was already setting off after his nephew. He looked at her, took a step to one side like he might go round her, then stopped himself. He turned back to Rebecca, where she was still watching in silence. Maddie did too.

The smile that had looked like a struggle was all gone. Now there was something else on her face, a look that mirrored that of her son and the first time Maddie had really seen it in Rebecca Arnold.

It was fear.

CHAPTER 9

Monday

Monday morning and Maddie had a hangover, despite not touching a drop over the weekend. It was an emotional hangover, the aftermath of being hollowed out from their trip to the hospital the previous day and the evening that had followed.

Rebecca's deterioration was stark, enough that it had caught Maddie out, let alone the nine-year-old boy who had slunk to his bedroom the moment they got back, dragging confusion, fear and anger along with him. They had managed to get Sammy back to his mother at least, even got him relaxed enough that Maddie could step away and listen in to a hushed conversation between Vince and the doctor doing his rounds.

What she heard were things that Rebecca would never have told them, how she had been strongly advised to increase her pain medication and how it would take a lot of her suffering away, but also her lucidity. She had refused, knowing that Sammy was coming in and wanting to be as alert as possible. Vince had scolded his sister the moment he could, told her that she should have taken the advice, that her focus needed to be on doing what the doctors told her, on looking after herself.

Maddie could see that Rebecca's reply had hit Vince like a punch to the gut: *This might be my last chance to see him, to really see him, I mean.*

Vince had scolded her again for talking like that, for even considering it. Maddie had only ever seen Rebecca bolshy since her diagnosis, to the point of arrogance — *just something else to beat into submission!* she had said and Vince had been sold, they both had. But yesterday, that arrogance was gone, the judo master with all the trash talk had been caught out and a big hit had her staring aghast at the canvas.

Then Vince looked like he had taken another punch in the gut when, as they prepared to leave, Sammy said goodbye like he knew it might be for ever. Maddie was the one in the middle, the one supposed to be strong for everyone else, the outsider, but that final embrace between a mother and her son had shattered her heart in a way that twenty-four hours had done nothing to mend.

Now she was a tea drinker nursing a coffee that was shit-like in both appearance and taste. She was in the space that had recently been made for Major Crime to occupy. After the centralisation, de-centralisation, structuring and restructuring of the department, it was back where it had all started. The long, slim and totally unfit-for-purpose office that formed the top of what had once been a firing range, a soundproofed and oppressive extension to Canterbury Police Station. Maddie had taken herself off to sit in one of the empty chairs of a corner set aside by free-standing dividers to act as a briefing area, her latest attempt to spend a morning avoiding contact of any sort with anyone else. Eileen had been busy covering the dividers in case material. There were photos of the scenes and of exhibits, copies of statements and first accounts and a whiteboard with a handwritten VOWS assessment that Maddie herself had started and was still look-ing rather depleted. VOWS was a basic policing tool used to organise information that might be coming in fast into four categories — Victim, Offender, Witnesses and Scenes — and she lingered on the blankness of the *offender* column, allowing it to blur where her concentration slipped.

She heard Harry's voice, a growl that travelled whether it was directed at you or not. It wasn't, in this case. Maddie dipped her head, running her hands through her hair, lazily following the movement of a pair of dusky pink slippers with contrasting stuffed edges in white.

Another minute or two passed and the officers working the case started to shuffle in around her. Part of being a ranking officer meant that those serving beneath you always felt the need to offer a greeting on entering a room. Maddie started out lifting her head to acknowledge the first few, then she let her head drop and murmured at the next row before reverting to just shaking her mug of shit coffee at the final stragglers.

'Good morning.' Eileen's raised voice carried its usual authority, enough, even, to summon Harry back into the area. He sat next to Maddie, reaching across to take her shit coffee off her and replace it immediately with a fresh tea.

'Looks like you could do with it,' he said, his voice low where they both skulked at the back of the class.

'If I could have your attention!' Eileen continued, her voice cutting through the hubbub, then smothering it. 'We have had a significant weekend and there is much to bring you up to date on. There is a lot to do as well, much of which will be dished out at this meeting by DI Blaker and ADI Ives, so you will do well to listen now as they will not take kindly to having to repeat anything I am about to say.' Eileen paused and Maddie could feel her looking over for endorsement. She tried another flail of her hand, sloshing a cup she momentarily forgot was full. It was enough to get Eileen talking again.

Maddie's mind wandered in and out as she went over the crime scene that had been discovered on Saturday morning, the way it was reported and initially found, accounts from the first officers and how the scene appeared to be clean — although forensic work continued. The core of the team had been called in over the weekend and would know this already, but for major investigations such as this, resources were sent from every corner of the force and there were plenty of new faces. Maddie was glad she didn't have to concentrate.

Then Eileen moved on to something Maddie didn't know already.

'We do have a find, however, something that gives us somewhere to start.' Eileen was back looking over at Maddie, who sat up straighter. She held up a clear evidence bag, a black item visible inside, heavy enough to tug at the seal.

'This is a mobile phone,' Eileen continued. 'It was found on Saturday, not *at* the scene, but just a few hundred metres away. It was clean, dry and with no sign of dirt or decay. In other words, likely to have been dropped a very short time before it was found, possibly by a person leaving that crime scene.' Eileen paused for effect. She increased it further by taking out a shiny metal pointer that extended. The pointy end *thwacked* down on a piece of paper pinned to the sound-deadened board. 'This is an intelligence report submitted by a source handler in June. This report assigns this phone,' Eileen lifted the bag higher, like she'd won a fish at a fayre, 'to one of our local drug runners. A sixteen-year-old boy by the name of Connor Docker.'

Connor Docker!

A name.

A place to start.

A flash of anger: why was she only just finding out about this now!?

Eileen continued: 'Connor Docker lives in Margate but there are numerous sightings of him in all of the Thanet towns. He is known to use the train network to deal drugs on behalf of a county lines gang. This phone is believed to be the gang phone and, as you can imagine, has no place in rural Sheppey. Docker's PNC shows arrests for street robberies and he's been convicted for theft offences so we have an element of bad character that supports his involvement.'

'What robberies?' Maddie's mind swirled with a million questions; this was the one she couldn't hold.

'His victims were fellow drug dealers, it would appear, which might also explain the lack of a conviction. They don't tend to support police prosecution,' Eileen replied.

'A kid with the line phone out in affluent rural areas targeting safes?' Again, Maddie was thinking out loud, her hangover clearing, suddenly aware that the room had turned to focus on her. A "line phone" was highly valuable, it contained the numbers of a near-infinite number of local drug users and would be used to send a daily text out to each of the numbers stored to make them aware that sales were "online". The users would then respond and arrange to meet the person holding the phone. It could be worth thousands of pounds a day; more, even. The line phone stayed central, moving when required but always to a place where a lot of transactions could be carried out in a short period of time, so transport links and a high density of drug users were essential. A quiet country road out on the Isle of Sheppey made no sense at all. But nor did the murder of the family there. The phone seemed so out of place that it had to be linked to the only example of extreme violence ever reported in that area.

Connor Docker.

The briefing continued. Eileen explained how Docker had been stopped in possession of the line phone by a uniform patrol carrying out a street search. This gave them an official link, the way was clear for the arrest. Evidentially, the phone and its link to Docker was useless — a moveable object that was, by its very nature, passed around and last found to be in his possession months ago. But Maddie still felt enthused. She would get a full briefing, answers to all her questions, but no matter what those were, they suddenly had a place to start.

Sixteen-year-old Connor Docker.

CHAPTER 10

Their so-called "place to start" was under arrest almost before the briefing was complete. Harry had tasked the team with Connor Docker's arrest first thing in the morning the day after the link had been made, and at a time when his location would have been anyone's guess. The one thing you can be sure of when it comes to drug dealers is that they work the late shift. Intelligence had Connor anywhere between Margate, Ramsgate, Broadstairs or even as far round as Herne Bay according to the gangs matrix — a collection of every piece of intelligence linked to the county lines there was — and that same matrix offered up a far more reliable address for an early morning knock: a flat on Athelstan Road, Margate.

He had been asleep on the sofa when patrols arrived, his only movement to roll over so he was facing away from the sudden sunlight when the arresting officer pulled back a thick curtain. He was already used to police raids and this was tame in comparison. He was linked to at least four drug raids where his wake-up would have been to the sound of a front door being forced off its hinges, then determined shouts of *POLICE*! before being grabbed and roughly handcuffed in the same movement. Today the officers had knocked, been allowed entry and then stood over where he lay. It was hardly a situation that would cause a raise in his pulse.

His swagger through the custody suite of Margate Police Station was consistent with all the recruited dealers. It consisted of an exaggerated step with the leading leg, the foot turned slightly inwards, then the back foot dragged forward with a dip of the shoulder. Also consistent was the sucking of his teeth every time he was asked a question, like having to form words in an answer was a waste of his time and energy. Maddie watched him from behind the custody desk. The arresting officers had been held up searching the address while Connor sat on the sofa pretending to be asleep, so she had beaten them there. The two arresting officers standing either side of him highlighted his small stature, making his arrogance all the more ridiculous. He mumbled answers at the custody sergeant, ignoring a couple of the questions completely to further demonstrate his overall contempt. In his mind he was a loyal soldier repeating his name and rank under enemy questioning. The truth was that he was young, vulnerable and stupid and, to the people exploiting him, nothing more than a sales clerk who now needed to keep his mouth shut.

Connor Docker sucked his teeth at a question to ascertain if he had a parent or carer who could come down and sit with him while he was interviewed. He didn't. His age meant he would need an appropriate adult; there was a list of volunteers run by the local council and Connor demonstrated his experience in this situation by asking for one he knew by name. Maddie had seen enough.

It was two hours later when Maddie finally took her place opposite Connor with Harry to her right. Still Connor was giving no eye contact and Maddie had to give it to him — to be constantly talked at, asked questions of and given instructions to and not to make eye contact once, that was some commitment.

She finished the formal part, a script that preceded every interview that Connor probably knew as well as she did. The last part was to introduce the appropriate adult, who Maddie recognised as one of the regulars. The appropriate adult scheme was something that was called on when a juvenile — or anyone meeting the criteria that deemed them vulnerable — was the subject of a formal police process and where a parent or carer was not available or, very often, couldn't be bothered. They were vetted volunteers, usually with some sort of background in social work. The pink stripe in the woman's hair that was otherwise bleached blonde and a subtle nose ring certainly screamed social worker, while also making her a little more difficult to age — mid-forties seemed a fair guess. She looked a little bored, hardly surprising seeing as she had likely attended more interviews than all the people in that room combined. Her eyes did lift and shift at the sound of her name, enough for Maddie to notice that her right eye had an elongated pupil, like it had split at the bottom and leaked out a little. Maddie's first best friend at secondary school had had the same trait, something she had used as a conversation starter with boys she liked. The boys had responded positively then, but, in that interview room, Connor still hadn't looked up.

The appropriate adult introduced herself as Amelia Chagrin and confirmed her understanding that she was simply there to make sure Connor was being treated fairly, something that life had failed to do up to that point. Amelia then reached out to squeeze his hand and Connor Docker sucked his teeth and recoiled.

'You don't have a solicitor here to represent you, Connor. I need to remind you that this is your right. Why do you not have legal representation?' Maddie said.

'Don't need it,' Connor replied, leaning forward to talk directly into the tabletop.

'It's an ongoing right. That means that at any time, if you think you do need it then you just need to let me know and I'll stop the recording and get it arranged.'

'Takes bare time, though. I got no time to be here, I got earning to do.' He curled his lips into a sort of smile. Maddie didn't bite, Harry's fidget in his seat told her he would have.

'How have you been, Connor?' Maddie said, her first question open enough for Docker to determine the direction the interview took from there.

'That's what you want to know? That's why I'm here? Someone out there said I was arrested for like, conspiracy to murder or something and you want to know how I've been! Clowns, the lot of you! You want to tell me what the fuck I'm doing here for real? I ain't conspiracy to murder no one I can tell you that now, you show me what you got, you show me the proof!'

Maddie took her time. She sat back, crossing her arms to stare at him while he sucked his teeth so hard the strain showed on his face. Finally, she produced a piece of A4 paper, a printed intelligence report, taking her time examining it. The pink-haired Amelia craned forward; her misshapen pupil fidgeted like she was reading it upside down.

'This report was written by the last officer to talk with you. Seems you were sofa surfing at the time and at the same address where we found you today,' Maddie said, finally.

'So?'

'Why aren't you in Canterbury with your mum?'

'You live with your mum, do you?' he snapped.

'I'm not sixteen and unemployed.'

'I ain't no boy, you get me? I can live where I want and with who I want. Easier for work, people move to stay places where it's easier for work all the time, don't mean they get nicked for conspiracy to murder people.' He mumbled a word that sounded like *fafarsake*. He was starting to make eye contact now, albeit fleeting and he looked over at Harry for the first time. Connor was small for his age, the parts of his face that weren't spotty were pockmarked like they had been recently, his hair was shorn close to his head by someone far from trained — possibly even a DIY job. He was wearing a wrinkled designer T-shirt over tracksuit bottoms that didn't look like they had ever seen a washing machine, and of course the inevitable £200 trainers that looked brand new.

'So, not unemployed? What's your line of work these days?' Maddie asked.

'Same as the old days! I work at the carwash on Northdown Road. You should come see me some day, I charge double for gavvers!' That smile was back, this time there was genuine delight on the kid's face. *Gavvers*: A slang term for police officers that didn't seem to exist outside of Kent. It was a good one, you could get a lot of hate into the first part of that word: *gav*-ers.

'Who's your boss down there?' Maddie asked.

'What does that matter?'

'Because I know that carwash, I know who runs it and most of the lads who work for him too. They're from Afghanistan or Iraq mostly and every one of them Muslim, because he won't employ someone who isn't. He's quite open about that. Is that the carwash you mean?'

'Who says I ain't Muslim?'

'Are you?'

'He likes to get some English down there, unofficial like. It gets the punters in when they see a white boy stood there with a sponge.'

'Standing with a sponge got you those trainers, did it?' Maddie said, quick as a flash.

'Something about murder?' Connor sat up straighter now, finally making lasting eye contact with someone and Maddie had the honour. Then he looked over at Amelia Chagrin, whose expression was also one of confusion. 'That's what was said. What you saying, I killed someone with a sponge or what? I got no comment, yeah? That's it. No comment, you got anything else to ask me then it's no comment.' His head slumped again, his lips pouting just an inch or so from the tabletop and that was how he was to remain. Maddie asked him about the phone, about how he had been stopped in possession, asked him how it had travelled the forty-five miles from Margate over to the Isle of Sheppey and what the phone was for. She was wasting her time. It was all a waste of time. The first few questions got *no comment* as promised, then he leaned back, slid his bum as far forward as the seat would allow and pretended to be asleep.

They would get nothing more from him.

* * *

Harry left the interview room while Maddie was still wrapping up. It had been a waste of time, something they could ill afford, and his call to Eileen from Margate's back office confirmed that they would get nothing of use from the phone either. The network provider had confirmed that the phone had been switched off for at least a week and had never once connected with a mast in Sheppey. Eileen's good news continued when she reported that the phone linked to Docker had also been found on at least two other people as part of a stop and search operation in the Thanet area. The link had always been tenuous, Docker was only ever going to be a place to start, but now it seemed he wasn't even that. From the look on Maddie's face when she appeared in the back office, she knew it too.

'One of life's winners,' she sighed.

'Pretty much what I expected. Did you kick him out already?' Harry said.

'No, the appropriate adult wanted a couple of minutes to do her welfare check bit.'

'Ah yes, where she tells him all about getting a job and he turns his life around, starting now.'

Maddie slumped into a chair under a bank of monitors, each with a different prisoner in its middle. 'I'll hang around and kick him out. I've called ahead and there's a desk and a kettle for us in Child Protection. I shouldn't be long down here.'

'Sounds ideal,' Harry said and left his colleague looking deflated. His walk out of custody was timed perfectly to see the streaky-haired appropriate adult through a dirty window. She was walking across the front of the police station, towards the visitor parking and Harry had changed direction before the idea had fully formed.

'Amelia?' Harry was just in time to call out to an open car door that was pulling shut, faltering at the last like she had heard just too late. She came back out, instantly looking cold in just a blouse having shed the jacket she had been wearing a moment earlier. She held her arms tight across her front, there was a little disdain in her expression too, something that Harry hadn't noticed in the custody block.

'Help you?' she said. In the daylight she looked paler, her face certainly, the layer of foundation possibly to blame.

'I was just in the interview in there, I—'

'I know,' she snapped.

'I don't mean to keep you. I just wanted to see how our friend Connor is. I know he has some issues with talking to the police, he wouldn't talk to us even if he desperately needed to. Did he talk to you?'

'Maybe you should approach him a little different. Your colleague was hardly extending an olive branch in there.'

'Do you think he would have responded to that any better?' Harry countered.

'Probably not. He seems OK, a bit miffed that he was brought in for something that he doesn't know anything about. I guess he would say that, wouldn't he?' The disdain shifted for a moment for a smile to break through. A shiver chased it off. Margate Police Station and the visitor parking out the front came with an expansive view of the sea: beautiful in the summer, raw in the winter.

'I'm sorry, you're freezing. I was just wondering if he said anything that might help us. This is serious, what we're investigating and the only thing we have is that phone being found close by.'

Amelia reached out for the handle to the rear door of her car. Her jacket was on the back seat. Next to it a toddler was sitting in a car seat decorated with ladybirds. A man was in the front passenger seat, he was turned away, picking up a brightly coloured book that had been dropped in the

81

footwell. It was a snapshot that ended when the door was pushed back closed.

'I've been doing this a while, Inspector Blaker, long enough to know that I'm not there to ask questions, or to pass information to the police.' She pulled the jacket on, it was dark denim with buttons, she skipped the buttons to pull it tight across her front.

'You're right.' Harry held up his hands, then said, 'Cute kid' to move the subject away.

'Grandchild. I promised him a trip to soft play.'

'You don't look old enough. To be a grandmother, I mean.'

'Comes from not being old enough to be a mother,' she said, the answer quick enough to suggest it was practised. 'What happened, Inspector? With that family, I mean, seeing as we're asking questions that we shouldn't. We didn't really talk any details in there but I've seen what's on the news . . .'

'There's not much to say beyond that, to be honest. We have a mother killed, her daughter was there at the time and isn't a whole lot older than your little grandson in there so I'm sure you can understand why we're so keen to find who did this.'

'Not Connor,' she said.

'I know that, we both know he's part of something bigger.'

'I represent a lot of kids down here that are mixed up in *something bigger*. They never tell the police anything. He's a child too, no matter what front he puts up and whether he likes it or not, that makes him a victim too.'

'I agree. That front is for us, for the police, maybe that slips when we're gone, maybe these kids talk a little more to you?'

Amelia seemed to stoop, it was subtle, just enough to check back into the car through the window. 'Snitches get stitches, right?' Her grin looked like genuine humour. 'The amount of times I've heard that. I don't think these kids know anything at all, they're just doing what they're told to do.'

'Who by?' Harry pushed. 'There will be a name with a reputation so they know to keep in check.' She hesitated, her gaze moving beyond Harry to take in her surroundings for the first time. 'Off the record,' he shrugged.

'Is there such a thing?' She was still grinning, but it was tinged with suspicion. 'There is a name I've heard mentioned a couple of times, someone they all seem to know.'

'Go on.'

'It might not be anything, but I get the impression they're scared of him, like he might be in charge.'

'Might be someone we know already. The name?' Harry said, trying to damp down his enthusiasm. The woman hesitated, glanced back at the car like she was reconsidering.

'Liam,' she said. 'That's all I've got, nothing else so don't bother. Now I really am freezing! Good luck with your investigation, I hope you get the bastard.' She moved back to stand by the driver's door. Harry reached into his back pocket where he kept a few cards with his details on it. They were old, he didn't know how old, there were only a few left and the one he offered was dog-eared, with pocket fluff that he brushed off.

'Amelia, if anything else gets said, anything that might help me find who did this . . . There's a little girl now trying to come to terms with losing her mum, who would really appreciate your help.'

She took the card, her eyes suddenly watery as they ran over the details. 'I would. I can't imagine the pain . . .' She lingered, the emotion so real on her face that Harry sensed there was more to come. The spell was broken by a chirrup from Harry's phone and she used it as an opportunity to drop back into her driver's seat. The sound of the engine firing masked the caller's first words.

'Sorry, who?' Harry said, turning to walk away from the noise.

'Charley Mace, Harry, do I not even have the honour of being saved as a name in your phone?'

'Charley!' Harry was too loud in the sudden silence of the police station foyer. He waved at the old fella sat behind the high desk who wore the expression of someone surprised awake.

'Yes, *Charley*. You left me a voicemail message because you were too cowardly to keep calling until you could speak to me straight. I bet you couldn't believe your luck.'

'It's always a pleasure to speak to you,' Harry said, his voice tinged with humour.

'Now I know you're scared, you're being nice. You should be scared too, your message said something about me missing something at a murder scene?'

'Did you?' Harry said.

'I didn't miss a damned thing, nor did my colleagues. We took direction from the investigation team at that scene and in the areas where we were pointed to, I can assure you that we—'

'You're not calling to tell me what you didn't miss, are you?' Harry belatedly thought that it might have been ill-advised to cut across Charley in this sort of mood but she had something for him, he could feel it.

She huffed. 'I'm back at the address. I suggest you meet me here, if you've got the bollocks.'

CHAPTER 11

'What was that all about?' Russell Southam was naturally suspicious. It was a disposition that shaped his expression most of the time and looked all the more ridiculous to Amelia with him holding a copy of *The Very Hungry Caterpillar*. She had met him as part of a scuffle in a pub, where a young lad had fronted Russell up, asked him why he was looking at him *like that* and Russell had been confused, his reaction enough for the situation to escalate. They still talked about that incident a lot, it was a unique *how-we-met* story for sure and every time it came up Russell would insist he still had no idea what that lad had meant.

But Amelia did.

His standard way of looking at people just seemed to communicate that he didn't trust them, didn't like them even, and all before a word was said. His suspicion was peaking as he watched Inspector Harry Blaker walk back towards the entrance to Margate Police Station.

'Standard police, always wanting to know more,' Amelia said. 'I was repping some young lad who's mixed up with people he shouldn't be and that detective thought I might like to tell him who.' Amelia backed out of the space; in the moment she took to change the gear she sensed she was being looked at. 'What?'

'Did you?'

'I don't know anything worth telling him.'

'You didn't talk to him about what's been going on?' Russell said.

'We talked about this—' Amelia started.

'We did. We talked about how people are getting *killed*, Amelia! Families left *dead*! People just like us.'

'We don't know they're people like us, not for sure.'

'How much do you need to know? How sure do you have to be? Do they have to be kicking your door in, threatening your kid? Maybe stabbing me up in front of you? This thing you got us involved in is—'

'*I* got us involved in!? You think I want anything to do with these people? *They* found *me*, and I didn't exactly get a choice. I'm nothing to them anyway, I just keep them informed.'

'Nothing? What do you mean nothing?' Russell's words were spat now, his expression like he was back at that bar the first time they met: *I wasn't looking at you like anything!*

'Nothing, as in, why would they be interested in me?'

'*Think!*' Amelia was a little taken aback as his ferocity increased and he rapped his knuckles against his own cranium so hard it made a popping sound. 'They got you sitting in there with their little soldiers to remind them to be sensible, to keep their mouths shout and how you'll report back if any of them start squealing . . .'

'Right? So that's all I do. I'm not part of anything—'

'In a *police station!*' His intensity wasn't going away as she rolled the car up to a set of stop lines. Russell paused, for effect maybe, or to plan his next words carefully. 'Think about that? Those poor bastards that got hit, families and kids involved, you said it must be because someone's talking, right?'

'I don't know, OK, I don't have a clue. I just said that because it seems to be all that matters to these people. They're paranoid.'

'*Exactly*! And they think someone's talking to the cops.' She heard that popping sound again. She was looking away, towards oncoming traffic, hoping it might calm Russell down. It wasn't working.

'That was my guess, but just now that was a police inspector asking *me* questions. If someone is talking to the police then he wouldn't need to talk to me, would he?'

Russell sighed, and Amelia recognised it as him standing down. 'All I'm saying is here you are, going to a police station just about every day to sit in little rooms with cops. How long before they come round to thinking that maybe you've got the best opportunity of anyone to be spilling your guts? And these people, when they ask their questions, they spill guts for real.'

'I know what I'm doing.'

'Do you?' Russell hissed. 'You think those others did too, before they got that knock at the door, their kid in the house with them? We've got one of them too.' He jutted a thumb from his tight fist to point over his shoulder. Amelia lifted her eyes to the rear-view mirror where she could see Jacob was staring forward, his eyes wide. *The Very Hungry Caterpillar* had found its way back onto his lap.

'You're scaring him, keep your voice down.'

Russell sighed again, longer and harder. 'Maybe he should be scared.' He spoke lower, softer, still with menace. 'You should be too. You talk about these people enough, you know what they do. You can't just bury your head in the sand and hope they don't come looking for you.'

'They won't, OK? I'm not doing anything to upset anyone, I just do what I'm told. What would you have me do? Let's say you're right and they're on the warpath for someone talking; you would have me go in there and do exactly that, right now, become the person they're trying to find? Advice isn't your strong point, is it?' Amelia was back searching for a break in the heavy traffic, and when it didn't come, she forced it. The front tyres scrabbled and thumped under her, the grip coming all at once to propel them forwards. Amelia reacted with a furious middle finger to the sound of a horn from behind her. She accelerated away, taking a hard left off a roundabout that was quickly upon her, while furious honking went directly over, the sound reverberating back off the arcade fronts to dissipate over Margate's famous sandy beach. She negotiated a couple more turns until she pulled up outside a coffee shop she knew and turned off the engine. The atmosphere was instantly more oppressive, the silenced engine adding power to the silenced interior. Russell sat half-turned away.

'Let's just get a coffee . . .' she said, still gripping the steering wheel tightly, her focus forward. 'We can talk about this, but we need to be so careful, *I* need to be so careful.'

'I get that. I didn't mean . . .' Russell hesitated. 'I didn't mean for you to go in there and blurt at the first uniform copper you see, I just meant that I heard that fella, that suit who came out after you. I heard enough to know that he's the one trying to work out who's doing this. Maybe you could talk to him off the record? If he gets these people then they can't get us.'

Amelia shook her head. 'They don't do *off the record*. You should see it in there, in those custody areas, everything's written down or recorded on CCTV, they'll even stop you talking if you're not in the right place for the microphones.'

'What if you spoke to him away from there, outside of that place, on your terms? You don't have to give no details, just be hypothetical. I just don't want . . . I'm scared, Amelia, OK. I'm scared for you, for that little lad in the back and for us — for me. I don't want to get caught up in this shit.'

'I know—' Amelia started.

'So we'll go for a coffee, sure, but we don't need to be talking about this no more, not out of here. You know what I think and that's that. I saw that cop give you his card. Maybe a call to him is what stops anyone ever coming to our home, to Jacob's home and getting us into something we really can't get out of.'

Amelia still gripped the steering wheel. Russell's door opening was like a puncture in a boat's hull, the flood that came was street noise. The door shut firmly to turn it off like a tap. She checked her mirror again for Jacob, he was watching Russell then his head jerked to stare forward and meet eyes with her, his grandmother, all that he had left to keep him safe in this world. The car dipped where Russell sat on the bonnet. He shook a cigarette out of its packet then hunched forward to light it, every one of his subtle movements was communicated through her seat.

She unclipped her seatbelt and lifted her bum to reach the card she had been given. It was dog-eared, slashed by creases but good enough to read the information through the centre:

Detective Inspector Harry Blaker
Major Crime Investigation Team

Then a phone number that her thumb chased from left to right. She pushed the card back into her pocket and reached for her own door handle, lingering for just a moment, preparing for the world and its noise to flood over her again.

CHAPTER 12

The senior CSI for Kent Police, Charley Mace, was no longer the woman in white, this time she was the woman in various shades of blue. Her day-to-day uniform was a navy-blue collared T-shirt with the Kent Police bucking horse on one side of her chest and her name and rank on the other. This was tucked into navy cargo-style trousers with a pleat stitched down the front of each leg. The final shade of blue was far lighter and took the form of two layers of identical forensic gloves that she rolled off her hands from the wrist downwards between a pinched finger and thumb, reminding Maddie of her latest CSI refresher training and the mantra of the month: *Gloves are only as effective as the way they are applied and removed.*

Charley stepped out of the Mercer family home and into the Isle of Sheppey's idea of a *light mist*. The front door had popped its locking mechanism when it had been forced, Maddie noticed, rather than splintering, meaning it had remained functional and a round-shaped dint was now the only remaining clue of the violence bestowed upon it four days earlier. Maddie had to shield her eyes a little. The sun was weak as a heat source but the mist had distorted it into a wall of light.

'Firstly,' Harry called out as they approached, 'I just want to assure you that this was all Maddie's idea.'

'What was?' Charley challenged.

'The idea that something might have been missed and that we should send you back a second time to do it properly.' He said and Charley offered the start of a smile that turned mischievous when Maddie rolled her eyes.

'Well then,' she said, 'it's Maddie that you will have to thank for cracking this case wide open, isn't it?'

'Wide open?' Harry said, quickly.

'Well, ajar perhaps.'

'I didn't think you would call us all the way out here for nothing,' Harry said, almost starting to sound excited. Maddie wasn't feeling it, her CSI colleague wasn't acting like someone about to offer something key in a murder enquiry.

'Would I not? What if you had really upset me with a phone call suggesting my incompetence? Maybe I called you all the way out here because *I* had to come. We're still busy at your latest murder scene, there's a lot to do so if my time is being wasted somewhere else, maybe I thought I would do the same to you.'

'You said ajar. There's something here?' Harry said, ignoring her point.

'Fine then, this is new.' Charley led them all through the front door then pointed down to her left, to where a digital camera was set up on a tripod, tipped nose down, ten centimetres above the floor. The flash on top was angled for the light to bounce round the room rather than directly at its target. But the CSI camera was not what Charley was referring to.

'New?' Harry said, while Maddie was still watching Charley closely.

'The floorboards you wanted me to look at, the screws more specifically. I found a part fingerprint.'

Harry snapped straighter. 'A print?' he said. 'So this is why you called us out here?'

'The print matches the victim, not an offender.'

'What does that tell us?' Maddie pressed.

'Nothing.' Charley said, her smile now with an air of satisfaction to confirm Maddie's suspicions. There was nothing here that was going to help.

'It doesn't tell us nothing.' Harry insisted.

'Well OK, so it tells us that Maria Mercer lives here, has done for some time and it is highly likely that just about every inch of this place contains a trace of her. Maria Mercer's prints, or DNA for that matter, are of no interest to me or to your investigation. It's an anomaly we want, something that doesn't match — or, even better, matches with someone who wasn't supposed to be here and, like I put in my first report, I can't help you with that.'

'There was a hammer and some nails that were found in a cupboard—' Harry cut back in, his excitement seeming to deflate with every word.

'There was, and they were seized at the time, because that's what a competent CSI would do. We also dusted in situ. We got both prints *and* DNA from the hammer . . . Maria Mercer's.'

'Dammit,' Harry growled, barely audible, then moved away from the camera set-up.

'Happens all the time,' Charley said. 'We're both long enough in the tooth to know it.'

'What does?' Harry snapped.

'Detectives and their theories. I assume that's what this is about? You've convinced yourself what happened here and you need forensics to back it up.'

'I know better than to convince myself of anything.'

'I know you had a break, that you retired for a little while, maybe policing has changed, moved on since you left . . .' Charley paused, her mischief reaching new heights. 'One thing we teach all new detectives is that forensics on its own can never prove a theory, but it can disprove one.'

'We've disproved nothing,' Harry grumbled, ignoring the gentle mocking.

'This doesn't mean that someone careful didn't pick up that hammer and nails, someone other than the person who lived here?' Maddie was thinking out loud but instantly regretted voicing what had seemed reasonable in her head.

'Someone careless does nothing and we find trace evidence. Someone careful wipes it down and we find no trace of anyone; there is no in-between. At some point Maria Mercer picked up that hammer and some of those nails, we don't know when, we don't know why, but we do know that no one has since.'

'Can you age it?' Maddie said.

'Prints?'

'Prints, DNA, any of it?'

'Prints don't last. A fingerprint is nothing more than a grease residue. The surface, the conditions, how it was left and the environment will conspire to break it down. I can't tell you how long ago a print was left, not evidentially at least, but we do get a feeling for what a fresh print is, because it shows up as more prominent. That said, dip your thumb in cooking fat and press it firmly against an internal windowpane and that print will look fresh for months. Or, if I find you a print on the roof of a car and it rained an hour ago, I'll tell you that print has to be fresh. A print on a hammer discarded in a cupboard in a centrally heated house? No tellings.'

'And DNA?'

Charley huffed. All the mischief and humour now gone for only agitation to be left. 'DNA denatures over time, but will still exist where it was left. The restriction is more on the technology to pick it up rather than whether it's there or not. In this case, DNA on a screw head, that could have been there four days or four years. You can't age denaturation of DNA. That would be a gamechanger, Inspector Ives, so when I do find out how that can be done, I will be sure to call you from my Caribbean holiday home.'

Maddie was spent. Four days since this home had been filled with fear and panic and it didn't feel like they were anywhere close to finding out *why*, let alone *who*.

'I'm sorry I called you out again, Charley. I just needed to be sure. We're done here.' Harry said, confirming that he was spent too.

'Don't mention it. I would rather someone let me rub their nose in their mistake than have someone consider for a moment that the mistake was mine.' The mischief was back, Harry turned to meet her smile with one of his own. But it didn't last long.

CHAPTER 13

'He's here.' Amelia Chagrin was standing in her own living room, Jacob sat on the sofa to her right, remnants of beans on toast worn like clown make-up round his lips while he was transfixed by the television to her left. Her attention was out of the darkened window straight ahead.

Her voice had a little shake, the nerves had got to her heartbeat too, giving it a quicker beat that seemed to pulse directly into her ears. Russell appeared with a cup of tea in one hand and a Tommee Tippee cup of milk in the other. Their eyes met over Jacob's giggle.

'Thanks for this,' she said.

'You know me, always happy to help.' Russell's sarcasm was designed to be detected.

'I won't be late.'

'I know you won't.'

The evening was fresh, the sun not long gone and the darkness still pushing in. The interior light in the van was sudden and stark where the passenger door pushed open as if in greeting. The engine was running, her ex-husband the only other occupant, his tight grip and slightly awkward expression suggesting that he was feeling the nerves too. Today might mark three years since the disappearance of

95

their daughter, but the impact on them both wasn't diminishing at all.

'Hey Tim.'

'Hey yourself,' he replied. She closed the door to snuff out the harsh light, leaving just shapes, edges and outlines. Tim was looking back over to the house she had just left. She did too. Russell was in the open doorway, still holding the Tommee Tippee cup to give his silhouette an odd shape. The shadow that was his face suddenly had a red glowing tip at its centre and smoke moved upwards as a clump to catch the light behind.

'He really doesn't like me, does he?' Tim had a satisfaction in his voice that irritated Amelia.

'What makes you say that?'

'The way he looks at me.'

'He's easily misunderstood.'

'How's my grandson?'

'I said you could come in and see him,' Amelia said.

'I know, I would, only . . . I don't want to cause issues. I'll have him again though soon, just me and him.' Tim shuffled back into a driving position and they moved away. The shift in his focus killed the conversation and they were at the park before another word was said.

The parking area was quiet, the ground a slick mush of pebbles and mud, pockmarked with deep potholes where rainwater had gathered to lay out black mirrors. The van's headlights brightened on a low fence that marked the beginning of the parkland in front. Tim killed the engine.

'Back here again,' he said in the moment of stillness that followed.

'Back here again,' Amelia echoed. She reached down into a storage bin under her seat until her hand wrapped around the top of the lantern she had ordered online. It had looked ornate, beautiful even, in the pictures and had not disappointed when it arrived. The candle was already inside; she patted her pocket where she knew she had stuffed one of Russell's lighters. 'Let's do this.'

Away from the lights of habitation the darkness was thick enough to have its own form. It swirled around her, blacker around her feet so she couldn't see the standing water she knew to be there. She would light the lantern here. She flipped open the Zippo lighter, a collector's edition, she knew that from when she had bought it for Russell soon after they started dating. The sound of the lid opening was satisfying, she'd fiddled with it so much that she could do it one-handed. The gritty mechanism rolled, tutted and sparked but wouldn't take.

'Dammit!'

She tried again, the spark only lit up Tim in a flicker as he stepped closer to produce a strong flame of his own. He knelt down, patient, as Amelia fumbled over taking the lantern's top off. Tim was gentle with the flame, shielding it like an injured bird as he held it to the wick.

They had light.

Amelia led the way. The grass of the parkland was sodden and it was quickly obvious that wearing canvas trainers had been ill-advised. Then again, Amelia was never going to wear anything else. Their daughter had always worn canvas trainers, always Converse, occasionally veering away from her standard blue to a louder colour, even a paisley pattern once but always the same make and style. They were a part of her memory. So now Amelia wore them too as one of the few ways she had left to honour her missing daughter. The trip to this park was another. It was the last place they had seen her, Amelia and Tim, two parents meeting up with their then nineteen-year-old daughter. What could be more normal than that? They had met at the coffee shack in a clearing that all paths led to, sat on a gnarled picnic bench and made small talk. In truth it was far from normal, the real reason they were there was stalking them the whole time: *neutral territory*. That's what their daughter had called it when she had suggested the place on the phone. That still hurt. To think that she had insisted on meeting here because she couldn't bear the family home and was too embarrassed to admit she didn't have one of her own.

The bench was still there, still the same leathery brown with green spreading up from the legs like a velvety cancer, the same planks of the tabletop with a slight lift at each end that bore the same "*RR 4 TC*" carved into its centre; the hole for the umbrella acting as the centre of the heart shape surrounding the sets of initials. Amelia sat the soft light of the lantern down and the grooves of the graffiti got deeper, the message more pronounced. She couldn't help but wonder if *RR* and *TC* were still in love. She doubted it, three years was a long time. It had certainly been a long time to be left waiting for the confirmation of what she already knew: Kayla Goodyer — her only child — was dead.

Tim was carrying the poster rolled up in a cardboard tube. Amelia took it off him to flatten it down on the tabletop, taking a moment to study the last image they had captured of Kayla. It was from that last meeting here; three years to the day. The same trees that now stood silent in the darkness featured as a blurred haze of colour and sunlight to form the poster's background. Kayla's smile had seemed pained at the time, Amelia remembered having to coax it out of her, like it was an inconvenience for a daughter to be asked to smile at a mother holding up her phone for a picture. Now, in the light of the lantern, the smile seemed so genuine. She looked happy, healthy even, where the flame's soft light added colour to her cheeks, concealed the weight loss and the dry patches that had been prominent on her scalp and removed the sheen from her dark hair. Her green eyes were bright too, a combination of that flickering light and the fact that this latest *Missing* poster had a shiny finish. It also had a bold title: *WHAT HAPPENED TO ME?* and a number to call that no one would.

The sound of a staple gun dropped onto the table beside it made Amelia jump from where she had been lost in those eyes. She looked up at Tim and his version of a pained smile.

'Shall we?' he said.

'Go ahead.'

Tim took the poster. The tables making up the picnic area were arranged around any number of mature trees. The café was actually a wooden cabin, its serving hatches hunkered down in the darkness for now, but they would open out with the sun. Tim chose the tree that was most central, the same one as the previous years. The *clack!* of the staples forcing their way into the ancient bark disturbed something trying to roost above. Amelia counted five more *clacks!* in total.

'That's not going anywhere,' Tim said, taking a few steps back.

Amelia forced herself back to a stand, suddenly feeling ten times heavier. She walked the lantern over, placing it carefully at the foot of the tree, the light still enough to illuminate their daughter above. She felt a hold around her middle. Tim pushed himself in against her and she reached out to hold him back. With her free hand she took a picture on her phone — for her social media. She would put something out later, when she had the strength. Her posts had been hourly at first, a way of shouting out to the world that Kayla Anne Goodyer was missing. She had made the mistake of expecting a large response, like what she had seen when other teenage women had suddenly disappeared. Kayla might have had her troubles, she might have had a different lifestyle to what most of society considered to be *normal* or even *acceptable*, but Amelia had still believed that the world would care.

She didn't anymore.

Now they visited under the cover of darkness to avoid the stares and faux sincerity of those hanging out here during the day, and now the social media posts were just for her, a demonstration to herself that she hadn't forgotten, that she would never forget. And that she was still trying to find her answers, her remains, more like; something of her daughter that wasn't a tree or a graffitied bench. It didn't seem like much to ask for.

'What if she's here, somewhere close?' Amelia said the same thing every time they came here, she knew that, Tim knew it too. She felt his sigh through her hips.

'They searched high and low, they were here for days, they said that—'

'Not all of it. They couldn't do all of it and not soon enough. She'd been missing nearly a month before they even agreed to come here. I told them this was a place she came a lot, it was her favourite place away from . . . away from all that. And if someone wanted to . . . They could have followed her here and done anything they wanted, she could be buried right under our feet . . .'

'She could, we just don't know, Amelia. But one day we will.'

'We have to. I can't bear it. People said it would get easier in time, the more that passed but that's not right, not for the missing. Every day is worse, every day is another day wondering. I think I can cope with the fact that she's dead, Tim, I didn't at first, but I think I can. I just need to find her.'

'Me too,' Tim said and sighed again, 'more than anything.'

CHAPTER 14

Tuesday

Two flatscreen televisions side by side both played the daily update press conference for Tuesday — fronted by Superintendent Mark Hall, in company with Assistant Chief Constable Daniel Sawyers. The ACC had given his initial, scripted update and now looked far more settled in his seat as he directed specific questions about the investigation away from himself and towards his colleague. There were a lot of words, very few of which could be considered to constitute an *update*.

Maddie watched as Hall's cheeks burned in annoyance at being asked the same questions over and over by a gathered body of press refusing to acknowledge the phrase *we cannot disclose any more information at this stage*. The circling sharks of the press could smell blood; or bullshit, more like. A local hack might be batted off but the daily updates were now to a room filled by the nationals, who would not be abated by two officers fudging over the fact that the police were four days into an investigation and still had very little. The pressure had already been bad enough, but the suggestion of a second murder that might be linked had forced a move to a larger area and still with standing room only.

As I have said a number of times, we have not made any confirmed links between the two incidents at this time. Work continues at both scenes and we are keeping an open mind for all outcomes.

That seemed to be enough for Harry at least, who turned it off. There were some groans from colleagues who were enjoying the spectacle of senior management squirming under the lights of the media, but Maddie was a little relieved. The lack of progress had her squirming, too.

Eileen had not been watching at all, pacing instead, a mobile phone permanently pushed against her ear. She looked over at Maddie as her call finished, her neck and the top of her chest a cherry red and her eyes swimming with something significant.

'Eileeeen?' Maddie said, elongating her name into a question.

'Ma'am Ives.' Eileen looked to be fighting back a grin. Harry picked up on it too, moving closer.

'The bosses are downstairs getting a grilling right now, which means they'll be upstairs *giving* a grilling very soon. If you have something we can tell them . . .' Harry said.

'I may. I may not.' The analyst bristled with excitement. Whatever it was, she had already made up her mind that it was important.

'Eileen.' Harry's growl carried a warning.

'All you gave me was a name, Inspector . . .' she said, then stopped to lick her lips as she clicked a couple of times on her mouse. '*Liam*, right?'

'And?' Maddie prompted.

'Moran,' Eileen said, her delight peaking while Maddie deflated a little. She had been waiting for a big reveal and all she had was a name that meant nothing to her.

'Liam Moran?' Harry said like it meant a lot more to him.

'I thought you would know that name.' Her smile got wider.

'Not as well as some. Career criminal, part of a crime family. His dad used to be the go-to man for fencing stolen property, probably still is.'

'Ten points to Inspector Blaker!' Eileen blurted, before gathering herself back in. 'Previously the subject of a number of Theft Act Warrants, though nothing was—'

'What's the link?' Maddie cut in, her patience gone.

'Inspector Blaker came to me with the name *Liam*, which came from someone working closely with street dealers in the east of the county. I spoke to the intelligence asset responsible for the gangs matrix and also to—'

'Eileen!' Maddie interrupted and Eileen tutted.

'Liam Moran has been linked to drug supply in the county before. The gangs matrix team are aware but they only include confirmed persons. A stronger link came from the Source Handling Team. One or more of their sources has said that Liam Moran is controlling drug supply in large parts of Kent. Thanet included.'

'George Arthur.' Harry clicked his fingers, standing to pace as he did so.

'Liam's father,' Eileen called after him. 'He might be even more interesting.'

'Someone you know?' Maddie asked Harry.

'Not personally. He used to be a regular part of the daily briefing, linked vehicles and associates listed for disruption purposes. The feeling was that any stolen property from burglaries, commercial or domestic, it was all going through him.'

'Not just burglaries, sir,' Eileen sang. 'George Arthur Moran served six years for a violent robbery some time ago and in that case, violence was used as part of gaining access to a safe.'

'Well, that is interesting!' Maddie said.

'It was also a long time ago,' Eileen said, a little more muted, like she was suddenly aware that she was running ahead of herself. 'There's not much what you would call recent intelligence. Liam Moran has previous for assault too, an assault he made off from. The officer chasing him, who then went on to submit an intelligence report about the nature of his driving? PC Vince Arnold.'

'Always Vince,' Maddie murmured.

'Liam Moran might agree with you there, ma'am. PC Arnold has been the arresting officer twice and has led a couple of Theft Act Warrants at the Moran family home, which still shows as George Arthur Moran's address.'

'Is Vince in?' Harry said, his words like a prod to Maddie's side.

'Yeah.'

'Have him meet us in the yard.'

CHAPTER 15

Vince was just coming away from another concern for welfare, this time a suicide risk that he had spent almost two hours with, talking out the ways of the world, before leaving them at a mental health facility who could take over. His standard method of answering the phone with a burst of energy was muted, tired even, detectable in just a few words of agreement when asked to return to the station. Vince was acting sergeant for his response team most days since their substantive team leader had gone on long-term sick leave, something Maddie had encouraged to start with but was now concerned it might be something else to add to a mix that was thickening by the day.

Even his movement out of the driver's seat of his marked police car seemed laboured and the wide grin that had become a standard reaction whenever he saw Harry Blaker was missing.

'No matter what you lot got going on, it always falls to little ol' Response to crack your cases!' He did at least manage a jibe. It threatened to ignite a smile but instead stamped crow's feet either side of his eyes.

'You look tired, Vince.' Harry stated the obvious.

'Handsome too though, right?'

'Sure, if that's what gets you through the day.' Even a muted version of Vince Arnold could force a smile onto Harry's face.

'What do you need? Maddie said it was urgent, something about how I'm the only man for the job.'

'Liam Moran,' Harry said, the name like a blanket thrown over a flame — even a muted version — causing Vince to darken in an instant. His nostrils flared and his lips twitched like he was holding back a reaction.

'I know him, yeah. Might be best I don't talk about him too much seeing as I know you don't like the cussing, boss.'

'He might be linked to this job somehow, that's literally all we know. Would that make sense to you?'

'Liam Moran is all types of horrible. I nicked him for a road rage incident once. Some fella might have cut him up changing lanes so Liam forced him to stop then fractured the man's skull while his kid was strapped into a baby seat in the back. There were witnesses, broad daylight, middle of the day and guess what happened?'

'He got off, I didn't see a conviction on PNC.'

'No one saw nothing. I couldn't even get the driving offences to stick when he made off. Liam Moran's untouchable. I had other coppers telling me that and it gave me the hump so I went after him for a while after that, thought I could be the one to get something that stuck, but you know what, they were right. Witnesses don't talk about them and the SLT here don't want to put the time and effort into that family so they get left alone. Any police activity there and they always kick up a right stink, too.'

'Left alone to do what?'

'Whatever they want. Word is that the Morans are the place to go with anything hot. That'll be George Moran though, he's the old codger who'll tell you he heads up the family, but he ain't what he used to be. I hear he had a stroke, not enough to take him out unfortunately, just enough to make him a burden.'

Harry rubbed at his neat beard like he was thinking. He rested his gaze on Vince. 'We'll take your car?'

'Take it where?'

'To kick up a right stink.'

CHAPTER 16

The words "*The Grove*" were only just legible from the defaced sign twisted between two rusting posts. They were in Herne Bay, one of two seaside towns a few miles out of Canterbury, but seemingly the poor relation of the two, with Whitstable five miles down the coast a little further along in its gentrification. It was also a location that could be used to mark the halfway point between Margate and the Isle of Sheppey.

'Liam won't be here, he's never been found at this address,' Vince said, having already said it more than once on the way over. 'He's a nightmare to find.'

'This is the place to start, then,' Harry replied.

'What are you expecting from George Moran, boss? The only way I could even get him to open the door was with an enforcer and a power to do it under a Theft Act Warrant. Without that, this will be a waste of time.'

'We'll see.' Harry's tone was one that Maddie recognised.

'What are you thinking?' she said.

'I'm thinking of an intelligence report I saw from the last Theft Act Warrant executed here.'

'My report?' Vince said.

'Yes, where you said that he threatened you, told you that if you ever came back without a warrant he would beat you with a golf club.'

'Keeps an assortment of blunt weapons in an umbrella pot,' Vince said, his smile still looking tired.

'Well then, we'll stand you out front. He'll have to open the door to get a hit in.'

Harry led the way up the path. Maddie hung back a little, watching as Vince was positioned — in his police uniform — just right so he would fill the vision of anyone looking out through the spyhole. Suddenly, Harry's insistence on taking the marked car made more sense too.

'*Press the button!*' was the instant reply to Harry's knock. The voice was coarse, projected through the door, the final word prompting a smoker's cough. Harry ignored the instruction to hit the door again. Maddie noticed Vince was opening and closing his hands, making fists, a sign she recognised — he was rattled.

'We're not playing your games, George, not today.' Vince's bellow had real aggression in it.

'I don't have to let you in, do I?' There was a pause, maybe for confirmation. 'But I might if you press the button,' the voice said when none came.

Harry lashed out once more in frustration to show he had no intention of following instructions. Maddie took in the place overall. It was ugly. A detached plot, built over two floors where all the others that surrounded it were well-kept bungalows. The tiled roof of the upstairs drooped down in odd places, like a normal shape had been put on initially that had then sagged in the rain. Front and centre of the roof was a hump containing a small window that looked, to Maddie at least, like a tired eye — apathetic more like; bored at the latest police visit.

'Do you want me just to ring the bell?' Maddie said, recognising that they were now in a silent stand-off. Her step closer nudged a metal bucket, sloshing the water inside to set the endless dog-ends off on a synchronised shimmy across its grimy surface. The bucket was at the foot of a bench that ran under the largest window on the ground floor and was the only part of the garden that wasn't swamped by long grass, parts of which were flattened into curious round or square-shaped yellow stains. Back towards the perimeter fence — and the parked police car beyond — a child's slide was just holding its faded orange head above the grass, though its fate seemed inevitable.

The front door was cast in shadow where the first floor had an overhang propped up by a thick, wooden post positioned perfectly for Maddie to catch her elbow when she took another step forward.

'Press the button!' That insistence from inside came again. 'You, the big, brave man in the stab vest!' The voice from behind the door was louder; the cough that followed was louder too, sounding like it came with a layer of throat.

The one "button" Maddie could see was the doorbell. It was halfway up on the left side and in the deepest part of the shadow but now she was closer, she could see it was indeed labelled with the words *Cunt Button*. With no ego in her way, Maddie stepped forward to press it and George Moran was true to his word. The doorbell made its pathetic noise — like an asthmatic duck — and a man appeared to beam out a smile.

'You got a warrant?' His grin stayed but the eyes were disconnected. He already knew they didn't. No one presses a *Cunt Button* unless they have to.

'Nope.'

'Fuck off then.' Moran's grin dropping away and the shutting of the door were instantaneous. Maddie let him do it. Jamming her foot out would cause an immediate escalation, something she wanted to avoid, though Vince's huff from behind suggested he might have been hoping for that outcome.

'It's in your interest to listen to what we have to say.' Harry stepped forward to speak to the closed door.

'You reckon?' The voice was moving away, their opportunity with it.

'You think we would come here if it wasn't?' When there was no answer, Harry took to hammering on the door again.

'He's not going to talk to us, did you really expect him to?' Maddie hissed.

'He will,' Vince cut in. 'Like the boss said, we gotta piss him off. If there's one thing I'm good at . . .'

'Where are you going?' Maddie called out after Vince who set off walking. Harry exchanged a glance with her then fell silently in behind. The house was in the middle of its plot, and the outside space was all lawn. There was a fence that might once have prevented access to the rear but had long since died standing up and now leaned into the grass. The back garden formed the largest part of the footprint by far and contained two large outhouses, the closest one the larger of the two — almost barn-sized. It looked like it had been added to in stages, perhaps by various generations of Morans. The latest addition looked to be an extended front made out of pallets and a double door that looked like it had been ripped off a conservatory. The front panels of glass were frosted. Vince headed for it. The second, smaller outbuilding was so far back as to rest against a rickety-looking fence marking the transition to fields beyond. That one looked a little more standard in its construction, barn-shaped and adorned with wavy corrugated iron sheets rusted to the point where they would be chic in a different setting.

Vince reached for the door on the first outbuilding, his hand didn't even make the handle before the shout came.

'I SAID FUCK OFF! YOU GOT NO RIGHT TO BE HERE.' George Moran stood in the outline of his back door, concealed up to his middle by the rampant grass between them. He was only still for a moment, then moved out to make for the trampled path. He had a heavy limp that suggested Vince might have been right about his health.

There was a second bench in a flattened area with another receptacle next to its leg that swam in dank rain water and fag butts, this time a plastic saucepan from a children's tea set. Vince took a seat, crossing his legs and resting his hands on his lap to wait patiently. He was sure to fix a welcoming grin.

'Who is it!? Who's this!?' Another voice sounded at the door, the source shorter and Maddie could only see closely cropped, dark hair bobbing above the grass as it moved towards the same worn path that George was still stumbling up.

'Back in the house, ya little shit!' George bellowed without turning and the little shit in question ignored him completely.

'You're trespassing, I want your name and number. I got someone I can speak to with complaints!' George's fury had coloured his cheeks purple.

'I'm sure you have,' Vince said, calmly.

'I'll have your fucking job!' He hacked another cough, this one violent enough to bend him forward, merging into a retch. 'Boy!' he barked, 'get my fucking stick.' Maddie could see the source of the second voice now — who George was instructing — a little boy with bare feet stopped suddenly enough to squeak on the damp grass. He was ten years old at a guess, his scrawny chest also bare despite the cold and the only item of clothing visible were a pair of tatty school trousers on his lower half. He ran back for the house.

'I'm not sure you'd want it,' Vince said, looking up from his sitting position. 'I've had a hell of a morning and I'm in no mood to take your shit.'

'Take my . . .' George Moran had to stop to suck in a breath, his rage seemed enough to prevent words and Vince cut back across him. 'My boss here came to make your job easier, so you should really calm down and listen.'

George Moran didn't break from staring down Vince. 'I know you,' he said, his face a snarl. 'You came here last time, gave it the big man and found nothing. I want you out of here, I told you that last time.'

'And we know you, George,' Harry said. George didn't break from Vince. 'At least I thought I knew some things about you. You're clever apparently, savvy, and I have something you're going to want to hear.'

'And I've got a boot I'll stick straight up your arse if you don't get the fuck out of my garden!' George turned his snarl onto Harry. 'You the man in charge? You don't go to another man's house and sit unless you're asked to, and I ain't asking.'

Harry didn't reply immediately, he left George hanging, breathing hard, a bit of spittle resting between his lips. The small boy reappeared to hand George the stick he suddenly looked like he needed. George wore a vest aged to an off-white that yellowed in a patch on his chest and under both arms. His bottom half was a pair of light blue jeans, the knees and bottoms worn white, stained and creased in equal measure. The arms that hung from that vest hinted at the strength and ability Maddie had heard about on the way over, as did the broad chest with wisps of grey. He held his big hands by his side, both rolled up into fists that could have been hammers once, but now were reminders of another time, littered with scars and misshapen knuckles like medals from battles won.

'I heard about the stroke. That's nature's way of telling you to calm down, that your days of sticking your boot up other men's arses might be over,' Harry said.

'Is that what you think!? You wanna test that out, sunshine? A lot of people been making the mistake of thinking I'm done. You wanna know what happened to them people?' His fury was peaking, the next level was a lunge, whether he could back it up or not, and Harry seemed to decide that he could do without the paperwork needed to explain why three officers had been involved in restraining a man held up by a stick.

'I know who you are, George, I know what you're capable of. I didn't come here to underestimate you—'

'You did come here, though and just the two of you? Time was, your lot used to send a whole squad to pick me up and it still weren't enough. You think it's different now?'

'There are three of us,' Harry said. 'That's more than enough for a conversation.'

'You think I see your woman as a threat?' George jabbed one of his big fingers at Maddie, without the honour of eye contact. Vince reacted, snapping to his feet and lurching forward for their chests to collide. The force of it had George scrabbling with his stick to stop himself falling into the long grass behind.

'You have some respect!' Vince snarled.

'Your woman then, is she?' George smiled gleefully.

'Trust me,' Harry said, pulling Vince back by the shoulder to take over once more, 'Inspector Ives is the biggest threat here, I would advise you not to upset her.'

'These the filth!?' the boy chirruped; he had stayed just off George's shoulder. Vince and George remained locked in a stare, neither Harry nor the boy's voice could break it.

'Of course they are. You should be able to tell them by now, boy. Uniform or not, it's the stink.' His lips curled into a smile that Vince mirrored.

'Did they press the button!' The boy suddenly looked delighted, the finger he raised to point at Vince might have been smaller but the jerked movement was a chip off the old block. 'You pressed the Cunt Button!' he squealed. 'You know what that makes you, right!?'

'That's enough! Get in or you'll be the one on the end o' my stick.' The boy's delight was doused and he slunk away.

'We're investigating murder, multiple murder. Three people are dead.' Harry hit him with the reason they were there.

'So what?' George said, giving nothing away in his reaction.

'So, you have an opportunity for damage limitation.'

'What the fuck do I care about your murder?'

'I can link the Moran family to the scene,' Harry said.

'You fucking can't!' George replied, finally fixing on Harry. 'If you could there *would* be a lot more of you, you'd all be tripping over each other's hard-ons and I'd be in a cell by now. Bullshit, if you think you can come here and play me like some—'

114

'Robbery gone wrong, people hurt to get a safe open, does that sound familiar?' Harry cut back in, despite George correctly calling his bluff.

'Not to me. I did my time behind the door, but never for anything that went wrong.'

'I'd say it's gone wrong if you end up in a prison cell,' Harry pushed.

'I got out of that game a long time ago,' George replied.

'Maybe you only got out of the getting caught part,' Vince cut in, the venom in his voice like nothing Maddie had heard before. 'We know you're not so keen on thieving yourself these days. Who needs to be out doing the dirty work when you can send other people out to do it for you?'

'Are we done?' George snarled, his lean on his stick suddenly more pronounced.

'Tell me who I should be arresting. If this is something that got out of hand, something that went wrong . . . We can help each other,' Harry said.

George beamed. 'Let me tell you something, *gav*-ver, I'm more likely to admit to cold-blooded murder than I am to grass. I don't know nothing about it, and even if I did, I ain't gonna be the one making your job easier. I suggest you go figure it out, you and your bitch here.' He gestured towards Maddie and Vince shifted his weight to move forward, then thought better of it.

'Got yourself involved in drug dealing, I hear, managing the line phone for a bigger organisation. Or at least Liam has. He's in charge now, right? Seeing as you're past it,' Vince chanced and George locked back onto him.

'This is what you lot call fishing, right? Drugs ain't my thing, never has been.'

'But you're not in charge anymore, I was right about that?'

'In charge of what?' George grinned and Maddie recognised someone delighting in winding up a copper with Vince playing his part perfectly. 'Now, we're done. Fuck off,' George added.

'I bet you told Liam that you're not happy with his change of direction,' Harry said, holding his ground. 'You would have told him that drug dealing comes with a lot of heat from the likes of us, that you didn't want it to end up with the police knocking on your door with a drug warrant. But this is ten times worse, George, this is murder. Drugs and violence you see, hand in hand.'

'Still fishing, are we?'

'You need to do something for us if you want us gone. I need to talk to Liam. That line phone links him specifically to a murder scene, but if he's only controlling the kids carrying that phone then he needs to tell me that so I can rule him out.'

'Liam? You think I know where he is? I ain't seen him in months, he ain't been *here* in years!'

'My job is to keep coming back to check,' Harry said.

'You come back here you better make sure it's all legit. I was talked out of a harassment complaint last time, I won't be talked out of it again. My solicitor has all the information still, yeah, all the dates you've been here, all the times when you found nothing, the stuff you broke, the stress you caused to me and my family and with fuck-all reason to do it, just because you've got a hard-on for me, because you think I'm something I'm not.'

'I think you're a liar and a thief, don't think I'll be backing down from that.' Vince took another step forward, his stance that of someone squaring up for a fight. Maddie had seen enough, she reached for his arm.

'PC Arnold,' she said, 'Inspector Blaker here can talk out the details. Let's make our way—' She stopped when Vince threw her arm off, his anger turned on her for just a moment then flicked back to George. It was a moment of someone else, someone Maddie didn't recognise at all. George's grin was his biggest yet.

'You should do what your bitch says!' he gloated. 'Like a good little boy.' Vince shifted his weight again but when Maddie took back hold of his arm this time, he didn't flinch.

116

She was hoping for backup from Harry but he stepped in closer to Vince, the two of them forming a wall of aggression that had George's smile wavering just a little. He even shuffled a step back on his stick. Maddie waited out the stand-off that followed. She was angry herself now, but at her colleagues, enough that she walked away.

There was more said, another round of insults that further compounded a situation where George Moran was their only lead and a DI and a PC, both of whom should know better, were burying their chances of getting anything from him.

She got back in the car when Vince unlocked it from a distance, facing herself out of the window while the two men took their places. The car fired and pulled away. Ten minutes was enough for Vince to chance conversation.

'That went as expected.'

'Why would you act like that?' Maddie fired back.

'Like what? I was reacting to how he was.'

'Isn't that rather close to *he started it*? You men are all the same.'

'What are you talking about?' Vince was driving, Harry silent in the back.

'We pulled up and you said it was going to be a waste of time. But we got him out and talking. Then it became a waste of time with your dick-swinging competition.'

'It wasn't like that!'

'Wasn't it? What would I know, I'm just some bitch woman.'

'You're angry because I reacted to that?'

'Yes, I'm angry you reacted to that! You think I haven't heard that before, or worse? I don't care what he says or thinks about me, all I care about is what he knows.'

'He was never going to tell us a word of what he knows.'

'Not like that, not going there to pit yourself against him, to call him old and weak. What about appealing to him? You never even mentioned the fact that a child was tortured. Whatever you think about him, these old-school career

117

criminals have their rules, their codes, they don't stand for that sort of thing, they don't stand with having their name linked to it either.'

'George Moran only cares about himself, about what he can get from a situation. He doesn't care about no kids. You saw how he talked to one of his own back there. Appealing to a man like that is another way of bowing down to him and the moment you do that you give him the upper hand.'

'What's the problem with that? If it gets us what we need?' Maddie countered.

'People have been doing that his whole life, I wanted to disrupt that, to make him realise that I weren't there to bend to his will.'

'What were you there for?'

Vince allowed the car to slow early for a junction in the distance. 'What's that supposed to mean?'

'That wasn't police appealing to someone who might have useful information, that was three men and their egos butting up against each other. You're having a pop about him being used to getting what he wants and you just spent the last twenty minutes demonstrating just how similar you are. We're not supposed to be competing against him but that's exactly the position we're now in.'

'You would have handled that differently?' Vince said, jutting his chin out in defiance.

'I would. I would have told him that someone is out there destroying innocent families, killing a mother in front of her eleven-year-old daughter and I would have asked what sort of a person does that, if that sounds like Liam. He's either appalled at the very idea, or he considers it. Either way, we get to see that reaction and we're a step closer to under-standing what's gone on here. Then I would have asked for his *help* talking to Liam.'

'And you would have got nowhere. George knows what Liam is and he doesn't care, he's still blood. That's one way he is *old-school*. You heard what he said about grassing,' Vince said and when Maddie didn't reply, he continued. 'This ain't rock-paper-scissors; you have to meet them the same way they come at you. Anything else is just showing weakness and then you've already lost.'

'So I'm weak, am I?' Maddie snapped back.

'That isn't what I said,' Vince sighed. 'You have to threaten them is what I mean, their way of life at least, and they have to believe you mean it. For that man to do anything he has to see what's in it for him.'

'So, what now? All we achieved was making sure that George Moran's next call is to his solicitor to make damned sure that getting any warrant is ten times harder. Then he'll start making his own investigations to find out what happened with that phone and that could mean anything from setting someone up to take the fall, or driving Liam further underground.'

'He will call.' Harry spoke up for the first time. 'If he has any involvement. Even if it's just to find out what we know.'

'And if he doesn't?'

'Then I'll go back.'

'*You'll* go back?' She spun to face Harry.

'What are you saying, that you want to do it? You won't even get face to face with him, you saw how he reacted to you,' Harry said.

'And I saw how he reacted to you. You ever hear the fable about the wind trying to get someone's jacket off by blowing harder? It just meant the jacket got done up tighter.'

'This isn't a fable,' Harry said. 'And you won't even get that door open. He doesn't respond to anyone unless he sees them as having some sway . . .'

'And a set of testicles,' Maddie added.

Harry flashed a smile, perhaps believing it might help diffuse the tension. 'Seems to be a prerequisite, yes. The man's a dinosaur.'

'Dinosaur,' Maddie huffed, turning back in her seat to face back out of the window, 'and look what happened to them.'

CHAPTER 17

'You must be Maddie Ives . . . I have two names here . . .'

The woman was instantly timid. She was standing behind a desk in a foyer that was sparse in an unfinished way. The office space was among a row of commercial units that were all newly built, while the housing estate around it was still very much under construction, as were the roads that would feed it. Even the lawn that Maddie had cut across to avoid the roaring plant machinery still had the visible lines and spongy feel of new turf.

'I am, my colleague got called away so Mr . . .' Maddie paused to open her pocket book, 'Harding will have to make do with me, I'm afraid.'

The woman grinned. 'His name should be up on this wall by tomorrow, there'll be no forgetting it then. I'll give him a buzz, he's expecting you.'

Andrew Harding had found the time to get his name on his desk at least. The nametag was carved wood, a material choice that clashed oddly with the frameless glass and aluminium furniture and was either intentional or, as was Maddie's guess, an item that had followed him from a previous office — a good luck charm, perhaps. Andrew Harding then stumbled over pronouncing his own name as he stood to greet her.

'Mr Harding, my name is Detective Inspector Maddie Ives and I am led to believe that you know why I am here?'

'No! Of course not, how could I?' Harding's fluster would pass, Maddie knew — she had seen it a thousand times with people who had never had cause to speak to the police previously and whose reaction was to instantly feel under suspicion. He was a tall man, slim and long-limbed with a five o'clock shadow that didn't suit him and oil-green eyes that matched with the tie hanging from an open-neck shirt. His hair was lank, pushed over to one side and added to the impression she had of a man who usually looked smarter. He was smarter, for instance, in the only picture that hung on the wall: here his top button was done up, his tie neat and accompanying a suit with a matching pocket cloth, while his hair and face were styled and shaved respectively. Those eyes seemed a brighter green, too and he looked different overall; younger, but that wasn't just it. Looking at him now, stress hung like weight on his cheeks to pull him into a sullen expression. The picture had him in the classic handshake pose with a man Maddie recognised as Ron Blackman — the male victim from their second murder scene.

'But you are aware your business partner was killed in suspicious circumstances on Saturday?' Maddie pressed.

'Yes, of course I am aware of that.'

'Then that is why I am here, Mr Harding.'

'But I didn't have anything to do with it!' he snapped, his shock that of someone being directly accused.

Maddie removed her bag from her shoulder. A chair was pushed over to one side under another desk, it was high-backed and the cushioned bit at the top still had a layer of plastic protection on it. She pulled it over; the plastic crackled as she took her time taking a seat opposite him. She leaned forward into his space.

'Is it OK to call you Andrew?' she said, warmly.

'Andy . . .'

'Would you like to take a seat, Andy?' He had been standing over his chair, gripping it tightly with his right hand which he now snatched away like it was on fire. He took a breath, tugged at his shirt and sat down. On his desk was another picture of him, this one in a far more relaxed setting with his arms out to embrace two people standing one either side. A step to their right was someone dressed as a cartoon dog that looked familiar. Everyone had a smile — the dog the largest.

'Your family?' Maddie gestured at the photo.

'My wife and my daughter, Taliah.'

'Is that Goofy with you?' Maddie grinned.

'Euro Disney. He wasn't with us the whole time.' Andy managed a weak smile.

'This year?' Maddie said with her last effort at small talk.

'A few years ago. Taliah's twelve now.'

Maddie paused, holding her smile until it was reciprocated. Andrew Harding still didn't look comfortable in her company, but he looked less like he was about to run straight through the closed door. 'Murder investigations are massive and they are complicated,' she said. 'My job is to find out what happened to Ron and most importantly who was responsible. I don't stand a chance of doing that until I get to know him as well as possible. Talking to you is just part of that. Does that make sense?'

'That does, yes, of course.'

'I need to know Ron Blackman better, and I can do that by talking to his closest friends and work colleagues, of which you are one. That is why I am here.'

'OK. I did get that message when Anne said you were coming. She said there would be two of you, though?'

'My boss got called away. This isn't the sort of thing that needs two police officers anyway, is it?' Called away wasn't quite true, but it was all he needed to know.

'No! Goodness no, not at all!'

'OK then. So what I am trying to say is that I don't have to suspect you to have played any part in his death to be talking to you, I just have to believe you know something about his life.'

'I know, I'm sorry . . . This has all been . . . the timing of it all, it's a nightmare here, we're supposed to be expanding and now . . . Sorry! That sounds very insensitive, doesn't it? Ron's dead and all I'm worried about is what happens next with the business, that's not how it was supposed to sound. He's very important to me in many ways. I miss him.'

'I understand. How about we start with you telling me what this business is and Ron's place in it.'

'Well, Ron set the whole thing up, hence the company title: *Black Books*. It's a play on his name of course, he didn't want to use the whole of it because of misunderstandings around . . . well, it didn't have the same ring and so he played on the *black* part, because of course in accounting, which is the nature of our business, being in the black is highly desirable . . . and I'm rambling, aren't I?'

'A little.' Maddie did her best to smile encouragement.

Andy tutted, then took another deep breath like he was starting again. 'Ron worked for a big accountancy firm in the City and I joined his team. We were both from this part of the world so we shared a commute, a friendship developed and we realised that between us we had a portfolio of clients who might just join us if we went out on our own. That wasn't entirely the case, as it turned out, but Ron was very proactive, very good at the sales side of things, attracting new clients, and we were still able to grow. We moved here as part of the next phase in that growth. And now he's dead.'

'Do you have a client list that I can see?'

'A . . . yeah, I mean it's all here somewhere. I'll get Anne to send something over. Do you think it was related to here? The news said it was a burglary or something like that?'

'The media don't know so now their job is to speculate, we don't know either but my job is to find out. What he did for a living might be relevant, it might not.'

'I understand.'

'Does he have an office here?'

'Next door but he hasn't moved in yet. He was still working from home so it's pretty much an empty room.'

'I'll have a quick look anyway, before I leave.'

'OK . . .'

'Is there anything that stands out? Any difficult clients, any current disputes, or historic for that matter?'

'No! And we're accountants, we're not in the business of upsetting people, not to the extent that someone would go out and do this.'

'You deal with money, you'd be surprised how upset people can get over money. And you specialise in estate agents, is that right?'

Andy sniffed laughter, then mumbled a quick apology. 'That's not . . . no, I mean we do work with them but not as our clients. Mainly it's the developers who are the client, companies that build whole housing or industrial estates. They will have a sales team working for them but we'll deal with the management company overall.'

'When was the last time you saw Ron?' Maddie watched him closely as she shifted the focus back to his business partner. There was a flaring of the nostrils, his eyes flickered side to side and he took in a breath. His reaction could still be that of someone shocked at the sudden and violent loss of a friend and business partner, but he was wired with nervous energy about something, that was for sure.

'Must be two weeks. We only moved into the office a month or so ago but we split the workloads, I moved here straight away and supervised the move and he stayed away to make sure some actual accounting got done.'

'But you were speaking to him a lot?'

'Daily and often, five, six times a day easy.'

'On the phone?'

'No . . . it's a busy place, you know, we use email mostly. That way you can ping something off and go on to something else knowing there'll be an answer waiting. I find it to be a more efficient way to work.' His eyes flickered again, a sign of someone searching for the right thing to say, something considered.

'And he hasn't moved in yet, after a month?' Maddie lingered on him, enough to make him feel uncomfortable.

'He hasn't.' The answer was a mumble.

'Did you not get along?' Maddie said and the sigh that proved she was right was instant and heavy.

'You might as well hear it from me. There's nothing in it, but our relationship had soured a little. Enough that I've been looking at alternatives.'

'Alternatives?'

'A different place to work. Or at least a different way to work. It's ironic, I always wanted to be a partner in an accountancy firm, but the reality of that . . . you just have to have the right partner, that's all I'm saying.'

'And Ron wasn't it?'

'We were working through it. We have different ideas, different directions. We just needed to find some middle ground.'

'And Saturday, where were you?'

'Where was I . . . ? Are you asking me for my alibi?'

'Of course I am. A man you know well, that you don't like and whose death you might benefit from, is dead. What sort of a police officer would I be if I didn't ask for your alibi?'

'It had nothing to do with me!' His eyes had a far more urgent flicker now. 'We clashed about work but I didn't want him dead! I'm not capable of anything like that anyway, it's just not in me.'

'And my gut tells me you're telling the truth, but I'll have to write this meeting up, including why you're not someone we should be pursuing as a possible suspect, so a solid alibi would really help me out. The bosses don't generally appreciate my *gut feelings*,' Maddie added.

'Sure, I get it. My wife, I was with my wife all weekend, I think. I didn't go anywhere near his house, that's for sure.'

'Excellent. I'll need your wife's details. Your car details, too and access to your client list and email system, specifically your communications with Ron.'

'OK . . .' Andy suddenly sounded a lot less sure of himself. 'Are you allowed to just do that?'

'Of course, with your permission.'

'So not without?'

'Ah, *without* is my favourite!' Maddie smiled. 'Without your permission I'll have to arrest you for murder and formally interview you for twenty-four hours at the police station. That way's better, it comes with carte blanche access to anything I want, shutting the office down, searching your house, seizing your cars, clothes . . . but that *gut feeling* again tells me I'm wasting my time . . .' Maddie waited — she didn't have to wait for long. That flickering of his eyes was back, more urgent and for a longer period, until they finally settled on his desk phone.

'It's no problem, it just wasn't what I expected.' He cut a tired smile. 'I'll have my assistant give you access to everything you need. She replies on my behalf most of the time anyway.'

'She has access to your email account?'

'Of course. I've nothing to hide, Inspector Ives.'

Maddie's heart sank a little. She wasn't expecting much from ploughing through a month or so of accountant talk, but there had at least been a faint hope of something relevant. But no one planning a murder does any part of it on a shared email account. 'When did you last speak to Ron on the phone or in person?' she said, moving on.

Andy suddenly knocked on the table twice, like he'd had a realisation. 'I did speak to him on Friday! It would have been around 6 p.m., after hours for sure.'

'And what was that about?'

'Oh God, it was utterly mundane, he'd set up the utilities here and there was some issue. It was a thirty-second call to get a password for the account so I could resolve it. That was it, my last conversation with Ron. I'm sad, you know; I want you to understand that. We had our differences but we've been through a lot together, a lot of good has come out of working with that man and I shall miss him dearly.'

'I'm sure you will. Do you know much about his private life? Anything that might be relevant?'

'Like what? I don't think so.'

'Anything. Was Ron happy at home, was he involved with another woman, did he have investments elsewhere . . . Secrets, Andy, those are what can turn sour.'

Harding's head-shaking was emphatic. 'Ron adored Sandy, they adored each other. We took the wives out when the new company was first registered, it was a nice night. You can tell the chemistry with some couples, can't you? And they had it. They were just so comfortable with each other, you know? And besides, I don't see where he would have the time for anything like that.'

'Any investments, any business ideas or pursuits outside of here?'

'Not that I know of.'

'Do you think you would?'

'He probably wouldn't seek me out to tell me, not that I would have an issue with him doing something on his own.'

'Great.' Maddie had her daybook open in front of her, shutting it was a clear signal she was done. She hadn't made any notes. Andrew Harding was a task allocated to the DCs on the team, an enquiry she had used as an excuse to get out on her own while she was still upset with Harry. Vince had slunk back to his response duties. They would talk later when they were both calmer, at least she hoped so. Her team had tried to reach Andrew Harding a couple of times with no joy, which was why it was still outstanding.

'Oh, just one thing — why didn't you speak to us earlier?' Maddie fixed on him; the question purposefully direct. She had stood up too, forcing him to sit back a little and look up at her.

'I . . . I mean it's crazy at the moment, it wasn't like I didn't want to, there's just been so much to do with the move and with Ron . . . you can imagine, I'm sure.'

'Your assistant out there, *Anne*, right?' Maddie waited for the nod. 'She said you had taken Monday off last-minute?' Maddie left it hanging as a question.

'That's not quite true. I was working from home. The last thing I needed was to be here, to be disturbed with more problems about hot water or electricity bills. I needed to deal with the fact that this company has just lost fifty per cent of its leadership and clients are going to want to know my plan B.' Maddie took a moment, still studying him. It was a reasonable answer, just as all of them had been.

'Last question and I'll let you get back to it!' Maddie said and Andrew visibly relaxed, only to tense back up the moment it came. 'Do you earn the same?'

'Earn the same?'

'From the business. Is this a fifty-fifty profit share job? The private sector confuses the hell out of me.'

'It is a little more complicated than that . . . we take dividends and a minimum wage out of the business and—'

'The same?'

'Those elements are the same,' Andy said.

'And what elements are not the same?'

'There is a sign-on bonus or a *commission* as you might call it for finding new business. Like I said, Ron excels in this area—'

'So he earns more than you?'

'We have the same opportunities, you understand, but yes, Ron has attracted more new business in the two calendar years we have been up and running and he has benefitted from that. There is no ill will, the scheme is designed as a bonus scheme and of course, more clients are a good thing for us both.'

'Two years?' Maddie said.

'Two years?'

'Since you started out together?'

'That's right.'

'And fewer clients followed you over than you had hoped?'

'They did.'

'And yet here you are, expanding already to a bigger place.'

'We are an attractive proposition, Detective, we were careful to position ourselves as such. The first two years and the initial expansion are the easy part; you can undercut, even run at a loss with some of the tax relief and incentives offered to upstarts. The move here was to take advantage of a very pleasing rental agreement in exchange for filling a brand-new development that is still part building site. But it's all introductory rates and temporary reprieves and it's all going to run out. Starting the business was hard work but, from a financial point of view, it wasn't so difficult. It's the next two years that could kill us.' He suddenly seemed to realise what he had said. 'I didn't mean . . .'

Maddie let him off. 'I know what you mean. Thank you for your time. I'll speak with Anne about that client list.'

'Maybe I should. I've not long broken the news that we will need to be seven days a week.'

'You've just taken away the woman's weekends off?'

Andrew offered another tight smile. 'We were already a half day on a Saturday but we need to be steadying the ship. She's a good egg, I can't force her.'

'You'll come out the other side, I'm sure,' Maddie said and he shook her hand and thanked her for her time, going through the motions of something he must have done a million times at the end of a business meeting.

But there was no missing his relief at her leaving.

CHAPTER 18

'I missed your call?' Maddie was curt, she hadn't planned to be. It all fell away in a moment.

'I got called in.' Vince's voice was fragile. It was five missed calls, actually, and still Maddie hadn't considered that he might have been calling about something significant. Too wrapped up in her own thoughts.

'To the hospital?'

'Yeah. I'm here now. I flashed over, the way they spoke on the phone.'

'Is she . . . ?' Maddie couldn't bring herself to say the word, she didn't need to.

'No.'

'Is it bad?'

'It's worse. My mum's here, she came with Clara.'

'Oh, is she behaving?' Maddie made sure there was laughter in her voice. Clara was a bit of a standing joke — *family friend* could be her official title but Vince would often refer to her using other words, the most repeatable of which being *busybody*. She was Kathleen's best friend and they were good for each other. Clara was good for them too, to be fair, she was proving invaluable as a willing babysitter for Sammy.

'Yeah. I'm glad she's here actually . . . for my mum.'

'Yeah, of course.'

'I just . . . there's nothing to tell you really, I just wanted to speak, to say sorry for today. I don't want to fall out with you, not now.' Vince's voice was quiet when "booming" was the only volume she usually considered he had. She could hear his breath, and the picture in her mind was of Vince slumped forward, the phone pressed too tight against his lips, his eyes scrunched shut.

'We haven't fallen out,' Maddie said, gazing bleakly out of the car window. She was still outside Black Books Accounting. A hub of idle construction workers, the same ones who had accompanied her walk across the grass with whistles and heckles, were leaning on plant machinery, still staring at her through the windscreen. She turned the ignition for the phone to connect so she could move off.

'You were right. I should never have gone there, I turned up angry. Me and Liam Moran have history for sure, but it was more than that.'

'Tough week,' Maddie said, softly.

'Tough week,' he said back. 'Just doesn't seem to want to ease back, either. I went with you after another rough call.'

'The suicide risk?' Maddie said.

'Yeah, some young bird, not even twenty-five and already tried doing herself in a few times. Drowning, train, cliff and today she was out on a bridge . . . going for the full house I reckon!' He pushed out a laugh.

'She didn't, though . . . manage it, I mean.'

'Nah. I talked to her for ages, sat down a little way from her watching the traffic pass underneath 'til Traffic could shut it off. She was talking it out, don't think it mattered who was there. Saying how it all gets on top of her, all gets too much and she'll go somewhere like the sea or train track, or with legs over a cliff or motorway bridge and how she's just waiting for this moment of beauty.'

'Moment of beauty?'

131

'Sounds shit, don't it!' Another forced laugh but Maddie was suddenly aware that she'd never heard Vince talk like this and was desperate for him to continue.

'Not at all. Tell me what she said.'

'She was talking about despair, kept saying that word. Talking about how *despair* takes over everything, right, slows everything down, walks you to the place where you're gonna end it and makes you wait for this moment of beauty, a moment that can make you see it as the right thing to do. She talked about watching a train coming, said it was silent, how it was just like it was growing, not coming at her, with a mouth open to scoop her up, taking all her fears with her . . . there wouldn't be no pain.' He ran out of steam. She could still hear him breathing, it sounded deep. 'She got grabbed that time. Pulled out of some water too, said the way the light hit it, the way water feels when you're switched on and really feeling it everywhere, like a blanket and all you gotta do is wrap yourself up in it.' Vince sounded lost inside his own thoughts.

'But she's wrong,' Maddie said. 'Right?'

'It made sense to me,' Vince said and she waited for the follow-up, for a sign he was joking, taking the piss. She got nothing.

'Made sense to you like I should be worried?' Maddie's chuckle was nervous.

'No! No . . . I mean . . . I'm just trying to say that I've heard that sort of shit before and I sit and listen like we all do and then I'll kick 'em to the Crisis Team and never think about it again . . . but I . . . she just made sense to me. I think I can see how she got there, to that point.'

'If you're talking about *despair*, then yeah, it's definitely a thing. We've all seen it enough times but I guess you don't get to understand it fully until it has you by the hand. Is that what you're saying, Vince? That you're feeling it?'

'I'm OK,' Vince said, like he was telling himself.

'You're not, and that's OK. You need to take some time off. The job will support you, they know what's going on.'

'I think I will,' Vince said, when she had been expecting a very different answer.

'Promise?' Maddie wanted to push it home while she had her chance.

'You calling my bluff at a time like this?' Vince's laughter was far more genuine this time. He sounded lighter in general, the vision in her mind now of someone sat a little straighter, eyes open, pushing himself to his feet to dust himself down.

'Gotta take advantage when you're weak and vulnerable. It might never happen again,' Maddie said.

'That's right, you've seen the gun show!'

Her mind's eye shifted to Vince tensing his biceps for no one's benefit.

'I can head to you. If you want?' Maddie said.

'No!' Vince was quick and firm. 'There's no point. It could be . . . It could be soon or it could drag on a bit. There are people here, one of them might be Clara but it's all good! Can you be back for Sammy?'

'I'll make sure of it. Do you want me to bring him in?' Maddie had stopped at the junction, the way was clear but she stayed, waiting out the silence as Vince considered her question.

'I don't know,' he said, finally. 'He's at school, he likes school, let him have one last day where everything's normal, eh? Maybe . . . I don't know, Mads!'

'Don't worry. Talk to your mum, to Becks and work it out. I'll have my phone on. Whatever, we'll talk more later, yeah?'

'Thanks,' Vince said. 'Maddie, I . . . ?' He faded out when there were words left.

'What's up?'

'I . . . miss you.'

'Jesus Vince, I just left you!' she said, then when there was no answer, 'I miss you too.'

133

CHAPTER 19

Maddie wasn't concentrating when she reached her destination, but was presented with a need to switch on, for the sake of self-preservation. She was caught out by a flash of movement close to her driver's window that came from nowhere — a moped had mounted the pavement, its sound like someone had upturned a glass on a hornet. At first it stopped right by her driver's door, then moved forward in a burst of mechanical flatulence when she jerked her door at it. The engine cut and the driver was the first to dismount. He got close to her quickly, his sunglasses and their mirrored lenses dominating her outlook, increasing the intimidation level where she was forced to look at a distorted version of herself. She took a step back. He was wearing a long, dark coat, his hands pushed into pockets large enough to conceal anything he might be holding.

'I need to speak to George,' she said, gesturing at the Moran family home that was barely visible from where the passenger now stood close enough to his mate to form an even wider barrier.

'You got a warrant?' Always the same response.

'I don't need a warrant to speak to someone,' Maddie said.

'You need permission, then, and you don't have it.' Sunglasses was doing the speaking, he shuffled another step forward.

'I'll need the man himself to tell me before I can leave. I'm a stickler like that,' she said, holding her ground.

'No you fucking don't, love, we're telling you what he said!' The passenger spoke now, puffing out his pathetic chest as he did, his arms hung down like he hadn't realised someone had removed the two rolls of carpet he had been carrying from under them. Maddie grinned.

'Did he not tell you to stay on the bike while the adults talked?' She gestured at Sunglasses. She could see enough of his face to sense a greater maturity; certainly he was built far more like a man with a wider chest and thicker limbs. The glasses turned to take in the younger lad with all the mouth and she knew she was right.

'You can't be here,' the passenger spat back.

'You don't get to tell me where I can or can't be.' Maddie took a step sideways like she intended on moving around the obstruction.

'What the fuck are you doing?' The passenger moved to block her way.

'I'm going to speak to George.' The passenger was now close enough for her to smell him. He had the sweet and sour odour of a drinker; despite the cold day, it ran in the sweat down the side of his face, where it would be directed by the nape of his neck to pool on his back in the shape of a cape — shittiest superhero ever. The drink was a weakness; if this turned nasty she would put him on his arse first hit. Sunglasses would be a different proposition but his mate going down might give her the element of surprise, at least. She still fixed on the passenger and he suddenly looked a lot less sure of himself, even taking a half-step out of her way. She walked forward, no looking back, silently cursing the fact that she had been distracted and hasty getting out of the car and had left her radio and protective equipment in a bag on the passenger seat. She dug her hands into her jacket pocket and was able to grip onto her phone at least. She let it go again to hammer on the front door.

'He's already spoken to you once, he won't be speaking to you again. You're wasting your time.' It was Sunglasses who called after her.

'He didn't talk to me,' she replied, having detected a twang of nerves in his voice. George would have tasked them to get rid of the cops if they showed up again and they had failed.

'I'm telling you, he ain't answering no door to no copper.'

'Then I'll have to force it,' Maddie said.

The snort that followed was so firm it sounded like it might have brought something up with it. 'You think I'm dumb! You ain't got no right to go putting doors through!' Sunglasses sneered.

Maddie spun on her heels. 'You two have broken in yourself and tied him up and now you're trying to warn me off, at least that's what I'll write to justify my reasonable suspicion.'

'What are you talking about?'

Maddie shrugged nonchalance. 'A couple of strangers intercept me on my way to speak to an old man, a recent stroke victim who I know to be vulnerable, and I got every right to be worried. All you've done is give me a power of entry. Any copper with a day's experience doing this job would do the same.'

'You ain't got no power of entry, you're just trying it on.' Sunglasses started up the path behind her.

'Section 17 PACE,' she said. 'I'm now fearing for his life and limb, means I can kick his door in just to be sure you two haven't robbed him.'

'We ain't no strangers, we work for the man.'

'What's your name?' Maddie said, quick as a flash.

'You don't need to be knowing no names.' Sunglasses' lips twisted upwards in a dangerous-looking smile.

'So, a stranger then,' she said, turning back to hammer on the door again. The talking stopped. The two men had followed her some way up the path but they backed away, not too far, just close enough to block her exit.

George Moran arrived with a fury he directed beyond her to the end of the path.

'Ah excellent, Mr Moran, you're all right. I was worried when these two thick-looking blokes turned up on your property to turn the police away.'

'They told you to leave,' he growled.

'But you need to talk to me, George,' she replied. 'My colleagues approached this all wrong this morning, seems you rubbed each other up the wrong way, but someone is out there making a mess in your name and they didn't tell you the half of it. So far, you've had two police visits in the same day but this isn't over until you talk to us.'

'You need to come back with a warrant,' he snarled.

'Three people dead, George, and the Moran name smeared all over it.'

'War-*rant*.' He leaned in to deliver the second syllable. The cigarettes that tainted his breath smelled both stale and fresh at the same time.

'Or we can talk now, stop anything else happening.' The answer from George was to push the door shut, but Maddie's reaction was different this time, her foot already out for the door to catch. She could hear the two men walking closer behind her. Maddie still held her ground, the old man's gaze too, when he lifted it back up from her foot. 'The warrants executed here before, do you know what they were for?' Maddie kept up the talking.

'Of course I do! Some stuff got stolen and you thought it might be here. You should move your foot, before it gets hurt.'

'That's what you were told. Internally we call them *disruption warrants*. You'll never prove that and the police won't ever admit it, but I've seen it a million times. It's a message. Someone talks, tells us that you had something to do with a theft and those warrants are our way of making sure you know we're onto you. Sometimes it can force a mistake or

137

wind you up enough that we get a nicking out of it, but it's mainly about pissing you off, sending a message to all the scrotes out there that George Moran is being looked at closely and he's shut for business. Taking you offline.'

'What do I care?' George said.

'This isn't a series of burglaries and a rumour you're the one moving the goods on; this is murder. This is more attention than you can imagine, a shutdown that is a long way from temporary.'

'Cops come and go.' George shrugged.

'I won't be going nowhere.'

'We didn't hit it off, you and your *boss*, because he thought he could threaten me and yet, here you are, back at my door threatening me. You don't seem to really understand just who the f—'

'I'm not here to threaten you,' Maddie raised her voice to cut him off. His foul breath escaped through his shocked recoil. 'Just to make you aware. Someone is murdering families, torturing children . . . Do you know someone capable of doing that?' She studied him closely. His jaw clamped shut, then he licked his lips, his nose twitched and Maddie took her confirmation that this was not news to him.

'Not my style, love, never has been.'

'Liam?' she said, still studying him.

'You need to talk to him about that.'

'So, tell me where he is.'

'I don't know where he is. Even if I did, I wouldn't tell you.'

'I know people who might. People in your circle who talk to us regular and more than you know. They can get a message out too, if they're asked.'

'What are you talking about?'

'There's not much information out yet, not about what happened. But it's a simple job to task a couple of our grasses to ask about, to see what they can find out about the Moran family torturing kids to get what they want. Liam's overstepped the mark and everyone will know. Even if they could see past child torture, no one could ever work with you again.'

'Liam didn't torture no kid.'

'I need him to tell me that.'

'No, you need to prove he did!' The anger was growing in George, standing him straighter, his hands rolling back into fists.

Maddie shrugged. 'Proof doesn't matter. Thieves and drug runners don't like attention, they don't like working with someone under scrutiny, some of which you can see, like me turning up at your door, and some of which you can't see, like the tactics I'll deploy around you. Your phones, your bank accounts, undercover officers, better-paid grasses, surveillance — you name it. That's what comes with torturing children, with murdering families.'

George was shaking his head, his leer back. 'Go ahead, waste your time and money.'

Maddie shrugged again. 'It's not my money and, if nothing else, I'll wipe out your operation. That's not a waste of anything. Unless Liam had nothing to do with it, like you said. In which case, I need to be going after someone else.'

George's anger was focused in a stare that locked on to Maddie. She held her ground, staring back, waiting.

'Bring her round,' George said eventually. Then he gestured at the two men behind her, slamming the door shut in the same movement. Maddie had taken her foot out to turn and assess what was behind. She didn't know what his gesture might mean. As it was, Sunglasses strutted through the long grass to give her a wide berth and continued round the side of the house. The younger man stayed where he was, making it obvious that she should follow.

Maddie cast a longing look over at her parked car at the end of the path, considering jogging over to retrieve her kit, but it wasn't an option. Sunglasses had set off at pace, already he was out of sight and Maddie strode to catch up, hanging back just enough to keep a reactionary distance. He was in dark trousers to match his jacket and his chunky boots made short work of the tall grass.

The younger lad she couldn't see anymore. Maddie stuck to the same flattened path Vince had led them down earlier and, not for the first time, she wished he was here with her now. She had come back on a whim, not really thinking it through completely, just knowing that she didn't want to head straight back to the station. In her mind, this was a visit that could mark the start of repairing relations with George Moran and she had considered that her best chance of doing so was to head back on the same day. Now she was a long way from sure.

This time the outhouse they stopped at was the furthest one, easily a hundred metres from the house and a long way from anyone who could help. She thrust her hands back into her pocket where her phone was.

The corrugated iron that made up the structure was a ragged material, its poor fit obvious now she was closer. A large tree loomed above it, the trunk of which sprouted from the other side of the fence, its branches drooping over like they might add another layer of concealment in the summer months. For now, it was just spindly fingers that picked and scraped at the rusted hulk. Access was via tall, wooden double doors and Sunglasses pulled one open, then gestured inside.

'What is this?' Maddie said.

'Where the boss talks to people like you.' He grinned.

'I don't step into dark buildings.'

'Then you don't speak to him. You came to his house to talk, least you can do is follow his rules.'

'Why here?'

'Why not?' He was still grinning, revelling in her discomfort. She took a small step forward, enough to be able to see in. The building looked empty. It was dark too, darker than she might have expected, the only light coming from what was able to push in through the open door. The floor was swept concrete, light grey with patches of darker stains. The grinning man fed off her hesitancy, he reached for the

140

second door to make the entrance wider, his strain with its weight obvious. Then he started walking back the way they had come.

'That's where you wait for him. Inside,' Sunglasses called out without breaking stride or looking back. She watched him out of sight, he stayed looking forward, even lifting the over-sized hood on his coat. He went into the house via the back door, easily far enough that she could make it out in time if he turned to sprint back for the door. She felt confident enough to face into the building. The doors were as good as floor to ceiling, the opening of the second door had cast more light inside, enough that she could see that the inside was actually highly reflective with a silver shimmer covering every part of the surface like wallpaper. An old wooden barn with an ill-fitting metal render should be leaking light from everywhere but this one didn't. There were some tools dotted around to lean against the wall, a shovel and fork that were dark outlines, some others too that she couldn't make out. But that material on the walls — *what was it?*

She moved in, checking first that her chaperone hadn't reappeared. It was eight paces to the back of the small barn to investigate. She made the wall, lifting her hand to touch a surface that flexed and crackled under her fingers.

'Tinfoil . . .' she said out loud, 'even on the ceiling?' Her eyes chased all around the room, every inch was covered in the stuff. Her mind suddenly caught up, her hand jerking back to her pocket where she snatched up her mobile phone.

No signal.

'It's a Faraday cage!' She breathed out the words. Her legs reacted half an instant later, lurching her forward into the start of a sprint.

But she was too late, a force was already pushing the doors closed from the other side.

CHAPTER 20

His sister's hand was cold and clammy with veins stark purple against the shocking white of Rebecca's skin. The grip was looser, the fingers weak and slender and the eyes that tried to find Vince were wide, showing whites that were more a washed-out red. The black rings around them had grown too, like a shadow that was making its move to consume her entirely.

When Rebecca had agreed to see Sammy, seen what she had to live for, Vince had dared to hope for a miracle, that she would find the strength from somewhere. But the deterioration since then was terrifying, like it had only served to accelerate her illness. A miracle now was a coherent conversation. Rebecca was scared, too. Vince had never seen such fear in his big sister before. He'd seen her nervous, a rare touch of uncertainty, but never this.

Their mother fussed while Clara, her best friend, hung at the back seemingly unsure what to do with herself. Their mother had been a flurry of questions: *Do you want some water? Are you comfortable? Do you have enough pillows? Can I get you something? Are they giving you something for the pain?* and Rebecca had said nothing to any of it at first, seemingly summoning all of her energy to muster a smile that appeared in slow motion.

'You fussing?' she slurred. Their mother took her other hand in both of hers, massaging it with her fingers, lifting it to gently kiss the back.

'My girl, my little girl,' she said and her own smile was quickly tainted with a tear.

'It's OK, Mum, don't cry,' Rebecca managed between swallows, her head shaking too. She was still doing what she had done her whole life, even when she couldn't reach out and wrap her mother up in her arms, she was still cosseting her, protecting her, hiding her own pain and fear as best she could so it wouldn't spread. She was Vince's hero, always had been, just as big sisters should be, but it was more than that, she was a good person. Vince felt like he was in a position to judge, having seen enough of the bad. And now, for the first time, he was forced to face up to the fact that the world was about to lose one of the good ones.

CHAPTER 21

The door rattled, clanged and scraped. When it finally pulled open it had a wobble from where it had caught at the bottom. Maddie took another step back, readying herself to charge forward from her position in the middle of the barn — far enough back to get good momentum, while also being able to fully assess the threat that was entering. She'd picked up a pickaxe that had been stood on its head in the corner, the best of the tools for the purpose and she wielded it across her body, her stance directly towards the door.

A walking stick appeared. It hadn't been what she was expecting. George Moran scuffed his foot after it, shouting as he did.

'Who the FUCK locked this door?' His head was half-turned, there were mumbles from the other side, she detected a couple of different voices, at least one sounded like Sunglasses. Finally, he fixed on her.

'They were fucking with you, locking this door. That wasn't what I asked.'

'What did you ask?' Maddie said, the arid atmosphere of the sealed barn tripping out her voice and she coughed to clear it.

'To show you to here, to wait with you so you didn't go off snooping.'

'And what is here?'

'Here is just you, me — and, it would seem, a pickaxe. You won't be needing that.'

'I'll hold on to it for now,' Maddie said.

'Suit yourself. Do you mind if I shut the door? No locks.' He was softer, different, asking questions where the answer mattered. She couldn't explain the change, not right now, but the whole situation was odd. There was something going on here.

'I would rather you didn't. How about we go out into the fresh air, why waste that beautiful garden?'

His face lifted in a grin with no feeling. 'Your mate was right about something at least, I did have a stroke. Stuff I took for granted before, like mowing the lawn, they're gone for me now. Do you know what this is?' Moran offered a sweeping gesture with the walking stick, his eyes lifting to take in the ceiling.

'A cheap and effective way of making sure I can't call for help. It doesn't matter, a whole team of coppers are waiting just a small distance away and right now they've lost contact. I'm surprised they're not here already.'

The old man's smile held, still not lighting the eyes. 'You and I both have careers where you need to be able to spot a lie. I've become rather good at it.'

'Not good enough.' Maddie pushed her bluff.

He gestured again at the foil walls. 'You're right about cheap and effective, but it isn't the calling for help bit that concerns me.'

'You think I'm wearing something? That I'm transmitting our conversation out to my colleagues listening down the road? Why would that matter, I'm no undercover copper trying to fool you, I told you who I am, what I am . . .'

'I don't think you're wearing something, no.' George turned back to the door, running his scarred hands over walls that flexed and crinkled to the touch. He found what he was looking for, a hidden switch, a bright bulb hanging high in the centre of the ceiling lit up with a copper glow. Then he pulled at the heavy door, his struggle obvious enough to prompt assistance from the other side where someone pushed it shut. 'Now leave us!' he shouted, waiting to hear movement away from the other side.

Maddie waited too, standing out in the middle of the glow. The pickaxe had dropped a little but she brought it back up to show her readiness. He ignored her, shuffling to the left side of the barn — away from the shovel and fork — to where a small, wooden trunk was pushed up against the wall. Maddie had searched it already and knew it to be empty. He used it as a seat, the act of lowering himself onto it seemed to hurt him. 'Don't get old, love,' he said, the creases on his face moving from anguish to humour. He planted the stick out in front, then made a pile on top with both his hands.

'It's not me you're worried about,' Maddie said suddenly, 'it's them, it's your own people, isn't it?'

'We need to be talking lower now,' he said. 'I'm not sure I know who *my* people are anymore.'

'You need our help, don't you?' Maddie spoke more quietly as requested.

Another smile, this one laden with irony. 'You'd love that, wouldn't you?'

'You do want something.'

'What happened to the kid?' His voice was suddenly more intense to the point of being unsettling, even more so with the weak light directly above making shadows of his eye sockets.

'Kid?' Maddie prompted, hoping he might give up something he shouldn't know.

'You talked about a kid, torture, you said. What happened?'

'I was rather hoping you would tell me that.'

'You didn't come back here on your own without telling those two gorillas because you think I had anything to do with it, that would be stupid. You came here because you *know* I didn't, because you know I would be just as upset as you are.'

'For different reasons,' Maddie countered.

'Different?'

'I'm upset that a child would be tortured in any circumstance, you're upset because it might be bad for business.'

George grimaced as he leaned forward, his stick had a wobble where he struggled to his feet. His walk was clumsy, noticeably worse than even that morning. He might have noticed her questioning look. 'I get worse if I sit for too long.' Then he laughed, sudden and forced. 'I think I remember threatening to stick my boot up someone's arse!' His laughter continued until it morphed into wheezing. 'Turns out I'm barely capable of standing up. Wasn't so long ago I would have been a good dancing partner for those gavvers.' Maddie ignored the slur, *gavver* — the way he said it was just like it was a pet name, just what he called the police.

'They told me as much. Seems there's a grudging respect there, even if none of you can admit it.'

'I'm not sure *respect* is the word. But they don't know me, they both talked to me like I'm a man with no morals. That ain't right.'

'What did you want to talk to me about?'

'What did they do? This torture you talked about; I want to know.'

'Does it matter?' Maddie said, despite knowing it did.

'You'll never find Liam, but you know that. I bet you didn't even go looking, did you? Just came straight here. Your only chance of talking to that boy is through me and even then he's going to have to want to. Right now, I don't got enough to tell him, not enough that he'll see it as worth his while to speak to you. I need details, I need to know a bit about what happened, something I can use.'

'We need to talk to him about murder. Surely that would be enough? If he's innocent, at least.'

147

'He is innocent. Liam has his ways but not hurting kids. You're here fishing, no meat to the bones, he won't put his head up for that.'

'I came here to learn something new, not the other way around.'

'Then maybe this can be an exchange of what we know.'

'Why *would* you help us?' Maddie said.

'So you leave us the fuck alone. I ain't doing much these days, you can see why, but people still know, they still think what they think about me and that took a lifetime. I would rather that didn't change.'

'Bad for your legacy?' Maddie couldn't help but grin.

'Nothing you would understand. What happened?'

'I can't give you much. A family home was invaded, the parent killed and her little girl was forced to be part of it, kept close to where it happened—'

'Close?' George's gaze was on the floor now, his jaw tight, his chest puffed like the anger in that one word was real.

'Close enough that she won't ever be the same again,' Maddie said and it prompted a shuffling walk, his version of pacing, his head still down, his stick leading the way with a thump. 'Close enough to destroy a legacy,' she added.

'Why?' he growled.

'This is where the information *exchange* bit comes in. You tell me.'

'For access to a safe?'

'I never said that.' Maddie pounced, aware that the safe element hadn't been released to the press either.

'It's what *I* did. The gavver hinted at it when he was here earlier, talked like this is about something similar to my past. I'm a different man now, I wasn't so prepared to work for my living then, thought I could just take it. A safe in a family home is a good target, they give it up easy. I never tortured no one, mind, and there was *never* a kid about.'

'Maybe I can see why my colleagues have such a hard-on for you, that's the expression, right?'

George smiled another empty smile. 'Robberies . . . you gotta be quick, you gotta ramp it up, hit 'em hard from the start and it has to hurt. Not torture, just what gives you the control you need. That doesn't sound like what you're describing.'

'Maybe Liam has his own interpretation?' Maddie said.

George shook his head in reply. 'I know he plays it up for you lot, I know he's got a big rep, but putting a kid through that to open a safe? Never. That's someone desperate, someone blind to nothing but the cash and my Liam . . .'

'He doesn't need it. That's what you were going to say, right?'

'He sees himself all right.'

'You know anyone else with that M.O.?' Maddie chanced. 'It's come up a couple of times now, I would really like to make sure it doesn't come up a third time.'

'You've got two?'

'Two families,' Maddie confirmed.

'Same night?' he said and Maddie just shrugged. She'd said enough already, nothing more than was on the news, but she needed to be the one asking the questions.

George balanced on his stick with one hand, the other he used to grab his nose. It looked like a thinking stance. 'Same night could be some kid off his nut on something. I've seen it before, people react different to substances, I've seen people do despicable things, then wake up next day with a bundle of cash and no idea how it got there.'

'This wasn't someone on a substance bender, it was planned, well organised, forensically aware.'

'And you found this line phone at one of these places?'

'Somewhere it had no place being. Whoever dropped that phone was involved in what happened.'

'You don't know that, not for sure?' George was watching her close for a reaction.

'I need to talk to the person who dropped it, George.'

The man was still pacing, still struggling with it too. 'I don't know . . . I'll see what the word is.'

'But something else has been going on . . .' Maddie said. This whole set-up was about something more. George stopped his pacing, seeming to consider his next words and she kept up the pressure. 'You're not the main man anymore, are you?'

'Say that again!' George snarled, rounding on her and standing straighter as he did, suddenly those scars and damaged knuckles lined up into a fist. Maddie took her time resting the pickaxe headfirst on the concrete as a place to lean.

'Do you even have access to Liam anymore, or did he cut you off entirely? I don't have time to be wasting, George, I need to get back to work.'

'All that you've heard about me, that's all true, love, let me tell you that.' But he had to stop to catch his breath. 'I have people I trust, people who will know.' The hard edge to George Moran was back, but this time, Maddie was seeing it as a front.

'But not the men outside? The ones you locked yourself away from in a Faraday cage?'

'If you can't be strong, be careful. My da' told me that when he got old.'

Maddie eyed him closely. 'You do need my help. And I can help you, but you have to give me something first. I want Liam, I need to speak to him, I need him to speak to me, to tell me what happened in those family homes and who was there.'

George's movement was to the door now, it was another struggle to open it. He turned back to her, standing side-on like it was time for her to leave. She still carried the pickaxe as she stepped back out into the weak sun, just in case Sunglasses or his younger, dumber mate were still about. There was no one else around and she dumped it down for the heavy head to thud into the turf. She threw her card down next to it.

'That gavver boyfriend of yours was right about something at least.' George's voice was behind Maddie now as she continued her walk away. 'He might have reared up for you, but you are a bigger threat than he is.'

'My number's on that card, George. You call me when you have something worth talking about.'

CHAPTER 22

Light punctured the dark in bright strips and she lifted one of her hands to try and block it from her eyes. Her fingers, already sore with splinters, scraped against the coarse wood. With her other hand, she grabbed her own mouth, suppressing a scream that pulsated silently against her palm. Her eyes were drawn upward to a loud thud, the wood so close to her face it hurt to focus. It flexed inwards, shedding dust that she sucked in through her fingers to layer her throat. She choked on it, retching and coughing against her clammy palm.

Then a scream started, from above her, so close she couldn't be sure it wasn't hers that escaped. Her lips brushed against the wood, the scream louder and louder until it was everywhere and everything, cascading through cracks that ran red to soak her middle and thighs. The red glowed hotter, brighter until it was all she could see.

* * *

Jade Mercer snatched awake. It took a moment to realise she was already sitting up, her bedsheets pushed back, sitting in a soaking stain on her mattress. She shook her head to rid her mind of the last of the vivid red, until all that was left was the soft lighting from the Disney lamp Mac and Angie had bought for her. The screaming was her; she only realised when she stopped for air and silence rushed in with its own roar. A new sound came: footfalls towards her.

'Hey . . . are you OK?' A soft voice cooed through her open doorway, waiting to be invited in. It was Angie. Mac would be hanging around behind her, the same dance they had performed the night before. And the night before that. 'Shall we get you sorted?' Angie appeared to smile her words; she always smiled her words. Jade knew exactly what she meant.

The warmth she had felt to her middle had already cooled, her underwear and nightie sodden and the smell distinct. The bed-wetting was a nightly occurrence, something that had horrified Jade the first couple of times, but less so by now. Mac and Angie insisted from the start that it would stop, that it was normal, *there's no shame and it's no trouble*. They were good people.

Jade swung out her legs and heard Mac's voice as a mumble that said something about "leaving them to it". Spare bedding came from under the bed, a new waterproof topper for her mattress. The old one made a crinkle sound as it was folded inwards on itself. New Rapunzel pyjamas were next to appear, then crisp new sheets and duvet. The process now slick from practice, the old, soiled items whipped away before Jade could dwell on them. It might happen again; if it did the process would be just as slick, just as patient, just as low-key.

'All fresh!' Angie sang, then offered a hug with raised arms that Jade accepted. She had resisted the first few days, but a hug is nice and Angie always smelled like lavender and talcum powder, her skin soft, her nightie softer and at that moment Jade could almost fool herself that it was her mother holding her, making her feel better.

Angie backed off and Jade shook her head to the offer of a glass of water, then nodded that she was all right. The loose board on the landing lifted to clunk back down as Angie walked away. The stairs had a creak, too, where Angie made her way down to the washing machine. She always tiptoed this bit, closing the doors as she went so Jade wouldn't consider the inconvenience she had caused. But she knew. Her first set of bedding would be swirling itself clean in less than a minute — the last part of an ever-repeating pattern. The next part was Jade alone, reading one of her books, trying to fill her mind with images that weren't of confined places, of floorboards, cobwebs and dust, of the sound of nails being hammered into a place close enough to make her ears ring or a scream so strong it became as all-consuming as the red running through the gaps, dripping down onto her chest and arms, until it was all she could see.

Jade tossed aside her book to lie back down. It was half an hour since she had woken and, just like that, a new image filled her mind. *A new memory!* It had to be. It was like it was forming in the ceiling above her, taking its time, a photo negative gradually revealing itself in a dark room. Details were starting to come back, scaring her and exciting her at the same time. The searing red between the floorboards was there, but now, the vision projected by her mind's eye had something else: a kneeling figure. And they were looking downwards.

Looking at her!

This face appeared suddenly enough for her to gasp in fear again, but she couldn't break away, its emergence came with a force that held her down, holding her stare. She had to fight hard, using her elbows to sit up and focus on her breathing, tearing her eyes from the ceiling to fix on the Disney light. But this new memory wasn't fading, this memory of a stranger looking right at her, of a face close to the gap in the boards and of eyes that had stared right through. She dared to stare back at the ceiling, inviting the image back and it was obedient, appearing more quickly this time, clearer too. And this time the lips were moving.

The stranger had spoken to her!

More details clarified in her mind; those spoken words had vibrated the wooden slats so she had *felt* them through her fingertips. The memory of it had her lifting them for inspection where she could feel the same tingle. It had been four words, hurried and terse:

We need to go.

CHAPTER 23

Wednesday

The morning briefing meant centre stage for Eileen Holmans once again and already it seemed to be the only way the day could start for the Serious Crime Investigation Team. Her telescopic pointer had appeared on her desk, in its closed position for now as she tidied up the last parts of her presentation. Then she tutted, mumbled something and was still mumbling when she set off towards the briefing area.

'Hey.' Harry spoke to Maddie who was a heavy mess at her desk, then looked at her with a sympathy that always looked awkward, chiselled out of his stern features.

'Rebecca rallied, she picked up a little during the night.' Maddie's words took a physical effort.

'Vince?'

'They sent him home,' she said. 'They can only let one stay so they're taking it in shifts until . . . for as long as it takes . . .' Maddie faded, her mind taken from the conversation by the memory of her front door opening at close to midnight. She had been lying awake, making it to the bottom step by the time Vince had closed the front door. He had caught her out, stumbling straight into her to hold her tight, her hair caught up in his gulps for air.

Then they'd talked a little, their living room lit only by moonlight, explaining how Vince and his mother had been called in for the end, how that was the only time an ITU ward made the concession of allowing a number of family members to be at a bedside at one time. Clara too, of course.

But the shadow of death had slunk away and their permission to remain had gone with it, forcing them back into a waiting game. Only their mother had stayed. Vince's smile had looked strange in the moonlight when he explained how he and a band of whipped horses wouldn't have been able to drag her away. Vince had admitted to being a little relieved, said he felt bad about that but he'd had enough. Maddie had understood, she'd told him so, then told him to stay off work, to relax or go and swap with his mother if he must. He had refused. He was tasked with looking for Liam Moran, which meant shaking criminal family trees to see what fell out. It was a part of the job he liked, a part he was good at — even better, he insisted, when his mood was black. They'd argued a little, Maddie insisting that he wasn't in the right frame of mind, but he'd found a comeback she couldn't argue with, countering that his only other option was to sit home and spend every moment with his mind full of his sister's plight.

For Vince, the penny regarding his sister had dropped. Hope is always the final light to fade, but last night had been as sudden as an off switch. Maddie hated that there was nothing she could do to soften that blow.

'How's the boy?' Harry shook her out of her memories.

'We haven't told Sammy . . .'

'How do you feel about that?' Harry picked up on her hesitation.

'I tried to talk to him about that, but Vince, Rebecca too, they've both been insistent on how this plays out. I packed him off to school this morning like it was a normal day.'

'Do you have to be here? Maybe you have some things you could do with sorting at home, before . . . before it gets more difficult?'

'I'm better here. I'd rather not be there when Sammy gets back in, I might do something I shouldn't. It's not for me to go against wishes like that.'

'Even if you think it's a mistake,' Harry said, then nodded like he agreed.

'I know my place.'

'Then you've changed more than I thought.' Harry's face softened into a smile. His eyes had a sparkle when it was genuine — a rare sight, one that always made Maddie feel better.

Eileen appeared back from the soundproofed incident area, her movement deliberate as she picked up her pointer and tested the mechanism like a wizard picking out a wand. Then she was gone again and Harry's sparkle held as he gestured towards Eileen. 'Come on,' he said, grunting to stand, 'Jessica Fletcher's about to tell us whodunnit.'

* * *

Twenty-three miles away from the first thwack of Eileen Holman's pointer and while the Serious Crime Investigation Team sat down to listen in, Amelia Chagrin was standing beside her car, cursing at the fob that never seemed to work her central locking anymore and forced her to walk back to lock it manually, juggling everything she was already holding. She took a moment to peer over the top of her car, the rain was already settling in large patches on the blue metal, but there was something beyond that, a *someone* and they were standing still in the falling rain, facing directly towards her from the other side of the road.

He didn't deviate. Even when she stood straight to stare back. It was a *he*, no doubt about that, a tall man with broad shoulders, his shape wrapped in dark clothing, a hood up and pulled tight by hands in his pockets. The hood kept out the daylight enough that she could only make out white skin. This would be disconcerting anywhere, but Amelia was standing on her own drive, in front of her own home. She looked away to glance at the long window of her living room, to where the blinds were tipped so she couldn't see in and it was unlikely anyone could see out either. She ran over her options, quickly realising that the only one she couldn't accept was moving into her house, ignoring what was staring her down and just hoping it would go away. She had to know.

Her coat flapped in the wind where she hadn't bothered to do it up for the short walk to her door. She put her bag back onto the passenger seat to free up her hands, then did her coat up tight, forcing herself to slow her movements when her fingers fumbled over the zip. She took a breath, one last glace at her window and then she started to walk — away from the house — down her drive, directly towards the figure, still staring at the darkened void in the middle of his hood. There was no reaction. His shoulders were shiny in the wet. There were trees with an overhang a little further along the road, a bus stop too, with a curved, plastic roof — two types of shelter, both with a view of the house. But he had chosen to stand out in the rain. It was falling harder now, enough to make a noise against her jacket and to run into her eyes. She still stared straight at him, making it as far as the end of the drive before she got a reaction.

The figure turned away.

She was close enough to see his back stained with moisture, to see the drips when his hands were pulled from his pockets so his arms could swing to match a stride that was fast from the off. Amelia continued after him, glancing back to make sure she was far enough away from her home to be able to call out.

'Hey!' Her voice was strained, wrung out with tension. 'HEY!' She shouted and it had an impact, the black outline burst into a run. Amelia did the same, the sound of her footsteps clattering back off the bus stop as she sprinted past.

157

She lived on the outskirts of a housing estate that was a warren of paths and cut-throughs, and now the man took one that came up on the right, ducking through a slim entrance where two walls ended and for a moment he was out of sight. Amelia flung herself into the same opening.

It was a mistake.

She ran full pelt into the blow, her midriff bending around a solid fist, her head thrown forward for her cheek to collide with the man's shoulder, her nostrils swamped with a damp smell as her legs gave out. Her momentum was still forward but as a stumble downwards, the ground rushing up to meet her. There was no pain, not at first, just desperation as she gasped for a breath that wouldn't come, and the feeling of cold water soaking her side. Then came the sound of heavy boots clumping away. Black, with a red circle on the back, visible over rucked-up black trousers, a pocket flapping open on the side of the left thigh and a long, black jacket. She tried to shout again, to shout after him but only managed a short rasp, her hands instinctively brought to her middle where she was scrunched up in a foetal position.

Amelia didn't know how long she lay winded for, but it was enough that a search for her attacker was pointless. She moved to a sitting position, her legs pulled up, her knees under her chin. Her stomach hurt like hell and this was the only position she could stand for now; her cheek was throbbing too. Another minute or two passed, the pain subsided and her discomfort now came from being sodden and cold. And she was still being rained on.

She was able to stand but her walk was still a little bent over. She managed to be straighter by the time she made it back to her drive. The blinds were still tipped. She did her best to open the front door in silence but the sound of a surging car passing made her grimace.

'That you, hon?' Russell's voice. Amelia didn't answer straight away. The bathroom was at the end of the hall and she made for it, aware of the noise of approaching footsteps as her boyfriend came to greet her. She wrenched the bathroom door open, closing it and spinning the lock just as Russell made it to stand the other side. 'Amelia?' he said with puzzlement in his voice.

She needed a moment to recover, her stomach flashed with pain. 'Yeah, hey,' she managed.

'You OK?' Concern now.

Amelia paused to gulp a breath, desperate to sound normal. 'Yeah, of course. Just really needed the loo. How's Jacob?'

'Fine . . .' He lingered outside. 'I'm fine too and loving this babysitter gig.' Sarcasm: always Russell's weapon of choice. Amelia didn't want this battle, not right now.

'You're always fine!' She forced a chuckle.

'And then one day I might not be. Did you call that copper, that inspector yet?' Amelia wafted her hand under a round mirror on the wall and it lit up, lights all the way round to form a ring in her eyes that had a knack of making her look better. Not today. Today it just highlighted her mottled red and white cheek that throbbed in time with her raised pulse and might swell. She was soaked too, the water mixed with grit on her face and the side of her neck. Further down her body her jeans were torn over a graze to her hip and one of her trainers scratched down one side. She lifted her top. There was some reddening to her stomach where she had taken the blow, but it didn't look like much, considering how much it still hurt. She felt like she needed deep breaths but the pain was forcing them shallow and strangled her voice.

'Not yet,' she said, watching her tired features form the words, the bright rings in her eyes the only sign of life.

'Are you going to? You said you would.'

'I am,' she said, but there was no conviction; not in her voice, not in her reflection either and Russell must have picked up on it.

'What if they come here, Amelia? Even then, just you opening our front door had me panicking . . .' He faded out, the fear was clearer in his voice, it was becoming clearer in him day to day. It was like he could sense something bad was about to happen and now she had to believe it too.

Suddenly, her next move took on more significance.

She turned the shower on, pushing the temperature around as hot as it would go. Hot water made her flush red all over, her only chance to conceal her new injuries from her boyfriend.

* * *

Eileen Holmans was leading up to something, it was big and it was relevant. Maddie could read her by now, how she delighted in the process, the build-up just as much as the big reveal, describing what she had done to get there, demonstrating how clever she was while the room hung on her every word.

'An abandoned vehicle was found in a car park of a doctor's surgery in the Watling Gate Housing Estate, Sittingbourne. It's been parked there for a few days, we're not certain just how many but Watling Gate is a newly constructed estate that includes a row of shops, one of which is the surgery I mentioned and the other . . .' Eileen paused to hang out her big reveal.

'Andrew Harding's new place.' Maddie stole the moment and was the subject of a glare over the top of the glasses that they were all becoming accustomed too. 'I went there,' Maddie added with a shrug.

'Yes, you did.' Eileen took back control. 'Andrew Harding is of course the business partner of Ron Blackman, our victim from the Isle of Sheppey address.' Another pause, she was building up to something else. 'The report of an abandoned vehicle came in from someone at the surgery. It was parked across two bays and they said it had been there a couple of days with a window down and hadn't moved. I know it was a long shot, but as it was close to Harding's place of work I thought it might—'

'What's the relevance?' Maddie cut back in, her patience for showboating gone. Eileen snapped to her and she felt a pang of guilt. Eileen was an excellent analyst, her investigative powers as good if not better than any of the detectives sat in that room and no doubt her enthusiasm eclipsed them all. It wasn't for Maddie to flatten that. 'We don't have masses of time,' she said, apologetically.

'It was tagged for uniform to attend. I added a note on the CAD that it might be relevant to a Major Crime investigation, but as it was, they might have worked that out for themselves quite quickly. The car was unlocked and an item located in the boot that was wrapped in a tea towel. The item is described as a stainless-steel, single-piece corkscrew. The late-turn CSI attended to seize that item and to oversee a forensic lift of the vehicle, but we were warned that it appears to have been cleaned. They certainly detected a strong smell of bleach.' Eileen now spoke towards Maddie. 'The car's central screen, however, that was a smudge of prints, too much for them to resist it seems, so they dusted it in situ . . .' Eileen was back to showboating, her enthusiasm unaffected.

'What did we get?' Maddie said.

'Two good prints from the car's touchscreen infotainment system, both a match for a Liam Moran.'

CHAPTER 24

The briefing was a blur of horrors from then on. Maddie already knew *The Liam Moran Story* that Eileen launched into. She started with the street robberies when he was a child, the juvenile incarceration and how he seemed to have *wised up* since becoming an adult as no convictions had stuck since — despite his name being linked to a number of offences. Maddie knew how, though Vince had explained it best: Liam Moran, possibly coached by his father, had quickly realised that bully-boy tactics can keep you out of prison.

And if they weren't careful, it would happen again.

The briefing ended and, despite a significant development, the case priorities hadn't changed at all. Vince was already leading the manhunt for Liam Moran and with all the resources he needed. Maddie wasn't hopeful of a quick result, however, seeing as most of the recent intelligence had Liam Moran out of the county. It also told the story of a man trying to make a name for himself, looking to become the go-to man for drug supply in Kent, supplied from London. It had been explained to Maddie as a franchise model, like how someone might operate their own McDonald's.

Maddie was still convinced that their best opportunity to find Liam Moran was by prodding an old man held up by a walking stick. Harry Blaker didn't agree and he made clear a new determination to go out and rattle more cages alongside their uniform colleagues. Maddie waited for the briefing area to empty of detectives, leaving just her and Eileen present, before she opposed him.

'I'm just saying, if we go out there en masse knocking doors, we're letting him know that we don't have a clue where he is. We need him panicking, on the hop and moving, not bunkered down.'

'We've been out to George already, which means they already know we don't have a clue,' Harry said.

'That was the right thing to do. Word gets to Liam that we're looking, then he expects us to start knocking on the door of every associate — because that's what we always do. Let uniform do the splatter-gun enquiries while we wait until we learn something that means we can be more targeted.'

'Sounds like *do nothing* to me? This isn't hide-and-seek, Maddie, where someone like Liam Moran thinks everyone else has stopped playing and opens the cupboard door to shout.'

Maddie didn't rise to being patronised. 'I've looked at a million crime reports and looking for this bloke doesn't work, all it does is give up what we don't know.'

'And in the meantime, he goes to another family home, forces entry and drags someone out of a cupboard for real, stabs them ten times with a corkscrew and another kid gets to watch?'

'I just mean a more subtle response, that's all. I don't mean do nothing, just do more behind the scenes. Liam Moran is well used to being wanted, he knows this game as well as we do, so let's play it different.'

'Different how?'

'George Moran is different. Liam wouldn't consider for a moment that George might tell us anything—'

'And he's right,' Harry said.

'George can help us, with the right motivation—'

'The right motivation doesn't exist. He had his chance.'

'You didn't give him a chance,' Maddie said and Harry sighed, standing up to take a few steps away like he was considering his next words carefully.

'You want to talk about this again? People have different ways of approaching situations, different to you doesn't mean wrong.'

Maddie stopped short of pointing out how easy that was to reverse back on Harry. 'But we do try something different if the first approach didn't work. Let me go back and talk to—'

'No.' Harry cut her off, his voice raised. 'We're not going back to that man cap in hand. You're not. We've wasted enough time with George Moran.'

Maddie was working hard to stay calm. 'There are still outstanding lines of enquiry, we're waiting on the Met to come back to us with their own intelligence for a start. Let's get the whole picture first. We shouldn't forget that if Liam Moran walked in to front counter right this moment, we have a car we can't put at either scene, that just happened to be left close to a work premise linked to one of the victims, with a corkscrew that matches with what we *think* the murder weapon was. The only forensic evidence is a fingerprint on the screen of a car that was left with the window down. He'll come with a solicitor too, of course he will, who will very quickly point out that those prints aren't really evidence at all.' She couldn't hold her anger back any longer. 'I know I'm just a jumped-up DS only given a break because you left, but right now, a no-comment interview means releasing Liam Moran the same day and gains us nothing. All we would do is show all our cards, then send him back out to remind his network of mates that should anyone feel like talking to us, then there are plenty more corkscrews where that one came from.'

'Are you finished?' Harry's growl was laden with menace.

'I haven't even started,' Maddie replied, now standing, but not to face up to Harry, to walk away from him. Her stride was quick, unstoppable and it took her out of the

office, feeling as she did for her emergency packet of cigarettes, where this suddenly felt like one of those moments.

She jammed one between her lips, the hunt now for her
lighter, but the moment was to be stolen, her desire with it
— her phone was ringing.

It was the sound of opportunity.

CHAPTER 25

'Maddie Ives, can you talk?' Maddie's phone just showed a row of numbers and she'd considered ignoring it entirely while her heart still thumped in her chest, pushing the anger around her body. She couldn't be sure if she was angry that, after all this time, Harry was still not listening to her when it mattered, or if she was angry at herself for not telling him the whole truth of where she had been and what it might mean.

But she did answer, and to a voice that was familiar but took a moment before she could pair it with a name: George Moran.

'I didn't expect you would want to talk to me over the phone. The last time we talked you struck me as a little paranoid.' Maddie was in a hallway, heading for fresh air. When she did step out of the building her instincts still had her checking to make sure no one was around.

'I don't want to talk over the phone. You need to come out and talk to me. Just you mind, I don't need no pumped-up gavvers with testosterone issues.'

Maybe it was because she was still angry but Maddie didn't hesitate, she might even have agreed with part of his description.

'Not in your little Faraday cage. I don't plan on being in there with you again, George, no offence.'

'What if I said you could bring your own pickaxe?' There was something new in his voice, it might have been humour. It was gone just as quickly for his next words: 'Then where?'

'I'm at the police station right now.'

'I'm sure you are.' Despite herself, Maddie actually grinned; she didn't think there was a set of circumstances that existed in which George Moran would come to a police station voluntarily. 'How about somewhere a little more neutral,' he said. 'There's a park near me, a nature reserve with a car park no one else seems to know much about. We could take a walk.'

'How romantic,' Maddie said, 'but I won't be coming alone, not if you're choosing the venue. That's not a risk I am prepared to take.'

'And yesterday, what was that?'

'A mistake,' Maddie said, flatly.

'I have something you'll want to hear.'

'Then you can prepare to tell us both.'

'Someone I can trust?' George said and Maddie didn't quite know how to answer that. Since when would George Moran trust any police officer?

'Someone I trust,' she said, simply. 'I will call you on this number when I'm ready.'

Maddie ended the call, taking a moment to think. All that call had done was to justify her desire to delay the onslaught of more coppers going out in waves to knock on doors and demand Liam Moran. George was their best bet, she was certain of it. Still, she would keep this to herself for now, and she would take DC Rhiannon Davies along with her. *Someone I trust*. Then perhaps Harry would recognise that she was capable of getting results her way.

* * *

'Everything all right, boss?' Vince's question prompted Harry to look up from the paperwork he and Eileen Holmans were poring over. Both their expressions changed the moment they saw him, to obvious sympathy; Eileen the more obvious of the two. She bit her bottom lip, her head tilted slightly and she brought her hands together like she might crack out a prayer.

'Vince,' Harry said. 'How are you doing?'

Small talk from the boss — if Vince had a list of the things he could definitely do without, that would be pretty close to the top. 'Dandy. No luck on your man, I'm afraid. I thought I would come to the main table and see if you've got any more crumbs to throw me?'

Eileen's sympathy face contorted to confusion, and she turned it towards Harry. 'Intel update,' he said, gruffness back in his voice. 'Good timing, actually, Eileen was just about to talk to me about the very same thing.'

'I was,' Eileen said, recovering her enthusiasm. 'I'm not sure I can add to your table and crumbs analogy however? Maybe with some seasoning?' She smiled, it was awkward. Vince found Eileen Holmans awkward in general, out of place even, certainly in a police station setting. He liked her a lot though and had made it his business to crack her sense of humour. It was proving a real challenge.

They moved to a briefing area made out of free-standing sound deadeners, the inside of which was covered in case material. The most striking were the images from the crime scenes and Vince lingered on a photo of bloodied floorboards strewn either side of a void cast in shadow. The image next to it was clearer, it was of the same thing, only this time the void was lit by a cold white camera flash: the place where he had found Jade Mercer. Her suffering was still incomprehensible to him, the reason even more so.

'Vince? Vince . . . VINCE, you in there?' Harry Blaker's voice cut through the blur where Vince's own mind was starting to drag him back in time.

'Sorry, boss!' Vince managed a grin. 'I popped out for a moment, there!'

'Eileen here might have something you can use.'

'Thank you, Mr Blaker,' Eileen said. 'With reference to the car that was located, I tasked out CCTV enquiries and have drawn a blank. It is a brand-new estate, meaning there is nothing installed by the council and none of the commercial units have anything up and running yet. Most aren't even occupied.'

'ANPR, dashcams, sightings, doorbell cameras, personal CCTV, house to house along the most likely route in — maybe someone saw it moving or being abandoned.' Harry reeled off his list at Eileen who reacted by putting both her palms up.

'All in hand. ANPR is a negative, we know that much. . .' Vince detected that she was hesitating. 'And you are sure we cannot put out a public appeal for information with details of that car?'

'Maddie doesn't want too much of a noise around Liam right now, for whatever reason, so we can hold off on the public appeals for now.'

'Who's the registered owner?' Vince said, knowing it would have been the first check.

'Hire car. Enquiries show it's rented out to a company. I've run them through Companies House and they're listed but they don't have a digital footprint as far as I can see, so no idea what they do,' Eileen answered and Harry expanded:

'It's a common way of laundering money: set up a company with some made-up trade and then hire cars against its name. Sometimes they'll even rent commercial property. It'll be part of a bigger concern.'

'Something Mr Harding at Black Books might be able to help us with, perhaps?' Eileen said.

'He might. That'll be something for later when we're throwing everything and the kitchen sink,' Harry said, then turned to where Vince had reacted to his vibrating phone like a bee sting. 'Are you all right?'

'Yeah, I . . .' Vince snatched the phone from his pocket. It took two reads for the words to register, and when they did, they reached out from the screen to steal his breath. He gasped; his eyes fogged then cleared as he fought back his emotion:

You need to come back to the hospital, now.

It was from his mother. The lack of detail all he needed to know exactly what was going on.

'Boss . . .' Vince struggled with the word, struggled to get his breath even. 'I need to go.' He was already moving, his walk like a float towards the exit. He heard Harry's voice as a single tone, no idea what he was saying but he turned to speak in his general direction. 'Can you let Maddie know where I've gone.'

CHAPTER 26

Maddie didn't leave it long before making her call to George Moran, but she'd needed to call someone else first. The *someone* who would accompany her was always going to be DC Rhiannon Davies. Maddie hadn't expected any resistance. She hadn't got any.

Rhiannon was waiting in the driver's seat of a pool car that was ticking over in the yard of Canterbury Police Station. Neither of them could help the smiles that formed.

'You look smart!' Maddie said, opening the passenger door to lean in and talk, not yet taking a seat.

'You gotta make the effort when you're running a team.'

'Just not when I'm running the team you're in?' They both laughed. Maddie had called her young colleague away from her role as an acting detective sergeant running a team of newly accredited detectives which, despite her team dealing with the more minor offences, would be a tough job even for an experienced DS. It would also look fantastic on her CV however, hence Maddie herself taking the hit of losing Rhiannon as a constable in her own team to push her for the position. It had been a wrench, too. They were close, previously having been neighbours as well as close work colleagues, their relatively short time together forcing them into the sort of experiences that would always bind them together — no matter how far apart they lived.

'Are you staying out there?' Rhiannon said, where Maddie had stopped for a beat while hanging on to the door handle. 'What's this about?'

'You don't have to come.' Maddie had now pulled the door open and leaned in enough to gauge Rhiannon's reaction.

'So that confirms it, you have gone rogue!' Rhiannon replied. She was an excellent detective and excellent detectives ask the right questions. When Maddie had called her to ask if she was available, if she was happy to *come out on an enquiry*, Rhiannon hadn't hesitated. But she had asked *why*. Why no one else in Maddie's team? Why not Harry? Maddie had been vague, Rhiannon had been laser-direct: *Harry doesn't know, does he?*

'You have to go a little off script every now and then, just to keep everyone on their toes,' Maddie said, her smile still holding.

'I've never considered Harry Blaker as the sort of man who needs keeping on his toes. Are you getting in?'

Maddie did. 'He's the sort of man who likes results, breaks in cases. Let's see if we can't get him one.' She said, the door closing behind her with a thump.

'OK, then. You make it sound like this is going to be easy. Your phone call said something about a secret meeting with a dangerous criminal?' Rhiannon now seemed full of mischief; excitement, too, at the idea of the unknown.

'Just a walk in the park,' Maddie replied.

CHAPTER 27

'There are rules.' George Arthur Moran was on his own and already waiting in one of the smaller car parking areas on the outskirts of Blean Woods. The two detectives had held back to watch him struggle out of the driver's seat of a Mitsubishi Warrior truck.

This had been Rhiannon's idea; having been brought fully up to date with who they were meeting, she wanted to make sure he was the sole occupant and to give any other cars the chance to arrive. It also gave Rhiannon time to run the vehicle on PNC, which showed it to be a rental with no intel tags. No surprise. Criminals who get to a reasonable level will ensure any assets they have are on a monthly lease: houses, cars, luxury goods: all rented, a veneer of wealth that the authorities can never take away, only ever take back.

Accruing illicit riches seemed to have taken its toll, however. The picture of a ruthless and violent criminal that Maddie had painted on the way over seemed silly, almost. The only remnants of his power left on George were wide shoulders and big limbs now conspiring to pull his posture down. Something was missing from their earlier meetings, his bravado perhaps, and Maddie found herself considering how someone so fragile could be any use at all.

George was wearing a large, lumberjack-style shirt that looked quilted to double as a jacket with deep pockets. The collar was lifted on one side like a struggle might have taken place to get it on. After calling out his opening line he turned towards a path that led away from the car park and into the forest. A signpost carved out of wood labelled the direction he had gone as "*Green Trail*" and his stick tapped out his route. Rhiannon still held them back, checking the car park for the final time, keeping her voice low to point out the vulnerabilities to ambush. Maddie's response was to shake her head and share a belief that was only getting stronger: *He needs us.*

'Rules. Everything goes to shit without them, you lot should know that better than anyone.' George spoke again the moment he sensed the two detectives just off his shoulder.

'Even in your world?' Maddie said.

'Especially in my world. Those rules are the reason I'm here, not because I want to be.'

'Go on?'

'Who's the girl? She on work experience?' George stopped to give Rhiannon a quick once-over.

'It's always handy to have someone that people underestimate.'

'Someone you trust?' he said, still staring down Rhiannon.

'Why do I need to be bringing someone I trust?' Maddie countered.

'This is off the record, right? You and work experience understand that?'

'This is a line of enquiry,' Maddie said and there was a pause like George might have been considering if this answer was good enough.

'Where does your investigation take you next?' he said, turning away from them both to resume his walk. He seemed to be studying the ground, his heavy pit boots scuffing like he was struggling with the pace.

'I didn't come here to give you an update on my investigation, George. This might be a very short conversation if you think that—'

'My boy.' He stopped again, turning enough for his eyes to dart all over Maddie like he didn't want to miss a single part of her reaction. 'You have evidence enough to nick him, to keep him in?'

'Yes,' Maddie said, with all the confidence she could muster.

'There are a number of things pointing you in his direction, more even than when we talked yesterday?'

'Again, George—'

'You have been left things to find. Liam is being stitched up; evidence planted. You have to understand that. I don't make a habit of meeting in the woods, not with the likes of you, but this is something you need to know.'

'Someone?' Maddie said.

George started his walk again. There was a clearing ahead, Maddie could see snippets of benches — a picnic area perhaps. 'I don't know who, I know that's not gonna be good enough but I'm working on it. We've got competitors, enemies too, fuck knows that boy's got more than he even knows. I've always told him that the way he carries himself was gonna come back and bite him on his arse one day but . . . they don't listen, do they? Kids, I mean.' The silence that followed was long enough to bring them out into the clearing. Maddie wanted him to speak next, she was here to listen. He made for the closest bench, turning to lean on its table like he needed the rest. There were more tables than she had realised, all were centred around a circular wooden cabin that was labelled as selling refreshments. It was closed up; weather-dependent no doubt. The area was punctured by solid trees, one on the other side had a poster stuck to its trunk that was too far away to make out any details. Maddie's focus was on George, aware of just how much was different about him, even detecting a little sorrow.

'And I know what you might be thinking, that I've had a day to think about all this and this is what I've come up with. It's not like that. You can believe me or not.'

'I don't believe anything without proof.'

175

'You gavvers are all the same,' George said. 'I guess they don't see me as the one to go for no more. I'm already nobbled. If they go for Liam, get him out of the way then there's nothing left but the spoils. I tell you something, when I find out who this is . . .' The sorrow was gone, his expression hardened, he stood straight enough for just a moment that the stick was obsolete.

'They?' Maddie said.

'Every business has its competition,' George huffed.

'You can't, can you? Find out, I mean. If you could, we wouldn't be having this conversation. That's why you need us.'

George's focus was back on her. 'And you need to find Liam. So here's what I have. I will be at an address with Liam at some point in the near future. When I am, I will share that address with you. You will turn up with a story of how you saw my car parked outside, reason enough for you lot to knock the door. I assume you ran my car through when you pulled up here?'

'I didn't get the chance, what would I find out?' Maddie said, prompting a smile from George.

'Of course you did. So, when you tell my people that I've been seen driving it, it will make sense, I've had that motor a while. When you come to the house you insist on searching for Liam and I'll tell you to fuck off. You'll need to be insistent, pushy like what you're so good at, but you'll also need to give me time to talk to Liam. He will listen and he will come out on his own accord.'

'Liam doesn't know of this arrangement?'

'There is no arrangement yet.'

'But he won't know until we turn up?'

'No.'

'Sounds like something that can go very wrong, very quick. Why not just tell him to come to the police station and talk to me?'

'Because he won't! A man like that . . . you have to force his hands. Corner him like that and he will react, he will blow up, but I'll have him contained and I will be able to make him see sense. It's the only way.'

'You're turning him over,' Maddie said, testing him.

'He will turn himself over!' George spat. 'For his own good. Whatever you have is nothing, my solicitor will make sure of it and then you can leave us alone. You will have your explanation and you can stop wasting your time with me and my family.'

'There's more, more you aren't telling me, isn't there? More to why you need Liam arrested.'

'I know how you lot work, once you get it in your head that you want to talk to someone, there's nothing else good enough. Liam won't come and speak to you on his own accord, but he should give his side. I'm a father looking out for his son. He needs to better understand the game when it comes to you lot. Innocent people should have no fear coming in on their own terms to tell it like it is, or you lot might make up your own minds. Liam won't do that. He'll stay hidden and I know what you lot think of people that hide.'

'You need him arrested,' Maddie repeated.

'What do you mean? I just said I did, he needs to clear his name. *Our* name.'

'There's more. You talked about someone planting evidence, they're doing that to get him arrested. You think that the moment that happens, whoever stitched him up will make their play and then you will know what you're up against. Your solicitor clears Liam, with my help seeing as how I now know the evidence was planted, and he is released in time to help you deal with your *problem*. Which would catch your enemies out, right? This is a serious crime he is being linked to, they'll be expecting Liam to go to prison, remanded short term at the very least. I'm just someone playing a part in all that, right? Plus, you get rid of the police scrutiny in the process.'

'You're not interested in who *didn't* do this,' George scoffed. 'I could see how angry your mates were, your boyfriend particularly has taken it rather personal. You lot need to find who was responsible and you're looking in the wrong place.'

'You know I can't just take your word for it? If you really want Liam released and the scrutiny to shift, I need more.'

'Do as I've asked, take Liam clean, not a hint that we ever had this conversation and deal with him quick and I will have something for you in return.'

'Like what?' Maddie demanded.

George pushed off the picnic table to start walking, his aim for a different path, the general direction still back the way they had come. The terrain changed to something springy, a soggy mulch of wood chip, grit and fallen leaves that made for uneven progress.

'Who your victims are, their part in all this,' George said.

'What victims?' Maddie said, pushing him for detail.

George took long enough that Maddie didn't think he was going to answer at all. 'Accountants and council workers, Inspector Ives . . . the sort of people that have no place in this world. These weren't robberies gone wrong, they were targeted for what they did.'

'What did they do?' Maddie said.

'There's your deal, Inspector Ives. My boy arrested clean, released the same day back to me. Those people, what they did and who they upset, that is my side of the deal.'

'I need something now, George, something that tells me you're not bullshitting me. This is all give right now; I need some take.' Maddie was still pushing for something that confirmed he could be useful. The police had never mentioned the victim's occupation but that didn't mean it wasn't out in the public domain.

George stopped again, he chewed his lip, his eyes searching the ground for no reason other than to avoid eye contact. 'There was a family . . .' he said, eventually. 'Up in the city and they were brutal. They fronted up as legit owners of a lot of restaurants, Italian places. Legend has it that you knew you were in trouble if you turned up to find you were the only one invited. They'd shut the place down, sit you out in the middle and ask you questions. These restaurants got well known, even had their own merchandise, salt and pepper pots, pint glasses . . . corkscrews.' He paused like he was waiting for a reaction. Maddie was sure to give him nothing.

'What does that have to do with anything? Are they who I am looking for?'

'No, God no, they're ancient history by now. The stuff of legends, specifically their methods for getting information. You're out in a cleared space and you're surrounded, but the man asking the questions, he cracks open a bottle of wine with a single-piece steel corkscrew. You gotta have the knack with one of them. You'd be given a glass, that takes up one of your hands and all your attention, see. That's when the punishment would start.'

'Punishment?'

'A corkscrew at the right length is something you can keep nicking with for as long as you want and not do enough damage to end the day. And you'll get what you need, trust me on that.'

'Sounds like you're a fan,' Maddie said.

'Of the family? Sure. Every family wants a legacy.'

'Of the method.'

'I know a lot of people who are.' The bastard grinned at that.

'That's a nice story, George.'

'My boy, in and out clean, with me doing my part. He'll walk with you and he'll behave. Don't expect him to say much, but once that's done, I'll be in touch and I'll tell you another story about someone who has been keeping that method of obtaining information alive.'

'So, when you get everything you want, I can come crawling for what I need, with all my cards played.'

'Take it or leave it.' George started up his walk again, his breathing instantly more laboured. Maddie stayed put.

'I tell you how this works,' Maddie called after him, prompting a stop and half turn. 'I get your boy in custody clean, with your help. While he's in my cell, I'll call you and we'll talk again. You give me something worthy of my time and I'll get back to getting Liam out, same day. You don't and I'll lie, cheat and steal to remand him to prison. I might not make it, George, I don't have the power on my own, but one thing I can do is tell Liam my own story about how we knew where to find him.' George was fixed back on her. 'Take it or leave it.' She shrugged. The smile that formed on George Moran's face might have been genuine.

'If you ever consider a career on the other side of the fence, Inspector Ives, you should send me your CV.'

'I might do that, just so you can read all about my commendations for bravery, for outstanding service and my past of taking down whole crime families from the inside out.'

Maddie wasn't quite able to wipe the smile off his face. 'Liam will be where I say he is but it has to play out like a routine knock on the door. I will talk to him; he listens to me; I will tell him to go with you and get this straightened out. I'll have our solicitor meet you at the police station so the process is slick. Keep your boyfriend away and we have a chance. It needs to be you and it needs to be calm. Can you do that?'

'I'll do my part,' Maddie said. 'Who says he's my *boyfriend*, anyway?' She was more curious than amused.

'I saw the way he reared up, the way he looked at you and I recognised myself there for a moment. There was a woman I would have reared up like that for once; only one.' George Moran offered a scar-crossed hand to shake, his grip surprisingly firm. He offered the same exchange with Rhiannon. 'We have an understanding,' he said.

'We do,' Maddie replied.

'I need fifteen minutes to get clear. Enjoy the view.'

George Moran picked his way back along the path with his head down. Maddie and Rhiannon watched in silence. Maddie waited until he was out of sight to take out her phone. They had an encrypted messenger application with a group chat function. The group consisted of her, Harry and

Eileen, effective as a way of updating everyone at once. She tapped out a message: MORAN SNR GOT IN TOUCH. HE CAN DELIVER LIAM. EILEEN — THERE IS A LINK BETWEEN ALL THE VICTIMS AND THE MORANS SOMEWHERE, WE NEED TO KNOW IT. ON MY WAY IN.'

She hovered over the send button, hesitating long enough to change her mind about the recipients, removing Harry to add in Vince and the young DC standing next to her. For the time being, this was the tight circle of people who needed to know the George Moran line of enquiry. She sent the message. She would follow it up with a call to Eileen and ask her to keep it to herself for now; Vince too.

Harry would learn of her romantic walk at some point, when she could talk to him about it, which wasn't as a text message. By the time they got back to the car the message had two ticks next to it that told her it had been delivered to all recipients.

They still had ten minutes to wait.

CHAPTER 28

There was clucking and strutting like a mother hen the moment Maddie walked back into the office, all from Eileen. Even her walk was hen-like, and barefoot too, her feet out of her slippers.

'I'm working as fast as I can,' Eileen said, holding up her phone to make it clear she was referencing the message. 'There's stuff coming back all the time but we're still not talking anything that could be a link between those poor people and this Moran family—'

'I tell you what,' Maddie cut in, recognising the need to stem Eileen's stress levels. 'Let's go back over the victim profiles and see what gaps we have. If the answer isn't obvious in what we do know, then it has to exist in something we don't. Working out what we're missing is the first step.'

'That makes sense!' Enthused, Eileen set off towards the briefing area at once and both Maddie and Rhiannon followed to find a place among the untidy chairs. The victim profiles had their own place on the padded dividers. 'Victim one!' Eileen announced, the words followed by a solid *thwack!* from the pointer that had appeared as if by magic for her silent, barefooted dance. 'Maria Mercer, forty-four-year-old single parent of Jade Mercer. Maria Mercer worked for the council, housing was her bag, specialising in affordable housing, where she held a senior position. She was passionate too, her previous work was with social services, looked after children, emergency foster placements, that sort of thing—'

'OK, so we know a little about her history.' Maddie cut her off again; there wasn't the time for the complete history of Maria Mercer. 'What don't we know?'

'Actually, sorry, there's a little more to what we do know . . .' Eileen said, clucking again, 'her senior role with housing had her chairing a panel that sits within the Council Planning Department for the eastern area of the county. This panel are the last bastion when it comes to endorsing planning permission for large housing estates on brown belts and, more and more, green belts in the whole of the east.'

'So, she had some sway . . .' Maddie was thinking out loud.

'She did, and in an area where people could stand to make a lot of money on her word.'

'And we know the Moran family own land and property. Have they submitted applications to this panel?' Maddie said.

'The request is in for all applications that have gone to that panel since our victim took up the chair. In regards to the Moran family estate, it's small-scale stuff, a chunk of woodland here, a bit of field there and a couple of two-up-two-down rental places. None of it should bother a housing panel, and even if it did, this would be rather extreme bully-boy tactics for such a small gain, would it not?'

Maddie was pulling her cheeks down in a thoughtful stance. Eileen was right, this was murder, torture too, and for what? Refusal to grant permission to build on a small parcel of land? 'It would be stupid,' Maddie said, 'and George Moran is a lot of things, but stupid is not one of them.'

'And Liam Moran?' Eileen held Maddie in that gaze-over-glasses to continue. 'Forgive me for what might not be relevant, but I stood at the front of classrooms for a long time and I saw a lot of boys come through the school years — and it's always boys — reacting in the most alarming ways if they thought they were losing face. I don't believe this to be a trait that leaves them. Some men just can't accept being told *no*.'

'Liam would certainly fall into that category,' Maddie conceded. 'Let's hope you're right — if we see a Moran application to the council's housing panel that was rejected by Maria Mercer, I will be personally delighted.'

'But you're not expecting it?'

'No.' Maddie held back on the theory George had shared with her, that this was a stitch-up with the Moran family as the target. She still needed to be convinced herself.

'I also took the liberty of speaking to the Organised Crime Unit to see if they had anything more about our Moran family. They don't, they're not actually on their radar anymore, too small. But when I told them about Maria Mercer they were a little more interested.'

'How so?'

'Apparently there is a known money-laundering tactic involving property development. Criminal gangs have found a way to chip in to fund development projects: they become an investor in exchange for a percentage of the profits when the properties are sold.'

'And Maria Mercer could have stood in the way of those projects getting off the ground?' Maddie said.

'She could. This is all theory here, but we know land is far, far cheaper when sold without permission to build in the first place, or even before an application has been accepted for a change of use — the very first step needed. A piece of land where there is no permission becomes a very shrewd investment if permission were to follow on later.'

'So the Morans invest and Liam bullies the right people for what they need?'

'I think it has to be a theory.'

'But if the Morans needed Maria Mercer, why kill her?'

'Maybe they didn't need her anymore?' Rhiannon shrugged out her words. She made a valid point.

'Can you keep on that, Eileen?' Maddie said.

'Of course. One thing to add, Maria was chair of a panel, but it had to be a unanimous decision for any permission to be granted. Detectives have spoken to the four other members and none of them have had so much as *evils*.'

'Evils?' Maddie said.

'That's what the kids say, isn't it?' Eileen was back to taking in her colleague over her teacher glasses, her face stern but tainted with mischief. She was back to enjoying herself.

'Maybe all of the panel have been bullied or paid off. Or influenced by Maria without realising it?' Rhiannon offered.

'The detectives who spoke to the other members didn't get that gut feeling that you lot talk about so much. Like I said, I've asked for all the applications that have been approved with Maria's involvement as a starter for ten. I'll have a good ol' snoop through it and see if there are any patterns.'

Maddie's hope — excitement even — was starting to crash. This was beginning to feel like a dead end. 'What else do we know about her? What about her private life, does anything stand out?'

'She's never married, the father of her child remains a mystery to this point and I can't find much to suggest intimate relationships on her social media accounts. Her medical records tell of a period of depression that got quite bad while she resisted medication, but levelled out some time after she relented. Financial investigations . . . now these *are* a little more interesting.'

Maddie sat back straighter in her chair. 'How so?'

'Maria is reasonably well paid for her job, but more significantly, her home is her parents' house and is paid for entirely. She was to become the sole beneficiary of the house and was already in charge of her mother's finances due to poor health. She should be very comfortable indeed.'

'Should be?'

'She had a gambling issue. Her bank history shows money being channelled to a number of online betting companies. This peaked around the same time as her depression, no doubt they were interlinked. The poor thing got into quite the spiral, it would seem. This last year or so she seems to have got control but her finances took a hit. She has loans up to almost half the value of the house.'

'Why didn't she remortgage? The rate would have been nothing like what those loan companies will be asking.'

'She couldn't. The house isn't hers until her mother passes.'

'The mother, of course.'

'From her phone we have nothing that stands out. I spent a little while chasing a thread I thought might lead somewhere, Maria Mercer was part of the approval process for the new-build housing estate at Watling Gate in Sittingbourne.'

'Ron Blackman's business premises.'

'Exactly. I could argue that I have found you a link but it's tenuous to say the least, a coincidence really and I know that you detectives aren't keen on coincidences. This isn't even a big one; Ron Blackman was openly looking for a new build to move his business to as there are significant reductions in business rates for the first year and of course, any new-build estates in this area are likely to have involved Maria Mercer.'

'What about Ron Blackman, then?' Maddie said.

'Yes, that does lead us on rather nicely.' Eileen swapped the sheets of paper around in her hand. 'Ron Blackman is an accountant who started his own business two years ago in partnership with Andrew Harding. Blackman was murdered alongside his wife, Sandy. They have a son, Rhys, who is twenty years old and was at university in Cardiff at the time. Sandy worked from home as a television producer for a Spanish-based estate agent. She travelled out there a couple of times a year, the last time was four months ago. We're in the process of going through the information provided by Ron's firm to determine who they work with, but so far nothing's sticking out.'

'Why does an estate agent need a producer?' Rhiannon voiced what Maddie was thinking.

'They have a TV channel, daytime stuff on one of the Freesat channels. It's small-time, the company are expats who sell holiday homes to Brits so they use a channel over here to showcase their stock.'

Maddie slapped her knees as she got up to start pacing. 'There's nothing here, is there? No obvious link and no obvious gaps either.'

'Not yet!' Eileen said, bolshy, but her confidence quickly waned. 'I'll go over this again when I have all the information, with a fine-tooth—'

'Which will take a lot of time. Time we might not have. . .' Maddie continued her pacing. 'George Moran is our best chance, assuming he knows something that can move us forward.'

'Not a good thought, ma'am, that we're reduced to relying on a man like that.'

'I have no intention of relying on him, I intend on rolling him over a barrel until I get what I need. Something I can do just as soon as I have his son in the cells.'

'And you think he will help us with that, tell us where this Liam is?'

'Yes,' Maddie said, sounding sure and feeling it too. 'He needs us just as much as we need him. That arrest is everything. If we can get Liam clean we can make a break, I'm sure of it.'

'Let's just hope this Liam can behave himself, then,' Rhiannon said. 'Management won't need much of an excuse to push you towards a remand. Assault police would certainly do it.'

'It would. Which is why you and I are going to play it nice and calm.'

Rhiannon chuckled. 'I thought you told me this was just a walk in the park?'

CHAPTER 29

Jade spun the pencil between her fingers, having worn out one side entirely shading the main bulk of the thick lines across the pages. This was the first instance where she had taken the time to draw the boards in detail, using lighter touches and lighter shades rather than bristles pushed so hard as to bend double. There was even a swirl or two in the wood, just like she remembered.

Details were still coming back and she had a new determination to capture them. Her recall had been terrifying at first but it was getting easier. She knew it was important and she was somewhere she was starting to feel safe, which could be why the details were coming back to her in the first place. The drawing seemed to be helping, but the test was now, when moving on to the detail that had become the most vivid: that face. She'd never been good at portraits, her art teacher had told her that it was a niche in itself, that the greatest artists might never master it and how she should focus on what she was good at: colour and angles; contemporary and abstract. But she didn't want to be abstract, she wanted this to be right.

Jade had stalled, the lead of her pencil rested on the page, unmoving. She'd been staring down at the paper for

too long, the gaps between the floorboards she had drawn —
where she needed to recreate that face — looked to be closing
up, the gaps for her to work in somehow smaller than when
she had started.

The lead gave way, catching her out and jerking her forward where she hadn't realised she had been leaning so hard.
Jade huffed. She had another pencil, it wasn't the right softness but it would do. She just needed to get this bit drawn,
a first go at least, one last look around to remind herself that
she was safe now, that she was hidden away and comfortable.

This time she had a lighter touch and a pencil that
moved. Lines started to appear; lines that would become
details, details that would become features, features that
would become a face.

The face that had taken her mother's life.

* * *

It was the middle of the afternoon and Maddie felt like she
had wasted a chunk of her time lost in a black hole of associations on police systems, Rhiannon doing the same on the
desk across from her. She had started by bringing up *Liam
Moran*, then the extensive list of everyone associated to him,
before clicking on each of them in turn to bring up *their*
associates. And so on. An endless list of names, dates of birth,
last known addresses and a pick-and-mix of warning mark-
ers for violence, drugs, theft, contagion, domestic violence,
sex offences, offenders on bail . . . and still the list went on.
The worst traits of human beings listed time and time again,
stacked against the names; a who's who of the worst people in
the county and all of them associated in some way or another
to Liam Moran.

There were hundreds of intelligence reports too, mostly
generated from police stop-checks or third-party informants.
Put together, they painted Liam Moran as a man who took
personal pleasure in violence, in the intimidation of others,
lost in his own persona as the incumbent head of a family of

career criminals whose activity dated back more than three decades. But their strength was slipping, undermined even, and Maddie reckoned the old man who had met her earlier that day, standing out in the cold wind in a jacket he had fought to get on, could see it. On the drive back from that meeting, Maddie had considered that this was actually about George and his stature, that this could all be about using the police to get some control back over his son.

Speak of the devil.

Maddie's phone was ringing. She had labelled the row of numbers that George had called her on earlier in the day, but was still surprised to hear his gravelly voice.

'Sainsbury's in Westwood Cross, you'll need to flash your badge. I left something there at the police desk. You need to go now.' George sounded stressed, his voice wrung out, like he was talking with the last of his breath and this time it was him who cut the call. It didn't feel like a control thing, more like a man in a rush. She knew the supermarket he was talking about. It was part of a large shopping complex in a busy part of Ramsgate. She took a moment to take in Harry's desk. He had refused a return to the office he had once occupied, preferring to sit out among the team for the time being. This was the last opportunity to tell him what she had been up to, to give him the option to come along, to have his opinion.

'Rhiannon,' she said instead, standing up from her desk as she did. 'That was our call. We've got to go.'

* * *

Jade Mercer sat back, so far that her head found the wall of her bedroom from where she was sitting on the floor. The light was low, her curtains now pulled across the bright window, the ends tucked firmly down the back of her radiator to make them more effective. She had broken another pencil as her tension had increased, and pulling the curtains was part of what had relaxed her. She wanted to feel like she was

190

penned in again, that nothing could get to her, just like last time.

Jade knew she was being ridiculous. She knew that neither a memory nor a drawing could hurt her but she was now onto colour, and adding colour meant adding the life. The eyes she drew were suddenly wide and moist, they locked on to her, staring right into her. But that wasn't possible, *they couldn't be*!

Her panic came all at once to overwhelm her. She shoved the drawing pad, pushing it away so it fell from her lap onto the floor. The drawing landed face up, the eyes still staring straight at her. She lashed out again, this time with her foot to send the pad across the floor, it spun under her bed, colliding with something solid underneath. The sobs came all at once, powerful enough to have her fighting for breath. It was a fight she felt like she was losing.

Jade rolled onto her side, her legs and arms lashing out, catching her bedside cabinet and the items resting on it scattered and showered down. Everything felt like it was coming towards her, falling on top of her, the whole room closing in and she needed to fight it off, her rushed inward breaths were coarse, rattling the phlegm in her throat. Her door burst open.

'Jade! It's OK, sweetie, it's OK now, I'm here.' Angie moved in. She knew what to do by now, she knew to stay away and not to grab. She used her voice instead, telling Jade over and over that she was safe, that she was OK and in a safe place, that she wasn't trapped anymore, that no one was ever going to do that to her again.

Jade needed to hear it over and over, enough that she could slam her eyes shut and mouth the words along with Angie until she started to believe them. Finally, she got some control over her breathing and Angie moved closer to take her up in a loose hug, one that tightened the moment Jade grabbed her back.

'I'm so sorry, Jade, I'm so sorry, but it's going to be OK, everything's going to be OK . . .' Angie whispered from close enough that Jade could feel the breath on her ear. 'It's going to be OK.'

CHAPTER 30

The address was typed out in the middle of a sheet of paper that was far too large for the job and left in an envelope for a gum-chewing Sainsbury's worker with a crooked badge that said "Christine". Christine had an overall aura that she couldn't care less and Maddie was handed the envelope the moment she asked for it, not even needing to show any form of police ID or any mention of the name George Moran. She snatched it up and made her way back across a busy car park where Rhiannon was leaning on the car bonnet.

'Get what you need?' Rhiannon said and Maddie nodded, taking the piece of paper out to type out the address into the encrypted group for Eileen to pick up.

'I got an address, or at least let's hope so: Saint Nicholas-at-Wade. Seems he didn't make it far away from the family home after all.'

'This modern age and we're still messing about with love notes,' Rhiannon said, craning to see the address in full.

'Old-school,' Maddie said, 'deniability, see. Put it in a text message and he doesn't have that, doesn't trust us enough to say it over the phone — or he can't speak . . .' Maddie stopped to type out a message that would follow up the address, it was a reminder for Eileen of what they had discussed. This had to be done right:

USUAL CHECKS ON ADDRESS PLS, I'LL DO DOOR KNOCK. TWO PATROLS IN AREA TO COVER MAIN ROUTES IN/OUT BUT THEY STAY OUT OF SIGHT. MUST LOOK LIKE STANDARD ADDRESS CHECK.

Both messages had a tick appear instantaneously, confirming that Eileen had received them to her phone. She gave it another second to see if a second tick would appear. It didn't. An earlier message on the same application was still only showing one tick too. They only showed when all recipients had received it. Maddie knew it would be Vince's phone that was causing the issue; her message asking him to call when he had an update was still showing undelivered too. He kept his phone off at the hospital, his visit was now longer than she had anticipated.

She didn't think that could mean good news.

* * *

Rebecca's grip was loosening. Vince could sense it more than he could feel it, his sister's fingers were flushed white, her hands and arms paler than ever. Vince had been warned it was a sign of a body shutting down, of a heart barely strong enough to function. The most terrifying part was Rebecca's breathing. There was a definite cycle, it was quick and laboured, interjected with coughs and then she would just stop breathing at all. Vince had lost count of the number of times he had thought that was it, that his sister's life had ended. The longest may only have been ten seconds or less but it was long enough for sheer panic to merge into acceptance and even a pang of relief. Vince still felt bad about that. But this was suffering, right here in front of him, this was his sister suffering as much as anyone could.

Their mother had Rebecca's other hand. Clara had left them to it after a brief conversation with his mother around an hour ago and Vince found himself wishing she was still here. She might know what to say at least. Their mother was stroking Rebecca's brow with the thumb of her other hand, a constant movement. Rebecca had lost her focus, the ability to fix on anything and Vince wasn't even sure she knew who was there at all. Her leg twitched, the arm that Vince held did the same, her mouth which was now fixed open made a guttural sound that freaked Vince out.

'What's happening?' he said for the hundredth time.

The nurse his sister had lovingly nicknamed Nanny smiled, this time with only warmth, no mischief. 'It's OK, your sister's a fighter,' he said, then moved round the side of the bed to place his hand gently on their mother's back. 'With you all here, Rebecca will be fighting for you as much as for herself. She knows you're sad, she thinks it's what you want.'

When his mother turned her head to the voice, Vince caught the glimpse of a tear on her cheek. 'She doesn't need to stay, not for us. She's done so much.'

Vince had a reaction that he choked back, and his sister made another sound, her face screwed up in pain.

'Then telling her might help,' the nurse replied and he took his hand back. Vince locked eyes with his mother, another tear forced the first off her cheek.

'Mum . . .' he said, but nothing else would come. He wanted to tell her not to, a phrase thrashed against the sides of his mind: *Don't you dare tell my sister she can die!* But he couldn't say it, knew that he shouldn't. His mother wiped her face with the back of her hand, making doubly sure there were no tears for when she leaned in to peer down at her daughter, at her glazed eyes as another twitch rocked her body.

'Rebecca my love, it's OK now, it's OK to go, you've done enough. We're all here and we will always love you, my little girl, but you need to go where there's no more pain.'

The pupils moved, there was some focus. Vince had selfishly feared that his sister had already looked at him for

194

the last time, but he had been wrong. Rebecca met eyes with Vince first, her grip around his thumb — their greeting since hugging had become too painful — tightened. Then she looked at her mother, who was back to stroking her brow. Her eyelids were heavy, their movement protracted and slow, her breathing back to shallow and fast.

This time, when the breathing stopped, there was to be no starting up again.

* * *

Maddie was sure not to hesitate on sizing up the address on arrival, pacing straight up the front path instead, then slapping the door with all the firmness she could muster. The door knocker that was just above the part she had hit shuffled and rattled against it. Rhiannon hung back to ensure a view that covered all of the front-facing windows for any movement. Maddie hit the door again.

Just an address check, she mumbled, *routine*.

'All right, Jesus!' The voice instantly took on a grunt of exertion but nothing opened. 'What do you want?' Maddie recognised the voice: George Moran.

He had been as good as his word and she suddenly felt buoyed, daring to consider this might actually play out, that Liam Moran was behind that door and, once he was quietly under arrest, the answers they needed would follow from his father.

'Open the door,' Maddie called out, delivering the role of a police officer doing door-to-door enquiries. You never revealed the reason for a visit to a closed door, that just made it easy for them.

'What do you want?' The same voice only slightly louder, slightly more agitated. George seemed up for his part too.

'It's the police, George. I know you're here, your car's outside. I need to talk to you.' A longer pause this time, a pause that, in any other situation, might be read as time used

195

to contemplate ditching out the back. Of course she would also have officers braced at the back and this would be a good moment to radio through and have them step out and show themselves, so the occupants would know their options were limited. But today there were no officers covering the back, today this was just a knock on the front door by two passing detectives who happened to see a car linked to a close associate of a wanted man. The time for contemplation was over. The door scraped on the other side then shook open. It only opened a slit. George Moran peered out and Maddie detected a little humour in his eyes. He was enjoying this.

'Mr Moran, we meet again.'

'And so soon,' George replied.

'This one of yours?' Maddie lifted her eyes to reference the house, George Moran mirrored it to reply.

'Nothing to do with me, I'm just a guest.'

'Who of?'

'Now come on!' His grin was big and wide, his enjoyment increasing. 'You spoke to me at my home what, yesterday? Now you turn up at a friend's house? At what point does this become police harassment?'

'At the point that I'm satisfied your son isn't here,' Maddie said, jumping ahead in their game of to-and-fro to get to the point.

'My son?'

'Is Liam here?'

'What does he have to do with anything?'

'I need to speak to him regarding a serious matter,' Maddie said, now stating her intent.

'Bit unfair, ain't it? Coming to a house where I'm a guest and starting asking me questions about who might be kind enough to be giving an old man a cuppa tea and a biscuit.'

'So, he isn't here? Only you haven't said that.' George Moran lost his smile, there was a flash of anger too and Maddie reckoned he had hoped to play out his game a little longer. She didn't have the time or the patience. She needed Liam under control, under arrest. She might not have officers round the back but there were two marked cars further down the road in both directions, their engines ticking over, the passengers standing outside the vehicles to head off any foot pursuits. But she wanted to avoid using them, almost at all cost, or their bluff of *just passing* was dead in the water. 'Would you like to take a moment to check?' Maddie said, prompting the next stage where he stepped back into the house and talked to his son to convince him to walk out quietly and answer questions that were not going away. Just like he had said he would.

'I'll check, sure. But me checking means that you lot don't have to, right?'

'We'll see,' Maddie said, not wanting to concede the option. George pushed the door to close but it only bounced off her boot, the second time she had used this move on him and one he would have been expecting.

'If you'll give me a moment.' George turned away then mumbled something that wasn't for her. A moment later another familiar face appeared, still part-obscured by a pair of mirrored sunglasses. Once again he stared out with all the intimidation he could muster, lingering on looking down at her foot in the door. Maddie stared back. Her foot stayed where it was, and her lips formed a smile where she found herself enjoying this too.

'We have to stop meeting like this,' she said. No answer, just as she expected. It didn't matter, she didn't need anything from him, she needed Liam, then George.

So far so good.

Maddie used the moment to send a message to the group for Eileen to pick up. She updated them that the door was open, that George was there and she now believed Liam Moran was in the property. The message would be passed on to the patrols that were parked up. All that was left to do now was wait.

Nearly ten minutes passed until the doorstop was instructed to step aside. George appeared back at the door, he even pushed it a little wider.

'Seems I've found something that might be of interest. You need to give me a couple more minutes, time for a cigarette and a phone call to arrange for a friend of the family to meet you at the station, the best friend money can buy, if you know what I mean.' That gleam was back, George was back to enjoying playing his part in the facade. 'We don't want no excuse for this to be held up.'

'I won't just stand here forever,' Maddie said, then stayed put at the point where, in a normal situation, she might start pushing her way in.

George Moran disappeared again.

Ten minutes passed, fifteen minutes was Maddie's cut-off. That passed too.

'Any idea what's going on in there?' Maddie said to Sunglasses.

'No,' he said, without making any effort to look behind him.

'Maybe you could call through, I don't have all day.'

'I do,' was the reply and with no change to the man's expression. Maddie herself turned, but it was away from the house and to the sound of a car pulling up, its appearance loud and revvy, the braking hard and untidy so the tyres squealed as they bumped up the pavement. Someone arriving in a hurry. The driver's door burst open, the huge figure that stepped out of it instantly reeked of a fury that was directly towards her, emphasised by a door slam that rocked the car on its wheels.

Then the occupant started up the path towards her, two scrunched up fists swinging like wrecking balls either side of a pumped chest. Maddie made eye contact with Rhiannon, there was only time for a few rushed words.

'Something's wrong!' she said. 'We're in trouble here.'

CHAPTER 31

Rebecca's hand fell from his grip and Vince found himself backing away as if led by an invisible force, his periphery closing in, a pinprick of focus directly ahead while the rest of his surroundings blurred. Rebecca's face was the only part in focus, her glassy eyes, drooping lip, her chin now rested on her chest. There was blurred movement the other side of the bed, it came from his mother, a sound too, like someone forcing air from a blown-up balloon that merged into a scream. It should have been shrill, piercing, but it was muted like his ears were stuffed with cotton wool. He turned away, making for the door that took him out of the ITU ward and into the corridor beyond. He took a sharp right, where the overhead lighting soaked into the polished floor to give his whole outlook a glow, an impression of walking into a celestial light. Darker figures unmerged from a row of plastic seats to step in his way and a voice he knew punctured his internal buzz: Clara. She must have been waiting outside. Her face pushed right up to his, forcing him to focus on her lips. They were moving, the eyes above filled with questions Vince knew he couldn't answer. He bumped past her, the next sensation was a dull hit to the waist: Sammy; Clara must have been sent to get him. He arrived as a clump to wrap himself tight around Vince's waist, adding to the sensation of a man wading through deep water.

'Vince, Vince, VINCE!' Clara bellowed at him and he cowered away from it. Then Sammy's voice rose up to hit him like an uppercut.

'Uncle Vince, can I see Mum!?'

Clara replied when Vince couldn't, the volume too low to puncture the cotton wool effect and he felt the grip round his waist being pulled from right to left. Sammy's voice struck him in the chin again: 'You didn't save her, did you? You said you wouldn't let her die!' Vince was still wading, still down a corridor glowing white. Clara's voice rushed back into his ear.

'Vince, you need to talk to him, you need to talk to the boy and tell him what's going on. He's upset!'

A phrase filled his mind but he couldn't push it out as words: *I told you not to bring him.* He kept moving, someone came out of a door to his right and they collided, Vince barely felt it but the blur of a man spun away like he'd been hit by a wrecking ball. There was a shout too, Vince didn't know if it was at him. 'I'm so sorry . . .' he finally managed and not for the man shouting up from the floor, it was for everyone; his sister and her son, his mother and Clara. And for himself.

He heard Clara's voice again, from further away, calling Sammy back.

'I'm so sorry,' Vince said again.

He carried on through the hospital, his head down, people appearing as shapes that floated towards him like ghosts. Mostly they parted, he heard mumblings of complaint and confusion as he moved through them until finally making it outside. He'd abandoned an unmarked pool car in the police bay by the entrance, the closing of the driver's door made the buzzing louder in his ears.

His phone was still hooked where it had died — in the cradle on the dash — and starting the engine woke the screen. He moved the car out of its space and across the front of the hospital towards the exit. Vince stayed fixed ahead, his head jerking to his phone as it shook with notifications and graphics that littered the screen as blurs. Still his ears whooshed and buzzed like they were blocked, the only noises he could pick out were internal: his own pulse and shallow breathing, the sound of swallowing as he tried to lubricate his dry throat and a cracking sound when he worked a jaw locked with tension.

The road passed under him. On autopilot, he negotiated tight streets, flows of town traffic and motorway, the need to keep moving, to get as far away as he could taking over. Still his periphery was a fog of flared white, still his only focus was at the end of a tunnel. He had no idea how long had passed, how long he had been driving but it was enough for the numbness that had been instant the moment he had dropped his sister's hand to start to give way to realisation. Anger came next, anger that escalated to a rage that was unquenchable, that took control of the car, pushing the accelerator harder, working the brakes later, the steering more erratic as he cut his way through traffic, roaring nonsense at anyone who was in his way, anyone he saw. A sense of direction dripped into his conscious mind, some of his senses were returning, enough that he could feel phlegm spotting on his hands as he roared out at the world, his grip on the steering wheel like he was trying to crush it flat. Those same hands wrapped up into tight fists the moment the car came to a screeching, shuddering halt and lashed out at a door that flew open.

The next thing that registered was a woman's voice, nervous, scared almost, the words cutting through the buzz and the cotton wool:

We're in trouble here.

CHAPTER 32

Angie McIlhenny creeped up the stairs. She'd set Jade at the table with her favourite treat: homemade scones with cream and jam. Her husband had waited out Jade's emotional reaction and was now making small talk to keep her comfortable. He was good at that, he had a knack of carrying on like everything was normal just after an episode and in all her years as an emergency foster carer Angie considered there to be no other skill more important. It was the only way to de-escalate a child. Suggest that they had overreacted or been unreasonable and you could lose them altogether. Angie's skill with getting children past a trauma was not in her ability to understand what that child was going through, but in accepting that that wasn't possible, that no one child or situation was the same and that she was only there to help them find their own way.

But in this case, she also felt a responsibility to assist the police. Jade's mother had been a close friend, a good woman. If they had adhered strictly to their own rules they would not have taken Jade in at all, but how could they not? And she was such a wonderful child, so gentle, curious and creative by nature and she could still have a future, still become who she was supposed to be. Just as soon as the smokescreen of trauma lifted.

If it lifted.

But the person who had caused this trauma, who had taken Maria's life, was still out there somewhere and if Angie could do something to help, she absolutely would.

Angie paused at the top of the stairs to listen. She could hear her husband, he was talking back at the radio, answering questions from a competition and chuckling at himself for being wrong, doing his best to involve Jade. Angie was in the clear. She pushed open the door to Jade's bedroom. The items disturbed from the bedside cabinet were still scattered all over the floor. A stack of teddies had been unsettled too, caught by one of Jade's flailing limbs no doubt, as were her trainers that had been lined up against the far wall. But the item she was really interested in was what Jade had been recoiling from, the thing she had been fixed on, her feet scrabbling to ruck up the carpet like she was backing away from a coiled snake. But it wasn't a snake, it was a picture, one of Jade's. Angie had caught a glimpse of it under the bed while Jade was wrapped up in her hug.

Now she knelt to pull it out into the open, revealing a picture that, at first glance, was just like the others. The bright colours Jade had used this time were mostly yellow with a dash of pink and — as before — they contrasted with the darkness of thick lines. Angie's shiver was involuntary as she recalled the police and their breathy reaction: *floorboards!*

It was almost like Jade had heard Inspector Ives and set out to prove her right. The thick strips had detail confirming them to be slats of wood, they were brown rather than black and with swirls and knots, the brown a lighter shade at the edges. But that wasn't the reason Angie had known she needed to come back. Between the wooden boards, neatly drawn and standing out from a clump of washed-out yellow, two eyes peered down. There was part of a nose too, just the top where the bottom fell behind a floorboard.

She walked the picture back out into the hallway and through to her bedroom where the light was stronger. She took her phone out, laying the paper flat to take a picture.

She would be careful to put the picture back, then talk about it with Jade when the time was right. Or maybe she wouldn't, maybe sending it to PC Arnold would prompt him to return and he would talk to her about it. Jade had really taken to him and if she was going to talk to anyone then surely he would be her choice. But even if she didn't, Angie fixed again on the face, the eyes in particular. She took a second photo, this one held closer to what had her flushing a little with excitement. The drawing overall was far from perfect, the face generic-looking, but that might not matter because the way Jade had drawn one of the eyes was so distinctive that Angie didn't think the rest was going to matter at all.

'So this is him.' Angie couldn't contain her thrill and it came out as a whisper. 'This is our man.'

CHAPTER 33

The front door was the only part of the house in focus and Vince headed straight for it. It was ajar, Maddie had her foot stuck in it and was turned back towards him. Someone else was with her, to Vince, it was just another blurred ghost. The door widened, a face appeared from the dimly lit hall, a face that was part-obscured by sunglasses to peer out, sizing him up no doubt and eyebrows flickered their surprise. The door was then pushed firmly to close, flexing where Maddie still had her foot wedged.

Vince hit it full on. He must have been running, his shoulder took the impact for the door to fly inwards, the figure the other side stumbled away but came straight back at him, his outline wide and strong, his grunt might have been a shout as it was enough to puncture the internal buzz that still filled Vince's ears. Vince reached out instinctively, grabbing the man by his face, his momentum pouring him through the door. The wall was close to his left, Vince spun the man more easily than seemed likely, slamming his head into the wall and he dropped, spilling a shoe rack and all its contents beneath him. The stairs finished close to the door, the man rolled clumsily onto the bottom few steps and rocked like he was shifting to get straight back up. His sunglasses were lost, his face unobstructed, his right eye exposed as an opaque ball of white that rolled in its socket, an angry red scar jutting away from it to cross the bridge of his nose, stopping just short of his good eye. Vince threw his fist, aiming for that scar, his tunnel vision filled with just this head and face. The blow connected and he felt something shatter against his knuckles. The man straightened on the stairs, then slid downwards, folding like a dropped rug to make a pile on the floor.

Vince spun right, striding through an open door and into the lounge. Something firm struck him, the source was outside his tunnel of focus, there were blurs of movement and in different directions — *more ghosts*. The sound of someone pushed into his right ear and he lashed out towards it with the back of his hand. It prompted a grunt in pain where he had connected, then another shout came. He turned towards a man who was stumbling backwards to fall into an armchair, but he heaved himself back out to face up to Vince who lashed out again, meeting the man as he stepped towards him, his momentum increasing the power of the strike. The man slumped back into the sofa and stayed there.

More shouts. Straight ahead this time. A man came at him, stick-thin with flashes of red on his face to give away his youthfulness. His fist moved at him quick, the ceiling light flashed off something held in his hand and Vince lashed out to meet it with his forearm. The blow deflected to open up the man's body and Vince stepped in, bringing his left hand up in a chop motion aimed at his neck and another body crumpled for him to step over, this one twitching and choking. A table tipped towards him, shedding items that bounced off to fall under and around his feet. He could feel something around his waist pulling him backwards, he swung his hand towards it and the pulling stopped. The ghost of an older man appeared, he was shouting, his hand extended by a dark-coloured stick swung at Vince, striking him across his shoulder and chest. It registered as pain through the numbness and Vince instinctively moved his right hand to where it hurt and, in doing so, noticed his forearm was blurred a deep red that dripped. It only fuelled his push forwards.

The old man was knocked over with an elbow. Vince could hear something that didn't have to break through the buzz in his ears, it was internal, his own voice roaring outwards, he reckoned it had been there the whole time. He pointed it downwards, at the old man who had fallen and there was a moment of recognition: George Arthur Moran was cowering at his feet.

Vince lifted his roar to more movement in front of him, *more ghosts*. It was movement away, a pair of blue jeans and a white T-shirt running into the kitchen at the back. Vince followed until it came into focus.

Liam Moran.

Liam was right in front of him, spinning the key in the barrel of the back door. He kicked a full bin back at Vince and it caught him hard in the shin, though he barely felt the blow, stumbling over it as an obstruction. The kitchen had an untidy stack of dirty crockery, Liam grabbed what he could to throw, slowing Vince down as he tried to avoid the blurs that came at him. Liam pulled the back door open, Vince twisted away from the last saucepan that glanced him in the face and bounced off his shoulder.

When he faced back to the door, Liam Moran was gone.

CHAPTER 34

Vince followed out of the back door and broke into a powerful sprint. He'd never felt faster, it was effortless, his body pumped high on rage and adrenaline that powered him after a smudge of white that hit the fence at the end of the garden and then disappeared over it. Vince did the same, his right foot smashing straight through the panel halfway up, while he gripped the top to propel himself over in one movement. He landed in a tight alleyway. The movement away from him was on the left and he broke back into a sprint. The alleyway came out onto the same street where Vince had abandoned his car, only further up and Liam Moran turned away from it. Liam was fast too and still had his head start, so when Vince saw a car's indicator flicker, he knew he was too far back to stop Moran getting in. The car was a silver Vauxhall, parked on the end of a row, giving Liam a free run to pull out, the engine revving, the exhaust throwing out a clump of blue smoke in disdain. Vince turned away, desperate, reacting to a marked car surging down the road with its lights flickering, already starting its pursuit. It needed to brake heavily when an off-duty PC stepped out to fill the road in front of it.

'Vince!? Get in!' The driver leaned out; he was the only occupant.

'I'll drive.' The words were unleashed from a thorny throat, muffled enough to sound like someone else had shouted. The copper got out, he was vaguely familiar, the car ticking over as he jogged round to the passenger side, his uniform a black blur to Vince who fell into the car, scrunching himself up into the driving position of someone smaller. The rubber against the tarmac scrabbled and squeaked as he floored it away. The black uniform was left standing in the road behind, his arms raised.

Liam Moran wasn't just a fast runner; his driving had the same theme. He was no stranger to police pursuits either, this wasn't even his first dance with Vince. Their previous chase had been short-lived — Liam's style was to immediately resort to erratic driving, the sort that put members of the public at risk, knowing that the police would quickly call off their pursuit. Vince had called it himself the last time, a calm update on the radio, how he was cancelling the pursuit due to risk to others, then a thump on the steering wheel in frustration as the bandit car disappeared in the distance. That was then. A rational decision — the right one — when he had been capable of such a thing.

And this was now.

Moran's driving was more erratic than ever, more dangerous and the decision to continue this time would surely be taken out of Vince's hands the moment after his first radio update; his control room would call him off. But there wasn't an update. The radio in the car was turned up and monitoring the local channel, the operator knew a marked car was in a pursuit and was demanding PC Arnold update with his status. But PC Arnold couldn't update. He couldn't talk. His vision was unchanged, the focus at the end of the tunnel now fixed on a silver Vauxhall, his only movements were to swerve past the same members of public as Moran, to make the same last-ditch overtakes, to flash across the same junctions to narrowly miss those he had sworn to protect.

They burst out onto the A299, the Thanet Way, a two-lane carriageway where overtaking and excessive speed were both far easier and they chased down a roundabout as fast as their cars would allow. Moran's braking was late, his lights stark red in the outside lane, their movement suddenly unnatural where the car had begun a slide. Liam Moran had misjudged it. There was a car on the roundabout, Liam's brake lights flashed off and on where he was fighting a skid, but he was losing. Even through the cotton wool, Vince heard the squeal of a sliding car. The Vauxhall evaded the car on the roundabout — somehow — flashing across its front, the back squirming out to the right, throwing out a trail of tyre smoke, the front wheels turned in to try and wrestle back control, but he was beyond that now. The roundabout itself had a raised central island, the kerb sloping upwards as the perfect ramp for the right side of the Vauxhall to hit hard. Moran, somehow, kept the car upright; it squirreled and twitched, the right side thrown back in line, upwards too, so only the front two wheels had rubber on the tarmac. The next noise came from the back landing, the hit so hard the rear bumper was thrown loose.

Vince had reached the roundabout himself now, he was braking heavily too, but in better control, enough that he could look over in the direction Liam's Vauxhall had leaped. The raised central island blocked his view for the next sound — the loudest of them all; the sound of a car crashing.

Vince emerged from behind the roundabout to where the bandit car was at a full stop. A long horn sounded and bits of the Vauxhall's bodywork were still settling on the road. The front end had folded into an Armco barrier, its final resting place at the end of two thick, black marks smeared into the road. Vince pulled his car over roughly. The roof lights made a *snick, snick* sound direct into his ear as he stepped out of the car, their sound filling the void where the long horn died away with a sneer. Vince tried to shake his head clear, his vision was still blurred and pulsing a vivid blue. The only thing with any sort of focus was directly in front: Liam Moran's driver-side door.

Vince wrenched it open as easily as tearing a sheet of paper. The movement shook glass from the frame where the window had popped, the shrill sound of it scattering over the tarmac registered, but was muted. Liam moaned, his head was forward but moving, trying at least, it lolled like he was in a daze that was quickly wearing off and a moan of confusion was quick to turn to pain. Liam's hands reached forward to hover over his legs, clearly identifying them as the source of a pain that was too intense even for him to touch them. Vince could see they were crushed under a dashboard that had come back at him. The steering wheel pushed him in the chest, its airbag spent and limp like the tongue of a defeated monster. His whole body flinched in pain and his moan turned to hissing as he tried to move. The air was acrid, a burning rubber smell that Vince thought was from the airbags. But it was strengthening. The smoke was sudden, it puffed all at once, quickly pushing out either side of windscreen wipers that were broken to lean hopelessly against a bonnet peeled back. The windscreen was cracked, the pattern like a clawed hand, the view past it now hazy where the heat was intensifying.

The flame was inevitable. It was instantly large too; the whole front of the car reacted with a ticking sound to signify metal rapidly heating. The fire would move backwards from the engine bay, the interior was stuffed full of far better materials to feed the hungry flames. Moran flinched again, then roared his pain as he clawed at the doorframe, trying to pull himself away from the growing heat, his eyes wide enough to reflect the fidgeting mass of red and yellow that now threw itself against the windscreen while smoke arched from the footwell to run up his body. Vince still held the door.

'Get me out of here!' Moran squealed, 'My legs! I can't move them!' He reached out for Vince, his fingers opening and closing like a toddler reaching for a parent. He finally got a handful of Vince's top to pull him lower, further into the interior and Vince reacted by taking hold of Moran's hand, the fingers specifically, bending them back until they must surely break. Moran was vocal with his pain again and he changed his grip, grabbing Vince's hand and, for an instant, it mimicked the last grip he had had on his sister: Rebecca Arnold, a good person, a single mother who had spent every day being the best she could for her young son; now dead. And the Liam Morans of this world? They would live on, the privilege of old age would be theirs and it would come despite them ruining lives, taking lives even; a constant trail of mess and misery dragged behind them like a cyclone through a shanty town.

Not this time.

'Burn!' Vince spat the word with such venom at the stricken man that it seemed to stoke the flames. A part of the interior popped, the smoke instantly thicker to smear a black shadow on the windscreen like huge talons reaching out. The smell that had been rancid was now overwhelming. Vince wrenched his hand back and stepped away from the thick column of smoke.

And then he was moving backwards.

It was just like it had been at the hospital, floating away with no control. The blurred silver car in front of him was quickly turning yellow, another solid *pop!* and a black item skittered across the road. There were muffled shouts that came from behind him while his pocket vibrated with a ringing phone to add to the confusion. Two ghosts in police uniform ran past, one turned their face to him, a voice accompanied it but the buzz in his ears was louder than ever and he couldn't make out words. Still, he floated away. The ghosts pushed forward to wrench open the driver's door he had just slammed shut, their outlines merged with, then disappeared among the fidgeting mass of yellow and thick, black swirls of smoke.

Vince had turned away for the big sound. An explosion. The heat pushed him in the back. Ahead of him now was a mass of blinking blue lights, the movement towards him like all the ghosts in the world had arrived at once and with a sense of occasion, all, as they were, dressed in black.

PART THREE

CHAPTER 35

Saturday

'Can I come out!? MUM! ARE YOU THERE?'

Sophie Harding grimaced, her eyes locked on to her husband. They were both at the bottom of the stairs, and the voice was coming from the top, the words muffled but she could still make out every syllable. Sophie was gulping air but she didn't seem to be taking any in, the sound of their daughter in distress removing her ability to breathe properly. Andy Harding still had one arm out to block her from sprinting up those stairs and ripping the wall open to get to their daughter. The other hand he held across his chest, every ounce of his attention was on his watch, like if he looked away it might explode, taking them all with it.

Sophie had listened long enough.

She threw herself forward, catching her husband out enough to push past him. She took the steps two at a time, ignoring the cries from behind her. Their daughter must have heard the commotion, she must have heard the footsteps coming for her as, when she called out again, her words were thick with relief. She was in a space at the top of the stairs that had been an airing cupboard just a week or so ago, but now a pocket door was fitted on rollers and covered in wallpaper to ensure it blended almost perfectly with the rest of the run to conceal the empty void behind, a void easily large enough for a twelve-year-old girl to hide in.

Her husband had insisted the door be installed in such a way as to be pushed inward to open, something that could only be done from the outside — a deliberate failsafe so their daughter couldn't get out, even if she wanted to. And it was clear that she did.

The mechanism was clunky where it was new, the wheel on the top of the door was stiff to find the rails behind, the bottom hung loose to swing in a little. Her daughter's face appeared. She was bright red from shouting and when Sophie swept her up she could feel the strength of her heartbeat.

'Less than ten minutes!' Her husband's voice grumbled from behind.

'She was terrified, Andy, Jesus! Don't you think she's had enough for today?'

'We don't have time, OK, I told you that. This needed to be a full dress rehearsal, that means the whole time. The police take between fifteen to twenty minutes from—'

'We know! For Christ's sake, we know.'

Andrew Harding was stopped in his tracks to huff. The stress was etched clearly on his face too, the panic just below the surface. He had never worn stress well, it was how Sophie had worked out that the business was in trouble in the first place. But his levels were getting worse. She didn't know the last time he had slept at night, not for any more than a snatched hour, the rest of the time he would walk the landing or the living room with the house in darkness, constantly checking the road outside for movement. They were in a town, there was always movement.

'We need her to be quiet,' he said finally, his wide eyes taking in the image of his frightened family. 'The Blackmans knew that too. And Maria, she knew better than any of us and she *did* get her daughter safe. This is what we're trying to do here, that's all we're trying to do.'

'This isn't NORMAL!' Sophie's voice turned to a screech for the last word. It caught her by surprise, scraping the sides of her throat on its way out. 'What the hell are we doing!? *Drills* to keep our daughter safe in case someone comes knocking at the door and still with no idea *who*!'

Her husband took a moment, a sigh left him hanging on his frame like he had just finished with a heavy set of weights. 'We talked about this. We know what we have to do.' He looked away from her, fixing on their daughter who was still pressed against her mother's hip. 'We talked about this, Taliah, about how you have to stay quiet in there until someone opens the door. Us . . . the police, someone that means you are safe.'

'It's small and it's scary. I want to be with you, why can't I be with you?' Fear and upset gave the girl's voice a whine.

'You'll have to go in there with her.' Andrew was shaking his head as he spoke, but by his tone, he meant it.

'But what about you?' Sophie snapped.

'What about me? I don't matter, you two matter, that's all and I need to know that you're going to be safe and that means being quiet. If you're with her you can keep her calm, which means quiet.'

'Even if we are quiet . . . there are joins . . .' Her finger pushed along the raised edge where the wallpaper had an edge. 'If you know what you're doing, if you're really looking—'

'I won't let that happen,' Andrew snapped. 'As far as anyone who comes to the door is concerned, I'm here alone. We'll . . . we'll keep Taliah's room tidy so it looks like she's not even in it, your stuff too, Soph, your make-up and things, anything you use daily, put them out of sight. I'll tell them I'm staying on my own because of what happened with Maria, give them a quick tour if they ask so they can see for themselves and then I'll talk to them, find out what they want.'

'This is ridiculous.' Sophie was quiet this time, resigned, her throat still sore from her previous outburst. There were no other options, she knew that. They'd talked it all out before, about moving away, about her actually moving out for real or just Taliah going to stay with her nan. But Andrew wanted to keep the family together until they understood the threat better and he kept saying that he would soon. That was *all* he kept saying.

Sophie had to walk away. She took Taliah with her, coaxing her back into her room where her iPad was. That always calmed her down. Andrew stomped down the stairs, the movement a precursor to an argument where he would once again complain about being cast as the *bad guy*. Bad guy or not, this was his fault. He had put his greed before his family and now it was coming back to bite him. *Of course* it was. Had he asked her about it she would have told him exactly what was going to happen. But he hadn't. Her opinion had never mattered, even when it would have been something as important as putting his family first.

Sophie waited on the landing until she was sure Taliah was settled in her room, then, as quietly as she could manage, she moved down the stairs to the ground floor. Andy was boiling the kettle in the kitchen and she was able to slip out of the front door without being seen or detected. There was a single, tall tree on the edge of their front garden and she was sure to be hidden behind it before taking out her phone. This was a call she'd tried a number of times now. The phone always rang, no problem; it was getting an answer that was proving to be impossible. She deserved one too. This was a direct line to the person who had convinced them all to ensure they had a *drill* in the first place, a plan in case their house was attacked, in case *they* were attacked. Sophie remembered the first time they had all talked about it as a group. The shocked silence, the awkward laughter where no one knew what to say and where no one really took it seriously. Not at first. The conversations that had followed had been bizarre, *normal* families talking like they were planning the logistics of a garden party when they were actually talking hiding places in their individual homes. Ron Blackman had talked about the cupboard under the stairs and how there was no phone reception but it shouldn't matter. His wife wasn't at the meeting, he'd done his best to keep her in the dark about everything, but he had been sure he could convince her if the time ever came. He must have been wrong about that.

The tone of the meeting had changed quickly as the seriousness was stepped up. Maria Mercer had lost control of her breathing for a full-on panic attack and everything had stopped while she had been talked down. She was the only one who lived alone, or at least, just her and Jade. Eventually Maria had been calm enough to think, to talk about some damp work she'd had done recently and how there was just about space enough under the floorboards for a person, for Jade. She could leave it loose, she had said, a hammer and nails to hand, the holes were already drilled so it would just take one hit. Maria had even managed a tight smile as she had told them how the tradesmen who came to fix the damp had joked about it being the perfect place to hide a body. The irony hadn't been lost on Sophie when she had heard what had happened.

They had managed to talk it all out, plans had been set in place and the feeling of *never going to happen* and *just in case* had even returned by the end of the night. But that was before Sandy and Ron: stabbed to death in their own hallway, that was before Maria too . . .

Poor Maria!

She was just like her. Similar age, one child, a daughter who was also a similar age to Taliah. Their daughters were friends, trips to the park were irregular but talking face to face on their tablets was just about nightly.

Jade.

Sophie hadn't been able to say that name without bursting into tears. It was so sad, so desperate. She'd made contact with her godparents to offer up a park trip, Jade and Taliah, they hadn't spoken since what happened . . . not even through their devices. On their last park trip, just a week before Maria was killed, Maria had told her where Jade would go if . . . if the worst happened. It had been another conversation that had seemed ridiculous, like it was never *actually* going to happen.

But then it had.

And now she and Andrew were two of the three people who had been in *that* room, having *that* conversation, who were *not* dead — as far as she knew, at least. And still Sophie didn't really know what this threat was, the full extent of what her husband was into, and there was no way he was telling her. *For your own good*, he would say. Well, that wasn't good enough. But that third person, the only other one left alive, knew it all, Sophie was sure of that. And she wasn't going to stop calling until she knew it too.

The phone rang out to divert to voicemail. Sophie had been told never to leave a message but she was getting desperate. The beep caught her out, forcing her to blurt her words.

'For Christ's sake, Amelia! Please answer me! This is serious now, this has gotten out of hand. We need to talk!' Sophie ended the call and sucked in a lungful of air. She wiped away the tear that sat stubbornly in the middle of her cheek and pushed the phone roughly back into her pocket.

CHAPTER 36

The roar of a motorway seemed strangely out of place when hidden by a tall treeline, like a snoring monster in a movie scene that, once woken, would rise up for its big green eyes and gore-smeared jaw to appear above the trees to roar in full surround sound. But there was no rising up, no CGI monster and no change to the soporific lull of the white noise. Amelia Chagrin barely noticed the din. Her interest in this place was nothing to do with the busy road that passed it.

The expansive concrete flooring was brand new and beautifully smooth, the effect was such that she could almost convince herself that she was walking on something with some give, spongy even. Above, the central spine of the part-built warehouse was on show with no cladding or fitted internal materials yet to conceal it. A different noise lifted her head from where she was studying the floor: a small dumper truck moved across her distant view, bouncing like something empty, but with tyres inflated for heavy loads. The hard hat inside bounced too, its hi-visibility colouring meant it was the only part of the driver she could make out. Her anxiety heightened: she couldn't be found here. Usually, she came at night but the pull was getting stronger, she was getting more reckless. She knew that could cost her. She should go home.

Her phone made her jump, the vibration sudden in her back pocket and she snatched for it, knowing the second vibration was when the ringtone kicked in. She read the screen: *Sophie Harding*, then pressed a button to silence the call, rather than reject it, before pushing it into her pocket.

She took a deep breath. The air she inhaled had an arid quality unique to brand-new poured concrete. The layer of dust laid on its surface was powder-like, so fine it almost felt moist as she squatted to trace it with her fingertips. Her phone rang again. This time when she checked the screen it was her boyfriend calling. He would be wondering where she was and, if she explained, he would be asking what the hell she was doing being so blatant.

She ignored this call too. It wasn't something she could explain to him and goodness knew she'd tried.

I just want to be close to her, to our Kayla.

She took one last look around, her eyes falling to the smooth concrete at her feet.

'You could be right here, I could be stood right over you, my love . . . I thought I might feel you, I thought I might feel something . . .' She drifted out, lifting her eyes to the vast interior. Come Monday, this place would be swamped with workmen and they would be adding another layer of concealment.

'I'm going to find you,' she said. 'I promise.'

CHAPTER 37

The sudden change in the light on his patio door was what dragged Vince Arnold's attention. Maddie appeared first to step into a freezing mist that was thicker at ground level. She was shepherding someone out, a someone who remained concealed by a combination of Maddie's position, the poor visibility and the fact that whoever it was hadn't quite committed to stepping out yet. Perhaps they might change their mind. Vince hoped so. Trying to read Maddie's body language was hopeless at this distance. He could hear a hubbub of voices, both sounded deep, like two people purposely speaking low. Maddie finally stepped aside to go back into the house, leaving the visitor free to start walking towards him.

Harry Blaker.

Vince was on a wooden bench that faced directly back towards his house. He'd spent a lot of time sat right there over the two and a bit days since everything had changed. Time didn't seem to matter, where he was sat certainly didn't, he might as well be out there, on that bench, than in bed waiting for sleep to come. It was a rickety old thing that he had insisted they bring when moving from his Deal home. The wooden slats that made up the seat had movement in them, enough that it had quickly earned a reputation for pinching your arse if you were not careful how you got out of it. Vince had kept it for that reason, telling Maddie that he liked its attitude.

He felt the slats shift as Harry took his place beside him for it to become two people sitting, staring straight back up the garden. Vince could recall any number of conversations following tough jobs, the jobs that left their mark somehow and this was how he always found himself sitting to talk them out: side by side, looking straight out. It's easier to say difficult words if you can't see the person you're saying them to.

'First, you should know that you're good at your job, a good copper. Brave, bold and stupid, led by your heart — blindly. I thought it might get you killed but, as often happens, it's those around you that take the brunt.' Vince had no reply other than a tightened jaw. What Harry was saying, what he meant, none of it was as impactive as *how* he was saying it. His tone was warm, kind almost, the voice Vince used when responding to a call where a dog had bitten a person. A good-dog, bad-owner situation, where Vince had no choice. Vince's explanation while scruffing its head, the lethal injection waiting in the vet's hand, had felt just like this.

'Which bit was the compliment?' Vince said eventually. 'Because a good shit sandwich should have at least two.' His chuckle came out as a ball of breath that rushed to join the layers of mist. The temperature had dropped in the last twenty-four hours, the sun rendered useless by the mist to hang over them like a silver globe, never threatening to break through. Harry might have been feeling it too, he pulled his waxed jacket tighter. He might just have been looking for something to do with his hands.

'There's a couple in there somewhere.'

'OK then. So now it's time for the big finish, hit me with it. I'm guessing this is big, seeing as they got you in on a Saturday.'

'They're going to be fine, PC Steven Gilbert and PC Karen Allen. They were stupid, they shouldn't have run to the car, not when it was already on fire and when they saw that you had already come away. They should have seen that it was too dangerous and kept their distance.'

Harry stopped talking long enough for Vince to be back watching the mist. He was supposed to give a reaction, no doubt, but Vince didn't feel like he had one, he didn't feel like he had anything inside him at all. These last few months had been slowly hollowing him out to the point where he was starting to consider he might be numb forever.

'But they saved Liam Moran's life. They will be commended for that and they will deserve it.' Another silence, the mist seemed to swirl in the silent moments, stopping still the moment Harry started up again. 'Karen said she ran for the door because she saw you shut it. She said you didn't run away, you weren't beaten back by flames, at least you didn't react like you were. She said it was like you slammed the door shut, then backed away to watch.'

'She said that?' Vince's throat still tasted of acrid smoke despite the time passed, sometimes worse than others. Here, it was back at its strongest, the taste flooding back with the memory.

'And Liam Moran is telling anyone who will listen that you told him to *burn*.'

'Is he?' Vince said.

'Maddie's angry,' Harry said and not with the question Vince had been expecting. 'As angry as I've seen her and I once saw her kill a man.' Harry sparked, blink and you'd miss it, but a spark all the same. It was a punchline he could never use if Maddie was around, shouldn't, even though she wasn't, and one that felt like his way of demonstrating that they were now talking as candidly as they ever had.

'Stick around, you might see her do it again,' Vince said. 'I fucked up.' Just a few days earlier and Vince would have squirmed at the lapse, at cussing in front of Harry, but it didn't matter anymore, nothing mattered.

'So she said.'

'She had something going with the older Moran, Maddie did, she went back after we'd all been out to see him, used her charm, wore the old bastard down. She reckons there's more going on and he was about to reveal all, only she had a side to the bargain that had to be delivered first.'

'And you trampled all over it,' Harry said. 'So she said.'

'I trampled all over her,' Vince said. 'I dragged her through that house, even hit her to get her off me. I didn't even know she was there . . . I didn't know anything.'

'It's a mess,' Harry said. 'If Liam Moran had died . . . They'll still treat this like a death in custody investigation and every one of them I ever saw was a mess at first, but they can get sorted.'

'And what does *sorted* mean, exactly?'

'It means an investigation, a lot of used-to-be-cops all excited that they get to be cops again, who won't give a damn that we're supposed to be on the same side. A lot of the same questions asked over and over and your answers held up side by side to look for something they can work on. Maybe a courtroom — even if there's no prosecution, the Moran family will go for you, you should be prepared for that.'

'I don't care. Not about any of that.'

'That's what I thought.' Harry leaned forward, the wooden slats shifting as he did. He made a tight ball out of his two hands like he was still noticing the cold. 'But one day you will, and I mean you *really* will. Once . . .' Harry's deep breath in and out was audible. 'My wife died, killed by a piece of scum driving out of his mind, a nothing man and a nothing moment. I found that man . . .' Harry shuffled in his seat again, the slats shifting but not changing his position. He was inspecting his hands closely. 'And I went there. I told myself I was going there to confront him, to tell him what he did, to me, to my daughters . . . to my life.' The bench flexed again, Harry did shift this time, sitting back and out of Vince's periphery. 'I was going to kill him. I know that now just like I knew it at the time. You can't make someone

225

like that understand what they did or who they are. It was a flat in a building full of people, broad daylight, middle of the day. I kicked his door in and I was utterly lost, lost to myself. He was dead already, laid out on the floor with a needle in his vein and I remember . . . I remember being just. . . disappointed.' More flexing from the slats, Harry Blaker fidgeting but not moving. 'I wanted to kill him. Seeing him dead woke me up a little, brought me out of that place, even had me wiping down some surfaces on my way out and, if I'm honest, I did get some satisfaction. I didn't kill him, but I got to see him dead, I got to see how it happened, how it ended and I was glad he was living like vermin. I took that satisfaction away with me and I never told anyone that I was even there.'

'So why tell me now?' Vince said, his throat still sore, his taste buds still convinced he was leaned over a fire.

More fidgeting, more shifting slats without changing position. 'If you tried to kill that man, Vince, if you were lost in yourself when you did it, you can't ever say it, not out loud, not to anyone. Not to me and definitely not to Maddie.'

'But . . .' Vince was suddenly feeling again, he didn't know what, everything at once to totally overwhelm him. 'I'm the police,' he managed. It was all he could manage, but it was enough. It was the one phrase he couldn't shake, three words that had been rolling around his mind on constant repeat since the moment that explosion had pushed him in the back. *What have I done? I'm the police . . .*

'We're people, too. I'll tell you again, you can't ever say it, not out loud, not to anyone. And as for what you do next, the answer is nothing. Keep your head down, there are going to be plenty of people trying to take it off.' The slats shifted, with force this time, the pinching sensation in Vince's buttocks cut through his numbness and his mind whirled for something to say. Nothing came in time and he watched Harry walk away, noting how the old man never looked back.

CHAPTER 38

It was a frontage that made sense to Vince the moment he saw the door number and realised it to be the home address of Eileen Holmans. He'd never been here, didn't really know the area and knew nothing of Eileen's home life, but this place just seemed . . . *right* for the daft old bird. The sun had taken all day to burn away the mist and its last hurrah was spotting on its clean, white facade in blobs of dull yellow, a reflection from the upstairs window of the house opposite. Eileen's home might have been among two rows of identically constructed houses either side of a street, but it still managed to stand out as the most interesting. She had window boxes under the large window of the ground floor and first floor, both bursting yellow and purple and dripping water like they had been recently tended. The front door was a matte green with a vine that climbed a trellis beside it and the bristled door mat at its foot was in the shape of a hedgehog and declared him to be *Welcome*.

Vince wasn't so sure about that. He turned away. He'd had a feeling of uncertainty during the whole trip over here, telling himself that he would trust his gut when faced with the front door as to whether this was a good idea or not. He'd been there just a few seconds and his answer was as clear as the mottled sun. It was not. He felt a rush of relief that he hadn't knocked.

'PC Arnold!' Eileen's voice, shrill with surprise, before he made it back to the pavement. She was staring out at him over those reading glasses he had never seen her without. 'Just passing, were you?'

'Just leaving, Eileen. Seem to have this habit of bad ideas that I'm trying to shake. Starting now. Sorry to bother you.'

'No need to apologise. I actually have something heavy that needs lifting.'

'Oh?' Vince said.

'Just in here.' And she was gone, the door left to swing, its movement meant that its spotless surface toyed with the light. Vince took the invitation.

'Were you stood at your door, watching who was passing?'

'You can never be too careful, PC Arnold. I live alone. You have to confront things straight away, you see, put them on the back foot.'

'Not sure you should be confronting anything, Eileen, how about you call the Old Bill instead, eh?'

'A lot of good that would do me, based on what I've seen recently,' she said, quick as a flash and Vince was powerless to stop a grin spreading across his face.

'How is it you have this ability to instantly make me feel like some naughty boy asking for his ball back?'

'I think you should ask yourself that question. It might be rather telling.' She was moving away, Vince stepped in to follow her, and she rounded on him with such sudden-ness that they almost collided. 'You *are* an incompetent, dangerous, ham-fisted idiot, PC Arnold, but you've always respected me and your reputation is of one of the good guys. That gets you through the door, for now.' Her turn back to continue her walk was just as sudden. 'That reputation has to have come from somewhere, after all.'

Vince stared after her, a little caught out, frozen to the spot even and struggling to find words.

'What?' she snapped when she noticed, turning back to huff.

'Is that what they're saying about me?' he said.

'Well, yes. I might have added *ham-fisted* and possibly *idiot*.' She shrugged, before continuing to the kitchen. 'I assume you'll be wanting tea, or a *wet* as you call it, I don't recall you ever turning one down.' Vince was left, still struggling for words, to become aware that he was being held in the glassy stare of any number of silent animal ornaments. And they had him surrounded.

The animal theme continued in the kitchen. Even the tea-pot needed to be uncovered from a tea cosy in the shape of a cockerel, complete with a separate crop of shocking red under its chin made of thin rubber to mimic the movement of the real thing. It was almost enough to put Vince off his drink, but he accepted it silently, taking a lean against a work surface that had two neat stacks of puzzle books and an open TV Magazine with a cosy detective series and two different soaps ringed in biro.

'How are you, though? Overall, I mean?' Vince said.

'You mean in my sad, lonely little existence with just my TV shows and tea cosy to keep me company?' This time, as she peered over the top of her glasses, she also raised one eyebrow. If her scolding-teacher look had a scale, this was her nearing a ten.

'That isn't what I meant at all!' Vince tried to sound indignant, now concerned to look away at anything else. 'And was the kettle the *heavy thing* you needed help with?'

'I changed my mind, what with you being ham-fisted and all. No, you came here for something and it wasn't just to compliment me on my tea cosy now, was it?'

'It was not.'

'But while you're here, what's your opinion?' She stepped back, using one finger to repeatedly disturb the shocking red rubber under its chin and to make Vince feel a little queasy all over again.

'It's a beaut, Eileen, no doubt about it. Can't say I've ever seen anything like it.'

'ADI Ives is right about you.' Eileen huffed again, turning back away to get on with the tea.

'Right about me when?'

'When she told me you will say anything to get what you want. I hate the damned thing and no sane person would think otherwise, I mean what the hell is with the chin? It was a present from my sister and I never know when she's going to turn up, I got fed up of trying to find the blasted thing every time the door knocked. So, what *do* you want?'

Vince sighed. 'I want to say sorry. I know what I did and I'll get what's coming for that, but the rest of you . . . you didn't do nothing. I messed up and you lot got moved off the case too with knuckles rapped. So that's it . . . I came to say sorry.' Vince bowed his head, secretly impressed with how that had sounded. He was aware of a pair of slippers scuffed across linoleum where Eileen moved a couple of paces closer. Such was his performance, he considered, he might even get a hug here.

He left it another couple of seconds before he raised his sorry face, his eyes meeting with a stoic Eileen Holmans.

'Bullshit, Vince Arnold!' she said, immediately. 'You do realise I've spent a career listening to lies just as much as you have?'

'What do you mean?' Vince gasped.

'You came here to apologise as much as I intend to take up beach volleyball. What do you want?'

Vince took a moment. Plan A was out of the water and he hadn't considered he might need a Plan B, which meant all that was left was telling the truth.

'I've been cut off, suspended and now Mads is in trouble for running some operation off the books and Harry for being her boss . . . and none of this would have happened if I hadn't gone in there all guns blazing.'

'Ham-fisted,' Eileen corrected him.

'OK, so yeah, ham fists or whatever. But I can make it right. I got a lot of mates in the force, some buddies who work close to the source handlers and they were telling me they got

230

a result. Some of the grasses were starting to talk about the Morans. They didn't know the detail, just said that it would all be sent on to the Major Crime Intelligence Analyst by the end of the day. Only, that was the day . . . that was not a good day.'

'So you came here to ask me what intelligence was passed over from our source handler colleagues?'

'Yes.'

'I see. Then I am very sorry — you have wasted your time after all. I didn't receive any correspondence of that type and, of course, I did not last the day either. Acting Inspector Ives' operation that you mentioned was something I was involved in too, which has proven to be my downfall.'

'You're frozen out too?'

'Very much. We all are. I think the reaction to me in particular was rather unnecessary to be honest, it seems to stem more from Superintendent Hall not respecting his members of staff who happen to like being comfortable in the workplace . . .' Eileen visibly bristled and Vince had to crush his lips together to make sure his silly grin didn't come back.

'He didn't like the slippers, did he?'

'He did not. And you can take that smirk off your face. I cannot be any help to you, I'm afraid. I completed a full handover, as instructed, then it was made clear that any future developments in that case are none of my business.'

Vince's grin dropped away all on its own. He pushed off the kitchen side to pace. 'I really fucked up,' he said, then panicked. 'Sorry! This mate I talked about, this information that source had, it was going to give something of a bigger picture, the impression I got . . .' Vince faded out. He had never been good at the detective stuff. Maddie talked about it like it was easy, as simple as getting loads of people talking about the same thing and then knitting it all together to see which bits were true. Maddie could do it all in her head, but it was beyond Vince. Response was the job for him: turn up and deal with what you see.

'What?' Eileen prompted him, 'What impression did you get?'

'Liam Moran isn't our man. He's part of all this, no doubt, but it wasn't him who went into those houses, he might not even have known about it.'

'ADI Ives had the same suspicion, or at least Moran Senior was trying to tell her the same thing.'

'And he might have if I hadn't . . .'

'He might,' Eileen said.

'I was gone, Eileen.' Vince stopped his pacing to lock eyes with the old woman in slippers, whose face had softened to the point of almost warmth. 'It was like an out-of-body experience.'

'I'm sorry . . . about your sister, about Rebecca. Ma'am Ives spoke very highly of her, she said you were very alike, which I imagine to mean that she was a lovely person, one that the world is a little worse off for having lost. I'm sure the powers-that-be will see your actions as part of the bigger picture. I know Ma'am Ives will.'

Vince welled up, he felt like his whole face puffed up from pressure behind it. He turned away, his palms taking his weight, and his right hand made a fist to screw up Eileen's TV magazine a little.

'This isn't about Rebecca, or Maddie, or any of you really. I promised Jade.' Vince was fighting his own emotion. 'That little girl, I promised her I would be a part of finding out what happened, who did that to her.'

'Perhaps you shouldn't be making such promises,' Eileen scolded him. 'Giving out teddy bears for comfort, getting yourself emotionally tied up with the fate of a child who may never recover from what she saw. And that won't be your fault, that will be the fault of whoever—'

'Which is why we need to find them!' he snapped and Eileen fell silent. Vince took a moment to calm himself down, to turn back into the room. 'It was Sammy's idea. I got off a little earlier than Mads that day. We'd arranged to have the kid looked after for a few hours more but I went and picked him up. He's a good listener!' Vince had to stop, he felt his jaw shudder and he bit down, locking it shut, locking the tears away at the same time. 'Sammy knew I'd had a bad day and he asked me about it. I said I'd met a kid who'd had the worst day of all, who had seen something so scary that she might never stop being scared and I was worried that she would never get over it, never leave the house again even. He got up and went to his room, came back with his favourite cuddly toy. Herb.' Another shudder, another clamping down on his jaw that scrubbed out his smile. 'Herb the Tortoise. Sammy broke his arm when he was a lot younger, first time he ever got badly hurt and it scared him. He reacted the same, wouldn't leave the house. I had forgotten all about it. He was about to lose a whole summer in his room, then Becks bought Herb and said how a tortoise lives the longest of any animal, they have all sorts of adventures in their lifetime and how they carry their house on their back, just so they got somewhere to go when they're scared. It was her way of saying it's OK and that the whole world would still be waiting for him when he was ready . . .'

'What a lovely thing.'

'It worked for him. I told Jade that same story, told her how Sammy was insistent that she have it, that he wasn't scared anymore so he didn't need it. I felt a bit silly going back to that house with a cuddly toy, seeing Jade and handing it over with its neck all crinkled up from being held for five years solid. It smelled like the back of a cupboard too, I thought she would just roll her eyes and maybe leave it somewhere first chance she had, but she took hold of Herb's neck just as tight as I reckon Sammy did all them years ago — like she might never let it go.'

'I think I understand why you might have made promises to that little girl.'

'And why I have to keep them.' Vince still didn't dare make eye contact with Eileen. 'I'm sorry Eileen, again, bad idea to come here.' He strode to the door of the living room.

'She adores you, you know; Ma'am Ives I mean, more than she will ever admit.' Vince turned to where Eileen was thoughtfully tickling the rubber under a tea cosy's chin. 'So you'd better sort this mess out so we can all get back to work, or I'm going to find out where my sister got this monstrosity from and I'm going to arrange a delivery to your home on the first Monday of every month until the day I die.' One eyebrow was lifted above the glasses, as high as he had seen. Her serious expression on the verge of breaking.

'I'll fix it,' Vince said, but the words hung heavy, lacking any conviction. He turned away to be stopped again.

'I hear that nice sergeant, Alan Miles, is at the pub tonight, the one over near Nackington. One of his team's retiring so they're having a few beers to celebrate, like you lot need any excuse.'

'Alan Miles, the man who runs the Source Unit?' Vince said and Eileen wouldn't have seen his smirk as he was still facing away.

'Oh, does he?' Eileen said. 'I get mixed up with who works where. Now do piss off, would you? I ringed those television programmes for a reason.'

Vince's silly grin spread and he was back to the naughty schoolboy walking away from the headmistress's office, his progress through the living room watched by a hundred pairs of glass eyes.

CHAPTER 39

The sound of the knocking door tore through the room like a gunshot. Sophie Harding reacted by staring across at her husband, who was frozen in the action of unbuttoning his shirt.

'Deliveries?' Andrew hissed.

'It's ten o'clock at night and we don't order anything anymore, remember?' It was one of his rules, one of a million ways their lives had changed over the last few months.

'Get the girl, get her up!' he said.

'Just don't answer!' she breathed. His eyes were wide, his chest had a visible rise and fall and he oozed fear. 'Or call the police?'

'We can't, this is what we talked about, this is it!' His wide eyes flicked side to side. The door thumped again; louder, more urgent. Andrew was standing right under the main light in their bedroom. They had been just about to turn in, another night struggling to get any sleep despite their exhaustion. Now she had never felt more awake. 'Just get hidden, get Taliah and get in the wall and make sure she knows that this is the real thing, she *has* to be quiet. I'll go and . . . I'll go to the door and I'll tell them I'm the only person here, just like we planned,' Andrew breathed.

'Don't answer it! The others answered, they must have, look what happened!' Sophie said.

'We don't know that. And I have to, I have to face this. We can't keep living like this. Go get Taliah . . .' He faded out. 'I got us into this, I have to face up to it. I'll just go and talk . . .' He moved out of the room, a visible tremble in his hands had him struggling to do his shirt buttons back up. She followed him out, turning left to Taliah's room; the door was ajar, her sleeping face visible in the soft glow of a night light.

'Taliah . . .' Sophie was gentle, sitting on the bed caused it to dip and Taliah rolled a little towards her. She stirred, her eyes opening to meet with Sophie but with no focus or recognition where she wasn't fully awake. 'Hey honey, we need to get up, OK, we need to get up now.' Still gentle, Sophie ran her fingers through her daughter's hair, resisting the urge to shake her, to make her aware that they had to move *now*. She needed to be calm, to appear so at least.

'What's the matter?' Taliah's words were still thick with sleep. She sat up, looking around like she wasn't sure where she was.

'Taliah, what we practised, what we've been doing, this is it now, this is it for real. Me and you are going to get behind the wall and stay quiet!' Taliah shrank back in alarm, she'd inherited a lot of her father's traits but this was the first time Sophie had realised that she got scared the same. It broke her heart to see it.

'I need to go to the toilet.' Taliah's voice had a tired whine, pathetic almost and Sophie's heart broke a little more. This wasn't their daughter's fault, none of it.

'OK honey, but we just need to get in the wall first, we can use the toilet soon, I promise, but we need to hide first.'

'I need to pee!' The whine was more pleading now and she moved her hands to her crutch to emphasise the need. Sophie grabbed her arm, tight enough to make her yelp.

'OK, but we have to be *so* quick.'

The bathroom was the end of the hall, back past the door to the master bedroom, the gap for the stairs and the sliding pocket door with a join that she could barely see when they had first installed it but now looked huge to Sophie. Obvious, even. Again, she found herself fighting off panic. It was too late now, there was no Plan B. She pushed Taliah into the bathroom, pulling the door to, telling her not to close it completely. Sophie turned to the pocket door, leaning on it to push it in, waiting for the subtle click that told her the wheels on the back of the door had found the runner. It happened immediately. She had been practising, no longer applying too much pressure so the bottom of the door swung out and thumped against the back wall. The void appeared, dark and ominous even to her. Her eyes fell to the box pushed against the right side that had a few things they might need: a phone, Taliah's favourite chocolate bar — unwrapped and rewrapped in clingfilm that was quieter — and a torch with material taped over its front so it gave just enough light to navigate around the space. And away from the box, taped above the door, was a kitchen knife. The largest and sharpest they could find. A recent addition after deciding that Sophie would be hiding in there too. She hadn't wanted it, but Andrew had insisted: *Just in case. You won't need it if you're still and if you're quiet, no noise at all, no matter what you hear.*

There was a noise now.

The chain flushing!

Sophie spun to it, but she was too late. Her daughter appeared in the bathroom doorway, backlit by the strong light that she clunked off, the hanging switch bucked and swung on its string to bump off the wooden surround. The next noises were from downstairs. Voices suddenly louder. The loudest was her husband. She couldn't pick out the words but the tone was pleading, there was another voice, they were both coming closer. *Too much noise!*

'Get in!' She hissed and Taliah did as she was told. 'The phone, use it only when you haven't heard anything for ten whole minutes, just like we talked about, and *not before!*'

'You're not coming in?' Taliah's eyes contained more fear than ever and it was all Sophie could do to slide the pocket door across them, closing the door, trapping their daughter in the void behind. Her mind flashed with the idea that she had left the knife taped to the other side, that she should slide it back and retrieve it. But there was no time. The bottom three steps always creaked under someone's weight.

They creaked now.

CHAPTER 40

The saloon-style door of the pub clattered open, the sound loud enough over the erratic *tink-tink* of the rain on top of Vince's car to travel across the car park and penetrate its darkest point. Surveillance wasn't Vince's area of expertise, but even he knew to choose the shadows. He was probably too close but those emerging from a pub approaching last orders on a Saturday night didn't seem to be able to see straight, let alone evaluate distance.

The car park of the Crown on Nackington Road, Canterbury, was an expansive mass of chewed-up grit and stone. Vince had been based nearby early in his career and for long enough to remember this car park being freshly laid as part of the refit before last. He couldn't remember how many times it had changed hands in total, or complete identities even, from a gastro pub to a family place, then an attempt at a fine dining experience and all the way back around to a place for police officers to get quietly sozzled after a late shift. Every police station had a preferred boozer. When life was simpler, it was whatever place was closest; back then, nothing got a cheer like a prisoner released and desperate for a pint, stumbling into the nearest pub to find it full of the bastards who had forced them into the custody experience in the first place. That was rare these days. Now the choice for an off-duty pint was specifically chosen as somewhere tucked away, running into a freshly released punter these days far more trouble than it was worth.

The Source Handling Team, like every other team, were having a busy time. Murder investigations had a way of doing that. Source worked a four-day shift rotation, today being the last and, if Eileen was right — and Vince reckoned she always was — the retirement of one of their number could also be added into the mix to make this a big Saturday night.

The clamour of the door was replaced by the sound of hissing and giggling. One noise from each of the two men. Vince recognised them both without knowing their names. He had his window all the way down as a half-open window stands out more (perhaps he wasn't so bad at this surveillance thing after all) and he watched as one of them burst into a cheerful song that he only knew half the lyrics for. The song stopped abruptly as the same man then offered an emphatic hands-raised cheer that was lit up in white headlights as their taxi arrived to take them one step closer to their hangover. Vince left it a couple more minutes before moving. This was what he had been waiting for.

Alan Miles, Source Handling Team sergeant, was left as the last man standing; or sitting at least, up against the bar. The only other punters were a couple at a separate table. Alan was taking no notice of them, or anyone else for that matter, his focus solely on downing the last two fingers of his pint, using the glass on the way back down to gesture for another.

'Make that two. On me,' Vince said, the stool rucking up the carpet to catch as he took his place next to Alan. The man behind the bar looked the same sixty years old he had a decade ago when Vince had last walked in here. His nod might have been one of recognition through glassy eyes over a bright red nose, before he moved away to complete the order. 'And two chasers, surprise me,' Vince called out. No matter how this went, he needed a drink.

'Vince Arnold.' Alan spoke the words then scowled like they didn't sound right. 'You're famous!'

'Infamous, you mean.'

'Yep, you're right, I did,' Alan said. The rest of his reaction was all through the nose. Laughter perhaps, a scoff more like, whatever it was it wasn't enough to puncture the layer of sadness that seemed to have him pinned to that stool.

'You OK?' Vince chanced.

'You divorced yet?' Alan's head turned faster than his eyes could manage and it took him a moment to focus.

'No,' Vince said after a moment, the question like a jab to the side. 'I would have to get married first.' The drinks he had ordered were plonked on sopping beer mats to disturb the smell: a combination of wet dog and stale beer. Vince took a long drag on his pint.

'Don't do it!' Alan announced and seemed to find that funny. Vince waited for his reaction to die away.

'Shit week?' he said.

'Shit week. Shit month. Shit life.' Alan lifted his beer in a gesture like he would *drink to that* before it found his mouth. He smacked his lips, the glass made a clumsy thud when he put it back down. 'But of course a shit week at work and I guess I have you to thank for that. Someone always ends up shouting at the source team when one of our own gets hurt. *Someone must be talking!* they say. How many times have I heard that?'

'And are they?' Vince said.

'The boss, Supernintendo Mark Hall, he uses the gym at Nackington sometimes so I know who he is. He came into our office and do you know what he said?'

'I couldn't even guess.'

'He said that he knew we'd had a shit week, used those exact same words, funnily enough. Then he said that it could still get a lot shittier if any of us talked to Detective Inspector Harry Blaker or Detective Inspector Maddie Ives, or especially Police Constable Vince Arnold!' Alan put emphasis on each word that made up the full titles. He fixed on Vince, the alcohol heavy in his eyes.

'Actually, I probably could have guessed that,' Vince said. The pint was going down well and he drained another chunk, already eyeing the brown liquid of the "surprise shot" that looked and moved like pure syrup.

'You gonna want another?' The barman was back, his nose might have been redder still. 'Only I should be shutting up soon, the police around here get shitty otherwise.' He smiled widely, seemingly pleased with his own attempt at humour.

'Same again then,' Vince said. 'And if the police ask, I'll tell them I forced you.' The barman winked clumsily and turned away. Vince watched him move out of earshot before speaking again. 'I hear Hall's keen on Liam Moran for those murders.' Nothing. Alan just lifted his pint glass for another deep slug. 'I also hear someone on your team thinks he might be wrong. There isn't time to be going after the wrong people,' Vince chanced, 'and we have to believe this will happen again.'

'I hear Mark Hall really fucking hates you. I don't reckon you're his type of copper!' Alan pushed his empty pint glass away with an air of contempt that lasted while he also dealt with the syrupy-looking shot, his grip visibly tightening as he rode out a grimace before thudding it onto the bar firmly enough to really kick up the wet-dog-beer smell. The barman timed his entry perfectly, replacing Alan's empty glasses with full ones.

'What the hell is that shit, Eddie?' Alan was still smacking his lips. The barman had a glass of what looked like coke with a straw that he was constantly sipping from; he put it down to make jazz hands.

'Surprise!' And then he was gone.

Alan was disturbed from sizing up his next pint by movement from the couple at the other table, who scraped their chairs and then their feet on their way out. Alan watched them leave, then spun all the way round on his stool, using the spinning top to great effect before resting back on Vince.

'You really here to talk about running after the wrong people? Ain't no one ever ran after someone harder than you went after the Moran kid! Tried to kill the man, is what I heard. A lot of the grasses saying that, too. Do what I do and you learn that the truth comes best not from one person you think you trust telling you something, but a load of dishonest people who wouldn't piss on you if you were on fire, and all telling you the same thing. Turns out I'm getting both about you.'

Vince took another swig. 'I lost my mind for a moment,' he said.

'And me talking to you would equal me losing mine, and without the excuse you had. I'm sorry about your sister, yeah, I mean that, I'll do you the favour of forgetting you came in here as my way of showing you I mean it. I shouldn't talk about shit weeks with you about.' Another gesture with his pint — *I'll drink to that*. Vince mirrored it.

'I just came into my local for a beer and here you were. We can talk, can't we?'

'Local? I'm less than two miles from here, can't say I've seen you about.'

'Littlebourne,' Vince said, stopping himself from explaining how he hadn't lived there long either.

'Oh, so only about six miles and eight pubs away. And when you go to your *local* do you always sit out at the other end of the car park waiting for just about everyone to leave before you come in?'

'You knew?'

'Of course I did.'

'And you still stayed.'

'This or an empty house.' Alan pushed his hands out along with his bottom lip in a *what-would-you-choose* expression. 'Eddie's pretty good, he lets me hang around until he's done his admin.'

'I even thought I might have a talent for the surveillance thing,' Vince mused.

'Nope. Just about everyone who left has called me to tell me that the copper who's in the shit with the Supernintendo is sat outside the pub in his Volvo.'

243

'It's the missus' Volvo, actually. I thought if I used my own car someone might recognise it. Now I'll need to come get it first thing to save me explaining to her why I left it eight pubs away.' Vince could have laughed if he didn't feel so empty. Alan shrugged.

'All that effort just to talk to me? Makes me think you're not about to just walk away when I don't talk back. It's fine, I can get Eddie to make the call and when the patrol car turns up to see what's going on and you see sense and scarper, I get a lift home. Win-win.'

'I'm just here to ask what you know. I'm no threat.'

'Even if I don't tell you?' Alan said, seeming to take a moment to take in Vince's size. They both started their next pint at the same time; it seemed like a decent way to fill a silence. 'For the record I think Hall's a bit of a prick and I think he's wrong about you. You been about long enough to have a reputation; a thief-taker and street smart. Some of the people we talk to say they trust you, too, I think you've put a few sources our way.'

'I have. The source team do a lot of good work, it's a two-way thing.'

'You blowing smoke up my arse won't make a jot of difference, either!'

'They got Liam in custody and he's not talking. I know that's my fault, but it also means they're wasting their time with him, trying to wear him down, thinking he's who they need. But someone on your team knows better, right?'

Alan made a gesture with both hands like he was sprinkling dust about the place. 'No one on my team ever *knows* anything. Welcome to source handling! We get told things, usually by people you wouldn't trust as far as you could gob and we pass them things on. That's it. If you want to *know* something, you need to speak to someone further down the line. Right now, I guess that means Supernintendo Mark Hall.' Alan smacked his lips after another deep slug of beer. He couldn't have been drinking at this pace all night, he must have sped up, sensing that he was running out of time.

'If Hall turns all that he has towards the wrong man, all that time, all those people, and whoever did do those things gets a free ride . . .' Vince stopped as Alan swallowed the final gulp of his pint, already fidgeting forward to stand up off his stool. He picked the refilled shot glass up from his standing position to down it in one. Another scowl.

'Eddie . . . that is *fucking* horrible.' He grinned then gestured at where Vince hadn't touched his two shots. 'You going to drink those?' and then scooped them up, one after the other when Vince didn't reply quick enough. 'The only thing worse than going home alone to an empty house is going home sober, alone and to an empty house.' Alan's grin was wider than ever but still the sadness hung from him like a cloak he hadn't noticed being clipped to his back. He was unsteady, patting his pockets like it was part of a search and seemed satisfied. 'Eddie, I will catch you later my good man.'

'One for the road? I got plastic glasses?' the barman called back, caught out with the straw in his mouth.

'Not tonight. I think I'm just about there.'

Vince leaned back on his stool, trying to hide his disappointment. His last opportunity was now making untidy progress out of the door and all that was left was for Vince to call out after it. 'It's going to happen again to some other family. I was there first, I saw what they did.'

Alan stopped, his left arm out like he needed the door frame to keep him steady. His voice came out gruff, like maybe the foul shot still lined it. 'Moran's an evil piece of shit, we all know it, but Hall needs an open mind. You remember what I said? Well, we got a lot of dishonest people telling us the same thing . . .' Alan turned a face flushing red back towards Vince. 'This weren't Liam.'

'Do they know who it was?' Vince was trying to hide his desperation.

'We don't *know* anything!' Alan's attempt at a smile never really caught. 'You want anything else, only Hall himself can tell you that, and that's where you'll have to go . . .' His face suddenly lit up, the cloak of sadness shrugged off for a just a moment as he lifted both his hands into the air to exclaim: 'To Hall and back!' The door crashed shut behind him, the sound had a finality to it, like it was a warning that he would get no more. Vince knew better than to chase a drunk man out of a pub.

'Eddie,' he said, 'any chance I could sit and have another while you sort out your admin?'

CHAPTER 41

'Amelia!' Sophie slumped forward for her knees to meet with the coarse carpet of her landing, her strength leaking out as relief rushed in. She reached out to steady herself, her left palm resting on the pocket door she had just hurriedly closed. She used it to pull herself back to a stand.

'Sophie, sorry, I know I've been avoiding your calls but I just thought it was best, what with all that's been going on.'

Andrew turned the hall light on and the soft edges of the shadows were revealed in a stark white. He called up, nervous energy leaking from every word. 'There, I told you she was here, now, how about that tea?'

'I just had to know. God knows I've thought about running away but until we know what we're running away from . . .' Amelia was still facing away from Andrew, towards Sophie, shielding her eyes from the sudden light. She was wearing a black denim jacket over blue jeans with a white shirt underneath. Her shoulders were spotted with rain, her light blonde hair had a little frizz to it too from exposure to moisture, despite being tied up into a ponytail. The pink streak running through it was new. Her Converse trainers, too, looked dusted with rain.

'Did you walk?'

'Walk?' Amelia looked blank, then caught up. 'Oh, yeah. Not far, from where I could get parked,' and she smiled, something that suited her very well with her pretty eyes. 'Tea then?' She turned back towards the stairs. Andrew waited for their guest to start back down the stairs, then pointed furiously at the cupboard, as if he thought that Sophie might have forgotten they were hiding their daughter. She waited for the footsteps to move away then pushed the pocket door open to reveal Taliah with a frozen-on smile formed out of shock. Sophie knelt to hold her in a tight hug.

'You did so well!' she said, her voice just above a whisper. 'Well done. That was just another test, OK? Just another drill so now we know what to do. But the next time we can't be flushing the toilet or turning on lights, OK? It has to be like me and you aren't even here, so your dad can concentrate on what he's doing.' Taliah reacted like she was being told off and Sophie hugged her again, telling her that everything was going to be all right with no confidence that Taliah believed a word of it. She didn't say anything, just tiptoed back to bed when her mother suggested it.

Sophie headed downstairs to the kitchen to find the tea already made and a tension hanging in the room that was thick enough to reach out and encompass her. It took a number of glances and some shuffling of feet for Amelia to speak.

'You've been calling me. I didn't want to talk over the phone, I must be getting suspicious in my old age but I don't trust phones. I thought I would come round and see you instead.'

'Maybe next time find a way to call ahead,' Andrew cut in. His voice still had a shake like nervous energy was leaving him. 'A public phone or something, that's what they do in the movies, right?'

'Noted. Sorry, I didn't think . . . I can see why this might have upset you.'

'Upset is one word,' Sophie snapped. 'We just shoved our daughter into a cupboard.' Andrew's eyes flicked up to meet with hers. They had been the only one of the group not

248

to reveal their hiding place and now she had blurted it right out. She shrugged back at him — if they could reveal it to anyone, then surely it could be to the woman who told them to make sure they had one sorted in the first place.

'What is it you wanted to talk to me about?' Amelia said and Sophie bit back her first reply, taking a breath instead while a voice in her mind screamed *why the hell do you think I've been calling?* Her husband was back to glaring at her, this being news to him.

'An update, anything. We can't keep living like this, we're a bag of nerves, but it's our daughter, I worry about the effect it's having.' Sophie cussing inwardly that her voice sounded whiny and weak.

'I know, God, I know. My Jacob's young enough not to understand but I still think he picks up on it. I do know a little more, that's why I came here.'

'What?' Andrew said and Amelia turned to him, suddenly looking a little awkward.

'Did you want to talk to me, just you I mean, then we—'

'No.' Andrew cut her off, getting in before Sophie. 'She should know everything, everything I do. It's only fair.'

Amelia shrugged: *whatever.* 'Information, that's it, that's what they want.'

'Who?' Sophie blurted, 'Who's they!?' and Amelia rounded on her.

'The drug dealers who put up the money in the first place.'

'Drug dealers! Fucking brilliant!' Sophie pointed her foul mouth at her husband whose head slumped forward, his chin against his chest. To this point all she had heard was *bad people* and *it's better if you don't know.*

'Surely you're not so surprised? All this.' Amelia gestured out into the air. 'It was never going to be about some bad debtors or a client dispute.' She was so matter-of-fact, smug even and Sophie felt her hands bunching up into fists.

'I guessed he had involved us in something bad, but I also thought him to be a better man than drug dealing,' Sophie spat.

'I didn't know either, OK, not at first.' Now it was her husband who sounded whiny. 'Ron saw a way to save the company—'

'Oh, don't you go blaming him!' Sophie spat. 'You're partners! For years you've been telling me how being a partner means you get complete control, how you can have the final say in what the company does and how it does it. So what are you telling me now? That Ron did all of this?'

'He got us involved in this deal, yes. We were just layering the money—'

'Layering? What the hell is that? And please, feel free to talk to me like I'm stupid.' Sophie's anger was only rising, she felt like she was close to the point of no return.

'Soph, please, calm down.' Andrew's voice was soft, but Sophie didn't react well to being told to calm down. She fought back her first response, an explosion of words and movement when their daughter was upstairs trying to get back to sleep. 'Layering, you get given a clump of money from one source and you split it up to make it look like it's come from a number of sources in the case of any audit.'

'*Laundering.* That's what you mean, isn't it? You're not fooling anyone, Andrew, not even your dumb wife.'

'Please, Soph, I don't think you're dumb.'

'Then you should listen to how you talk to me sometimes.'

'It is absolutely money laundering.' Amelia cut back in, her voice raised enough to shut both of them up and for Sophie to glance over to the foot of the stairs like Taliah might appear. 'Ron and Andrew are laundering money, they took money sourced from drug dealing and have been losing it in construction, paying a good number of labourers and tradesmen cash in hand, for example, or hiring plant as another. In return, these drug pushers were written in as stakeholders, which assured them a share of the monthly rent from the completed units and a cut when they eventually sell and, just like that, a legitimate source of income moving forward. Maria Mercer worked for a part of the council that granted permission for the construction to start in the first place, as well as for housing estates and property conversions all over Kent. The drug money paid her and your husband's firm. It wasn't just one site, it's a good few so, over the course of nine to twelve months, these drug suppliers moved large sums of money from the street to a place where it comes back for evermore as perfectly legitimate.' There was a stunned silence until Amelia continued, 'So now you know all there is.'

'Drug money . . .' Sophie sobbed the words. Andrew had told her that he was involved in something he didn't want to be, that Ron had pushed for it and neither had really understood the implications. It was always going to be something to do with money based on what Andrew did, what he was good at, but she'd thought tax evasion, embezzlement — something illegal for sure — not *drug dealers*. That was something you saw in television dramas or on the news. It was another world. One that her husband had brought right to their door.

'We just had to be creative with the accounts, we only dealt with the money. These people dumped a load of it into a couple of construction companies and we had to hide it, we had no choice! All we could do was spread it out to make it look like they were reinvesting any profits or gains into the next project, when really it was new money every time. To any inspection it would look like savvy businessmen living on a pittance for bigger benefits later.'

'Why didn't you go to the police? Right at the start, when you first realised what you were doing and who you were doing it for?' Sophie already knew the answer, it was written all over her husband's face. He was scared, he was weak and he was greedy.

'I don't think I need to remind you what these people did to Ron and his wife, and to Maria while Jade was there, in the same house! That tells you why, doesn't it? Ron got us in deep, and quickly.' Andrew jutted his palms out. 'I'm not blaming the man, that's not what I mean, but he was naïve. We both were. And it just keeps getting deeper. Even the rent on our new office is paid for by their dirty money. It's like there's nothing I can do to stop it.'

'What about you?' Sophie suddenly rounded on their guest. 'Are you a drug dealer?'

'I work personnel.' Amelia suddenly had a knowing grin that Sophie wanted to punch until it was gone.

'So, you work *for* drug dealers?'

'Not by choice, just like your husband, *they* found *me*. I'm part of making sure the initial money keeps coming in with no issues—'

'So you are a dealer!'

'No!' Amelia's anger was sudden and clear. She took a step closer, her body tensed, then she shook her head, shaking away her intentions, perhaps. 'I'm part of the custody process. The people out selling the stuff on the streets are just kids, fourteen, fifteen at best; never over eighteen. Kids are treated different by the law, a lighter touch. When they get caught my job is to go down to the police station and sit with them. Officially I work for the police, or *with* them at least, but really I'm there to be a reminder for these children that they need to keep their mouths shut and to report back if they don't.'

'And the police let you do that?' Sophie was aghast.

'No, they don't know, that's why I'm there. Any kid who gets arrested has to have someone like me with them if their parents can't make it. And they can never make it — when these kids are taken on, they all agree to call me, to ask for me.'

'So you're just there to throw these kids to the wolves if they talk?' Sophie snorted.

'I don't recruit them, I don't make them go out and sell drugs on the streets and I don't agree with what they do. These boys are not forced either, not like I was, they *want* to. Actually, I keep them safe. The police can be persuasive, they can make it sound like talking might be a good idea when it really isn't and with me sitting in there with them, not one of them has.'

'So what has all this killing people and hiding in cupboards got to do with this construction scam that my husband is now solely running?'

'It's not a scam—' Andrew was cut short by a look from his wife. He was wise to stop talking.

'I don't know for sure. What I do know is that these people needed someone they could trust with money. When you're paying forty per cent of a workforce building an entire industrial estate in physical cash, that's a lot of trust.'

'Forty per cent?' Sophie scoffed. 'Why don't they just do one hundred per cent if they have all this money to get rid of?'

'They would have, trust me, I had to talk them out of it.' It was Andrew who spoke now. 'We have to show a payroll, a workforce being paid the normal way, paying taxes the normal way. Wages are a huge cost in construction, but when half the workers get cash in hand, any overtime paid the same, it's . . . it's just as easy a place to lose money.'

'Information?' Sophie said as Amelia took a slurp of her tea, her demeanour maddeningly calm. 'That's what you said, that's what these people want?'

'That's what they want.'

'What information?'

'I was just going to explain. This person they chose, the person trusted with bags of their cash to deliver—'

'Let me guess. They did a fucking runner!' Sophie ran her hands firmly over her eyes.

'They're currently uncontactable.' Amelia shrugged.

'Well of course they are! Still, what does this have to do with us, with Andrew and Ron? With Maria and her daughter?'

Amelia took another slurp of her tea; all the while she watched Andrew expectantly. He got the hint to answer.

'We worked closely with this person, which meant we knew the sums of money that were going out, we also knew when and where to. And the circle of knowledge around those trips had to be very small . . .' Andrew faded out, clearly carefully selecting what his next words would be. Sophie didn't give him a chance.

'Did you steal their money?' She watched her husband closer than ever to study his reaction.

'Of course I didn't!'

'Tell me you didn't, tell me this isn't why our daughter was cowering in a cupboard tonight?'

'I didn't, Sophie, I'm telling you. I wouldn't do that to us.'

'Did Ron steal their money?'

'No.' Andrew was firm. She knew when he was lying; he wasn't. 'It's likely they think Ron or Maria, or both, may have had something to do with it or at least know where their money — and the person holding it — has gone.'

'What person? Who is it?'

'I don't even know!' Andrew was incredulous. 'We never got a name, we never met face to face, never even spoke . . . There was just an encrypted messaging system with how much, where to pick it up, who to and where to make the drop. I never even saw any actual money.'

'Which is likely why you are still alive,' Amelia said, still matter-of-fact.

'But you know who this missing person is?' Sophie rounded on Amelia.

'I do. And you don't want to know. If these people do come here it will be to get everything you know and that cannot include this person's name. The moment you say something you shouldn't know they will convince themselves of your involvement and they will not stop. These people live on their instincts, on their ability to be ruthless.'

'Come here? They're still coming here!' Sophie's chest was suddenly so tight she could barely speak.

'Actually, I don't think so,' Amelia said, still with a maddening calm to her. 'They questioned Ron and Maria hard, right to the end, they will have left certain that they got everything they knew, which is more than what Andrew here knows. It is true that Ron set up this agreement at the start;

he was the instigator, not your husband. I think they will be happy to stop at Ron Blackman.'

'You *think*!?'

Amelia shrugged, she *actually shrugged*. 'They would have been here already.'

Sophie took a moment to consider. 'And you're still laundering their money?' She spat her words at Andrew.

'Yes. I have no choice . . .'

'Jesus . . .' Sophie sighed.

'You cannot relax, OK,' Amelia continued. 'This doesn't mean you should get lax. They will find another Maria and they can just as easily find another you.' She talked directly at Andrew for this last word. Strain now seemed to have his face in a constant grip, it tightened on the word "you". Sophie could hardly remember what he looked like when he wasn't scared.

'Your husband needs to continue with his work, he needs to be useful. They will not want the hassle or the risk of replacing someone as important, having already lost Ron.' Amelia took another maddening swig of her tea. 'For now at least. He needs to carry on as normal and not do anything stupid.'

Sophie snorted sarcastic laughter, glaring at her husband.

'There's something else,' Amelia said. 'Part of what I was able to find out is that there is still one loose end, one I *know* they're going to want closure on.'

'What?' Sophie felt her chest tighten again.

'Maria's girl, she was there when they murdered her mother. Do you know what she saw?' Amelia said.

'Jade? She's eleven years old!'

'And they won't care. Did she see what happened?' Amelia asked, raising her voice a little.

'I don't know, I haven't been able to speak to her since. . . I did try. Taliah and Jade are close; *were* close. I've offered Taliah for a play date, I thought it might bring some sort of normality.' Sophie was shaking her head, trying to remember just what *normality* felt like.

'Where is she?' Amelia's tone still flat and firm.

'Why would I tell you that? What is this, what do you mean by *loose end*?'

'She's the key for us all now, she's all that's left that can cause us problems. I told you that I work as an appropriate adult so the fact she's eleven gives me an opportunity. The police haven't spoken to her formally about what she saw, they are giving her space, which means I can lobby to be sat in there with her when they do. I can keep her safe—'

'But she's with her godparents. The husband's a counsellor in Sandwich, a real pillar of the community type, why would they use you?'

'They won't!' Amelia snapped but was quick to go back to calm and dry. 'That is my point. We need to manufacture it so Jade is with me, that way I get to talk to her in private before the police can talk to her formally. She has no idea the danger she is still in. The police think it was a robbery gone wrong, but if she starts talking to the police . . .'

'What?' Sophie squeaked, holding her breath for the reply.

'There will be no hiding for her this time.'

'You're going to terrify her, even more than she already is. Maybe she should talk, the police can protect her, they have ways of protecting people, you see it all the time on tele!'

Amelia's head was shaking now, firmly. 'They can't, trust me on that, and if you think I'm going to cause her more upset, you should hear what Witness Protection does to someone. And a kid? No, she wouldn't make it. These people will be looking for her already, but if I find her first, I can tell them that I was with her the whole time, that she kept her mouth shut, even that she didn't see anything anyway. It shouldn't take much to convince them she's not worth the risk.'

'Why would they listen? Why would they believe you? You said yourself how ruthless they are,' Sophie whined.

'Because this is what I do for them, this is why they have me working for them. They won't want to hurt a child, the attention that comes from that could be their undo-ing. Murder a couple in their own home and the police do everything they can, but the effort fades. Another adult gets murdered somewhere else, the focus sharpens, but again, it can still go cold. Murder a child and that focus never goes away. They will never give up, the public outcry would be too loud. These people don't want that, think about it, this whole thing is about them getting clean money, that means going legit, keeping their heads down.'

'And you expect me to believe that you're doing this because you care about Jade?'

'I don't care what you believe when it comes to my moti-vation but something you won't know about me, I lost my own daughter. I can't tell you how much that hurts.' Amelia stopped, as if to ride out the first sign of any emotion. 'I didn't do enough to protect her and I lost her. This Jade, she might not be mine but I won't let anything happen to her.'

Sophie's hand covered her mouth while she took a moment. When she spoke, it was through her fingers. 'OK, OK . . .' Among the noise in her head, it was starting to sound like sense, like a way out at least.

'You already said that she's in Sandwich?' Amelia's tone was softer now, encouraging.

'With her godparents, she's staying with them. They used to foster a lot, vulnerable kids, the man's practically a saint according to Maria. She was always so proud when she talked about him. His name is McIlhenny, I remember she pointed him out on a campaign poster before, but everyone calls him Mac. I know his wife better, Angie, just through our girls being friends. We met at Maria's, she did a barbecue and we went to something over there with both the girls. Taliah and Jade really hit it off—'

'Where in Sandwich?' Amelia cut back in but she still sounded warm, soothing and confident. Maybe she really could make everything OK.

'I can't remember the door number, around forty? It has a blue door that stands out as the nicest and it's Strand

Street. The back overlooks some big, fancy golf course. I know it when I drive there, but I just can't . . .' Sophie was starting to fall apart now, the tension and adrenaline that had been holding her up leaking out and she pulled out a chair to fall into.

'That's fine, you did great,' Amelia said, her tone warmer than ever, her hand moving to rest on Sophie's shoulder.

'Please . . .' Sophie managed, 'please, just make this all go away.'

CHAPTER 42

'You sure, mate?' The heavyset taxi driver peered back over his shoulder, the bright white of the interior light swamping his bald head so it looked like a cue ball; the rest of him was difficult to pick out from the seat, like he had been sitting there so long he'd merged into the fabric. Vince kept his observations to himself.

'Yeah, I reckon I could do with the walk.'

The taxi driver's chuckle matched his gravelly voice. 'It won't make no difference, mate, she'll still know you've been on the sauce, they always know when you've been on the sauce!'

He was still chuckling when he pulled away, taking all the light with him. This could become a bad idea very quickly, Vince realised. The last sign of life they had passed had been the Six Mile Garage on Stone Street, its forecourt vibrant, the huge LED downlights reflecting in the standing water bright enough to force Vince to look away. Now the only light source was the A2 cutting through the countryside in the middle distance behind him, the light from it dissipating out into a night sky that was heavy with the promise of more rain. Home was about a mile in the opposite direction and via country lanes that Vince knew well as part of his regular jogging route. Tonight, however, it was just a wall of darkness.

The moon made a fleeting appearance from behind quick-moving clouds, its weak light hit bare branches to cast shadows like long fingers on the tarmac. The rain had fooled him, hiding in the breeze and he could feel spots now, the first few serving as a reminder that he had come out with nothing more than a light jacket. He pulled it tighter, lifting the collar as he started his walk.

The idea of being dropped short of his home was to clear his mind. He'd stayed on at the Crown for another couple of pints — solace could come from the most surprising places and, in this case, it had come from a red-nosed barman who had no doubt heard it all before. Vince had talked about his sister, about how unfair the world was and how he felt like he had lost all motivation at a time when he needed to be up for his job more than ever.

You lot are always after bad people who do bad things, comes with the territory. Eddie had sucked thoughtfully on his straw, his eyes without focus, his head with a subtle shake as he spoke the words of bar-wisdom. *I reckon you gotta use that to get you out of bed in the morning and back on the horse, sounds like you lost a good'un in your sister, that puts your side one down and you can't let the bad'uns win. You got to even it out, make sure there's more good'uns than bad'uns.*

Eddie the barman might not have been the most eloquent, he might not have been fooling anyone with that glass of "coke" either, but he was right. Policing was simple when stripped down to the sum of its parts. It was about good and bad, right and wrong and Vince's motivation had always come from catching the bad'uns.

The heavier rain came with a five-second warning, the tree canopy took the first wave of droplets but was unable to hold it back for long. Vince liked the noise at least, even when the droplets ran together to form something big enough to make him shudder.

The conditions sobered him up enough that, when he finally arrived home, he could find the lock with his key at just the second attempt. From the outside it looked to be in complete darkness. Once inside, the hallway glowed with light borrowed from the moon. The whole ground floor had enough for him to navigate through, even with an excited collie dog thinking it best to weave between his legs. He made it to the kitchen, pulling out the drawer where he kept his work phone, and prodded to turn it on with water running into his eyes. It was dead, of course it was. He had thrown it in the drawer the moment he had got home two days ago, still in a daze from the events of that shift. The rummage for a charger was a little more difficult in the dark but he didn't want to turn a light on, nothing that might disturb Maddie and bring forward the questioning about what the hell he had been doing all night. Finally, the phone came to life. The lead he had found was too short, forcing him into a lean on the kitchen surface, his elbows taking his weight as the phone pinged with a barrage of notifications to make Vince swear as he tried to turn the *fucking thing* to silent. He managed it and the notifications continued with just a shake in his palm. He waited it out, the text messages, missed calls and emails appearing as a growing stack on his screen. He wasn't there to check his notifications, though one voice message caught his eye: *Angie McIlhenny*. There was a text message from her too, with a paperclip symbol that meant it came with an attachment. He opened it up.

'What the hell . . . ?' The image leaped out brightly from the darkness of his kitchen and he had to narrow his eyes or look away. Police don't issue good smartphones to clumsy rough-and-tumble coppers like Vince, they issue pissy little things with rubber sides, small screens and little zoom. He turned it on its side, which only made it slightly bigger; enough, at least, that Vince could make out he had been sent a photo of a drawing. There were thick, dark lines at the forefront and brighter colours behind. Jade must have done it, Angie had taken his advice literally: *Let me know anything you think might be relevant, even things you don't!*

If there was relevance here, he couldn't see it but he was still glad she had listened. His sausage fingers tried again to pinch and zoom: *A face!?* The drawing wasn't great, lacking detail, but just the fact that Jade had seen a face had to be something. The eyes, too — one in particular — there was some extra detail but the zoom was on maximum, he did get it bigger but it lost its focus and zoomed back out again the moment he took his fingers off the screen.

'Like a keyhole?' Vince muttered, referencing the shape of the pupil in the right eye; Jade had drawn it elongated, strangely shaped. No way of telling if she had done that on purpose.

'What the hell do I do with this?' he muttered again, then put the phone down on the side, its glow still the only light source, looking away for a moment to rub his eyes with the heel of his hands. He wasn't thinking straight, it felt like the alcohol had worn off but he knew better. He didn't even know who still had access to Jade, he only knew who didn't. He felt helpless, the whole thing was hopeless.

And it was all his fault.

Vince lashed out, catching the phone to push it away where it clattered against the back wall. He started the kettle. Drink had taken him to the point where he had felt the urge to face-plant his own bed while sat back at the pub but the walk back in the cold rain and his sudden anger had him wide awake. He would make a hot drink, something soothing, see if he couldn't bring that feeling of exhaustion back.

With the kettle on he scooped his phone back up. Closing down the image for now and moving on to the reason he had powered up his phone in the first place. He brought up his email, ignoring the reams of messages in bold font — mostly from duties — baying for his attention and opened up a new message that he addressed to Alan Miles, then stared for a few moments at the cursor blinking in the subject box. He wasn't very good at this, he couldn't even think how to label it, so skipped straight to the main message box:

Hope you got home OK. Sorry I hijacked the end of the evening but you're proper important. Not to me, I don't matter,

but to that 11yo girl. Like it or not you're in the middle now,
you can be the change of direction that this investigation needs.

They're not going to look past Liam Moran. We both know
they should.

Jade Mercer doesn't have a say in any of this, you're going
to have to do the talking for her.
VA.

There was no hesitation in sending, but there was instant
regret. A wise mate of his had once told him to assume all
police mailboxes were monitored and if Vince were a DC in
the Professional Standards Department right now, he would
sure as hell be monitoring this account. He shrugged in the
darkness: *So what?* He was right. Alan Miles had the ability
to change the course of this investigation, to make sure it was
focused right and, worst-case scenario, PSD would see his
message and ask the same questions.

That feeling of exhaustion returned all at once, even
before he had finished making his drink and he skipped it,
leaving the cup out on the side. He was mindful enough to
head for the spare room so as not to wake his girlfriend, a
room he had started making up for his sister as part of his
plans for her recovery.

Maybe it was a fitting end to the day; it was certainly a
sudden one. It wasn't quite a face-plant, but he didn't manage to get fully undressed either.

CHAPTER 43

Amelia Chagrin waited for Sophie to close the door behind her, to *thank* her, before allowing her smile to bloom. Amelia had been enjoying holding it back almost as much as she did letting it go. In truth, she had been enjoying herself from the moment she had arrived to knock on the door, knowing the impact that would have, even pressing her cheek up to listen for furtive movements and hissed whispers. She wasn't sure if she had heard them or if it was just her imagination filling them in, but she hadn't imagined the panic and upset etched all over Andrew Harding's face when the door had pulled open; that was as a clear as day.

Amelia had enjoyed that too — *the power!* She felt it right down to the tips of her toes, feeding off Andrew Harding's fear, then again when Sophie had appeared, having hurriedly stuffed their daughter in some adapted cupboard.

The strength Amelia had now was a million miles from where she had come. She had been left distraught, weak and empty when her own daughter had been taken from her. And helpless. A helplessness that somehow became worse when she found out who was responsible, the information coming with a stark warning: *you don't get close to people like that.*

But you can.

Bide your time, build back your strength, find their weakness.

That was what Tim had said. She had never seen him so intense. Three years later and that cold determination still formed his expression as he leaned over to push the door open for her. He was right where she'd left him, parked round a corner, hidden from the Harding house.

'Did they tell you where she is?' he said, instantly.

Amelia nodded, taking her place in the passenger seat of his van and pulling the door shut: 'Sandwich, Strand Street.'

Tim nodded. His eyes shifted away, they were cold and focused, the same non-expression as when she had opened the front door to let him back into the accountant's home, when he would have been faced with a river of blood.

Her questioning of the fat husband was done by then, she had her answers and Tim had taken the stubby corkscrew from hands that were shaking in her excitement.

He had no such shake when he had dealt with the wife.

Tim worked a mapping application on his phone, its white light made him look washed out. It only took a few moments and he closed it back down. There was no more talking, he was back in work mode, back to the issue of tying up their loose end.

Loose end.

Tim's turn of phrase. His response when she had finally buckled to tell him her truth. She had expected him to be angry, but there was no anger, no blame or panic, just coldness: *loose end.* But Amelia was still angry at herself. She had been so careful with the preparation, obsessing over every detail and Jade had been one of them. She was not supposed to have been home, due away on a school trip, contactable by phone if Amelia needed that as an option. But a white paper bag on the Mercers' kitchen table date-stamped from the pharmacy that very morning offered an explanation as to why Jade might have stayed at home at the last minute. A leaflet was also stuffed in the bag, a guide aimed at young women who were experiencing changes to their bodies, new feelings, new experiences and how to cope. A sample box of sanitary towels was the final item, purchased by a mother ready to support her daughter through the next phase in her young life.

The bag had resonated with Amelia, brought on a moment of weakness. She had hidden it from Tim, knowing it meant Jade could well be in the house and, of course, Maria had already told her the hiding place she would use. Amelia had let Jade live, even passed her a ringing phone where a floorboard had lifted, when Tim was already on his way out. That moment of weakness was one where she couldn't leave a young child suffering any longer than was necessary.

But it had been an error of judgement. Kayla — *her daughter* — had been innocent too. And that stubby blade had opened a flood of information as to who the guilty really were. Kayla had been forced to drive huge amounts of cash by a criminal family led by George Moran, an old man facing up to the prospect of his own son taking advantage of his weakness. His reaction was a plan, one that would see him rob Kayla as part of undermining his son, while getting richer at the same time.

Kayla had been nothing to them, a pawn in a game. And for George Arthur Moran to win, Kayla had to die.

But one thing the street would tell you about the Morans is that they were untouchable. That was the first thing she had been told, long before any blood had been spilled, before she knew the truth, when she only knew that the key to what had happened to her daughter would be within that family. The idea that those at the centre of the organisation were so untouchable was what gave Amelia the idea of targeting those on the outside in the first place. All she needed was a way of finding out who those people might be — and for that, she had an idea.

Getting the volunteering role as an appropriate adult was easy enough. She had a clean record and a useful contact in the drug worker she had reached out to when Kayla's issues had been at their most desperate. Amelia had a believable line too: *I just want to help, my own daughter got sucked into a world that destroyed her and I want to help others make different choices.*

Everyone fell for it.

Amelia had other contacts too, Kayla's old friends, people still in the middle of the drug scene and she used them to get word back that she was available — for the right price. Drug gangs have one big fear, one big weakness: wagging tongues. For a fee, she would sit in a room and act as a failsafe, ensuring any street dealers careless enough to get themselves arrested were not careless with what they said after. No one knew who she was to Kayla, she changed her surname to further distance herself from her daughter, but in truth, no one cared to ask. From there she earned trust, learned names and increased her network of contacts until she got to hear about other people just like her — *normal people* — trapped in the same web, working close enough to Liam Moran that they might just have the answers. It hadn't taken long to find them, nobodies who had sold their soul for greed. As far as Amelia was concerned, they were no better than the men sitting at the top of the tree and she had no guilt about her own delight when she found they had children — a weakness — that would ensure they would talk.

And talk they did.

The accountant had been the most useful. Fat with greed, he had bled well. He knew Kayla, tellingly, he knew her role and how vulnerable it made her. He stopped short of saying that George had killed her, but something was odd about him. Liam was running the drug enterprise, the accountant was aware of his dad but only in the background. Until George had approached the accountant, came out to see him, said he wanted to know more details and, tellingly, told him that their conversation was not to be discussed with Liam. She'd heard from other places that George was feeling threatened, that he didn't want to be involved in pushing drugs because of the risks attached. It all fell into place, it all made sense. She left those houses with just one question still unanswered: *where they had dumped Kayla's body*.

The fat accountant hadn't known, she was sure of that. But he talked about how the Morans were building whole estates, sinking tons of concrete into the foundations for huge warehouses and how George had delayed one site around the time her daughter went missing. He'd thrown a tantrum, kicked everyone off, deemed at the time to be a show of power, of petulance.

But Amelia knew better. He had cleared the site of witnesses.

The image of her daughter sinking in cold concrete, discarded like someone might flick a fag butt to be swallowed for the rest of time had been eating at her ever since, keeping her angry, feeding her obsession. From that moment she had known that she would need to make George talk, the way she had made the others. But getting to him was never going to be as easy as it had been with the others.

The fat accountant was already out of his depth when Amelia knocked on his door out of the blue, timing it ten minutes before she knew his wife was due home, to tell him he was in danger. She spun a story of how someone was giving information about a drug gang to the police and they were closing ranks to try and flush out the culprit and it meant that anyone who wasn't part of the gang could expect a visit. He didn't question her once; after all, she knew a lot about it and she was only concerned for his safety, never asking for anything in return. He had offered up his partner too, Andrew Harding who would also need warning.

Would you be able to inform him? Oh, and there's a nice lady at the council that Andy knows, she sorts out the permissions, she's normal too, she needs to be warned!

But Amelia had a better idea: *How about we all get together, all us normal people and talk about this threat and what we can do about it?*

Fine! he had said, his wife due home any moment, and the die was cast. Amelia led the meeting that followed, but she didn't get what she needed. She got a room that shut down, unwilling to reveal their roles in any detail, to even mention the name *Moran* and with no real reason for Amelia to force it. Instead, an idea forming in her mind as she went, she ramped up the risk and the fear, pushed them towards discussing what they would do if their door knocked and made them understand that calling the police was not an option. They were scared too, that room was thick with it.

Amelia's plan evolved. She gave them time to marinate in their fear, to drive themselves mad almost, with not knowing what and when, and then she struck Maria Mercer first. Amelia had the impression she was going to be the least informative — she had been right about that — and more useful as a bloody statement, a sample of what might come for the others. When Ron Blackman's door knocked four days later, he was already half-beaten, beaten entirely the moment she revealed herself as the big bad wolf all along. He told her everything she needed, his murder wasn't necessary, but by then, the statements she was looking to make were aimed at those higher.

Today was different, today was about getting away with it all. She didn't deserve to be the subject of police attention, the same organisation who had given up the search for her daughter, who had forced her along this path in the first place. Today was the day they both made sure of a clean break.

This murder was necessary, it was tying up the last *loose end*.

CHAPTER 44

Sunday

Vince always woke early when he had been drinking, part of his body's way of scolding him for having a drink in the first place, perhaps. He was forced out of bed by an overpowering need to urinate and a sudden flush of heat where he was wearing his shirt and underwear from the night before. He tried to be quiet, partly due to his own muzzy head, but mainly for Maddie, asleep in the next room. A peek around the bedroom door revealed her to be laid in a puddle of her own hair, messy enough that it took him a moment to determine which way she was facing.

He checked Sammy next who was also showing signs that sleep hadn't come peacefully, laid out like he had been knocked sparko in a fist fight with one arm lolling over the side to lean dangerously close to the floor. Vince picked him up to lay him straight, sorting the cover as he did. Sammy's eyes opened and his mouth smiled but it didn't count as awake. He murmured and sighed and his eyes were back shut before Vince made it out of the door.

Vince hoped he slept the rest of the day. Sammy's return to the world was going to come with far worse than a hangover.

The mug and teabag were still out where he had left them. He touched the side of the full kettle, almost expecting it to still be boiling hot. It was cold, of course. Outside, the daylight was strong enough to make a strip of bright light where the curtains met. He would keep them closed for now. His legs ached too, a side effect that had followed him throughout his career of drunkenness. A career he had abandoned more than a decade ago.

The kettle's noise was enough to make turning on the small television in the room pretty much pointless. A talking head appeared to mime disdain from a face screwed up and bloated above a tie tied too tight, while a headline in bright yellow swarmed left to right in the space underneath him: *POLICE INCOMPETENCE RAP OVER CONVICTION RATE FOR RAPE CASES*. A clumsy caption appeared to label him as a former barrister and his jowls shook with glee as he put the final boot into the entire police service then sat back like he was ready to dust his hands.

'Wouldn't want to be a police officer right now,' Vince mumbled, flicking his wrist as he pressed the remote like it might make the TV turn off harder.

'You talking to newsreaders now?' Maddie's voice. She was leaning on the doorframe, her gown held tight across her front, her hair still messy but a divide cleared at least so she could see out. She looked tired too. 'What time did you make it in last night?'

'I'm not sure. Not long after closing,' Vince said.

'Closing?' She lifted an eyebrow that was subtle and then it was gone.

'Yeah. Had a couple to blow off a little steam, that's all.'

'That explains last night's shirt.' Vince had it unbuttoned but hadn't yet taken it off. He looked down his front.

'Last night's pants, too,' he offered.

'I didn't need to know that bit. Where did you go?'

'An old stomping ground actually, the Crown, over by Nackington.'

'The Crown, what's that, seven, eight miles away?' Maddie said, the question loaded.

'About that.'

'I sent a message to your phone, about Sammy.'

'He OK?'

'Yeah. I think he was just . . . he was missing you.'

'I'm sorry. I should have been here, I didn't mean to leave you with that.'

'He cried,' Maddie said. 'Straight out refused to for a while, but it happened and then we had a lovely chat about death and how it can come from nowhere and take anyone. I wasn't leading the conversation, I should say, but it's a little difficult to sugar-coat that one.'

'Sorry . . .' Vince said again.

Maddie shrugged out the first hint of a smile in more than two days. 'He set me off too. You were definitely better off at the pub.'

'I should have been here, I know he's suffering.'

'He needs time to grieve, same as you do. The pub might not be the best place. Just keep your phone charged. I worry.'

'Noted.'

'Did it work?'

'Work?' Vince said.

'Blowing off steam, right?'

'Oh. Not really. All I managed to achieve was a taste in my mouth that just won't go and leg ache.'

'I see. That's not good, especially as you're going to need your legs this morning.'

Vince was running the tap for a glass of water. He turned it off half full. 'My legs?'

'My car isn't outside. I guess that means it's around seven or eight miles away. I'll drop Sammy to your mother's in yours and you can go for one of your runs to get mine back. Sounds like the perfect hangover cure to me.'

'Could you not drop me on the way?' Vince whined.

'I could if I wanted to,' Maddie said. 'And I'll have that tea you started. I'll be in the shower.'

* * *

272

It was still raining. It wasn't the heavy drops that slap you in the face as you run, more a tiny net of hanging drops that wrap you up to soak you in secret.

The Crown looked a lot more beaten up in the grey light of the morning. It was still a welcome sight, however, as Vince's chest was burning and his leg ache — unsurprisingly — worse for the jog. The curtains on the first floor were firmly shut, the bar area only visible through a criss-crossed window that made up the top half of the entrance door. The part of the bar he could see looked untouched from closing time, with a bag of nuts toppled over on the nearest table and a scattering of dirty glasses on windowsills, tables and the bar itself. One smaller glass stood out on its own, with a straw sticking out the top and a dark shadow for a bottom: Eddie's "coke".

Maddie's Volvo was still parked under the thickest tree at the far end of the car park. It looked even more ridiculous now it was the only car there and was left at a jaunty angle away from where parking bays were marked out with sawn logs. His steps towards it burned with lactic acid and a sudden feeling of nausea.

That's it, he was never drinking again.

The Volvo was covered in large beads of water which sprinted for his hand to deliver a shock of cold as he tugged the driver's door open. He then had to sit with the engine ticking over where his wet, warm body conspired to fog the windows and he dipped his head to search the glove box for a cloth to help it clear, scrabbling around until he sat back up again to the sound of an approaching car.

It was a small Skoda estate and it was making right for him, the running lights on the front bright enough to burn through the morning mist like eyes made of phosphorus. It pulled up at its own jaunty angle, this one so the driver's window was close enough to Vince's door to keep it shut. The window whirred down to reveal a set of bloodshot eyes that nervously flickered over Vince and then the rear-view mirror.

'Sergeant!' Vince said, trying to sound cheery. 'How come you didn't warn me that drinking made you feel like shit?'

'Did you walk here?' Alan Miles, his drinking companion from the night before, presented as far more urgent.

'Ran. The missus insisted, I think it's her way of getting even.' Vince cursed inwardly at the mention of *missus*, it might have shown itself as a grimace.

'I thought I would be waiting for a taxi to bring you back. A few more minutes and I could have changed my mind, I still might . . .' Alan's eyes glazed, their snap back to focus was sudden and he checked over his shoulder. 'Look, I can't be . . . I just wanted to give you this.' He lifted something into view, it was black and A4-sized. Vince reached out for it but Alan hesitated, keeping it just out of reach. 'But I didn't, OK, give it to you, I mean. I can't lose my place in the Source Unit and Mark Hall will have me for this. You know about parallel sourcing, right?' All coppers did, Alan would know that, the question was more as a reminder for Vince.

'I do and I'll find a way,' he said. Put simply, whatever was in that file, Vince would need to find a way of knowing it that didn't involve Alan Miles and a hungover conversation in a pub car park. Vince couldn't know how difficult that was going to be, not at that moment.

Alan moved the folder close enough for Vince to grab before he could change his mind. It was nondescript, gloss-black plastic and he flipped it open hungrily to reveal four documents inside that were turned over to reveal blank backsides. He pulled them out, twisting them in one movement and instantly recognised the format. 'Intel reports?'

'Intel reports, yeah,' Alan called out from his car which was already moving away. It stopped suddenly, like he had stepped heavily on the brakes, his bloodshot eyes again meeting with Vince. 'Mark Hall has them too, he gets to ask me follow-up questions, but you don't. It won't do you no good anyway, that informant isn't on the books no more and we can't find her. I don't want to see you again, not here, not at work. This is all there is.' Alan's window whirred closed and the Skoda was quickly swallowed up by the soaking mist.

Vince's attention moved back to the file. It was only four pieces of paper, four separate pieces of intelligence that he read in a hurry. They were all from the same source and all graded $E,4,1$ — police coding that told him that the information he now had in his possession had been assessed as highly likely to be correct.

And if that was the case, Vince needed to get back to work.

CHAPTER 45

Amelia's phone woke her — a call, not an alarm. It was Margate custody, a juvenile had been arrested as part of an early morning drugs raid and they had asked for her to act as appropriate adult (of course they had) and could she come down. She confirmed that she could (of course she did) and the cheerful jailor told her not to rush, that the solicitors were currently all tied up and it wouldn't be until later in the morning. Amelia was relieved. It had been a late night. Even so, there was no way she was going to be able to get back to sleep. She swung her legs out, looking back over her shoulder to meet Russell's staring eyes locked on her from where he was still lying on his side.

'Jesus, Russell, you freaked me out!'

'Is that you going back in?' Russell said. 'On a Sunday!'

'Yeah, not for a couple of hours though, they were just making sure I'm available.'

'Good ol' Amelia's always available. You didn't finish 'til 1 a.m. down there last night.'

Amelia turned away from him to lie. 'It's the way it happens sometimes, you get two together just like that and then I'll have a week with nothing!' She snorted a laugh through her nose then allowed herself a grimace where she was still facing away. Too much.

'It was getting late last night, you were taking ages . . .' Russell said and Amelia sat still, waiting for a next part that didn't come.

'That time of night nothing runs quickly, you have to wait for a solicitor for a start; she looked like she had literally got out of bed to come in. Then the copper doing the interview went missing for like—'

'I called the number you gave me for custody.' Russell cut her dead and she bit her lip, this time waiting him out. 'I was worried about you, I had visions of you walking out into Saturday night idiots and getting into some sort of trouble, or . . . or worse. Sometimes I feel like I'm sitting here waiting for the cops to turn up at the door to tell me they found your body. Turns out I needn't have worried last night . . .' Another pause. She reckoned she could feel his glare in the spot between her shoulder blades. 'After all, I assume you were out with Tim. And we both know he will keep you safe.'

'Russell, I—'

'Whatever you say now, next, ever . . . no more lies. They just roll out of you, you do it so often, it's like it's second nature, like it's OK to sit there and lie to me. It isn't. It isn't normal, none of this is. Think about what you did.'

'What I did?' She turned back, he was still lying down, combined with his melancholy expression and watery eyes it made him look beaten, like life had knocked him down and there was no energy left in him to recover.

'You lied to me, then met your ex-husband while I babysat your grandkid so you could spend the evening with him.'

'It's not like that.'

'Like what?'

'Seedy, like I'm stealing an evening out with an ex, like I'm cheating. You know it's not like that with Tim.'

'So why tell me you were somewhere else?'

'The anniversary . . .' Amelia turned away again; time for more lying. Her hands fell together in her lap and she toyed with her fingers. 'It's just been a strange time, it's brought it all back.'

'*Back*? Doesn't something have to go away for it to come back?' She felt the mattress move where Russell shifted behind her. She fought to quell a surge of anger forming at him resenting her grief for her only daughter. It dissipated quickly — his resentment came from her lies. Her fault. It wasn't like she had a choice.

'You're right, but I guess grief is like that.' She turned to face where he sat up, his eyes still watery. 'Most of the time it's just this dull ache, always there, though there are some moments when I can forget it. Something will make me laugh on the tele, or I'll be with Jacob when he's being silly, or with you when you bring me a cup of tea and from nowhere you kiss me in that way you do sometimes, like I'm all that matters. But it comes back, that ache, always. Just recently though, it's been more, it really fucking hurts. It has to be the anniversary, the realisation that it's been three years since I saw her face, that I'm never going to see it ever again and you know what? *Ever* is a long, long time. This ache will only get better when I know what happened, for sure, I mean.'

'Where did you go? Back to the park?' The anger was out of his words.

'No . . .' Amelia's answer was instant, she stopped herself before another lie came out. She should at least stay close to the truth. 'We just went for a drive, we just talked, ended up some place called Sandwich! You don't forget the name of a place like that.' Another snort through her nose. 'I *was* with Tim, I needed to talk to someone and sometimes he's the only person I want to talk to about it. He's in the same boat, but it's not just that, it isn't fair to constantly put this on you.'

'It isn't fair to lie to me either.'

'You're right. I guess I didn't want you to worry, to even consider that this is anything more than two people helping each other through grief. He's nothing more than that to me, you do know that.'

Russell sighed long and heavy. 'Just don't lie to me, OK, you don't need to. If you want to talk to someone — even Tim — I don't care, but when you lie . . .'

'I know—' She had more to say but Russell grabbed her firmly by the shoulders to pull her onto him. She squealed, the last part muffled as he kissed her hard, and his hands moved, one to rest on her cheek, the other to gently hold the back of her head. He pulled away, locking on to her with a new intensity.

'Please . . . call that number that copper gave you, that inspector. Talk to someone off the record, talk to them about how you can get out of this situation. This constant worrying about you, about us all, I can't do it anymore. The only way we can all be safe is if you do something.'

Amelia shrugged him off, more laughter, dismissive this time as she took a few steps away, making sure she was back facing away so she could lie again.

'I will,' she said. 'Promise.'

CHAPTER 46

The house was empty by the time Vince made it back. Maddie would have gone in to work, dropping Sammy on her way where he was spending the day with Vince's mum at her insistence. Vince had known it was coming, his first time left alone, and he had been desperate for something to keep him occupied. He hadn't expected for a meeting with Alan Miles to give him the perfect solution.

'PC Arnold?' Eileen picked up on the first ring, then managed to contain a scolding entirely within his name.

'Eileen, are you with Mads?'

'Not at this moment. How can I help you?'

'Is Harry with you? What about Mark Hall, is he near?'

'PC Arnold,' she said, then paused like she was steadying herself, 'did you really just call me to ask the whereabouts of other people that you most certainly have direct numbers for?'

'No . . . sorry, no. I need to come in, I need to see the boss and Mads, but without being seen. Just for a few minutes.'

'I really don't think that's a good idea. We've all been told very strictly—'

'I reckon I know what you've been told. This is important, it's about the job, something that might make a difference.'

'What?'

'I can't tell you over the phone.'

'Email? Fax, posted letter? For your protection, you understand.'

Vince bit down hard on his first reply. 'Thanks for the advice. I'm coming in, it should be OK on a Sunday but I thought . . .' He struggled for his next words, the delay gave Eileen an opportunity to jump in.

'You thought we were friends now, allies even and I could cover for you?'

'At least direct me somewhere out of the way so I don't get kicked out or nicked . . .' When there was no answer, he continued. 'Please . . . I have to sort this out, that tea cosy, Eileen, it was *chilling*.' Laughter; concealed, but not enough and Vince knew he had a chance.

'We're not at Canterbury, we've had to head over to Margate. Ma'am Ives was tasked with finishing up with Liam Moran, seeing as no one else wanted to. He's come back from the hospital and she's in there as the scribe. They have a DC leading the interview, which didn't go down too well. Once Liam is kicked out, we have been told in no uncertain terms that our involvement is over. Mine already should be.'

'Kicked out?' Vince said.

'And very soon. They couldn't get enough to charge him so everyone's had a bit of a rocket to go out and find more.'

'Bail?' Vince said.

'With all due respect, I really shouldn't be—'

'You didn't, Eileen, if anyone asks! You can trust me.'

'Yes, then. With a condition of residence and a requirement to sign two times a week. It's only a seven-day bail.'

Seven days wasn't going to be long enough to find more evidence linking Liam Moran to a job he didn't do.

'Do you know where they're housing him?' Vince said.

'No. Seems there's a small circle of knowledge and I am very clearly on the outside.' Eileen's disappointment was clear.

'Is there a kettle?' Vince said.

'A kettle?'

'At Margate.'

There was more hesitation, Vince bit his lip, waiting to be scolded again as part of telling him to stay away.

'Dormant, unfortunately. No milk, see.'

Vince grinned into his phone. 'That sounds like an assistance shout, if ever I heard one!'

* * *

The journey took an hour, the traffic heavy and slowed by sporadic rain carried in the wind. Vince took the last space out the front of Margate Police Station, not even bothering to try the vehicle gate, being in no doubt that his access would have been removed. He stepped out into a gust that was part salt, two parts other-scents-of-the-sea. From his position, the ocean was visible as a scruffy expanse with breaking white froth. Two spaces over from him, a long van was ticking over, the side door slid open to show glimpses of a bench seat that faced away from the driver. The van was black in colour with all the windows tinted to the point where he could make out the shapes of men, but none of their detail. Vince ducked back in where he had left a pint of milk on the passenger seat and started his walk towards the entrance with the bottle swinging on his finger. At almost the same time a man was pushed out of the entrance in a wheelchair that seemed an obvious match for the idling van.

Liam Moran.

Vince should have stopped right there, turned back even, to sit in his car until he was gone — at least changed direction. Vince's hood was up, he had a hold of it in the wind and ducked away as best he could but it didn't make a difference. Vince's walk might have looked like a swagger, like he was mocking the man he was responsible for putting in that chair, but it was unintentional, his strides stiff-legged with tension. Liam clocked him just as they crossed, Vince trying not to look at him directly but aware that he turned in a jerked movement for a shout to follow. Ahead, Maddie had appeared to stand at the entrance door, her crossed arms and expression leaking her fury. In any other circumstance her direction was not the best way to walk.

In any other circumstance.

Vince locked on to her and, for a moment, he didn't think she was going to move out of his way. Moran's shouts were as nonsensical as they were livid: profanities jumbled with threats, his rage too much for structured sentences and Vince couldn't resist turning back to face him. Beside the van, Vince saw a tall, slim man in a fitted suit, holding a phone like he was taking a picture of Vince — the Moran solicitor, it had to be. Vince gestured with the pint of milk like it was lager and he was greeting a friend across a pub.

'What the hell are you doing here, Vince?' Maddie hissed.

'Eileen said there was a kettle.'

'Jesus Christ!' Maddie set off at a pace that had Vince clawing to catch the internal doors she was opening with her card, aware that he couldn't. It was two doors and a short corridor until they made the stairs and she took two at a time, getting off at the first floor. Here she stomped all the way down a central corridor to an extended part at the back, through double doors marked *CID* that clattered open for Maddie, then for Vince — only he, it seemed, was dragging a sound-deadening cloak behind in with him.

The whole office stopped.

You don't realise just how loud typing, clicking of mouses and the *whirr-kerchunk* of a photocopier can be until it is all sucked out of a room at once. Vince kept his head down, delighted that following Maddie meant moving into a side room. It was small and with no windows, the only light source the numerous monitors that cast just enough glow for him to make out a silent stare over the top of a pair of reading glasses.

'Eileen!'

'PC Arnold,' she replied, 'and you remembered the milk.'

'Yes, he remembered the milk,' Maddie said, the word *milk* hissed out of her by the force of her flop into her chair. 'And showed it to Liam Moran's solicitor, so, having literally just listened to his complaint about how both his client's legs were broken as part of his arrest — and that's before we talk about the burning car — that I am forced to assure him we are taking very seriously, the man suspended for causing that mess turns up for a lovely cup of tea.'

'If you're offering,' Vince said and Maddie shot him a warning look that could have boiled a kettle right there and then. Eileen saw it too, she got to her feet, picking the milk up off the table on her way out. Vince's grin fell away.

'What the hell are you playing at?' Maddie's tone was different again, resigned almost, like she was at the end of her tether. Vince might have preferred angry.

'My job,' he said. 'I can't just sit on my hands at home.'

'Tough shit, Vince, that's what suspended means.'

Vince had an answer, it was something about how she knew him better than that, but he wasn't going to get his chance to give it. Harry Blaker crashed through the door, seemingly to stop and stare.

'Boss,' Vince said.

'I didn't believe her; I didn't believe you would really be that stupid. You can't be here.'

'I can't not be here!'

'You're suspended, that means you're in enough trouble already. I've just ignored a call from the superintendent on his day off; word's out, this isn't about you getting in trouble, Vince, this is about me and Maddie not being able to control our staff.'

'I'm not your staff,' Vince said, then put his palms out in surrender. 'I get it, I know. But you two aren't supposed to be having anything to do with the investigation either, so what's all this?' He gestured at the darkened wall behind Maddie that was covered in case material.

'Eileen,' Harry huffed. 'She's trying to stay up to date. At least we were sensible enough to hide it in here. We got told to bail out the prime suspect because no one else wanted to deal with Liam Moran at his worst and now we're done. Hall has reassignment plans for us that probably involve looking for badly parked cars.'

Vince had been studying the material more closely, he had stopped on a picture. It was hand-drawn, bright blocks of colour and glitter all but obliterated by thick stripes of darkness. The style identical to what Angie had sent to his phone.

Eileen reappeared walking backwards, then spun to reveal hands full of tea.

'Kettle had just boiled,' she explained. 'Mr Hall called when I had my hands full. What do I do if he calls again?'

'The same thing I've been doing,' Harry growled. 'Ignore it for now.'

'What's this?' There was a photo laid out on Eileen's desk, Harry was squinting at it like it was his first time seeing it.

'Ah!' Eileen said, suddenly delighted, the teas abandoned on the tabletop. 'Charley Mace came here while you were dealing with Mr Moran. She said she had mentioned these to Ma'am Ives and wanted to drop them over personally.'

'And you told her that we're not working the case any-more and that everything has to go to Mark Hall?' Harry said.

'She knows that already,' Maddie answered. 'But I thought this was something you should see.'

'Me specifically?' Harry moved to take it in closer, Vince did the same. It was a photo of the inside of a family home; not the Mercer home, Vince was sure of that, which meant it had to be from the Blackman place. The photo contained a number of yellow, numbered triangles used by CSI to mark anything of significance. One was showing a ruby-coloured stain on the wooden flooring, another was by a door in a cupboard fitted under stairs that was swinging open. 'What is this?'

'That is Charley shooting down your theory,' Maddie said, her tone casual enough to be irritating.

'My theory?' Harry said.

'The one you dragged her out to the Mercer house for. It was *our* theory for a while, I suppose, I thought you might have been onto something.'

'Can you be more specific?' Harry said.

'We were running with the idea that Jade Mercer had been hammered under the floorboards as a torture method, torture for Jade *and* her mother. A way of getting information.'

'This isn't Jade's house.' Harry said.

'It isn't. What it is, is a neatly stacked cupboard.' Maddie slurped at her tea and even for Vince listening in, it was maddening and it was deliberate.

'And what does a neatly stacked cupboard mean?' Harry said.

'Time!' Maddie said, apparently enjoying herself. 'Look at the stacked items in the right cupboard.'

Harry did, Vince did too. He could make out boxes in two neat stacks, high enough for the coats hanging above to fall over them. Some of the boxes had liveries on the side that he recognised as classic board games: *Operation, Guess Who?*

'Board games, so what?' It was Harry that asked the question.

'And on the left side?' Maddie said.

'The left side, I don't see anything on the left side?'

'There isn't anything in the left cupboard, which is where Sandy Louise Blackman's fingernails were found, it was where she hid. Those boxes looked out of place to Charley and I have to agree. They have a grown-up kid who lives away so no need for quick access to *Guess Who?*, which means they would normally be stored in the smallest part of the cupboard on the left, the least convenient part, used maybe on the odd Christmas Day. You can't see what's behind those stacked games, but Charley tells me it's a shoe rack, something that would be constantly in use.'

'So, this woman moved the games to hide in a cupboard?' Vince cut in, trying to work out what was going on and why it was relevant.

'No, she didn't,' Harry said, his speech like a penny had dropped.

'In reaction to a door knock?' Maddie continued. 'How long would that take? And look at how they are stacked, that's not someone panicking, that's someone who prepared it as a place to hide in advance.'

'Yes, it is,' Harry agreed.

'Which makes it very likely that Maria Mercer hid her daughter under the floorboards. Jade wasn't forced there at all.'

'She was bruised,' Vince said, lifting his eyes to meet with Maddie's, his words lacking conviction where everyone else in the room seemed to be a step ahead of him.

'She was, but not badly. When it came to it, her mother might have needed to apply some force and they would both have been panicking. We know Maria had some damp work done not so long ago, she would have seen the floorboards up, the space underneath. As far as hiding places go, it's the last place I would think to look for someone.'

'They knew it was coming.' Harry's growl rumbled with anger. 'Both families.'

'They did. Do you remember what Angie said Jade was having nightmares about, what she was calling out?'

'The drill.'

'*Drill*, that's another word for *practice*,' Maddie said. 'Those boards probably lay loose for however long they've known about this threat, then, when it arrived, she used the nails and hammer we found to hide Jade. That was why we only found Maria Mercer's traces on that hammer and why it was screws everywhere else. That could also explain why it all happened in that room, Maria might have changed her mind and tried to get to Jade, or even used her own body as another layer of concealment, making sure she laid over the top of her.

'Jesus,' Vince said, ignoring Eileen's disapproving glare. 'These two families musta been mixed up in something big, something to do with the Morans and you were just about to

287

find out what.' Vince felt overwhelmed again, his emotions now a tap that was either off or fully on.

'Maybe. Maybe not,' Maddie said, but he knew what she really meant.

'Whatever we were going to get from Liam or his dad is gone, all we have now is silence from that family, from everyone around them too, I bet. We've got nothing,' Harry said.

'Not necessarily,' Vince said. The intelligence reports handed to him by Alan Miles were folded over in his inside pocket. He took them out and dropped the first of them on the desk. It was Eileen who reacted fastest when Vince's money would have been on Maddie. She stared right at him to ask:

'Who on earth is Kayla Goodyer?'

CHAPTER 47

Amelia wasn't prepared for Liam Moran to appear, just like that and *right in front of her*! The rage was so quick it caught her out, sitting her straight in her car and scraping her knuckles off the door handle in her haste to get out. She got as far as standing up, one foot out, but maybe it was the door knocking into her chest where it was caught in a gust, or that the solid rain drops were like a slap to the face, that stopped her long enough to think again. Her change of mind was prompted by the woman standing in the doorway like she was watching Liam leave — Maddie Ives. Amelia remembered her interviewing Connor Docker, how she had been like a dog with a bone despite the fact she was interviewing a child. She had been sharp too, sharp enough that Amelia couldn't risk her seeing a reaction to Liam Moran.

She ducked away. Maddie Ives only seemed to have eyes for straight ahead anyway. Liam Moran was distracted too, his attention on a figure who was walking towards him, hood up, the side of which was scrunched up in a fist where the wind toyed with it.

The two men passed. The hooded man continued making straight for Maddie Ives and Amelia dared to sit a little straighter for a better view. The hooded man was holding milk, he used it to make a gesture aimed at Liam, his half turn enough for Amelia to see enough of his face.

The copper from the news?

Local news at least: front and centre, the man who had run Liam Moran off the road in a police chase and was suspended as a result. So what was he doing here at the same time? Liam's reaction left her in no doubt it was unexpected. His voice was squeezed higher to penetrate her sealed car, even as the rain started to pour down heavily again. Profanities mostly, angry threats too while he pushed himself to the very front edge of his wheelchair. He flailed his arms, his legs were locked out straight under trousers to make him look ridiculous. Amelia dipped her window just an inch, enough to be sure she could hear every word. The man that had caused the upset disappeared into the police station, but still Liam continued with his threats and foul language. There was no reaction, no entourage of uniform bobbies to come out and meet the aggression, just a cold, stone frontage lashed in rain.

This was a side of Liam Moran that flew in the face of what she had been told, of what she had built up in her mind. He was beside himself, out of control and she watched him lash out at two men trying to lift him into the side door of the van. The impression of a cold, calculated and careful killer was melting in the rain in front of her.

'He's nothing!' She spoke out into the interior of her car, her throat dry, the voice someone else's. Her eyes fell to the ignition and the keyring that hung from it, containing the last picture ever taken of Kayla. The side door to the black van slid closed and the van moved smoothly forwards.

Amelia Chagrin followed.

As previously, an idea formed in her mind, an opportunity and she had started to trust her instincts all the more. This was an opportunity that was only possible if she knew where the injured Liam Moran was going to be staying, however. It might even be with his dad, back in the family home. She smiled to herself at the thought of the two of them together, one in constant pain with his legs useless and broken, the other only able to stand up out of his chair with the aid of a walking stick. A wave of excitement had her laughing out loud.

The Moran family would never be this vulnerable again.

CHAPTER 48

Intelligence Grading E,4,1

17 March 2018

SOURCE INTELLIGENCE — SENSITIVE

Kayla Goodyer 02/02/1997 is handling money on behalf of County Line gangs operating in Kent. She collects and distributes cash made by street dealers. She swaps her vehicles regularly but is careful that all documentation is correct.

Kayla Goodyer is of no fixed abode.

Kayla Goodyer is aware that she is currently reported missing by her mother, Amelia Goodyer 15/04/1981, but DOES NOT want police to update Amelia with any information on her whereabouts, or that police have spoken with her.

Kayla Goodyer performs this role under duress.

END.

Vince had put the first sheet down and then stepped back like it was the first ultrasound and he was the proud and expectant father. Maddie responded next.

'OK, so this is a new name to us.'

Vince put the second intelligence report down on the table and the room fell silent again.

Intelligence Grading E,4,1

SOURCE INTELLIGENCE — SENSITIVE

1 September 2019

Kayla Goodyer is regularly carrying cash sums of £50,000 or more concealed in the spare wheel bay in the rear of a small van. This has been adapted to a false floor. This is money earned by a County Line gang operating in the Thanet area. Liam Moran is leading the line in Kent on behalf of London based nominals. Liam Moran uses juveniles as street dealers, solely males, and all are recruited and operate close to their home addresses.

Kayla Goodyer works with a locally based accountant she knows only as 'Mr Black', white male, mid fifties, local accent, balding hair and dark features. Mr Black is responsible for moving the cash into a legitimate stream. He will direct her to locations where she pays over sums.

Kayla Goodyer performs this role under duress and believes her life is at risk if she refuses. She also fears that other criminals have knowledge of her role and she could be targeted.

Safeguarding advice to be recorded separate from this report.

END.

'Mr Black,' Maddie uttered, 'Ron Blackman.'

'Washing their money,' Harry said. Vince was almost enjoying himself as he produced a third sheet to lay on top of the other two for silence to fall over the huddle again.

Intelligence Grading E,4,1

SOURCE INTELLIGENCE — SENSITIVE

2 November 2019

Kayla Goodyer recently paid a senior member of Kent County Council's Planning and Land Consultation Board the sum of £100,000 in cash.

Kayla believes she is under threat of being violently assaulted as members of a rival gang have become aware of her role.

Safeguarding advice to be recorded separate from this report.

END.

'Maria Mercer?' Eileen said.

'I think it has to be,' Maddie said and Vince was aware she was looking at him expectantly.

'The last one,' he said, then placed down his fourth printed piece of paper.

Intelligence Grading E,4,1

SOURCE INTELLIGENCE — SENSITIVE

17 June 2020

Liam MORAN is identified as being at risk of serious harm. He is known to regularly be moving large amounts of cash through county lines. Rival gangs pose a threat, either to seriously assault MORAN or to plant evidence that will see

*him removed from the streets. It is believed that the preference
is for MORAN to be murdered in prison.*

*OSMAN warning OSM/W/112/2020 issued and coun-
tersigned with no response.*

END.

'Osman warning?' Eileen said, 'I've heard that before.'

'You'll hear it again, too,' Maddie said. 'R V Osman
is now part of case law, has been since 1998. If the police
get to hear about a credible threat to life, we have to let the
supposed victim know, by law.

'And we did? Let Liam Moran know, I mean.'

'We must have. *Countersigned* means by him, *no response*
means he had nothing to say about it.'

'Is that it, or have you got any more case-breaking material tucked in your jacket?' Maddie turned back on Vince.

'Sorry, Mads, all out. And as far as anyone else is concerned, I never did have, yeah? We all need to find another
way of knowing this, a way that isn't me being handed it in
a pub car park.'

'Been keeping your head down and staying out of trouble since your suspension, have you?' Harry said and Vince
recognised the need to stay quiet.

'Pub car park . . .' Eileen said, 'wouldn't happen to be
the Crown, Nackington, would it?'

'My memory ain't what it used to be.' Vince grinned,
though it dropped away when he saw Maddie's expression,
one she was flicking between him and Eileen.

'What's been going on?' she demanded, the question
aimed more at Eileen who shrugged it off.

'Depends, PC Arnold and I have either been pursuing
relevant lines of enquiry or discussing the best places for a
quiet drink of an evening. Some places are worse for gossip
than others.' There was a twinkle of mischief under those
reading glasses that Vince loved to see.

'Source Unit?' Harry said.

'The skipper in there. He's having a tough time out of work at the moment, it seems, drinking a bit too much.'

'And you took advantage?' Maddie snapped. 'Jesus, Vince, there's no self-preservation with you, is there?'

'He was stone-cold sober when he gave me this!' Vince was indignant. 'And don't tell me you wouldn't do the same for a break in this case, for a break in any case! All the attention is on Moran, but they need to be looking beyond, there's a bigger picture here, this tells us there is. I can't run with this and not because I'm suspended, because I don't have a clue what I'm doing! So, I came here.'

'Mark Hall will have this same intelligence, which means he will be acting on it anyway, right?' Eileen said.

'Mark Hall has enough to stick this all on Moran and to look no further. From what I'm hearing, he's happy to do that.' Maddie sighed.

'Why would he not want to take this further?'

'Because the successful prosecution of Liam Moran is quick and easy, two words that sum up Mark Hall and his career to this point. And he would be the hero swooping in and clearing up a mess *and* he will take out one of Kent's most notorious with it. No way he'll risk expanding an investigation he wants to shut down as soon as possible and that might give him a different result.'

'If you were still running this investigation, what would be your next move?' Eileen said.

'Arrest Andrew Harding for money laundering,' Maddie said, without hesitation. 'And force his family into police protection so he understands his situation. I met him and trust me, he folds under that sort of pressure and gives us the next place to go.'

'That sounds easy enough, maybe Hall will do that?' Vince offered but Harry was already shaking his head.

'He won't. Blackman isn't actually named for a start and Maddie was given access to their email system and their books with no argument. You could argue that he's been assisting with

296

our enquiries. Arrest is hard to justify, what you might call a *Maddie Move*.' Harry met eyes with his colleague. 'No offence.'

'I take it as a compliment,' Maddie said, then rubbed at her face like she was getting agitated. 'George Moran was right.' She turned away to pace the dim room. 'Liam's running drug supply for a County Line and he was using our victims, he didn't rob their houses and murder them. Why would he? They're part of the same enterprise. This intelligence states that he paid one of the victims a lot of money to be useful. She's no use dead.'

'Even if the Super goes for Moran with this, there's not enough to convict him, is there?' Vince said.

'No. He's scrambled all his troops to find out what they can. I think he intends to get him remanded at least, then it won't matter when the case falls apart further down the line as the press attention will have moved on to something else and he can still claim to have led Major Crime through a difficult time. He'll have someone to blame, too.'

'You mean us,' Maddie said.

'There has to be something we can do! Sir, you have a lot of influence, I've seen that. Is there no way you can get to those above Mr Hall and make them aware? Perhaps even be put back in charge of the investigation?' Eileen said.

'No,' Harry said. 'Not judging by the tone of the conversations I've had since Vince kicked a door in that no one knew about.'

'Sorry, boss.' Vince could feel himself burning up.

'I was right and I was just about to prove it,' Maddie said, suddenly animated. 'I still could, too . . .' She reached back down to snatch up one of the reports. 'But we can't do a damned thing. I can't even do a simple search on any police system for, say . . .' Maddie lifted the paper to read a name, 'Amelia Goodyer, whoever the hell that is. Hall is monitoring all of our system usage so the moment we do that, he'll know we have intelligence we shouldn't have. We can't do a thing!'

'Actually . . .' Eileen said, for the attention of the whole room to fix on her. 'The misper system is web-based. It is accessed via the Intranet, but still based out there on the world wide web.' Eileen's excitement seemed to be growing with every word. They meant nothing to Vince.

'And that's a good thing?' Harry said.

'The internal police systems have inbuilt programmes to log key strokes, we all know that from what we signed as part of our contract, it tells us directly that every action is traceable.' Vince nodded, despite having never really having taken the time to read what he was signing. 'All they have to do behind the scenes is put in your username and it shows them every key you have ever pressed. But anything run via an external website doesn't have that.'

'Please, Eileen, for one moment pretend I'm stupid,' Harry said.

'I'll try . . .' Eileen said, then composed herself. 'Use a police system like HOLMES or PNC and every action is logged against your username, it's inbuilt into that system. Use a web-based system that has an external server however and you *can* still be monitored in real time, but only if you're using a system computer. One that is plumbed into the police network.'

'Eileen, the point!' Maddie got in just as Eileen was really starting to enjoy herself.

'The missing persons system is hosted externally,' Eileen huffed. 'It's a website. The intel report says that this Kayla Goodyer was reported missing so we can at least access that report. I know it's not exactly—'

'But we look at people's computers all the time and we can tell what they've been looking at and when.' Maddie got a glare for cutting Eileen off.

'Yes, when we know to. But if I was out using a laptop on some coffee shop WiFi, I could access a limited amount of information and no one would ever know.'

'Are you talking about breaking rules, Eileen?' Harry seemed to be containing a smile.

'I am talking about solving a murder,' she said. 'For example, there's a Kayla Goodyer mentioned as the source for this information, so if we can find her—'

'Assuming Mark Hall hasn't done that already.'

'He's tried and failed.' Vince suddenly recalled what Alan Miles had said to him in the car, it made sense now: *Mark Hall has them too, he gets to ask me follow-up questions but you don't. It won't do you no good anyway, that informant isn't on the books no more and we can't find her.* 'Alan Miles just about told me as much.'

'Ah yes, but he never tasked me!' Eileen said, with more than a hint of arrogance. She was already taking her laptop out from its carry case. She lifted the lid, then fiddled with her mobile phone. 'I'll have a quick look here, I can hotspot from my phone and stay off the network, it's not the quickest but it will give us an idea if there's going to be anything of use.'

It took a few minutes to get up and running. Maddie went back to pacing. Eileen's fingers were a blur of keystrokes the moment the misper system came up. She opened the record labelled *Kayla GOODYER* and it came with an image. Kayla's cheeks were sunken, she looked a little too skinny and her pallor was creamy white to stand out against a woodland background. Overall, she looked exhausted, her smile half-hearted.

'She looks familiar,' Maddie said. 'I can't place her, though.'

'Looks like a user,' Harry said.

'She is.' Eileen was scrolling through a block of text, the movement too fast for Vince to keep up. 'Class A, suspected heroin user. Regular misper when she was young enough to live with someone who could report her. This was the first report in a couple of years, but it's from the same source as the others: *Amelia Goodyer.* Her mother.'

'They would have spoken to her already, that would be the first thing I would do,' Maddie said.

'Which means we can too,' Harry said.

'Does it?'

'If we were to beat Hall to her then he finds out we've spoken to her the instant he turns up, but if he's been there already—'

299

'Then he never gets to know!' Eileen sang her words to cut over Harry.

'Maybe.'

The printer came to life with a clunk, a piece of paper rolled through it almost without stopping. Eileen scooped it up to thrust it at Harry.

'The home address from two years ago when she last made a report. With a bit of luck she'll still be there. If she isn't, call me and I might have another option by then.' Harry took the paper off her. 'I thought I should print it, rather than send it to your phone. Leave no trace,' she said, her enjoyment clear as she rocked up onto her toes, toes that were still pushed into dusky pink slippers.

'Good thinking,' Harry said. Maddie was scooping up the keys to the car.

'What can I do?' Vince said, the excitement that had suddenly grown in the room enough to sweep him up for a moment.

'Go home, Vince,' Harry said.

'I'll keep you informed, but you have to stay away,' Maddie added, her head cocked to one side, her voice that of a parent speaking to a child.

'I can be useful. Angie McIlhenny sent me a photo, Jade's been doing more drawing, like you have up on the wall, there might be something in that, I can go round and—'

'We've been already, Angie knows to call us with anything relevant. You can't be out on police enquiries, Vince, you know that.'

Vince did know that, but it didn't stop him burning with frustration, anger even at Maddie dismissing him. 'The face she drew, typical kid's drawing, but she might have been trying to draw something distinctive, she needs asking about it.'

'Face?' Maddie snapped back on him, Harry did too.

'A face, yeah. Kid's drawing, but . . .' Vince took his phone out to bring the message back up. Again, he tried and failed at pinching and zooming. 'It's probably nothing . . .' he said, now doubting himself with the two detectives looming over him. 'Just a blob of yellow, a bit o' pink and then one eye's different, shaped like a keyhole.' Maddie took the photo off him. 'At least I think so,' he said, aware that he was now lacking conviction.

Maddie showed it to Harry who took a moment. 'She's a kid and hardly an artist. You're right, she needs speaking to about it,' he said and flickered a smile, then Maddie did too. They were back to parents reassuring a child.

'Can you make this bigger and print it? We'll head over there too,' Harry said.

'Of course!' Eileen replied. 'I'll do some social media snooping too. No one can trace me if I'm using my own logins . . .' She rubbed at her chin in thinking stance. 'But it's no good here, I could go out and find some decent WiFi. And maybe a sweet Americano!' She was back to delighted again.

'Do what you can,' Harry said, 'and be careful.' He lifted the printed sheet of paper. 'Tim and Amelia Goodyer,' he read out, 'let's hope you can give us something.'

CHAPTER 49

The black van had taken it easy, driving smoothly to get up to speed, no overtaking, no sudden diversions, no chance of throwing around a wheelchair-based occupant and no idea that someone was following. It had been simple.

Amelia slowed down when it pulled into a housing estate. The properties were all similar in style, most semi-detached, bunched together in twos, but the van continued through until it reached the outskirts and properties that were a little more spread out. It slowed in front of a detached place — the only house among bungalows — the brake lights glowing a deep red through the rain that had become persistent and Amelia kept her speed constant as she continued past. No one was taking any notice of her anyway, she was confident of that. She even dared cast a glance over at the house to see a snippet of an untidy lawn, long enough for the grass to be leaning over where it was heavy with moisture. She got a broken-down fence too, yellow patches in the lawn and a child's slide, its bright red steps and yellow top barely visible. She also saw untidy bins, one fallen into a lean against the other, both with a big white number painted on their sides: 54.

The rain was heavy enough to keep everyone's head down, their focus on the van's sliding door on the pavement side and Amelia felt confident enough to do another drive-by. She turned off to spin the car round out of sight. By the time she was back to the junction she had a distant view of a wheelchair being pushed up a concrete path that split the unkempt grass up the middle.

But the biggest reward for seizing her opportunity was yet to come.

She pulled away evenly, building her speed like anyone might when making their way out of a housing estate. She needed to look to her right this time, the wheelchair had made it to the door, it was being manoeuvred around a thick, wooden post that supported the first-floor overhang. Two other people had now appeared at the door: George Moran was one, his arms by his side were slim, his bulk wasting away under a vest now a size too large, his right hand gripping the door surround like it might be keeping him up. Next to him a man with a larger build stepped out, sideways so he would fit, wearing a long coat with deep pockets over dark trousers. He moved towards the wheelchair but reacted to an angry gesture from Liam that spun him away and had him walking back towards the house. His turn gave her a view of him from the back, of his long, black jacket and dark trousers, of the back of his black boots and the glimpse of a red circle on the heel.

It was enough for the penny to drop.

'They're onto us,' she said out loud, 'they're fucking onto us!' She sang it this time, a strange feeling of delight flooding through her. The man in the jacket had been outside her house. He'd run away, punching her in the gut as part of his escape. She knew why, too. Someone had dropped a drug-dealing phone outside of a home where the occupants had been murdered. Someone had also taken Liam Moran's hire car, the one he used daily, and parked it up outside an accountants' place with the murder weapon wrapped up tight in the boot. A trail of breadcrumbs that was meant to lead Liam to prison, away from his father — divide and conquer. This whole time she had been working towards getting George on his own; George Moran: old, weak, vulnerable. She had failed, the police had let Liam back out and, it seemed, the Moran family were closer to her than she had realised, close enough to be watching her home, planning their own invasion perhaps.

But she had all the cards now, all the power. She could feel it, it was back and even more intoxicating. The big man in the jacket hadn't come knocking on her door, he had run away, maybe to regroup, to come back stronger. But they had got *weaker* since then!

Both of them.

But this was not an advantage that would last long. Amelia's mind was racing. She would need something to make it work: money, a lot of it and quickly. She clicked her fingers, laughed out into the cabin as she rolled up to the stop lines on the edge of the housing estate. She had an idea, someone who could give her what she needed, even if they were going to need some persuasion.

CHAPTER 50

Amelia smacked the door as hard as she could, taking two steps away in the same movement, her eyes all over its grimy, scuffed surface. It was a basement flat just off Athelstan Road, Margate. The steps down to it were tight and even she, at five foot four, needed to stoop. There was a window next to the door, the net curtains that filled it seemed to be in direct competition with the pane of glass as to which one could hold the most filth. A sound came from the other side, subtle but definite.

'Connor!' Amelia leaned in to hiss at the door. 'Connor, you gotta let me in! They're after me!' She thumped the door again, it opened as she hit it a second time; just a fraction, enough to make out Connor Docker staring out.

'What are you on about?'

'I'm in shit here!' Amelia hissed. 'This is the only place I know to go. You gotta let me in!'

'Can't be doing that, ain't no one comes in here.' The door shut, 'get gone' called through it.

Amelia leaned back in. 'One word from me and you know what happens. I say one word, how you sat in that station and you arranged to talk to someone official without me present and you know what happens. It won't be me running away, looking for a place to hide!'

The door made more noise. It didn't move, not at first, but it was the sound of someone unlocking it at least. Amelia resisted the urge to kick it, waiting instead for Connor to pull it open. He did so wider this time, wide enough that she could see he was dressed in a black tracksuit with gold stripes down the side, his top was hooded, his feet in white socks that looked bright against the bottoms and navy sliders. He had a phone in his hand, it looked cheap, no doubt the one he was running his business on for the day. She moved forward, chancing it, but Connor held his ground.

'You wouldn't do that, I know you wouldn't. You're all about keeping us safe, you always tell me that. And I don't take you for no liar.'

'And now you gotta keep me safe!' Amelia retorted. 'Someone else was with me, I gotta get out of sight but he knows to come here. When he does, let him in.' This time her move forward was more aggressive, pushing past Connor who was caught a little off balance and he shouldered the wall.

'Someone else, who else you been telling about this place?' Connor demanded, slamming the door behind her.

'Look, if they get caught, I get caught, OK? Liam's got me on errands, someone picked up on it, some rival and they rushed me. I don't know what they want but Liam would want you to look after me here.'

'He won't want this place found! Do you know what this is, what's here? If someone finds this place there'll be all types of shit.'

'Is the money here?' Amelia widened her eyes. 'Shit, it is, isn't it!?'

'Yeah, the fucking money's here!'

'Shit!' Amelia said again, then pulled her phone out of her pocket. She pressed to send a message that had been prepped, then lifted it to her ear for show. As she did so, she carried on talking to Connor. 'I'll find out where he is, tell him to go somewhere else.'

There was a knock on the door. Connor spun to it, his limbs hung stiff and straight, then he mouthed words of panic over at her, something like *What do we do now*? She put her phone away to hiss back:

'That's him, we can't send him away now, they might be right on him. Let him in!'

Connor reached for the handle. It was polished metal, there were several locks all the way up the door, all of which looked brand new. He hesitated, turning back to Amelia who jerked a nod of encouragement. 'There's no time,' she hissed. He twisted the handle. The door came in at him all at once and he stumbled backwards, his hand lifting to his nose as he cried out in pain. Amelia grabbed his hood, yanking it hard to further unsettle him and his stumble turned into a fall. Tim bundled through the door in front of him and was instantly on the attack. Connor Docker had no chance to defend himself. The blows were quick, the sounds of something heavy hitting his chest and his raised arms. Then a blow made contact with his head and he ceased all resistance. Tim leaned over him, a stubby, blunt weapon still gripped tight in his fist, waiting for any movement from the floor. There was nothing more than a moan that faded away and Tim took it as a cue to look up at his ex-wife, a spark of something in his eyes quick to die back to cold. His whole body seemed to be moving in and out as he caught his breath.

'It's here,' she said.

'Where?' Tim replied.

'He didn't tell me exactly and I could hardly ask. But it's here.'

'How long do we have?'

Amelia knelt down, she took hold of Connor's head, pulling it back so he wouldn't swallow his own tongue, feeling slightly disturbed by his fluttering eyelids and the rolling movement behind them. She patted him down, pocketing both the phones she found on him. 'Who knows,' she said. 'Not long.'

Seven minutes. That was how long they took and it was perfect timing. By the time the money was located in a zipped compartment sewed into the underneath of a single-seater sofa chair, Connor had reset enough to try out movements. His eyes still rolled in their sockets, his voice back only as moans, but he could be back with them at any moment. Amelia stepped over him on her way out. The money was in a cheap nylon holdall, black with a blue motif on its side. She didn't count it, there was no point.

It would be enough.

CHAPTER 51

'What are you doing here?' The voice was from an upstairs window on the right side of the first floor, the side where Maddie was standing and she stepped towards it, out from under the porch she and Harry had huddled under to shelter from the heavy rain.

'Police, we just need to speak to you if possible,' she replied, her tone pleasant to counter the aggression in his.

'What about?'

'Do you mind if we do this inside?' Harry snapped, his tone not pleasant. 'I'm getting soaked here!' He stepped out into view for the rain to beat out a tune on his waxed jacket and the eyes of the man hanging out of the window shifted to take him in.

'Oh . . . it's you. Did she . . . did she call you, then?' His aggression was all gone.

Maddie fixed on Harry whose face didn't change. 'I'm trying to get hold of her, is she in?' he replied.

'No, but hang on . . .' And then he was gone. The window slammed shut and the only sound was the falling rain. Both officers got back under the cover of the porch.

'She called you?' Maddie said.

'No idea what he's talking about.' Harry shrugged.

The door opened and Maddie half expected the man to swear, admit his mistake and slam it shut again. But it didn't happen. Instead, he nodded at Harry like he was right on time for an appointment and stepped to the side to show them both in.

'Did you know what she wanted to talk about or should I come back when she's here?' Harry said.

'I'm not sure she will come back, to be honest. She went out last night, said she was at work but I know she was with Tim.' He spun away to set off at pace, giving Maddie an opportunity to whisper.

'That isn't *Tim*, then.' Which had Harry shrugging again.

The man had headed to the back of the house and they found him leaning on the kitchen side, shaking his head and huffing like someone struggling for a place to start. There was another internal door, large with an arch over the top and it led into a living room that was dark from pulled curtains, dark enough for the TV that faced them to dictate the flicker of the whole room: cartoons, the sound right down.

'Are you OK?' Harry said. 'And I'm sorry, but she didn't mention anyone else . . . ?'

'Russell,' he said, picking up on the question in Harry's tone. 'Russell Southam. I'm her boyfriend.' He snorted enthusiastically like the idea was ridiculous. 'For now, at least. I just don't know what's going on with her. And you know what?' He stood straighter, his expression suddenly stern. 'It might do me a favour if she walked back to that prick. Just a bit of a piss-take that I'm here looking after their grandkid while they're out rekindling the old flame. It has to be that, why lie about it otherwise?'

'And she didn't tell you that we were coming round?' Harry was clearly still bluffing — and it was clearly still working.

'No. She's at work again today, I heard her take the call for this one so I know that's where she went. She should be back by now but you can never tell. You know that better than me!' He forced a laugh and Harry reacted with a subtle smile.

'You seem to have an idea what she needs to talk to me about, though?' Harry said.

'I . . . it's better coming from her. I told her to call you a couple of times, this isn't just about her, see, this is about me and Jacob in there. She got mixed up with the wrong people, that's all, it happens.'

'Like her daughter.' Maddie now took a turn at chancing her arm. The man calling himself Russell turned to her so fast he had to adjust his feet to keep his balance.

'Well, of course you would know all about her. That was where it started, Kayla got herself in deep with people that you can't trust as far as you can throw, I'd never say it to Amelia, but I'm not surprised she ended up dead.'

Maddie hid her reaction, not that it mattered — Russell was lost in his own thoughts, his eyes cast down to the pitted tiles.

'Kayla's dead?' Maddie prompted. 'And you know that for sure?'

'Oh sure, she's *missing*, right.' Russell made the bunny-ears symbol around the word *missing*. 'The official line from the police, but you lot don't seem bothered enough to do a bit of legwork and put us all out of our misery. Her and Tim, though . . . finding out what happened, it's become this obsession. I mean, I get it, you'd want to know, but there are some places I wouldn't go to find out.'

'Like where?' Harry said.

'Like getting close to the wrong sort of people on purpose, just so you can get your answers. That doesn't end well, not well at all. Now I'm sat here at night waiting for someone to kick our door down. You'll be back here, you mark my words and it will be me and Amelia you find stabbed up in our own home, just like what happened to those others on the news.' His agitation was peaking, he seemed to recognise it too and took a moment. Maddie waited, intent on saying as little as possible, knowing that her next word could be the one that showed this all up as a misunderstanding. 'The news said you lot were in trouble, Amelia thinks it's something to do with this case. Police brutality, they said?'

'Misunderstanding.' Harry accompanied it with a smile. 'We still need to be carrying on with our investigation. I came out because Amelia asked for me personally. I want to help.' His lie was flawless.

'It's not her fault. I mean, she approached them in the first place, she'll say that she didn't, but I know that's not true. I think she thought she could get close enough to get answers. But they don't know, OK, they don't know who she is!' Russell suddenly lifted panicked eyes to meet with both detectives in turn, like he was terrified that the police might tell whoever *they* were.

'You can trust us, we're here to help and to keep everyone safe,' Maddie said, doing her best to sound reassuring.

'They don't know she's Kayla's mum, this gang. And she's just a face, a reminder, that's all she does. She sits in on the interviews with their little wannabe drug dealers to make sure they know not to say nothing to you lot. She has to, you understand that, right? She has to do it, if she says no then who knows what they'll do. But someone's talking, that's what this is all about and it's a matter of time until they think it's her.' His panicked eyes were still hunting the floor, then lifted again to run over both officers.

'She sits in on interviews?' Harry said. 'Police interviews, you mean?'

'That's what appropriate adults do, isn't it? Don't tell me she's lying about that too?'

'Appropriate . . . of course!' Harry recovered. 'She didn't say much on the phone and I'm trying to understand . . .' He broke off and seemed to be looking around for something specific. 'Did she change her name, by chance? Maybe that's part of my confusion?'

Another snort of derision. 'Too many times. She was married as a Goodyer, told me she was going back to her maiden name, but then when Kayla . . . when all that happened she changed it to Chagrin. You tell me why. A lot of things I don't understand about her since . . . are you OK?'

Harry had turned away, taken a few steps too and didn't seem to be listening anymore. His attention was on a group of pictures on the wall, the frames made out of twisted steel that looped round to make up the rough outline of a butterfly. Maddie moved closer to see what he was looking at, close enough to see the photos were all of people. The top right was the largest, it showed a woman with a little boy she assumed to be the "Jacob" Russell had mentioned complete with a dripping moustache of whippy ice cream above a wide smile. The woman was smiling too, a length of her mousey brown hair was caught between her lips and the rest lifted by a breeze that might have been coming in off the sea that provided the backdrop. The eyes were smiling too, the unique, misshapen pupil prominent in the right eye adding to her intrigue.

Maddie had seen those eyes before.

She had seen that face too, even if the hair had been different, bleach blonde with . . . *a blob of yellow, a bit o' pink and then one eye like a keyhole*! Vince's description as they had been leaving the office; pretty much spot-on.

'Where is she, Russell?' Harry spoke, his voice strangled so she knew his realisation was the same.

'I don't know! This is what I've been telling you. She's probably with Tim again, probably winding each other up over Kayla, plotting some obscene revenge but with no one to take it out on, just like usual. She could be home any minute or she could be back over in fucking *Sandwich* or wherever it was she ended up!' He flapped his hands in exasperation.

'Sandwich?' Harry said when Maddie couldn't speak. She felt a tightness in her throat that moved downwards to grip her gut.

'Last night, apparently. I know, sounds like a made-up place, but it isn't. She came in late, said she'd just been driving with Tim and happened to end up there. Bullshit.'

'Sandwich,' Maddie managed, the word aimed at Harry. 'We should go.'

CHAPTER 52

Sophie Harding was exhausted from the constant anxiety, it felt like all her muscles were constantly tense. Her back ached, her neck ached and was starting to catch her out with occasional cracking sensations. That was new. Her thighs ached too, as she climbed the steps up to Angie McIlhenny's house on Strand Street, Sandwich. A row of pretty flowers bent away from her in a hanging basket, all caught in the same breeze to lean back like they were taking in the purple sky that glowered ominously above them — a drink was coming.

She hesitated at the door, lingering on her distorted reflection in the brass knob that jutted out of the middle with an oversized brass knocker like a bull's nose ring. She turned away, perhaps seeking one last reassuring *go on then*! gesture from Amelia, but she was nowhere to be seen. A car trundled past, its driver elderly and fixed forward.

'This is the only way to keep her safe.' Sophie's muttering to herself was the only reassurance she was going to get but it did serve to steel her a little. She would walk Jade to the park, tell a little white lie that her daughter was already there, that they had come over to walk along the canal and have a spot of lunch and would love it if Jade would come out with them, all as they'd discussed on the phone before. But it was Amelia that would be waiting for Jade, not Taliah. Then, between them, they would make sure that Jade knew the danger she was in and how she shouldn't even consider talking to the police. She repeated the same phrase: 'This is the only way to keep her safe.' It had come from Amelia, she'd said it first on the phone when pitching her idea, then numerous times on the way over. This time, the word *safe* was accompanied by a firm swing of the brass knocker. The sound resonated through the empty space on the other side and signalled the point of no return.

Angie McIlhenny's anxious expression dropped away immediately. 'Sophie!' she exhaled, crumbling in front of her like she had been expecting a man with an axe. 'Nice to see you.'

'So good to see you too!' Sophie beamed as wide as she could, hoping she was looking convincing.

'But what on earth are you doing here, in the nicest possible way, of course!'

'I . . . I'm with Taliah, actually!' Sophie blurted, then stopped herself, conscious to come back softer. 'I left her at the park, I wanted to surprise her.'

'Surprise her?' Angie said and some of that anxiety was back.

'With Jade. I wondered if I could borrow her for an hour . . .' This was it, this really was no return. 'Or less, even. I mean, if she wants to . . . I just thought it might be nice . . . I know we talked about it and you said we could and I thought it was a Sunday and the weather's not so bad and it could be a good time . . .' The more she spoke, the more she was sounding nervous, she knew it too; unnatural. There was no response, Angie had frozen solid, like Sophie might need to click her fingers to bring her back. Instead, it was the appearance of her husband that was to revive her. He was tucking his shirt into his trousers, his cheeks flushed like he had hurried to get there.

'Sophie,' he said, 'everything OK?' He eyed her closely.

'Better than OK!' She could still hear her own nerves. 'We decided on a family trip down here, a walk along the canal and a bit of a play in the park. I just left Taliah there, I was hoping to surprise her by bringing Jade out.'

'Oh,' Mac said. 'Is Andy with you?'

'Of course!' *Of course, Andy!* She could have slapped her forehead, she should have mentioned him from the start. Who leaves their daughter on their own in a park in a strange town? Of course she left her with her husband.

'I mean, we could ask her.' Angie spoke to Mac. 'She might quite like a walk to the park and I've got nothing else on this morning, I can bring her back if it's all too much.'

'Oh, see, I was thinking that maybe I could give you a break, you know, take Jade off your hands for just a little bit. I wonder if it might be good for her too, what with all she's been through. Playing with someone her own age and not being chaperoned by the people who stepped in straight after . . .' Sophie stopped, it had made sense in her mind, they had talked it out on the way over, what she might say to get Jade out on her own. But out in the wild it didn't seem to sound right at all. 'I just mean a break for you all,' she added.

'I'm not sure that's such a good idea,' Mac said.

'Actually, I think it is.' Angie stunned them both, judging by her husband's face. 'Maybe we are hindering her recovery, I've been thinking that she's been spending too much time in that darkened room. We're the only people she sees, it can only do her good to see her friend, someone of her own age and for us not to be there.'

'I don't know, I'm just not comfortable . . .'

'What? What are we not comfortable about? We know Sophie and Andy, Jade knows them too and her and Taliah were friends before, when her world was just normal. Maybe she can get some of that back for an hour.'

Mac huffed again, his head had a little shake. 'We'll ask Jade. If she wants to then she can, but only if she wants to. She has been out, just trips to the shops . . . this is quite different.'

'Good idea,' Sophie said with a sudden urge to crack her neck. The tension was like a rod through her heels, rigid all the way up to the base of her skull. She was still holding her smile.

'Why don't you step inside and we'll see what the Lady of the Manor says!' Angie's smile, by contrast, was genuine.

CHAPTER 53

Maddie already had her phone to her ear by the time they made it back to the car. She was ahead of Harry and standing by the passenger door when the locking system clunked open.

'Angie!' Maddie cut off her greeting then took a breath, trying to quell her urgency. 'How's Jade,' she said, a little calmer.

'Inspector.' The greeting was warm and bright. 'Nice to hear from you. She's doing OK, thank you for asking, the nights are still a challenge but she's engaging with us a little more. She's even talked about speaking to you, to the police at least, after the picture—'

'The picture, yes, you sent it to PC Arnold.'

'A few days ago now, I must confess, I expected a more prompt follow-up, a call at least. Am I to assume you don't see it as significant? I thought maybe the way she had drawn the pupil in the right—'

'Yes!' Maddie again took a moment to calm herself down. 'It's important, of course it is, it's just been . . . we've had a lot going on.'

'I'm sure you have.'

'With Jade's case, I mean!' Maddie blurted where she considered she was being misunderstood, then tutted to slow herself down. 'I was hoping to come and see Jade actually, about that drawing, is she there to speak to?'

'Now?' Angie's tone had a marked change, a little unsure, her cheeriness falling away.

'Yes. I'm with Inspector Blaker and we are heading over your way . . .' The pause was maddening, Maddie could almost hear the contemplation, her mind already turning to what they could do if Angie turned them down. She would need to call in what they knew and explain the threat towards Jade, which meant she would need to explain how her team were in possession of information they shouldn't have. That wouldn't matter, she tried to tell herself, this was about Jade, she needed to be safe.

'She's not here, actually. But if you're heading over any-way . . . ? She might even be back by the time you get here, she's only at the park.' It was Maddie's turn to pause now, the low rumble of a man's voice asking who was on the phone in the background confused her.

'Is that Mac I hear?' Maddie said and Harry snatched to stare over at her, his attention dragged where her voice had tightened again. The car slowed.

'Of course?' Angie replied.

'Who did Jade go out with, Angie?'

Angie's chuckle now had a touch of nerves. 'Ah yes, it's OK. I know the police gave us lengthy safety advice about keeping her in for now, but I think that was only having a detrimental effect on her—'

'*Who*? I don't mean to cut in, we just need to be sure she's safe.'

'That's my job, you understand that, right?' Angie's shift from cheery to angry was complete.

'I do,' Maddie said, then bit down on her lip to stop her screaming the same question back at the woman: *WHO*? 'We're constantly assessing for any threats, the people that get in touch with Jade need to be part of that assessment . . .' Maddie said, grimacing at the huff.

'Sophie came by. She's taken her to the park with Taliah and Andy. That's all. We decided that Jade spending time with someone of her own age might be a good idea. She needs it.'

'Sophie Harding? And she just came by, you say, so it wasn't a planned visit . . . ?'

'No, actually, she was in the town with Taliah and—'

'And you saw Taliah, she was with her?'

'No, she was waiting at the park with Andy — is there something wrong?' Angie's tone changed again, now it was thick with concern.

'I'm sure there isn't, but could you do me a favour and head out to check on her? We're a little further away than you, just check everything's OK.' Maddie expected more questions but just got confirmation, then sounds down the phone like Angie was already moving towards the door. Maddie wasn't hiding the urgency in her tone so well anymore. There was a threat, it was serious. Angie said she would call her back the moment she got to Jade and gave the name of the park she had gone to, for their satnav: *Gazen Salts*. She would type it in later, first she needed to make another call. It was picked up on the second ring.

'Black Books Accounting, Anne speaking.' The woman's voice was nasal, bored-sounding.

'Anne, thank you, is Andrew Harding there to speak to, please?'

'He is, but he's with a client right now. He only takes scheduled calls or meetings on a Sunday. Can I ask who's calling?'

Maddie hung up. In the same movement her hand shot out to find the panel for the blue lights. Harry reacted by thumping the horn that activated the siren and, as the traffic in front of them parted, he started to pick his way through it.

CHAPTER 54

Jade walked with her head bent. She had appeared like it was her first day at a new school, hesitation at the door, a flicker of nerves, a new-looking rain coat and a stiff-legged walk down the steps with her eyes narrowed where the weak, winter sun was forcing its way through the cloud cover. She had doubled back too and, for a moment, Sophie had thought she was changing her mind. But it was to come back with a stuffed animal, a cuddly tortoise that came in a made-to-measure rucksack, its head out the top and loosely bouncing against her back with every step. Her change of mind had been about taking that out, rather than coming out at all, and Sophie had quietly sighed out her relief.

Jade had looked beyond Sophie at first, trying to catch a glimpse of Taliah, no doubt; that was who she really wanted to see, after all. This was a big step for her. Sophie hadn't needed to be involved with her since her mother's murder to know that; it was obvious from her demeanour, from the reaction of Mac and Angie who, in another nod to a first day at school, stood at the door to wave her off.

Sophie almost aborted it right there and then. There was no Taliah, there was to be no meeting, no playing at the park. They would not even be making it any further than the car park, where Jade would meet with someone she didn't know, had never met before; a woman called Amelia who worked for a drug gang and who would tell her the most important story of her life. And, if she listened and did as she was told, she would be walking back here full of lies for Mac and Angie.

This is the only way to keep her safe. The reassurance was internal this time.

'So how are you?' Sophie's first words since they had rounded a corner and moved out of sight. She regretted it instantly — it was stupid, a stupid thing to say. She knew exactly how Jade must be: broken, alone, scared.

'OK.' There was no conviction, of course there wasn't, it was the only answer she was ever going to give. Jade's eyes lifted from where they had been chasing the floor, following her own blue, Converse high-tops, one with a trailing lace. She was wearing skin-tight blue jeans with holes cut for both knees, her rain coat was a black hiking-style jacket one size too large and with holes in the sleeves for her slender thumbs to poke through. She was wearing her hair down, using it as a thing to hide behind. The pause that followed was awkward, just the sound of passing traffic and scuffing feet. They made it to the car park of Gazen Salts and the sound of the footfalls changed where Jade now dragged her Converse over tightly packed stones and chunks of grit. Sophie's phone shook with a message at the same time as Jade spoke again.

'Taliah knows, right, she knows what happened?' Jade's eyes were laden with fear, almost panic, her pace slowed too, like she had just considered that she might have to talk about what happened.

'Yeah, it's cool. She just wants to play on the swing . . . see that you're OK.' Sophie didn't like lying, never had, but she was turning out to be rather good at it. She looked at her phone, the smile she had for Jade dropped away the moment she read the message on its screen. It was from Amelia.

Bring her to the back of the van. We need control of her, we can't risk her running away.

322

The car park was busy with cars, but they were parked and empty. An elderly woman was the only person she could see, tipping out three yapping white dogs from the rear of an estate car, while a man she presumed to be her husband had a watching brief. She hooked leads on each of them and they turned towards the paths leading into the park, their heads bent, both digging their chins into their collars. Sophie picked out Amelia's van two spaces up from the estate car, the van that had brought her here, a cramped and awkward journey in the middle seat while a container sloshed and bumped against the back of her legs and the whole thing stank of fuel. The man driving, who had been introduced to her as "Tim", kept his hand on the gearstick the whole way, necessitating a lean across her and adding to her claustrophobia. "Tim" hadn't said a word, just sat rigid, his arm out, his only movements those required to operate the van.

'I need to get something out of the car, quick,' Sophie said, obediently leading Jade towards where the van was parked nose-in for the solid black double doors to face them. She guessed they could open up to provide a sort of screen, a place to contain Jade just long enough for her to understand that she needed to listen to Amelia very carefully.

This is the only way to keep her safe.

The sound of Jade's footsteps changed again, now they echoed back off the muddied metal. It took just two more paces for the doors to burst open.

It was all so fast.

Sophie might have been grabbed first, something emerged from down the side of the van to grab her hair in a tight fist and she was yanked back, her stomach exposed to take a solid blow that forced every scrap of air from her body, and with it, any opportunity to scream. She was helpless as she was shoved forward, her view now of the car park floor. She saw a flash of Jade's Converse high-tops, the lace trailing in a stumble, she heard a squeak in panic. Sophie tried to lash out, but with no oxygen in her body there was no strength either. She felt another punch to her side, then a kick that was more a scrape down her right shin and was excruciating, enough for it to register over the panic of not being able to breathe. She was forced forward, the top of her head banging into the metal door.

'Get in!' was hissed into her ear, then another kick, this time to the back of her legs. She stepped up, unsteady, and would have fallen were it not for the fistful of hair that she was terrified might come out as a chunk. Another punch, this time in the lower back as encouragement. Finally, her hair was released and she stumbled into the rear of the van. Someone followed her in and gave her another shove, this time letting her fall onto the bare metal floor, her feet catching on something laid out in front of her. The door slammed shut and darkness was instant. It lasted just a few seconds, a white light in the centre of the roof spluttered on as the engine started and a door at the front slammed shut hard enough for her to feel it through the floor.

Sophie tried to get back to her feet, attempting to take in her surroundings at the same time. Someone was standing by the back door, their right arm lifted to hold on to a strap hanging from the roof. They wobbled and shook as the van lurched backwards. Sophie wasn't holding on and the momentum threw her back to the floor where she landed painfully on her forearms. She lifted her head to where Jade was revealed as the lump she had tripped over, now rolled onto her side, the whites of her eyes catching in the frigid light. Sophie tried to get to her, but was unable to move as the van changed direction. She looked up, the figure standing over her was leaning forward, enough for her bleached hair and subtle nose ring to catch in the light: Amelia.

Amelia's feet were close enough that Sophie could touch her Converse trainers, identical almost to the ones she had seen Jade wearing. Amelia's right trainer was pulled back and Sophie could only watch as it rushed back towards her.

And then the blackness closed in on her.

CHAPTER 55

Any hope that Maddie had been wrong was gone the instant she saw Angie McIlhenny react to the flashing blue lights of their car as they surged out of Sandwich's medieval centre and Gazen Salts Nature Reserve came into sight. The car park was on their side of a river, the park the other, the terrain on this side loose gravel that scraped under them where Harry was too hard on the brakes. Angie was beating on his window before they were stationary. She stepped back just enough for Maddie to get out, her face was red, her eyes wide and moist, her stance rigid and her limbs flailed like someone else was controlling them.

'Where is she!? Where is my *Jade*!' Angie squealed.

Maddie tried to take in the area around her, someone else was moving fast towards them, at first she thought it might be a member of the public coming to the aid of the screeching woman, but then she recognised the lumbering outline. It was Mac.

Maddie put her palms out. 'It's OK, we'll find her,' she said, doing her best to conceal her own panic.

'We need to call this in, I'll do it.' Harry was next to her. They'd discussed it on the way over; if Jade wasn't here they would need to raise the alarm. Mac got to them, his face just as red as his wife's, just as shocked. He was breathless and pale, needing to lean forward, his hands flat on his thighs, like it was stopping him from keeling over. Angie took a hold of him while he recovered.

'What are we calling in?' Maddie was talking out loud to get her thoughts straight.

'Jade Mercer missing with people who mean her harm.'

'And we think one of them might be Amelia Chagrin?' Maddie said. 'That's going to set the cat among the pigeons, Harry, she works for us. Are we sure?'

'She has to be involved, Sophie Harding isn't capable of something like this on her own.'

'I'll call Eileen again, she can head back in and use all the systems she needs, there's nothing to hide anymore,' Maddie said and took a step back, shifting her attention away from Harry Blaker and the distraught couple bent forward in the car park. She allowed her eyes to roam beyond, taking in the stationary cars lined up in front of her and the parkland beyond with small groups of people dotted in the distance. Closer by, a young family were strolling along a path that ran alongside the river. The child was in a pedal-powered tractor holding them all up; their black lab had the energy and lolloping run of a puppy as it ran circles around them. An elderly couple were walking towards them, they had three small, white dogs on three small leads; two shied away from the exorbitant energy as the puppy made a beeline for them, the other yapped, rising onto its back legs as part of a tug-of-war with its owner. A car entered the car park, obscuring the barking dogs for a moment before pulling up.

These people were all potential witnesses, ones that they needed to control but Maddie couldn't even be sure that Jade had been anywhere near the park. Sophie had lied about her intentions, it made sense to assume everything else she'd said was also a lie.

Maddie pressed to dial for Eileen. Despite the ringtone in her ear, she could still hear Harry confessing the whole mess to the control room. He said a name twice then spelled it out: *C.H.A.G.R.I.N.* The balloon would go up now, a rush of resources coming their way and with a sense of the direction in which to point them.

Amelia Chagrin was the key to all of this, she had to be, even if Maddie still had no idea how or why.

CHAPTER 56

Coffee shops should be buzzing and busy, yet quiet and calm. At least according to Eileen, who would then find a good vantage point from where she could pass the time people-watching. The right establishment had to be chosen wisely and small, independent places usually had the most personality. She was delighted that this theory seemed to have proven correct once again.

The door accompanied her entry with a pleasant tinkle that prompted a warm smile from a woman that Eileen reckoned to be of a similar age to herself. She wore a crisp, white shirt over a spotless navy apron, stitched with the name of the place all over again: *Orchard Lane Coffee*. It was a fine name too, seeing as she had just marvelled at the orderly beauty of the rows and rows of apple trees blurred through her window in the run-up to the turning.

'Take a seat, I'll be right with you.' The voice was laden with delight, the woman in the apron beamed another smile and gestured out to where Eileen had a good pick of where to sit. The tables were chunky wood, each with a small vase of fresh flowers and chairs that were tastefully mismatched. There was a sofa too, but she steered away from that. Sofas were for living rooms.

A table at the back offered a fine vantage point. Next to it was a door with a frosted porthole and a stern sign stating *Staff Only*. All in, she counted ten tables inside, a third of them occupied and a few more scattered outside to intrude on the parking area. One of the outside tables supported the rump of a hardy smoker whose head was dipped like he was trying to hide behind his upturned collar, his trail of swirling smoke and rosy-red cheeks giving away the blustery conditions. Back inside and the closest occupant to Eileen was a man with a laptop, his fingers clacking and clicking, all his attention sucked into that glowing box. He had even moved the lovely fresh flowers from his table to crowd the next one over, making room for his workday.

Eileen was regularly annoyed at people in public places who covered their tables in laptops, tablets and documents and, more often than not, went on to make loud telephone calls. She remembered when people used coffee shops to meet with friends in nice surroundings, when coffee shops were for a break. She would normally feel even more aggrieved that he was behaving in such a way on a Sunday.

Today, however, she could hardly judge.

This was her second coffee shop in an hour or two and, in the first, she had opened up a laptop that had sucked her in, she'd even laid out a pad for notes beside it — just like the worst of them. And, of course, she had taken the inevitable phone call, although with far more decorum than most. That had been on the outskirts of Thanet, in a place that was loud and sterile, chosen only because it was the closest to Margate Police Station where she could be sure would have good WiFi, rather than for any sort of character or for its view out over Matalan's car park.

But here there would be no laptop, no notes and, seeing as the woman with the cheer in her voice was now using it to tell her about the homemade brownie just out of the oven, this would be the place where she simply enjoyed a coffee with a slice of warm brownie. The woman winked like she approved and hummed as she walked away. When Eileen dug around in her bag this time, it was crochet that she took out, immediately picking up at the point in the pattern where she had left it last night. She tutted at the inevitable vibration from her bag just as she was getting into her rhythm: the world trying to push its way back in. She considered ignoring it, even turning it off. It was Acting Inspector Ives and it seemed like she'd only just got off the phone to her and the last, very earnest update.

'Ma'am Ives,' she said, aware that she was sounding unimpressed.

'Eileen, Jade isn't here, we have a high-risk misper. The balloon is about to go up. Did you make it back to the police station?'

Eileen sighed. No matter what detective she worked with, they were always so intense. No wonder so many of them suffered burnout, though this didn't feel like the time to discuss it. 'I've not headed back in just yet; I'm still making progress away from the office.' She was leaning forward to speak, her voice as low as she could get away with. She peered out over her glasses, suddenly self-conscious.

'What progress?' There was anger now.

'The sort of progress that requires patience!' Eileen snapped. 'I need to be left to my work.'

'We don't really have the luxury of time here!' Maddie said and Eileen sighed again. From the moment she had started working with the police it had been clear that *time* was not a luxury that would be featuring in her working life. 'I need you back at the police station. I need you focusing on Amelia Chagrin; we need vehicle associations and any movements, we need people associations too, all addresses and everything you can—'

'Ma'am!' The word was hissed, impatient, enough to cut her inspector off in her stride. 'I understand. First, however, I have a warm brownie to devour and some crochet to catch up with.' The inspector's voice came back all at once. Fortunately, Eileen had moved the phone away from her ear in order to cut it off — and just in time — as she was able to greet the beaming woman now obscuring much of her navy apron with a laden tray. She set down the order and referenced Eileen's work in progress.

'Very colourful!' she said, 'I really need to get back into it. I used to find it so relaxing in the evenings.'

Eileen nodded her agreement. 'I've only just got back into it myself, I realised I needed a new tea cosy.'

'And you thought you would make it yourself! What a wonderful idea!' The woman moved to the *Staff Only* door and popped her head round for a brief conversation that ended with her laughing heartily. Eileen hungrily chopped a wedge of brownie with the fork provided and stuffed it into her mouth.

'Oh, that is stunning!' she exclaimed, loud enough for the woman to turn back, her face lighting up again.

'I'm so glad you approve,' she said.

'You said home-made, one of yours?' Eileen asked.

The woman suddenly had an air of mischief. 'I could lie and say it was, but we're close enough to the kitchen that the true genius might hear my white lies!' She was also talking loudly, but for the benefit of whoever was beyond that door.

'And would be out here like a shot, I bet!' Eileen chuckled.

'Absolutely she would, setting the record straight.' The woman turned to where the bell tinkled over the entrance. 'Duty calls,' she sang but Eileen stopped her.

'I know this is a little cheeky, but would I be able to have a brief chat with your chef extraordinaire? Baking is another of my hobbies but I can't quite get the moisture right. I would really appreciate a few pointers from the creator of this delight!' Eileen put her fork down to reach back into her bag. From here, she took out a pair of dusty pink carpet slippers and replaced her outdoor shoes in a slick movement. The woman watched her, the change in her expression subtle, though she kept any thoughts to herself. Eileen knew what people thought about her choice of footwear and cared very little. She cared even less for shoes, detested them and had done for some time now. She preferred to be barefoot, of course; her move to slippers had been grudging: getting old, it seemed, required a lot of padding. This way, at least, she could still take her feet out easily enough.

'I'll stick my head in and see if she can spare a moment,' the woman said, her smile now carrying a little uncertainty.

'Very good,' Eileen said, picking her fork back up for another dig in the brownie. She was as good as her word too, the aproned woman again leaned around the *Staff Only* door, this time the conversation was quieter and without the laughter. Then she moved away to greet whoever had tinkled the bell. Eileen dipped her head, giving the opportunity for the chef to peer through the porthole and size up the crazy woman who had just changed into slippers in a public space — if she felt the need. Eileen sensed the door pull open but no more movement. She didn't look up, waiting to be approached instead. She took another forkful of brownie, smacked her lips and, still chewing, took up her crochet to carry on with her tea cosy. A young woman moved to stand over her, she was wringing her hands together, leaning in with her head bent.

'Mary said you were interested in a recipe?' The woman's voice was meek, uncertain, verging on shy and Eileen felt like she could sit back and take her in.

'Sit down, dear!' Eileen said, delighted. She put her crochet back down, covering her phone on the table in case it lit up to disturb them. 'Are you the genius that created this taste and texture sensation? It's the texture I'm interested in most, I just can't seem to get it right.'

The woman sat as offered, though she took the edge of the seat and leaned forward on her elbows. She was pretty: rosy-cheeked, with bright green eyes that looked all the brighter shining out from where long, straightened, dark hair fell like it was framing her face. She could do with a good meal, though, Eileen thought, maybe sampling her own cooking a little more.

'There's not much to it, to be honest. I find recipes always have it too hot so I knock ten or twenty degrees off whatever temperature they say and take it out halfway to sprinkle it with water or, depending on what it is, a little squirt of oil or butter. Also, disturb the bottom, make sure it's well-pricked and let it rest for a few minutes before you put it back in for the rest of the time. And don't cut corners on the mixing and beating parts. It's trial and error, really. I get a feeling for what stuff needs by now.'

'A feeling?' Eileen chuckled with delight. 'That's another word for *talent* in my mind. You're quite the baker, you should go on one of those cooking competitions.'

'Oh, that's not for me. I'm quite happy out the back there, out of the way.' The smile that forced its way through was a pilot light that threatened to light up the room.

But Eileen was about to remove any spark from her entirely.

'Where no one can find you,' she said, her crochet suddenly still so she could study the woman closely. That uncertainty rushed back, washing over her to squash her smile into a tight scowl.

'I suppose so. And I had better get back to it.' A nervous chuckle.

'Do you know that *Chagrin* is French for grief?' Eileen said, restarting the crochet hook, her working hand a blur of twisting and fidgeting.

'I . . . I don't really see what that has to do with anything?'

Eileen stopped again to fix on the woman who had stood up, but was compelled to stay. 'I think you do.'

'Who are you?' the woman asked. 'What is this?'

'Your mother is in a lot of trouble. And all in your name, Kayla.' Eileen paused for a beat, long enough for the use of her name to have its full impact. 'Right now, Amelia has abducted a child that she means to harm. Now, you might think that's impossible; you might think Amelia *Goodyer* is not capable of such a thing and you know what, you could be right. But Amelia *Chagrin*? A bitter woman, twisted by vengeance, by loss and grief? You would be horrified to know what that woman is capable of. But you can stop it, if you

333

want to.' Eileen put her tea cosy down. 'You can make a call, direct to your mother and tell her to stop, tell her that no one else needs to get hurt in the name of the daughter she believes to be dead — or, you can go back into your hidey-hole, *continue* to be dead, and I will finish up and leave. But, by the time you give life to that next batch of brownies, an eleven-year-old girl will have lost hers at the hands of your mother. *Because of you*, Kayla. The choice is yours.'

'I . . . how did you . . .' the woman stammered. She sat down again, her landing heavy, her eyes darting around the interior like she was looking for someone else, a way out perhaps.

'You can't run and hide, not anymore. You always knew you were going to have to face up to this at some point, you must have,' Eileen said.

'Are you the police? You don't look like the police.'

'I don't, do I, nor do I look like a member of some violent gang of drug-dealing thugs. In fact, I bet I look like the only person in this world that you might risk stepping out of that kitchen to talk to. The slippers did it, didn't they?' Eileen grinned, enjoying the irony, even if there was no one else there to enjoy it with her.

'How did you find me?'

'It's what I do.' Eileen took another bite of brownie. It truly was delicious. Kayla Goodyer waited her out, her wide eyes seemingly focused on Eileen's lips as she chewed and swallowed. 'Social media.' She wafted the last of the brownie. 'It's so often how I do it. I started with your mother. She might have changed her name, but she has a lot of the same friends as Amelia Chagrin as she did as Amelia Goodyer. Amelia Chagrin's profile page is just a shrine, really, a shrine to a murdered daughter. She got a good response when you first went missing, a lot of shares, words of encouragement, people *sending hugs*. But it dwindled. Everyone else gets to move on, see. She still posts, at least once a week, mostly pictures of Jacob; he's your son, right?' Eileen stopped for a response. All she got was a flutter of the woman's bottom lip.

'Well, someone called Suzy Lamplugh never lost interest, she still likes just about every post Amelia Chagrin makes, even a heart emoji for every mention of Jacob. That stood out to me so I had a look at *Suzy Lamplugh*. No profile picture, no pictures at all, but that name, I'd heard it before.' Kayla shrugged for Eileen to continue. 'Another benefit of being old, you see, means I was around in the eighties when the Lamplugh case was in the media. I don't think I've heard that name before or since. Suzy was a young estate agent who went out to a viewing in London and was never to be seen again. The story was instantly a national obsession, head-lines for months, forty years later and there are plans for a documentary.'

'So what?' Kayla said.

'It resonates with you, doesn't it? Suzy Lamplugh was a similar age to you when she went missing and it captured the heart of the world. But she was from a privileged background and the world was appalled that someone like her, someone just trying to live a decent life, couldn't be safe. But you . . .'

'The police only cared about me when I was giving them information. Even then, I was telling them I was in danger and they did nothing. They told me to take my own measures to get safe, they gave me no other option but to leave my fam-ily behind!' It was anger now that was fuelling that pilot light behind her eyes. 'I could have been dead for all you lot knew.'

'You're right, it's not like you were hard to find. Your friend with the apron is *Gwen Havard* if I am right. Gwen took a picture of a brownie to promote this place and tagged *Suzy Lamplugh*; just once, but that was enough. That gave me a coffee shop, a brownie and a very famous missing person determined to associate herself with—'

'I get it. You're smart.'

'I am. But I also had the advantage of not being convinced you were dead. Your mother is looking for a body, not a chef.'

Kayla slumped back in her seat, the anger — and any energy with it — seeming to leave all at the same time. 'I created the Suzy account so I could still watch. It was so hard reading all those posts about me, the *missing* posters, the things she said . . . I don't deserve any of that. The life I chose . . . It wasn't fair on her. Truth is, she's been expecting to find a body since I was fourteen and she always knew no one else would care when it happened.'

'For a person, death is sad. For a junkie, death is inevitable.' Kayla's expression hardened. 'A saying I heard at the police station once. I tore a strip off that officer, I should add. We all have our weaknesses, multiple paths in front of us and we all test out the wrong ones at some point. The strength to change our path is what makes us.'

'Well, I'm not a junkie anymore.' There was a determination in her tone, it sounded well-practised, like maybe it was something she said into the mirror at the start of every day.

'I can see that.' Eileen picked up the last of her brownie. 'Now you're a master baker.' She crammed it in, inwardly cursing herself for not leaving anything to wash it down with.

'It's ideal for me. I used to be up a lot in the early hours of the morning fighting the desire to go out, and I started baking when I was a kid with my mum. Somehow it turned into a job. I've been very lucky . . . Baking saved my life . . . I guess it was brownie, or *brown*.' She snorted at her own reference. 'I'm sure that's lost on you.'

'Don't make the mistake of seeing someone old and wise and presuming they were never young and foolish,' Eileen said, licking her fingers and stabbing up the last of the crumbs. 'I know your *brown*. It wasn't my choice, but it was in my circles. Bare feet saved my life.' Eileen stopped, her eyes losing their focus. 'You're not rock bottom until you're barefooted, it's 2 a.m. in the middle of winter and you're walking the streets to find an off-licence still open. I finally found a humiliation powerful enough to stop me going out in the first place. I got rid of all my shoes. Every single pair, figuring it would keep me sober, get me through those first few months. I have shoes now, but I step out of them the moment I can, always in stressful situations. The feel of the earth reminds me who I am, how far I have come and just how easy it would be to step back.'

'And now, here we are,' Kayla said and Eileen regained her focus.

'Here I am, trying to understand you, Kayla Goodyer, so I can help you. The police might not have tried to do that in the past, but the more I work with them, the more I realise I'm not like them at all! This is just me and you now, two addicts now baking and shunning footwear. Make me understand.'

'I had to disappear.' The sadness was back, Kayla's mouth fell open to let out a sigh, her eyes suddenly watery. 'I wasn't a good daughter, not an easy one at least. I had my problems, my addiction, and I used that to justify a lot of what I did. It was never an excuse. I got involved with some people, some bad people, got in debt to them and they . . . they took advantage of that.'

'How?' Eileen pushed.

'They were earning a lot of money selling drugs, money they needed to get into the system somehow. They had some investment scam, paying construction workers and trades-men in cash. I got the job of transporting it. Honestly . . . I've never seen so much money. It was obscene.'

'Sounds like they trusted you. That's not taking advantage.'

Kayla scoffed. '*Trust*! You sound just like *he* did. Trust doesn't exist, not in that world and definitely not at the point when the cash comes to the surface.'

'Go on.'

'I've known Liam Moran a while. Liam had some deal going with these people up in London, I don't know the ins and outs, but he got me some work, said I was the only one he could trust to do it.'

'What was it?'

'Courier. Cash, a lot of it. Picking it up from one place and taking it to another. Simple.'

'So what happened?'

'His dad happened.'

'George?'

'George Moran. He has a big chip on his shoulder, that one. He didn't like that his son had changed their direction overnight. They've always been a family of thieves. Everyone knew the Morans, if you had something hot to sell, that was where you went. Suddenly they were out of that business and running an army of drug dealers and, I bet, making a lot more money out of it.'

'That's good then, right?'

'These men, it's a power trip. Egos come into play. It was running fine, but George Moran didn't want it to work, he wanted it to break.'

'And it broke with you?' Eileen said.

'I got told that George was setting me up to be robbed. By that time I had a few ears out, a few people looking after me. George knew where I was, what I was driving and what cash I had on me so it was an easy job for someone like that. And I was supposed to be dead by the end of it. Dead men tell no tales, that's what they say, right? It had to look like a robbery, like a rival had got hold of me. That way these people up in the city might have lost faith in Liam — maybe even enough to cut him off — and George would be able to take his place back running things his way. Also, he would've had a nice one hundred grand or so from the job, less after he'd paid off his team.'

'But you found out,' Eileen said.

'I knew for a while but I couldn't do anything about it. I was turning up every day expecting it.' She started to break, Eileen was surprised it had taken that long. The upset changed her appearance to a more ashen pallor and even her cheeks seemed a little more sunken, like her previous life was so powerful it had the ability to change her appearance back just by speaking about it. She was back to the Kayla Goodyer in her missing poster, back to the hopeless addict. 'I couldn't go to Liam, no way he would have believed his own father was planning a betrayal like that, not from me. And I couldn't stop doing it either, you don't quit jobs like that, so I disappeared. And now you're telling me my mum's . . . because of that?' She couldn't hold back her sobs any longer.

'It's OK, you did get away and you can still fix this. You just need to call off your mother then talk to us. We can help.'

Another snort. '*Help*! Why would you lot help someone like me? You're only here now to save someone else, this isn't about me.'

Eileen sat back and steepled her fingers on the tabletop. 'Then save yourself.'

'Saving myself was never what mattered . . . my son, my mum and dad . . . at first I just intended on letting it happen, let them kill me. Great plan, eh!' She lost a tear now, it caught them both out it seemed, spurting from her right eye, prompting a jerked hand to meet it. 'But I know George would have made an example of me. He's a coward at heart, scared of his own son and after blaming me for stealing their money, I know he would have gone after my family to hide that it was him all along. I had to stay alive, I had to disappear. I did run off with their money, but only to give it back. I got in touch with George and told him he could have it, that Liam didn't need to know he was getting it back either. That was part of the deal. He still got the money, I still disappeared and Liam never got to know. All George had to do was leave my family alone.'

'And your family, why do they think you're dead?'

'They had to. I made sure it was known among the people I used to hang around with, I wouldn't call them friends, it was a scene. My mum knew some of them and I knew it would be the first place she would go looking and I thought if she was told I was dead, she would stop looking. I didn't want her poking a hornet's nest.'

'It didn't work. If George was trying to scupper the agreement, I mean, it still seems to be in place.'

'I still heard a few things after, before I cut myself off completely. I think Liam smoothed it out, reduced his cut maybe, who knows. But they'll still be on thin ice and the fact that George took that money, effectively stealing from some really bad people, is good for me. That little bombshell should keep my Jacob safe.'

Kayla jerked back suddenly, a reaction to someone standing over them. Eileen looked up to the woman in the apron. Her beaming smile was gone, her hands on her hips, and those warm, sparkling eyes now carried a hint of fear.

'Gwen,' Eileen said, in greeting.

'Is this it?' Eileen was totally ignored, she spoke directly to Kayla, all the warmth gone. Kayla nodded, her eyes falling to the table like a scolded child. 'So, it's all over, is it?'

'I didn't think . . . I'm sorry,' Kayla said.

'You said it would either be the police or it would be much worse. I assume this is the police?' Confusion flickered on the woman's face now and Eileen grinned at her.

'A version of.'

'You don't look much like a police officer to me.'

'I don't look like the *much worse* either. You both should be delighted it was me who found her,' Eileen said, starting to pack away her belongings.

'And you have to go with this woman?' Gwen was back talking to Kayla.

'I think I do,' Kayla replied, her shyness back. 'I just need to get a few things,' she said in Eileen's direction. Eileen nodded, watching as Kayla stood and looked like she was readying herself, then slipped back through the door with the porthole. Gwen now had hostility in her stare and Eileen met it full on.

'She's about to do something amazing, the right thing. I reckon we can get her back to you one day, maybe even a version that doesn't have to hide in the kitchen,' Eileen said and the woman's stern front seemed to drop away a little. The warmth that had been her first response to Eileen was her natural state and couldn't be held back for long.

'I've become rather fond of her,' she said. 'Make sure you don't let anything bad happen.'

CHAPTER 57

There was no way of telling if the van stopping prompted the whimpering or if the sudden removal of the chugging diesel engine just meant that Amelia could now hear it. She didn't know which of them was making the noise either, but it didn't matter. It was time to finish what they had started.

The door thumped twice: Tim. He struck it so hard the metal made a flexing sound and she thumped it twice back, confirmation that they were still on course, that she still had control of the back. Both doors tugged open to flood the rear with light. Tim's stare in was back to cold and business-like.

'Any problems?'

'No, just like we said,' Amelia replied, catching herself out with how she was handling herself. 'Swap, then?' she said and Tim stepped aside to let her out. She narrowed her eyes further; the cloud cover was holding back the full effect of the sun but, compared to the weak interior light, it was still a dramatic change. She turned back to where their two captives were also reacting to the flood of light, both laid out on their sides to face her. Sophie's eyes looked to be completely shut but Jade was different. Her focus was all on Tim, her eyes better adjusted, wider than looked natural. She was staring at the gnarled twist of steel that jutted out from between Tim's fingers where they were bunched into a tight fist. The sort of fist that made stab wounds with every punch. It was an image that froze itself in Amelia's mind before the door was slammed shut, then dissipated, the details peeling away like petals in the breeze.

Amelia let out a breath. The next part was on her. She opened the passenger door of the van. The bench seat had a void for luggage right below where Sophie had sat. She leaned in, her chest almost touching the dirt-encrusted floor as she thrust her hand under to grab a handful of cheap nylon. The bag made a high-pitched whir as it slid over the van's lined floor. She tugged the zip and the black sides fell open like a wide mouth to show bundles of cash inside. The cash she had taken from Connor Docker, cash that was owed to the Morans. She allowed herself a moment to enjoy the irony.

She was shaken from her thoughts by a sound from the back, a shriek and then a thud that was firm enough to shake the van. She zipped the bag back up, took the weight through a strap over her shoulder and started her walk.

She crossed the road with no issues. The area was quiet, she could hear car engines but none close enough to see and there was no foot traffic either. She took in the house. It looked different from when she had passed it earlier, maybe it was just that it *felt* different. On her first pass, when she had seen Liam Moran struggling up the path in his wheelchair, his dad waiting for him while supported by his stick, she had felt confident — powerful, even — and that had only increased when that thick-limbed gorilla in sunglasses had appeared. She knew what she was capable of, she'd even had one of them on the run just a few days earlier.

The path was breaking up, the cracks large enough for her to feel them through the soles of her Converse high-tops. The same trainers Kayla had worn when she was still alive, the same trainers Jade Mercer was wearing right now, lying on her side, Amelia's ex-husband standing over her with his fist tight around a corkscrew.

Amelia hesitated. She was at the enemy's front door, she had all the cards, all the power and now was the time to reveal it: three years in the making. But something held her still, a niggling doubt perhaps. This was making her move, the element of surprise wouldn't give her an advantage for long. She turned to take in the van. She could see it rocking on its suspension where someone was moving around inside, fighting perhaps, begging more likely and suddenly found herself wondering how the hell this had become her world. She lifted her phone out of her pocket. She had turned it off, wanting to shut out everything but her task. But now she wanted a line back to Tim, back to help if this went wrong. She waited for it to find the network.

The door opened.

Amelia hadn't knocked, she'd been spotted. She cursed herself for handing over the upper hand. A pair of mirrored sunglasses confronted her.

'I'm not here to talk to them, I want to talk to you. It's in your interest,' she said, speaking quickly, her voice low.

'What are you talking about? We don't want any today, thanks love, now fuck off.' The door started to shut. Amelia pulled the bag apart, the wads of cash visible from its black mouth.

'*Who the fuck is it?*' Liam Moran's voice hollered from the back of the house. It steeled Amelia, made her more determined, stood her straighter.

'This is for you. You just have to walk back in there right now and tie their hands. Then you leave them for me. You know who I am, you've been watching me long enough . . .' She paused for a reaction, got two full lips lifting in a leer. 'And you have my word there won't be anyone left to answer to.'

'Can't do that,' he said.

'Me today and you walk with a bag of cash, someone else tomorrow who doesn't let you walk at all. The Morans are finished. The world knows it, I'm surprised no one's been here already. You get to walk off a sinking ship taking the last of their money. Last chance.'

'*Who THE FUCK!*'

Liam again. George shouted something after him, then a thump of a stick like he might be getting up.

'No one, they're just leaving,' the man with the sunglasses shouted back, then took a big step forward. Amelia held her ground, their noses almost touching. She felt him take a grip on the bag. 'How about I take it anyway, then drag you in to repeat what you just said?'

'You see that van behind me? Full of blokes. They knew you wouldn't open the door to them, but you would to me. Something about me having tits, they said. They also said to give you a simple choice. Take the bag and walk away, or close the door and be a part of the next part.'

His eyes lifted beyond her. The van was still making a noise, subtle sounds and shakes that Amelia knew was a struggle. But he didn't. She let go of the bag that he still held, then reached to her waistband, pulling out two lengths of rope long enough for two thick wrists. She stood back to show him. 'I have tape too, I can't be doing with begging or whining.'

He lingered on the rope, then on her. If he was looking for conviction then he must have been satisfied.

'There's a building down the end of the garden,' he said. 'You'll have all the privacy you need.' Then he reached out for the rope, still holding his bag of money in his other hand. He hadn't taken much convincing. That feeling of power was back, confidence and hate oozed from her in equal measure and she took a moment to gulp down a mouthful of the stale air that was pushing out of the house. The hall was dimly lit, the windows seemingly blocked. The man in the sunglasses led the way.

'*Close the fucking door then!*' Liam bawled.

They were walking towards the voices. There was a light on at the back of the house, a single bulb that hung from the ceiling, its light, in nicotine yellow, barely enough to show up

344

the two-seater sofa against the left wall where the two most prominent members of the legendary Moran family sat, one of whom was struggling to get to his feet. The same weak bulb was enough to project a shadow of quick movement against the wall, as the man with the sunglasses and a whole bag of money threw his first punch.

CHAPTER 58

Maddie paced. Even the time for a call to connect was agonising, then, after ringing twice — two times too many — her intelligence analyst picked up with a two-word answer that was maddeningly cheery in the circumstances.

'Ma'am Ives?'

'Eileen, I missed your call.'

'I found her, she's here with me right now.' Eileen's cheeriness teetered towards smug.

'Found her, found who?'

'Kayla Goodyer. She works in a coffee shop out in the countryside. It's a lovely little place—'

'Kayla's alive!' The words came out louder than Maddie had intended. Harry was close enough to halt his conversation with a uniformed officer — the first and only to arrive so far — and to lock eyes with her.

'Very much so and, it would appear, quite the baker,' Eileen added.

'And she's with you right now?' Maddie felt blindsided, trying to catch up.

'She is. I've talked with her, told her what her mum is up to and how she can stop her. Amelia Chagrin is doing all that she's doing because she believes her daughter's dead, now—'

'You told her?' Maddie grimaced at an expectant Harry.

'Yes, I mean, I told her our situation.'

'Eileen, Amelia is doing what she is doing because Jade is a witness, she saw Amelia through those floorboards.'

'Well, yes, but why was she at that house in the first place? It's all about Kayla and now, well, Kayla can talk some sense into her, tell her to stop what she's doing, that there's no point anymore.'

Maddie bit down on her fist. Eileen liked soap operas — she talked about them in the office — and that was all this was to her, only playing out live. In those soap operas, bad people stopped being bad when they were fronted up and given a monologue about how they're a good person, really. It wasn't Eileen's fault, of course she was naïve, no one can join a police force with their eyes fully open. 'I'm not sure how we get them together, Eileen, that's all, seeing as we don't know where Amelia is. Where are you?' Maddie pressed.

'Leeds, the village, not the city! I passed the main entrance to Leeds Castle on the way in . . .'

'So, near Maidstone! You're a fair way from us.'

'Yes, but we just need them to speak, Kayla and her mother, then all this madness stops. We have a phone number for Amelia, I know it's on the wall in custody if—'

'I have it already, it's switched off.'

'So what do we do now?' Eileen's cheer had quickly become exasperation. Maddie felt it too.

'There's not much we can do,' she said. 'I'm sitting on my hands at the last place Jade Mercer was spotted. We have a witness who saw her enter the car park area with Sophie Harding. The car park has an ANPR system but that's hardly an effective way of tracking anything fast . . .' Maddie sighed again. 'Everything now needs to be going back through Mark Hall. We've been ordered back to Headquarters, where I imagine our hands will be tied tighter. You need to call Mark direct, tell him what you've got, *who* you've got and he'll take it from there.'

347

'So that's it?' Eileen said. 'You're just giving up. Handing it all over to Mark Hall and walking away?'

'Eileen . . .' Maddie said, her tone designed to carry a warning. 'The superintendent has all the resources, all the intel, he's best placed to manage this from here. Tell him what you have, it's good work, I'm sure he'll tell you the same.'

'Perhaps I should call PC Arnold instead?' Eileen harumphed. 'At a time like this I could do with a dangerous, ham-fisted idiot.'

'Vince? What are you talking about?'

'What was it Jade said to you?'

'Said to me?' Maddie said, caught out by Eileen's sudden aggression.

'Lock up the bad people and throw away the key, right? Are you going to tell her that you walked away? Or PC Arnold, for that matter?'

Maddie sparked angrily, but it was just that, a spark that died along with any energy for a reply. A number of images triggered in her mind, some from Vince's bodycam, some from her own visit to the Mercer home. Maria Mercer's corpse dominated, only outed by the memory of Jade's mournful eyes peering out of the shadow at the top of Mac and Angie's stairs. More images came of blood-soaked floorboards, of panicked video footage, *that* scream. She remembered Jade's words too, in all their softness:

Will you lock them up, the bad people? Lock them up and throw away the key, that was what Vince said?

'I'll try her phone once more,' Maddie sighed, swallowing where her throat felt dry. 'I'll patch you in, stay on the line, just in case.'

'That's more like it!' Eileen whooped but there was no time for a reply, no time for anything.

It was ringing.

Maddie held her breath. 'It's going to ring out,' she said and her eyes fell shut, tension crushing her chest like it was in a giant fist slowly closing. It did, as she'd predicted, but an idea coursed through her like a bolt of energy. 'Did you give her your number?' she spluttered at Harry.

'Who? What's going on?'

'Amelia. Did she put it in her phone?'

'Not when I was with her.'

'But you gave it to her?'

'My card, yeah.'

'She's not answering me,' Maddie said.

'What makes you think she'll answer me?' Harry said, disbelief thick in his voice.

'Give it to me.' Maddie held out her hand for Harry to do as he was asked. 'Eileen, I'll call you back on Harry's phone and when I do, we will need Kayla's voice right from the start. Amelia's going to take some convincing.' She hung up before Eileen could answer, switching phones, her fingers clumsy.

'Why would she answer me?' Harry said, again.

'She will . . .' Maddie said, hoping her voice carried some conviction. 'Because she has to.'

CHAPTER 59

'Kayla!' Eileen sang towards the door with the porthole, 'time to shine!' Eileen's attention had been on her phone and she'd missed Gwen changing her position, moving to stand right in front of the kitchen door, her hostility suddenly more pronounced, her arms crossed. She didn't budge, either, when Eileen took a step towards her.

'You look awful pleased with yourself. Did you ever show us any identification, you police carry it, right?' Gwen said. Eileen still held the phone tight against her ear while a ringing tone played out.

'Really? You want to do this now? This is it! This is when our Kayla saves the day.' Eileen gestured to the door beyond.

'You could be anyone. Kayla needs to be careful, what sort of a friend would I be if I just let her go off with anyone?'

Eileen harumphed. She trapped the phone with her shoulder, plunging both hands into her bag to commence a search for her lanyard ID, a search that she paused when the phone suddenly fell silent. The call had been cut. Maddie had given up. It fuelled Eileen's frustration and she began searching more frantically, spilling items that skittered and clattered across the tabletop. The man with the laptop was long gone, there was no one at all left in the rear half of the coffee shop to upset, not that Eileen cared anymore. A packet of mints leaped from her bag, catching the edge of the table to roll and bump into Gwen's foot. Eileen was no longer looking in her bag, she was watching for her chance; it came when Gwen bent forward to pick them up.

Eileen moved as fast as she could, barrelling forward, able to push through the door, barely touching the woman who had been blocking it a moment ago.

The kitchen was small, neat and tidy, two walls of work surface and overhanging cupboards, another of ovens, hobs and the door with the porthole. There was a second door too, directly opposite, this one led to the outside. It was hanging open. Gwen spoke from behind Eileen, she was standing so close that Eileen could feel her breath on the nape of her neck.

'She was always going to run, I was always going to help. Been planned a long time.'

Eileen didn't have time to argue. Her phone was ringing.

CHAPTER 60

Amelia stepped out through the back door. The back garden was a mass of sodden, untamed grass, but with a path worn through it on the right side that led up to two outbuildings in the near distance. Just like the man in the sunglasses had described before taking his bag of money and fleeing his sinking ship. He had also said that she would have privacy there: *Do whatever you like in them four walls, no one can hear a thing.* But it wasn't those four walls that had featured in her fantasies for the last three years. The levels of violence had changed over that time — increased — but never the place. The end of the person who had taken her daughter's life always played out in the back of a darkened van. It was messy and it was loud, having driven him to the middle of nowhere where he knew what was coming and where they could take their time.

The fact Liam would now be coming along for the ride was the icing on the cake where she had previously considered him so dangerous that using the police to get him out of the way had been the only feasible option.

The end result was still going to be the same. It wasn't just revenge; George was going to tell her what she needed to know and Liam wasn't going to be able to stop her.

But then a simple text message did just that:

Kayla is alive. She is with me. This is Inspector Blaker, we spoke out the front of Margate Police Station. Call me back, talk to me, talk to your daughter.

The message was from a different row of numbers to those that she had ignored moments earlier as a call. It was a trick, it had to be, someone trying to get her attention. She snatched the card that was still in her back pocket:

Detective Inspector Harry Blaker
Major Crime Investigation Team

And a phone number that matched. It was still a trick. Three years obsessing over the death of her daughter and suddenly, from nowhere, she was supposed to believe that the same police force who had failed at finding her — stopped looking even — now had her ready and waiting for a chat on the phone. The moment she called that number back they would trace her somehow, just like she had seen on the movies, some SWAT team or whatever ready to move in.

But why were they even tricking her?

Why were they even contacting her *right now*?

They knew.

They couldn't.

She was being paranoid, everything was heightened, her fear, her senses, everything.

But why now? She couldn't think.

Her phone buzzed again, another message from the same source stacked itself neatly underneath the first.

Call this number back, it's the most important call you will ever make. Kayla is ready to speak to you.

How could they be so cruel! The police, the people who had already let her down so badly, who had given up any sort of a search for her little girl, were now using Kayla's name to bait her into giving up her location.

Amelia snatched the phone up to smash it back down again on the floor, her temper getting the better of her, but all the energy drained out of her at the edge of her moment of no return. Her arm went limp, her phone still in her hand to fall to her side and bump her in the hip.

That message meant there was a chance. It was slight, highly unlikely, but a *chance*.

There had been something about that inspector, something genuine, something different. He had seemed rattled when he was talking about Jade, like he really cared. Maybe it would have been different if he had been in charge of looking for Kayla? Maybe he *had* taken it on, maybe he had gone looking for her.

But she was dead. She'd been told so by multiple sources, all people who would know, all part of that same lifestyle, some of them had been close friends and she had pieced together a detailed story: Kayla was dead. She had been robbed, betrayed and used by George Moran in some kind of power play. It had all made so much sense to her.

Had.

'*Amelia!*' a voice hissed, enough to make her jump where her eyes had lost her focus, her state dreamlike, her vision blurred to a swirling green. Back to reality and Tim was close, his face red with exertion, his chest rising and falling in movements big enough to see and his brow slick, shining in the weak light. There was blood too, a hint on his right forearm, revealed by rolled up shirtsleeves, a larger clump on his right hand, a hand that was now open and missing the weapon he had been holding earlier. 'We need to get this finished,' he said.

And he was right. Three years to get to this point, three years to get control of the people who could give her answers and no trick or smokescreen from the police was going to stop her.

She turned back to the house. Tim was already bundling through the back door to the two men restrained on their sofa. It was time to tie all of the loose ends together, to go somewhere quiet and isolated, to get her answers.

And then to burn whatever was left.

CHAPTER 61

'Dammit!' Harry's phone was still laid out in Maddie's palm. They were back in his car, Harry driving, moving away from what had turned into a frenzy of activity in the car park of Gazen Salts, Sandwich. He had orders to return to police headquarters, they both had — Hall had tried calling both their phones, more times than Maddie could recall, his frustration at being ignored boiling over into a broadcast over the radio, a spitting demand for *Inspector Harry Blaker to return as ordered* and a reminder of the GPS function on personal and car radios meaning he knew where they were. There was even a demand for all officers to report sightings of either Inspector Blaker, or *Acting* Inspector Ives.

Maddie didn't care she was upsetting a senior officer, it was hardly her first time. She considered turning the radio off to cut the tracking function, but they needed the updates. She did care that they were becoming a distraction, however. If just one officer expelled energy on finding them, rather than Jade Mercer, then their presence was counterproductive.

They did need to leave.

Mark Halls' team were starting to arrive anyway, minus their superintendent — for now at least — and she watched as they swarmed to Mac and Angie. Their opening gambit, no doubt, would be to explain how Maddie and Harry were no longer part of the investigation, undermining their presence. There was nothing to be gained from staying.

Their movement had no real direction, torn between returning to the station as asked, floating towards Eileen or pulling over and waiting for some clue from Amelia as to where she might be. But Amelia wasn't about to offer that up for nothing. Maddie needed the right prod to get a reaction. She brought up their text conversation, it might have been one-sided to this point, but the two ticks next to the message told her that they were getting through. She tried again, this time for one that couldn't be ignored:

You don't have to harm Jade. We already know what she saw. Call this number. Kayla wants you to stop before it's too late. She's hurting too.

The phone made a *swooshing* noise to confirm the message had been sent. Maddie watched the screen, waiting for ticks that appeared almost instantly. This was it, the last roll of the dice and a risky one. She'd just confirmed that Jade was a witness who could positively identify Amelia as committing murder. From here, Amelia either panicked and realised she needed to stop before she made this any worse, or she realised the truth: that Jade hadn't yet given a formal account to the police.

And a dead witness was far more useful to her right now than a live one.

Maddie had been hasty. She flushed with regret, turning to take in Harry's side profile. She stopped herself from telling him, holding her tongue and opening the window a little to get some air moving, her breathing suddenly felt laboured where her chest had ratcheted tighter.

She'd just taken a massive gamble; her stake a child's life.

CHAPTER 62

'They know!' Amelia's voice came out as a wheeze, her lungs burned like she'd sprinted the length of the garden to tell Tim, but she hadn't, she'd ducked behind the door of the van to read the latest message, ensuring Tim didn't see. He couldn't have heard her words either. Some of her wheeze was left over from carrying George and Liam Moran to bundle them into the back of the van, but that wasn't why she was struggling to recover. Both Morans had kicked and squirmed at first, Liam the worst despite his broken bones and Tim had needed to quieten him down with the same cosh that had silenced Connor Docker. Tim was enjoying himself, told Liam as much, begged him to kick off again *so I get to beat you to death right here*. The cold, emotionless exterior of Tim Goodyer quickly replaced by the glee and enthusiasm of someone also sensing the culmination of three years of violent fantasy. There was a time when she would never have believed it.

'You OK?' Tim was looking at her now. Her phone was behind her back and she forced it into her pocket, considering that if Tim was now capable of glee, he might also be capable of anger. This was all her fault. She knew Jade had seen her and she had been weak, leaving her alive. She was back to doubting herself again, doubting everything. She wished she could go back to being that confident, cold killer who had knocked on the front door just a short time ago, who had been thinking straight and clear. Her mind was now overrun with the last part of that message, it dominated like a breaking news banner running behind her eyes: *Kayla wants you to stop before it's too late*.

'It's already too late.' Another wheeze.

'What are you saying?' Sure enough, Tim's voice carried anger. 'We have to go, we have to finish this.' He gestured to the back of the van, to where Amelia was no longer so keen to step up into its darkness. She just needed to cling to the strap, make sure no one got their gag free to shout for help before they could get to the burn site Tim had already identified.

She moved forward, now on autopilot, the breaking news banner still sliding from left to right in her mind.

Before it's too late.

She stepped up and the door slammed so fast behind her she felt the breeze on the back of her neck. The floor was slippery, slick from blood. The weak interior light flickered to the tune of the starting engine and she reached up to push the little black switch across to turn it off. She didn't want to see what was in the back of that van, she didn't want to see what they had done.

But the darkness couldn't hide it. There were mumbles still, murmurs of pain and of anger, the scuff of scattered limbs against metal and the cloying smell of blood. The van started moving. The journey from here was ten minutes, twenty in traffic. It wasn't much time.

She took her phone back out.

CHAPTER 63

The phone was suddenly like a freshly caught fish in her hand as it burst to life, and Maddie couldn't hold it. It squirmed, then jumped to bounce off the centre console and slip under her seat.

'Shit!' It was still ringing, the buzzing maddening as Maddie tried to contort enough to get her hand far enough under to grab it. She took her seatbelt off to assist. Harry must have seen the problem, he braked hard and sudden, the momentum bringing the phone shooting out from under the seat and into the footwell, and crashing Maddie sideways into the solid glovebox. 'Thanks,' she grimaced, scooping the phone up and pressing to answer, holding her breath that she had got it in time.

'If you're lying to me, if this is a trick, they're all dead.' The voice was strong, determined and low like a growl.

'Amelia,' Maddie said. 'You have to listen to me—'

'Who are you?' The voice came back higher, the emotion clear.

'Maddie Ives, we met in the interview room, Harry Blaker's here but he's driving . . .' She petered out, the background noise through the phone was like a whirring sound, the white noise of vehicle movement, Maddie thought.

'You put my daughter on, you put my Kayla on this phone *right now*, or this call is over; this is all over.' A voice through gritted teeth, rage wound tight around every word.

'I don't have her here, not with me, but my colleague is with her, I can patch the calls, you just have to give me a minute.'

'You have less than that.'

'Amelia, Jade has nothing—'

'You don't say another *word*!' That last word sparked, threatening to blow. A couple of heavy breaths followed and Maddie gave her a moment for it to pass. 'My daughter speaks to me next or this is all over. You will never find me, not in time, no matter what you think you know.'

'OK, OK,' Maddie said, 'I'm doing it now.' She took the phone away from her ear to put it in her lap. Harry had pulled them over, they couldn't afford the signal to drop. Maddie pressed to activate the speaker. She had to focus to work her hands, first pressing *Add Call* on her phone, then selecting *Eileen Analyst* from Harry's contact list. A ringing sound merged with the murmur of white noise. Amelia would be hearing it too, she would then have heard Eileen answer it, but what she couldn't have realised — that Maddie did in an instant — was that there was something wrong.

* * *

Eileen just stared at the phone to start with, letting it ring in her palm, then lifting her eyes to scan the interior of the coffee shop like Kayla might have changed her mind and suddenly reappeared. She hadn't. She could see the vacated table where the man and his laptop had been, still cluttered with dirty cups, her own the same. There were only two others occupied now, both at the front against the window. The man who had been leaning on the table outside for a cigarette was gone too. It was just her and the woman in the apron in earshot. Eileen had been out of the back door to peer out into a farm shop, two open barns and a unit in use as a salon. Then she had carried out a search of the kitchen while Gwen followed — tutting constantly — but doing nothing to stop her. It was no use. Kayla Goodyer had gone, leaving no obvious clue as to where.

'Ma'am Ives . . .' Eileen answered the call finally, her eyes locked on Gwen.

'Eileen, I have Amelia on the phone, you have to put Kayla on, and you have to do it right now.'

'Ma'am Ives, Kayla is very scared, I—'

'I knew it, this is bullshit! You're tricking me!' A woman's voice cut across them all, surely Amelia's and she sounded angry, the last word high in pitch like tears were next.

'No trick!' Eileen was quick to answer, to realise the situation, her eyes chasing back round the interior of the shop, desperate for something that could help. She found something that might. 'Just give me a moment!' Eileen pushed her phone into her pocket, the call still connected. 'Now you're going to help me make this right.' She spoke low, but her determination was clear, her words hissed at Gwen who snapped straight like a schoolgirl scolded. Eileen stomped to the two occupied tables. 'Out, we're closing, out!' That same tone, still keeping the volume down. The first table was two gossiping women who were instantly appalled.

'Gwen?' one of them said, looking past her to the shop owner.

'A health and safety issue has come up, we need to clear the shop for just a while.' Gwen backed Eileen up. The next table over got the hint, they stood, one of the occupants picking up the final piece of that delicious brownie to take with them. Eileen shepherded them out, ignoring utterings of *well I never*! She was firm in closing the door, then made her way to the counter where a landline was over to one side. Eileen took her mobile back out from her pocket, checking it was still connected.

'You need to call me on the landline here, the signal's not great.'

'This is a trick!' The same woman's voice again, her disbelief clear. The counter had takeaway menus stacked next to the phone. Eileen swiped the top one, read the phone number out and then, before anyone could cut back in, said 'call that number straight back.'

She hung up.

Eileen slammed her eyes shut, sucking in a deep breath that she held on to, feeling the cold floor through her bare feet, her familiar technique when she needed to be calmer. It had been important not to give Amelia the opportunity to respond, she could only talk herself into hanging up. Now she needed to hope that Maddie Ives had realised the same thing, that she didn't get into a conversation and just dialled the number; if she did that, Amelia would stay connected. Surely.

But the landline stayed silent.

Thirty seconds passed, a minute. Something was wrong. Eileen used the time to fiddle with her mobile phone. Then she met eyes with Gwen, who shuffled in her own awkwardness.

'We made a mistake, didn't we?' Gwen said. 'Was that really her mother, is she really in trouble?'

'Do you know where she's gone?' Eileen seized on her immediately.

'If it's where we talked about . . .' Gwen shrugged.

'Is it far? Can you get her back here?' Eileen's urgency was unabashed.

'I don't— maybe.'

'Can you try?'

Gwen bit her lip, her eyes fidgeted from side to side in their sockets like she was contemplating her next move. She seemed to make a decision, her arms suddenly lifting as she swept her apron up over her head and discarded it on a table. Eileen watched her as she hurried towards the back of the shop.

Until the landline rang.

* * *

'Eileen, you have us both but only just. Please, put Kayla on.' Amelia heard Inspector Ives' voice and clamped her jaw shut

363

so tight that it had an ache. She turned the volume up one-handed, the other still clung to the leather strap that creaked and strained under her weight as Tim's driving got more and more erratic. The van would lurch forward like a kicked football for him to then stand on the brakes. They had kept moving the whole time, the traffic must be light, the diesel engine droned like it was flat out and she knew they had to be clear of town traffic and out on the country roads. Their destination was close.

Inspector Ives sounded desperate and Amelia liked it. Finally, someone was desperate to help her — no matter the circumstances. But she wasn't getting any reply, just the murmur of a connected line.

'This is bullshit,' Amelia said, her jaw flashing pain as it came apart. Any hope that had built in the last few minutes was flooding out of her far faster. But there was another sound. It was distant, a little tinny, artificial almost, a voice but like it was from a television set overheard in the background:

'*I had to disappear.*' Four words were enough for Amelia's legs to give out and she nearly dropped the phone as she swung at the mercy of the leather strap. She couldn't get her knees to lock, the van was braking hard again to conspire against her, it turned too, the right side dropping like they had hit a rut and the bodies around her scraped and slid in the darkness. She was still standing, but only just. She managed to get her balance back, enough to be able to push the phone firmer against the side of her head. That voice that had taken her legs continued:

'*She had to think I was dead, everyone did, you couldn't possibly understand . . .*'

'*Try me.*' This was a different voice, that of the woman who had answered the phone, only a little tinnier.

'*I wasn't a good daughter, not an easy one at least. I had my problems, my addiction, and I used that to justify a lot of what I did. It was never an excuse. I got involved with some people, some bad people, got in debt to them and they . . . they took advantage of that.*'

Kayla.

It was her, her voice . . . it just was, and in that moment everything Amelia thought she knew was thrown up in the air to come back down in pieces. The floor bumped Amelia's knees where her legs gave way and she hadn't even realised. She was hanging from one arm pulled straight, she felt tears on her cheeks that ran along where her lips were pursed together in a tight smile. The van lurched again, she had to use the hand with the phone in it to steady herself. She had a breast pocket in her shirt, she put the phone on speaker, turning it up as loud as she could, then dropped it into the pocket, using her now spare hand to push out at the van's side as the ride became more violent. She'd missed some, the conversation was still going, she held her breath to listen.

'*So what happened?*' The shrill voice of the old woman again, before Kayla took back over.

'*His dad happened. George Moran. He has a big chip on his shoulder, that one. He didn't like that his son had changed their direction overnight. They've always been a family of thieves. Everyone knew the Morans, if you had something hot to sell, that was where you went. Suddenly they were out of that business and running an army of drug dealers and, I bet, making a lot more money out of it.*'

Another lurch of the van, the engine surged in a downshift, more of the conversation lost.

'*George Moran didn't want it to work, he wanted it to break . . . I got told that George was setting me up to be robbed. By that time I had a few ears out, a few people looking after me. George knew where I was, what I was driving and what cash I had on me so it was an easy job for someone like that. And I was supposed to be dead by the end of it. Dead men tell no tales, that's what they say, right? It had to look like a robbery, like a rival had got hold of me. That way these people up in the city might have lost faith in Liam — maybe even enough to cut him off — and George would be able to take his place back running things his way. Also he would've had a nice one hundred grand or so from the job, less after he'd paid off his team.*'

There was fear in her voice, desperation too. But there was something else. She'd heard Kayla like this before, when the grip of her addiction was at its tightest. It was resignation, acceptance. It had broken her heart then; it broke it now. There was more from Kayla, how she was being set up, how she was helpless to stop it, then she spoke about her family:

'*Saving myself was never what mattered . . . my son, my mum and dad . . . at first I just intended on letting it happen, let them kill me. Great plan, eh!*'

Then a sniff that became a break where she sobbed. It was a recording, Amelia knew that, a voice played back, but she still couldn't stop herself responding.

'Oh, Kayla . . .'

'*But I know George would have made an example of me. He's a coward at heart, scared of his own son and after blaming me for stealing their money, I know he would have gone after my family. I had to stay alive, I had to disappear. I did run off with their money, but only to give it back. I got in touch with George and told him he could have it, that Liam didn't need to know he was getting it back either. That was part of the deal. He still got the money, I still disappeared and Liam never got to know. All George had to do was leave my family alone.*'

'This conversation happened today, Amelia.' Maddie Ives spoke to fill a silence where her daughter had been stopped. Amelia couldn't answer, not at first, her words were lumps in her throat that wouldn't shift. Instead, she lifted her hand to feel for the little black switch. The weak light was enough. Liam Moran was laid out on his side, he had been groggy when she had doused the light, still suffering from the whack to the head that Tim had given him. He wasn't groggy anymore, his bloodied head was shaking, his eyes wide and he was soaked in sweat from the pain of being tossed around with broken limbs. George was sweating too, but his reason would be different. His expression behind his gag told its own story. Every drop of sweat leaking from his pores was mixed with something else, something unmistakable: fear.

Amelia was overwhelmed by any number of emotions at once. The van's lurching got worse still, the suspension grinding and squalling complaint as it pitched and rolled at low speed and Amelia knew they had pulled off the road and were some way down the track identified as the ideal kill site. The timing was perfect, it steeled Amelia just as the diesel engine clattered its last. Behind her, against the doors, was another pile of limbs where Sophie and Jade had rolled together, but it was the two men she squatted over to speak.

'I was looking forward to telling you, but the idea that Kayla just told you herself . . . perfect!'

The van door popped. The light as bright as it was sudden and both men slammed their eyes shut. They opened them again pretty quick, a response to the stench of petrol that rushed them from the green container making a sloshing noise in Tim's hand.

'And this is Tim, Kayla's father,' Amelia said, ending the call and stuffing the phone back in her pocket. 'And it seems we can skip the questions.'

CHAPTER 64

Two photos arrived together from Amelia's number, both screenshots of a map. The second a zoomed-in version of an area shown in the first. There were no words of explanation, nothing more at all, leaving just the fact that it was sent from Amelia's number to explain its meaning. Maddie tried to call back, but only got the reaction of a phone switched off. She could only assume that the pictures were instructions, telling them where to go. Maybe even where Jade was.

'It looks like a track, rather than a road,' Maddie said. She had found the location on Google Maps and changed it to a street view that showed nothing more than a rutted entrance. Harry was already heading in the general direction, following signs for a village called St Nicholas-at-Wade on the outskirts of Thanet, as the closest named place.

He planned to wait for Eileen first, the rendezvous point on the edge of an industrial estate, and they were due to arrive at around the same time. Eileen was a minute after, then wasted precious seconds by reverse parking, even edging back forward to make sure she was lined up right in her bay. Maddie didn't mind so much; the moment she saw who was in the passenger seat she knew it had been worth the wait.

Kayla Goodyer.

She looked sheepish, like Eileen had spent the entire journey going full schoolteacher on her, but how she looked didn't matter, what she said might not matter either. The fact she was there, the fact she was breathing meant that used right, she might be enough to stop the loss of any more lives.

But Maddie couldn't know how far that was from the truth.

They all bundled into the car, Harry driving, the blue lights already going, the siren following the moment the doors shut. Three minutes of silence passed until the police radio erupted, calling Harry direct. It was Mark Hall. He had seen their car stop on the GPS mapping, now he could see it moving again, towards Thanet, the opposite direction to Canterbury. Hall was demanding an explanation. Maddie replied, not with an explanation, just with a request for all available resources to follow to where they tracked. Then she turned the radio down as low as it would go.

'How are you feeling, Kayla?' she said to finally break the silence.

'Is my mum OK? Are you going to arrest her?' Kayla was sitting in the back, her head bent, her hands resting in her lap.

'Yes,' Maddie said, 'I have to.' Then she turned to where Kayla lifted her eyes.

'And it's serious. A kid abducted, right? Can we sort this, I mean, she's got it all wrong. When I explain she'll see; she wouldn't take a kid, not in a million years, only . . .'

'My job is to arrest her. Your job, Kayla, is to make sure she doesn't do anything that can't be sorted after. Can you do that for me?'

'I . . . I don't know . . . What do I say to her? This is all *my* fault.'

'We'll see when we get there,' Maddie said, keeping to herself the fact that she wasn't going to let Kayla say anything. Amelia was going to get a glimpse of her daughter and a promise of more when she let Jade Mercer go. And Jade was going to be there, unharmed and released at her request.

Then Maddie would arrest Amelia and keep a promise made to a little girl.

Jade Mercer safe was Maddie's focus. Anything else would be a bonus.

CHAPTER 65

A black van, muddied and pulled off a rutted track at an angle, the back doors facing the approach, those solid types with no windows and a steel step running along the bottom of them both. On this step, a lone figure sat, shoulders rising and falling in a slow rhythm. Both rays of sun and spots of rain hit the windscreen as Harry brought their car to a stop some ten metres short and Maddie recognised the woman she had met in custody: Amelia Chagrin.

Or a version of her, at least.

She was filthy, it was the overriding first impression. Her hair looked slick, her fringe stuck down, her sleeves stained black to blend into dark jeans where her hands rested on her lap. The only flash of colour to her was a spot of red against the bright white surround of her high-top trainers. Her shirt pocket had a phone-shaped dint.

'Mum!' Kayla squealed at the seated figure from the back seat, immediately trying to open the doors and falling foul of the child locks utilised on all police cars.

'I need to talk to her first,' Maddie said, 'and you need to stay here.' There was no real protestation, just shock as Kayla slumped back. Maddie stepped out, careful to close the door behind her. The angle of the van meant that she could see all the way down the left side to where the front had rolled into ferns tall enough to consume the wheel and push against the side window. The track was lined with trees that shushed and clacked, a disturbed bird performed a calamitous take-off almost directly above and the frigid blue of the grill lights caught on the washed-out pallor of the seated woman.

Maddie didn't take her eyes off Amelia, she knew she shouldn't. Her conversation with Vince came back to her, when they had talked about despair and how this job meant you got to know it well. It was here for sure, its head bent, refusing or unable to make eye contact. Maddie stepped closer, the trees shushed louder, the breeze that ran through them now engulfed her, carrying thick fumes.

Petrol.

Amelia Chagrin had fidgeting hands. They remained twisting in her lap, her glassy eyes downward to the move-ment. Her eyes were bright red and seemed to almost bulge with moisture. Maddie continued to edge closer with easy steps, her hands by her side, her palms out towards the seated woman. It was an approach straight from negotiator training — she'd had *some* at least; recognition that the woman in front of her was not in a good place and again, the conversation with Vince played out in her mind. The explanation that had made so much sense to him suddenly made sense to her too: *Despair takes over everything, right, slows everything down, walks you to the place where you're gonna end it and makes you wait for this moment of beauty, a moment that can make you see it as the right thing to do.*

Amelia Chagrin had her pick of beauty: all around her the trees were dancing, their movement manipulating the winter sun to mottle the rain-soaked ground. It was quiet too, the only sounds the shushing leaves and animal calls. She had the means as well, if that moment arrived, in the form of a lighter held in her hand. Maddie could see it clearly from where she was just a few paces away. The lighter was a Zippo, oversized and box-shaped and Amelia was turning it over and over in her right hand. She finally lifted her head to tell Maddie not to come any closer in a voice that was rough and delivered with a grimace. The words were probably painful; petrol fumes are aggressive, they force their way anywhere oxygen goes: throats, woodland scenes.

The insides of vans.

A single spark from that lighter's mechanism and the air would combust. And there would be no stopping it. That was what Maddie had seen as a layer of dirt and filth from a distance. Up close, Amelia was soaked in petrol.

'Amelia,' Maddie said, splaying her hands even more where she was still showing her palms. 'I want to help you, that's why I'm here.' Another line from a training manual, but she meant it.

'You can't help me. It went too far.' Those glassy eyes fell to her left side, to a metal object blending with the metal step. It was lying on its side, a polished metal bottle opener with a rounded handle — the body like a flattened pebble, she thought — and a corkscrew part that was stained darker than the rest. The sun was getting stronger, its position was at the front of the van to make a shadow of the back, but Maddie didn't need bright light to know what that dark staining was.

Amelia was back to focusing on the lighter that still tripped over in her filthy hands. It had a lid that flipped up with a satisfying sound, something she was able to do one-handed, her thumb pushing down one end to flip the other and reveal the mechanism, then clunking shut again. Beside her, moisture dripped, running from under the van's rear door on the right side. More petrol. The inside had to be soaked for it to have found its way back out. It wouldn't take much, not for a small space like that. Fumes would be swirling in the darkness, pushing against the sides and the roof, hungry for that spark, ready to consume everything that was in there.

'I can help you; I want to help you,' Maddie said. 'I think I understand.'

Amelia smiled, it was only the mouth, more like baring her teeth. Her eyes, too, were glassy and cold, drained of all emotion. Despair had her deep in its spell, her moment of beauty could come soon. 'I went too far . . . and you couldn't understand.' She said it again, gently, like she was whispering it to herself. 'And no one cares, not about me.'

'Grief . . .' Maddie said quickly, then took a moment. 'It can have you doing things you wouldn't normally, it can make you a different person almost. We lost someone recently, my boyfriend did at least, and I hardly recognised him. He did something stupid and now his life is going to be different because of it, but it was going to be different anyway, because of what he lost. But you . . .' Maddie paused for the right words. 'You have another chance. Kayla's still here, she's alive and in that car, you don't need to be that person changed by grief. But if you hurt Jade, if you *kill* Jade—'

'It's too late!' Amelia's voice was rougher when it was raised. 'It's too late for me now. Maybe I wish Kayla *was* dead.'

'You don't mean that.'

'You shouldn't have brought her here . . . I shouldn't have told you. I don't want her seeing this, seeing me. This was all for her, for the *murdered* Kayla . . . I thought I could do anything for her, because of what they did to her. If I had known that all along . . . she has to understand!' The tears that had been building were suddenly unleashed. Both cheeks flooded at once.

'Where is Jade, Amelia? Is she in the van?' Maddie glanced at the bloodied corkscrew as she took another step forward, stopping as Amelia's head dropped again and the lighter clunked back open with that same smooth movement. This time she lingered on it. Maddie turned to give a hurried signal and Harry was ready. He had got out of the car, by the back door and he opened it now for Kayla to get out. Maddie knew the risk — this was stepping away from any training manual ever written, you never bring a loved one to a situation like this, it can only add to the unpredictability. It was something the police had learned the hard way, from people who had promised to come down if their loved one was brought out to greet them, only for it to be discovered that this was what they had been waiting for.

One more glimpse: their *moment of beauty*.

It was the only play Maddie had left.

Kayla stood still. Harry had her loosely by the arm to stop her moving any further forward, but she didn't try to, it was like she couldn't.

Maddie jerked back to a scuffing noise, it wasn't Amelia, she was as still as ever. The van rocked slightly, then the door thumped weakly. A second thump was a little stronger. Then scraping, someone scratching at the door from the inside.

'Who's in there, Amelia?' Maddie said. 'It's not too late! Someone's alive in there.'

Another lifeless grin, Amelia still baring her teeth. 'It doesn't matter anymore, nothing matters.'

'Everything matters, Amelia. Jade saw you, didn't she? But you saw her too and you left her there. You didn't want to hurt her then and you don't want to hurt her now. Amelia Goodyer doesn't hurt children.'

'You shouldn't have brought her, my Kayla. You shouldn't have brought her here; this was a mistake.' Amelia was looking beyond Maddie, the lighter in its open position and she wasn't playing with it anymore.

'Mum!' Kayla's voice seemed closer.

'You shouldn't be here, you shouldn't have come!' Amelia's tone was empty, like there was nothing left of her.

'Just stop it. Just stop all this and let's go home! What are they telling me about a little girl? That's not you, Mum, what are you doing?' Kayla's voice was a mixture of surprise and anger, where anger was starting to win. And Maddie was feeling more and more that this was a bad idea.

'I thought I had lost everything when I lost you.'

'Did you hurt her? That little girl? Not in my name, Mum, what would make you think I would want that?'

Amelia stood up and Maddie resisted the urge to step back. Amelia turned enough to slap the van door twice, firmly. The reaction was instant. The front passenger door pushed out into the ferns and a bundle of something fell out. There was furtive movement, like a panicked animal released into undergrowth, moving towards them.

Jade!

She was crying hard, her eyes flitted around like she was unsure where to go. Maddie held her arms out to capture her attention, Jade's face flickered recognition and she threw herself into Maddie, forcing her to step backwards. Maddie couldn't help but dip her head, holding her tight, inhaling the scent of her hair as Jade wept into her chest. There were no petrol fumes from her. Maddie took hold of her by the shoulders, moving her back enough to take her in.

'Are you OK?' she demanded, searching all over her as best she could.

'I'm OK, I'm fine.'

'There's blood!' Maddie said, she could see flecks in various places and with no obvious reason.

'It's not mine,' Jade said, looking over to the rear of the van where Amelia still stood. Maddie turned back to her car, to where Eileen had appeared to move out into the middle of the trail, her hands out, her feet bare despite the soaking woodland floor.

'Come on, child,' she beamed. Maybe Eileen had a way about her from all those decades teaching children, but Jade didn't hesitate, pushing away from Maddie to run to where Eileen scooped her up and moved her back to the car, the doors closing, the reason for Maddie coming here now safe and sound.

Only that wasn't the entire reason.

The scraping noise was there again.

'Who is that, Amelia? Is that Tim? I heard you call someone Tim on the phone, just before you hung up. Tim Goodyer, your ex-husband. He's here, isn't he?'

'Dad?' Kayla called out from behind her. There was still blood unaccounted for, accelerant too, dripping from the same place that someone was knocking to get out of. Amelia looked through Maddie to her daughter. 'You shouldn't have

376

come,' she said. 'Your dad wouldn't stop . . . and we had to. You're still here, there's no justification for what we did anymore. I'm going to hell now, Kayla, but it's OK, I know what to expect, I've been there already.' Those eyes glazed, then dropped to the open lighter, her thumb lifted.

Her moment of beauty had arrived.

CHAPTER 66

The white flash consumed Maddie with a *whoomph*! The heat came a moment later and was gone just as quick. The next thing to puncture the atmosphere was a shout, loud, going up in pitch all the time to become a shriek, a sound that moved away as a ball of furious orange. Maddie realised she was on the floor, she lifted her head to the van where flames now clung to the back door. A dark figure swept past her holding a red blur and an explosion of white powder hissed and spat from it.

'Vince!' Maddie gasped, her palms nicked by a patch of brambles as she scrabbled to get back up. The powder stopped, the extinguisher hung limp in his left hand, his right reached for the van door. 'Vince . . .' Her voice was coming back a little, 'NO!'

Maddie sprang to her feet but she was too late. The door was pulled open for a rush of oxygen to mingle with the fumes and the flames consumed it all. Another white flash, this time Maddie's stumble was towards it and it was Vince who hit the floor, his arm raised across his face, the extinguisher thudding onto the woodland floor for Maddie to scoop up.

The powder erupted, beating back the flames that seemed to be everywhere. A man hung out the back, his head by Maddie's foot when she jumped up onto the steel step, her hand constant on the trigger as she covered the blackened insides in powder. Another two men were lying on the floor on the left side and in the chaos she couldn't be sure if they were moving. She doused them in the powder, soaking them, only stopping when a hand reached out towards her and she grabbed it to heave it backwards. The man slid easily enough over the slick metal floor, his momentum enough for him to fall out over the step. Vince was back on his feet to push past her and reach in for the other writhing body, dragging him to the edge by a fistful of belt. She watched Vince give a final heave that tipped him out.

The third man who had been laid out over the back was toppled out last to make a pile of the three men. The two on the bottom squirmed and moaned against gags while Vince slapped their clothes where new fires threatened to break out. Maddie went to squirt again but she was out. They pulled the top man clear. There was no movement from him, just a lot of blood. Maddie pulled his head back to feel for a pulse and got nothing more than a jagged wound, a throat just about ripped out.

Just like they had seen before.

'Dad!' Kayla's scream identified the body. Harry was now full-on restraining her and behind them the theme of noise and confusion extended where police cars were arriving, their sirens accompanied by lights flashing angry patterns. Vince had George Moran sitting up, he lifted the man's arm up to hook him under the shoulders and drag him away from where flames were growing again. George's heels pushed and flailed, kicking out a trail in the ground.

'It's going to go up!' he bawled as he came past and Maddie turned back to where Liam Moran was thrashing on the floor, his broken legs useless in bright blue casts, his fingers clawing at the ground where he was trying to drag himself away. The fire had surged back brighter, hotter, its progress from front to back was fast, hungrily moving along the wooden inserts in the walls and roof of the rear compartment, the threadbare carpet already well alight. Vince had dumped his first casualty and was already back to roll Liam over, ignoring his cries of pain. Maddie could see him struggling to hook the injured man under his shoulders. His lean away and the grimace on his face told a story of near unbearable heat. Maddie tried to move in to help but she couldn't get any closer, a searing force field was now rapidly pushing out and Vince still couldn't get hold of the casualty in its centre.

'VINCE!' Maddie screamed. 'Leave him!'

There was another flash which beat the sound by a split second and this time there was movement with it. The van seemed to hunker down, then shake with the power of an explosion that rolled outwards as light, heat and sound. Then came the smoke, sudden and thick, acrid and gritty, the breeze rushing it forward like a wall of black as Maddie stumbled backwards, her eyes narrowed, her vision down to nothing.

'Vince!' she bellowed again. His black hoody appeared, its movement the only reason she could separate him out from the whirling smoke. His head was bent, his eyes firmly shut, still with Liam Moran in his grasp whose useless legs dragged behind him. Vince got clear enough to fall backwards, exhausted, a police uniform now alongside him to assist, rolling onto his side to choke and hack.

Maddie stared back at the roaring van and the flames that had grown to replace the black smoke and beat against the walls and ceiling. She could now see the prone figure of Tim Goodyer as an untidy mess on the forest floor under the van's doors, still unmoving, his eyes morose and cold. For a moment Maddie thought she saw movement from a mouth twisting into a scream shape, but it was just a trick of the light, a flickering shadow cast by the flames that had easily made the leap to crawl along his back, the hood of his jacket shrinking away to nothing in a moment.

More officers arrived with the fire extinguishers. They huffed and puffed but the white powder was sucked into the heat, ineffective, and they were beaten, forced to retreat, forced to leave the fire to its feast.

CHAPTER 67

There was nothing for Maddie to do but sit and watch. She was swigging from a flask of tea that a uniformed officer had provided from somewhere. It had been a silent and very British exchange; a colleague turning up at a scene to find a shocked face coated in a layer of sweat and ash and — with no words needed — an understanding formed that tea was the answer. He'd dumped a sachet of sugar in it too. Maddie didn't take sugar, but she didn't stop him either.

Maddie felt OK. She was faring better than Vince who was suffering from smoke inhalation and the after-effects of a field medic giving him three eye baths in a row. But his discomfort wasn't enough to drag him away to hospital on the medic's advice either and Maddie didn't have the energy to try and convince him. She didn't have the energy for Mark Hall's blustering arrival either and, from somewhere, her reaction to his opening question — *What the fuck did you do?* — was a snorted laugh.

Mark Hall didn't stick around to ask any follow-ups. Instead, Maddie, Harry and the blinking Vince found a seat on a fallen tree, the bark rough against Maddie's bottom but preferable to standing on her exhausted leg muscles. Eileen was a little further away, inexplicably still barefoot, offering some sort of an explanation as to how the team who had been moved away from a major murder investigation had ended up being there for its fiery end. Hall loitered like he was listening to some of it, then crossed back in front of Maddie, Harry and Vince, his face like thunder, his gaze turned down to ensure no eye contact. He marched past them to stand over the charred remains of Amelia Chagrin, who had sprinted into the midst of a patch of ferns, scorching her own clearing in which to lay herself to rest. From there he moved to inspect what was left of the van, his white suit and blue booties already stained with soot picked up from somewhere. Soot had a way of doing that, it got everywhere, including the back of Maddie's throat, and no amount of coughing, spitting or sweet tea seemed to be budging it.

The van was cooling now and Hall loitered by its passenger door. It was wide open, and the door itself looked untouched when compared to the rear compartment of the van, which was now just twisted roof struts and a steel chassis, like a fallen animal in a clearing, its bones picked clean by woodland scavengers. *Which one do we think this is?* she heard Hall say, pointing into the front of the van.

'Sophie Harding.' The reply was from a detective sergeant that Maddie vaguely recognised, who had spent his time scurrying too close to the boss. By a process of elimination it had to be Sophie, although formal identification was going to be a lengthy — and rather unpleasant — process. Hall tutted, briefly stared over in Maddie's general direction to shake his head. She resisted the urge to wave back with her tea.

She turned away instead, her eyes lazily moving over what was a hubbub of activity. The roller shutters on the side of a fire engine clunked shut, the final kit checks complete and it was ready to rumble away. There was still one ambulance left, two others having left already with a Moran each. The one that had remained still had its lights flickering, one of the back doors open, the angle so that Maddie could just see a police constable smiling into the back.

DCI Jim Kemp was the last arrival to the hubbub and stepped out of his car for just his head to appear over the roofline, then came flashes of arms where he put a jacket on. He then stopped to look for something, some*one* as it turned out and he stopped when he was fixed on Harry. His expression might have soured a little, then his head dipped back beneath the roofline. When he appeared in full from behind the car he was carrying four coffees in a cardboard holder.

'All we need is a campfire.' Jim Kemp's opening line came with a strained smile.

'I think we may have had enough fire for one day, sir.' Eileen was back among them to give a retort from over the top of her reading glasses.

'Never a truer word said,' Jim said, quickly. 'Are you OK, Eileen? I've been hearing stories on the way here, seems some of the things you've seen today go above and beyond what I would expect for my civilian employees.'

'I'm just fine, thank you, sir. A coffee might help, I suppose . . .'

'Ah!' Kemp had clearly forgotten what he was holding. He thrust them at Eileen now, who took the hint, busying herself with sugaring and sorting.

'Talking of expectations, this is the first time I've had to consider what I should expect from a suspended police officer. It seems that sitting at home with his feet up is a little too much to ask.' Vince's reaction was a sort of smile and a flutter of winks, with both eyes taking turns.

'Not a big fan of daytime tele, boss,' he said.

'I see. And before I start ripping you a new arsehole, are you OK? You look like you've been forcibly inserted into a chimney.'

'I feel like I've been forcibly inserted somewhere. A little beaten up, it got a little hot but I've never been a fan of eyebrows anyway.'

'How are you here, even?' The DCI cut straight to the point. 'I assume the abandoned civi car back there is yours?'

'Yeah. Still had my radio, boss, I know it only pops up for attention if you transmit so I kept quiet.'

'Quite a struggle for a man like you,' Harry added.

'Yeah. I listened and followed, but I was in the area anyway, so first on scene.'

'In the area?' Kemp wasn't falling for that, not for a moment. Maddie wasn't either. With all the activity she hadn't stopped to think about Vince and his arrival from nowhere. She was listening now.

'Actually, sir . . .' It was Eileen who would expand. 'I was keeping PC Arnold up to date on our movements. I happen to know that he's rather invested and, it would seem, there are times when you need—'

'A ham fist,' Maddie cut in, her head shaking but she couldn't stop a smile. She tried to hide it by swigging from the flask.

'Well . . .' the DCI started, his eyes moving over the whole team one by one. 'I look forward to reading all about it in your duty statements. Why aren't you back at a nick writing those up by now?'

'Mr Hall suggested we stay *right where we are*,' Harry said, then shrugged his big shoulders. 'And this team does what it is told.'

Movement caught Maddie's eye, the officer at the back of the ambulance suddenly more animated, his movements like he was helping an elderly relative out of a car; but it was Jade Mercer who appeared. She had grudgingly agreed to be checked over, despite no signs of injury. The ambulance barely flinched as her slight frame dropped off its steps. Instantly she looked over at the upturned tree acting as a makeshift bench for Maddie and the team. She fixed on the stooping hulk to Maddie's left who was still ignoring medical advice by trying to rub the smoke out of his eyes. Vince hadn't seen her, he could barely see anything. He didn't see her walking towards him either, the uniform constable went with her for the first few steps then stopped to let her continue. Jade made straight for Vince, her soft features bunched up into something that looked like fear — but gentler than that — trepidation, more like. She reached out, a fragile hand that looked all the smaller when it rested on Vince's bandaged forearm. He was still leaning forward, cussing, fidgeting and pressing his eye sockets with the heel of his hands.

Her touch stopped him like it contained a magic power.

'I'm so sorry.' Her voice was the gentlest part yet, like the breeze might blow it away. Vince straightened, his eyes streaming and ringed with red and he forced them open.

'Jade!' he said, the smoke adding gravel to his words. 'I didn't know you were still here, love.'

'They want to take me away again, but I wanted to tell you I was sorry.'

'Sorry!?' Vince moved his hand to rest gently on her cheek. His thumb slid outwards to wipe away a tear.

'Herb . . . he was in that van, when they set it on fire. I couldn't . . . I didn't know where they put him. I'm so sorry, I lost him . . . Please . . . Can you tell Sammy that I'm sorry.' She was breaking down, the way that kids do, where they start from their bottom lip. It was too much for Maddie, too much for Vince too and he found his feet, pulling her in tight for a hug with his eyes scrunched tightly shut — and not just from the smoke damage. His next words, and the emotion that propelled them, disturbed Jade's hair that was loose over her ear.

'You don't have to be sorry, not to me or Sammy, not to anyone, do you understand?' He pushed her back a little, both his hands on both her shoulders now, squinting and blinking eye contact. Jade smiled, her lip still had a quiver but she got it back under control for the smile to win out. 'We'll get you something else that will keep you safe.'

'Thank you.'

'For what?' Vince chuckled.

'That was her, that was who hurt my mum and you found her.'

'I said I would lock her up,' Vince said, a half turn, a flicker perhaps, towards Amelia Goodyer's scorched corpse. 'I'm sorry you were here, that you saw that.'

'That's why I don't need Herb, I don't need anything. She can't hurt me now, no one can hurt me. I know you won't let them.'

I know you won't let them. Maddie grimaced, turning her head away so no one could see it. She knew what those words meant, she knew Vince had heard words just like it and that they were still so raw: *You won't let her die, will you, Uncle Vince?*

Vince was thinking the same, he must have been, it was a big part of what happened next; Vince Arnold fell apart. The big man sobbed on his knees, tipped so far forward that his forehead found the woodland floor and an eleven-year-old girl slumped over him like she was weeping on a rock.

That woodland clearing finally had a genuine moment of beauty and Maddie, frozen to the spot, was pretty certain she could feel her heart hurting.

THE END

ALSO BY CHARLIE GALLAGHER

DI MADDIE IVES SERIES
Book 1: HE IS WATCHING YOU
Book 2: HE WILL KILL YOU
Book 3: HE WILL FIND YOU
Book 4: HE KNOWS YOUR SECRETS
Book 5: HE WILL GET YOU
Book 6: THE DEADLY HOUSES
Book 7: LAST ONE ALIVE
Book 8: THE GIRL UNDER THE FLOOR

LANGTHORNE POLICE SERIES
Book 1: BODILY HARM
Book 2: PANIC BUTTON
Book 3: BLOOD MONEY
Book 4: END GAME
Book 5: MISSING
Book 6: THEN SHE RAN
Book 7: HER LAST BREATH

STANDALONES
RUTHLESS

Thank you for reading this book.

If you enjoyed it please leave feedback on Amazon or Goodreads, and if there is anything we missed or you have a question about, then please get in touch. We appreciate you choosing our book.

Founded in 2014 in Shoreditch, London, we at Joffe Books pride ourselves on our history of innovative publishing. We were thrilled to be shortlisted for Independent Publisher of the Year at the British Book Awards.

www.joffebooks.com

We're very grateful to eagle-eyed readers who take the time to contact us. Please send any errors you find to corrections@joffebooks.com. We'll get them fixed ASAP.